THE NIGHTINGALE
AND SPARROW CHRONICLES

TSARINA'S JEWELS

JERENA TOBIASEN

her story and keeps the chronology accurate, a worthy indication of an author in command of her genre.

Love becomes a central theme in the story, giving weight to the characters' emotions and connections.

An element of romance sparks between Simon and Mary, allowing characters to maneuver not just external conflicts but inner ones as well, pushing them to grow as people. Simon Temple is a character to cheer on, with admirable boldness and determination. The supporting characters are memorable and well-wrought too, adeptly playing their role in moving the story forward.

Tsarina's Crown: The Nightingale and Sparrow Chronicles is a striking start to a promising series, and one of the best espionage stories in modern historical fiction.

Tsarina's Crown by Jerena Tobiasen won First Place in the 2023 CIBA Hemingway Awards for 20th Century Wartime Fiction.

Chanticleer Book Reviews

DEDICATION

THIS BOOK IS FOR JPL, GCL, SIL and CGL,
all of whom inspire my writing.

OTHER BOOKS BY JERENA:

The Prophecy

The Crest
The Emerald
The Destiny

The Nightingale and Sparrow Chronicles

Tsarina's Crown

ACKNOWLEDGEMENTS

In 2018, while visiting the Fabergé Museum in St. Petersburg, Russia, I found the seed of *The Nightingale and Sparrow Chronicles* and wrote *Tsarina's Crown*. *Tsarina's Jewels* carries the story forward with adventures in England, as well as in Türkiye, during the Turkish War of Independence (1919-1923). I hope I have written my story well enough to capture the beauty and history of Türkiye during one of its most significant moments.

Türkiye is an ancient country. As a result, its people and culture, as well as its name have changed many times throughout history. This story is written during a tumultuous time in that history. I have opted to write it using the simple spelling of 'Turkey', as was common then. In 1923, however, the official name adopted by the country was *Türkiye Cumhuriyeti*, often referred to as Türkiye.

Regardless, I could not have written the adventures of my characters without some help along the way. For their insight, guidance, and suggestions, I am truly grateful. Specifically, I'd like to thank:

- The kind folks of Hebburn and Jarrow Local History Society, who shared their knowledge of the town of Jarrow, South Tyneside, England, including Jarrow Hall and Hylton Castle.

- Ben Coles, who helped me bring structure to my manuscript. I'm also grateful for Ben's commitment and service to the Royal Canadian Navy and to Canada.

- Michelle Robinson, Judith Sanvicente, and the gang of talented individuals at Cascadia Author Services, who help me turn my manuscripts into marketable novels.

- Jay Ritchey, my alpha reader, who always has great feedback.

- Robert McKellar Douglas, an artist with vision. He not only encourages my writing but helps me with the research. He has travelled with me, listened to my ideas and concepts, and provided feedback.

PART ONE

CHAPTER 1

Simon Nightingale-Temple and his companion, Artyom Egorov, entered the War Office off Horse Guards Avenue. Although the September sun had risen, the dew drops that clung to their high-polished shoes from their jog across the grass in St. James Park had yet to evaporate. Friendly banter filled the space between the two lanky men as they strode with purpose through a maze of offices, until Simon stopped abruptly at an unassuming door.

"Here we are," Simon said, pointing to the name plate, which read *Captain Sir Mansfield Smith-Cumming, Chief of the Secret Intelligence Service.* He rapped lightly on the door and turned the knob to enter.

A uniformed clerk sat behind a desk, typing. He looked up and nodded toward the two men.

"Lieutenant Simon Temple and Captain Artyom Egorov to see Captain Smith-Cumming. We have an appointment."

"Of course, sir," the man replied, "I'll tell him you're here."

A moment later, the young clerk reappeared. "Captain Cumming would like a private word with you first, Lieutenant Temple," he said, ushering Simon into the office. "Captain Egorov, may I offer you tea while you wait?"

The office was larger than Simon had expected. *Of course, it would be*, he thought, scanning the collection of accreditations displayed on bookshelves, the desk, and two walls, before his eyes fell on the man himself: Captain Sir Mansfield Smith-Cumming. The man who had honoured his wife by adding her surname, Cumming, to his. A brief flash of his own surname if he were to add Nikolaevna to his already-hyphenated name made Simon blink twice to rid himself of the apparition. *Mary would be aghast if I did that!*

"Lord Simon, welcome," Cumming said, rising slightly from behind his desk and extending a hand in welcome, indicating a chair for his guest.

"Please, sir," Simon said cheerily, "Lord Simon is a bit pretentious, don't you think? Lieutenant Temple, even Simon, is fine."

Having recently spent three years in the company of the Romanov family, as well as a lifetime in the company of various members of British aristocracy, Simon sat with ease in this office. The man piqued Simon's curiosity but did not intimidate him—although rumour had it that the captain had an overbearing personality.

Cumming took his seat and stared at Simon with a level expression. He was clearly not intimidated, either.

"You wanted to see me, sir?" Simon said, prompting his superior.

"Yes," Cumming replied, shuffling an assortment of pages on his desk. "It's come to my attention that, during your recent sojourn to Petrograd, you found yourself caught up in certain intrigues"—Cumming cleared his throat with a subtle cough—"to state it mildly."

"Yes, sir."

"I also understand that you spent considerable time with Bruce Lockhart, and that the two of you enjoyed a few … adventures together."

"Yes, sir." *He's well informed,* Simon thought. *I wonder where he's going with this.*

"I'm obliged to tell you that, in addition to high praise from King George, I have received reports from members of the Admiralty, Ambassador Sir George Buchanan, former Consul-General Bruce Lockhart, and others, of their great admiration for you and your support of the British Embassy in Petrograd, despite certain of your inadequacies and failures. Regardless, they have all recommended you for a position in this office."

"Excuse me, sir?" Simon said, a flush of red beginning to stain his cheeks. His fists impulsively clenched with anger. Unable to control his agitation, he jumped to his feet. "Inadequacies? Failures!"

Captain Smith-Cumming glanced down at the pages on his desk, then raised his gaze toward Simon, removing his monocle and twirling it between his fingers. "Please sit down, Lieutenant."

Once Simon had resumed his seat, Cumming overlooked Simon's outburst and continued. "As I'm sure you're aware, these are turbulent times. The fiasco in Russia hangs over Britain's head. There are those higher up who would gladly drop responsibility for the execution of the Romanovs and the Bolshevik revolution on your head alone."

"I've heard," Simon said angrily. He faced Cumming, his rigidity clearly expressing his objection to the accusations. Fingernails dug into the palms of his hands. "I was not to blame, and I will not *be* blamed. Excuse me. It was a mistake for me to come." He rose, nodded stiffly, and turned on his heel.

Smith-Cumming rose to his feet and cleared the side of his desk in three long strides, despite the limp inflicted by an artificial limb. "Hang on, son." His hand clamped on Simon's shoulder. "I said those higher up ... not me."

Simon swivelled and glared at Cumming.

"Please resume your seat," Cumming said kindly, pointing toward the recently abandoned guest chair. "At least give me a chance to explain." His eyes calmly challenged Simon's hasty response.

Several beats of his heart passed before Simon nodded curtly and returned to the chair.

As if Cumming saw Simon's rigidity ease, the man began to speak again. "Thank you." Cumming rested his elbows on his desk and linked his fingers. "Now where was I? Ah, yes: trust. Based on the recommendations of those I just noted, trust is key to our conversation. There is no lack of trust where you're concerned. I'm confident in that. It's the government's trust and poor judgement, as well as those in higher stations, that come into question. There sits the root of the blame."

Simon's stare softened and met Cumming's with curiosity.

"Government trust is at an all-time low. We can't trust our own citizens, let alone immigrants. Anyone could be a spy. And we certainly can't trust other governments. Other countries. There's treachery afoot, and spies and turncoats aplenty. We need men in the field: good men, men upon whom we can place our trust to be loyal to king and country. And we need them now."

"All issues of trust aside, sir, are you suggesting that I become a spy?" Simon said, incredulous.

"We prefer the term 'intelligence agent' or 'intelligencer'." Cumming replaced the monocle and studied the pages on his desk. "And not at the moment, but soon … yes." He removed the monocle again and directed his attention to Simon, clasping his hands on the desk as he leaned toward the young man. "After a period of training, I hope you will. I doubt it will take long, however. Lockhart has reported that you are quite competent in every aspect. We just need to endorse it officially."

"A spy?" Simon sat agog, unable to believe what he had heard.

"*Ahem.* Yes. Just so." Cumming's finger tapped on the pages. "I'd like you to start training as soon as possible. My clerk will help you organize that. Speak with him on your way out."

Simon scratched his ear and shifted in the uncomfortable guest chair. "Are you saying that Lockhart is an intelligencer, sir?" Simon said.

"He is employed by this office," Cumming said, "and he has been working in Russia on our behalf. That is all I am permitted to say just now. Please do not press me for more information. Investigation of your clearance has not yet concluded."

"Investigation of my—"

Smith-Cumming lifted his hand toward Simon, palm forward. His raised brow caused Simon's question to freeze in his throat.

"And where exactly would I train?" Simon said, clearing the remainder of a croak from his vocal cords.

"That information will also be provided by my clerk."

"I see." Simon grabbed his chin. "Your offer sounds fantastical, sir."

"Be that as it may," Cumming replied with a shrug. "You've been abroad for some time. Are you aware that the Secret Service Bureau was created in 1909, a product of a joint initiative between the Admiralty and the War Office?"

"I believe the idea came about as a means to control the flow of intelligence," Simon replied, keen to hear more, "both within the country and overseas."

"Indeed," Cumming replied. "In 1916, administrative changes resulted in the establishment of an *internal* counter-espionage office known as the Directorate of Military Intelligence, Section 5, or MI5, and an office to monitor *foreign* intelligence known as the Directorate of Military Intelligence, Section 6, or MI6."

Cumming rose from his chair and paced across the

window behind his desk, his gait exaggerated by the limp. A light rain had begun to fall again, obscuring the park view beyond the foggy window. "Deciphering code seems to be the primary focus these days. We need well-trained individuals." He paused opposite Simon and raised a questioning eyebrow. "I understand that you are also familiar with coded messages. Is this correct?"

Simon contemplated his service aboard RMS *Guardian* in 1915, with sinister submarines and secret messages. He nodded, struggling to swallow a chuckle as he recalled the merry chase upon which he had set his father, using coded messages tucked inside Russian souvenirs, during the early days of that country's revolution.

"Excellent!" Cumming replied. "We are hoping to broaden the scope of tactics employed by our agents in the field. In addition to the usual subterfuge, we will be improving safety training and training with unknown weapons. Preparing for the unexpected, and so on. These are all things of which you are aware, according to Lockhart."

Simon rose from the uncomfortable chair, jamming his hands into his pockets. He paced slowly across the spacious office on his side of the desk, churning through his thoughts.

"I appreciate your confidence, sir," Simon said, "but I'm curious why you would take the word of Lockhart alone as regards my capabilities."

"Your profile alone recommended you as a candidate," Cumming replied. "Lockhart was directed to, shall we say, test your mettle. His report supported our suspicions." He eyed the young Lieutenant thoughtfully. "I've been advised that you were instrumental in certain communications between the Tsar and King George; you thwarted the efforts of a man named Vasiliev; you protected the entire royal family during a red army conflict; you rescued the only surviving member of that family and brought her out of Russia safely …" He gazed at the ceiling as if clues might be written in the plaster. "*And* you know how to keep secrets, to list a few." Cumming peered at Simon from beneath wiry brows. "Enough said?"

"Enough said." Simon surprised himself as he extended his hand. "I believe we have an arrangement."

Cumming smiled, rising to accept Simon's hand, and shook it heartily. "Now, let's see what your man, Egorov, has to say."

He reached for the knob but turned to face Simon. "A word of advice, my boy: don't dwell on the sour position of the administrators. It will pass in time. They know they've made bad decisions; let them stew in their mess. Before you know it, they'll be forced to agree that your efforts, although unsuccessful, were well intended, and that your work here will be invaluable."

CHAPTER 2

Simon introduced Artyom to Captain Smith-Cumming and both young men accepted the captain's invitation to sit opposite him.

"Captain Egorov is mentioned in detail in the report that I filed on my return from Russia," Simon said.

Cumming nodded. "I've read it."

"Then you'll recall that he was captain of the Tsar's Imperial Guard, and during my stay in Petrograd, he became a close friend and confidant. In fact, he and his uncle helped me corner Major Ivan Vasiliev before I could be set up to take the fall for some of Vasiliev's covert operations."

Cumming planted his elbows on his desk and tented his fingers. "Captain Egorov, what can you say for yourself?"

"Sir." Artyom took a deep breath. "My friend Simon Temple, he speaks the truth. I was captain in Imperial Guard. I believe it to be this, and my accent, why no one wants to employ me."

"However," Simon said, "he has an excellent work ethic, and he's loyal and trustworthy."

Artyom grimaced as a red flush crept up his neck. "I am too Russian, and my English is not so good."

Cumming waved his hand, dismissing Artyom's comment. "Do you speak other languages?"

"Yes, sir," Artyom replied. "Several Russian dialects, including languages spoken around the Crimea and the Urals, some Slovak and Turkish, French, German … and basic English, of course, which improves daily."

"Given that your former employer is unable to provide a reference," Cumming said, "I suppose I'll have to take your word for it."

"And mine, and Lockhart's too, sir," Simon said. "Artyom has spent many hours with us; even worked a few adventures with us, too." He winked at Artyom.

"Very well," Cumming said. "Leave it with me. We'll need approval first, of course, but I can think of a few positions where Captain Egorov's expertise might come in handy." He rose from his chair and walked around his desk. He shooed the two young men out of his office, following them into the hall. "I'm off to meet the War Secretary for lunch. Your enquiry is timely. Come to my office later this afternoon."

———

Mid-afternoon, Simon and Artyom enquired at Cumming's office and were promptly shown in again.

"You'll be pleased to hear," Cumming said without preamble, "that I met with the War Secretary, and I discussed placing Captain Egorov with the cipher clerks. Given your language abilities, the level of security that you would have had with the Imperial Guards, and the recommendations of Bruce Lockhart and Lieutenant Temple, we believe you could be an asset to that department. You'll be expected to complete the department's training program and take the *Official Secrets Act* oath, of course."

"Yes, sir!" Artyom said, grinning broadly. "I am most grateful, sir!"

"Lieutenant, take Captain Egorov to Room 40. Alastair Denniston is waiting for him." Cumming rose and stepped from behind his desk. "Don't let me down!" he said, his voice deep and stern.

"I won't, Captain Sir Smith-Cumming," Artyom replied, tripping over the name with his Russian accent. "I am honoured to be of service to this great country and will do everything I can to help keep it safe! I loved Russia, but it is no longer the home that I served with my life. My loyalty is here now, with England."

Following the interview, Simon led Artyom on a brief tour of the War Office as they made their way to Room 40. There, Artyom was introduced to Alastair Denniston, deputy head of Room 40, an organization responsible for intercepting and decrypting enemy messages. Denniston, a slender man of average height, proudly advised that he had helped form Room 40 during the Great War in 1914.

"Room 40," Denniston said, "has recently merged with its counterpart in the army and is in the process of being renamed the Government Code and Cypher

School. We've simplified the name to GC & CS."

He introduced the new candidate to members of the department, informing them that Artyom was to be trained as a cipher clerk.

"We've a few hours left in the day. I invite you to remain with us and begin your orientation," Denniston said gruffly, eyeing the Russian dubiously. "Officially, your training will commence tomorrow. I hope you're up to the task."

CHAPTER 3

Two weeks later, Richard Nightingale-Temple dropped his fountain pen on a green ink blotter with a huff. Annoyed, he scrubbed his blue-stained fingers with a starched white handkerchief. His wooden chair screeched as he pushed away from its companion table and stood abruptly.

At a loss, he stepped first one way, then another. His casual dismissal by the Personnel Director an hour earlier left him agitated and impatient, his brain desperately trying to organize rapid-firing thoughts. He shook his head to clear the chaos. His father, Retired Commander Lord Charles Nightingale-Temple, had warned him often that his cavalier attitude toward work would eventually cost him his position, and now it had.

He glanced at the wall clock and kicked the table leg. "To hell with them all," he said aloud, casting about to be certain he was alone.

A remaining typist sat before another wooden desk at the far end of the room, fingers flying over the keys of a shiny black Corona typewriter. "Blast!" Her curse broke the silence that lay between them like a thick Persian rug. She reached to unlock two keys that had become entwined.

She glanced shyly at Richard, straightened the pages from which she was typing, and let fly her fingers once again.

Richard stood motionless, his brain still racing. An overwhelming sense of envy, this time for the young woman's skill, interrupted his laboured breathing. Mentally, he listed the skills he had acquired since his father had intervened in late 1916 and found him a civilian position as a clerk in the outer office of the Admiralty: sorting, filing, labelling, typing—albeit poorly. He hated the job, but his father insisted that he work his way up, first by earning his supervisor's trust. Richard was miserable and bored, and at a loss to determine what he would do otherwise. No one trusted him—and why should they?

The previous weekend, he had overheard his father accuse his mother of being over-indulgent, of funding his excesses. His belly had clenched when she asked what was meant by 'excesses.' His father's candid explanation elaborated on Richard's drinking, gambling, and womanizing. In his father's opinion, the twenty-one-year-old son of an earl had a duty to be more responsible. Richard's heart had softened when he had peeked into the room where his parents argued and had seen tears flowing from his mother's glistening hazel eyes.

Richard scrubbed his face to remove the latest image of his mother and scanned the room again. Bitter and angry, he wanted vengeance for the dismissal. He ran long fingers through his wavy, ginger hair. Then, like an automaton, he approached the filing cabinet marked 'CONFIDENTIAL'. The bold black letters stood at attention across the top of the cabinet as if they alone could protect the information within.

He eyed the typist, realizing that she had ceased her task and begun tidying her desk. She lifted her coat and hat from the tall wooden stand, hung a handbag over her arm, and nodded a farewell.

When the office door snicked shut, he yanked a drawer and began leafing through files, hoping for inspiration. Toward the back of the second drawer, his eyes snagged on the words: *Disposition of the Ottoman Empire*. Fingering through various maps, memos, notes, and supporting documents, a plan began to take shape.

Once more he glanced around the office, poked his fingers into the folder, and snatched its contents. Moments later, they were securely stuffed into his satchel, and he was reaching for his own coat and hat. As the wall clock ticked eighteen hundred hours, the office door clicked shut behind him with finality. Loyalty, integrity, and trust were the furthest things from his mind.

Simon and Artyom boarded the first-class car of the Friday evening train to Newcastle upon Tyne. Their animated discussion about their experiences during the week halted as they worked their way through the coach looking for their seats. Ahead of them, Simon spied Richard slouched in a corner seat, a sullen expression clouding his countenance.

"Richard!" Simon said with surprise. "I didn't expect

to see you on the train this evening. Don't you usually stay in town on a Friday night?"

"Hmph." Richard scowled at his brother, straightening slightly as he covertly slipped his satchel into the gap beside his seat. "I may as well tell you. You'll find out anyway … I've been sacked."

"Sacked!" Simon noted Richard's annoyance at his exclamation of surprise. "But why?

"You wouldn't understand," Richard said, slouching into the seat again.

"Say, what's with the satchel?" Simon said. "Stealing government secrets?"

"Why ever would I do that?" Richard said defensively, choking on his words. "I had to clear my desk of personal items, didn't I." He pulled the bag to his lap. "Want to inspect it?"

"No, no!" Simon said, raising his hands to wave off the need. "I was merely teasing!"

Richard dropped the bag to the floor, leaned back, and plopped his homburg over his face, ending any further discussion.

"What will you do now?" Simon said, grabbing the hat from his brother's face.

"I have no idea," Richard replied, appearing ambivalent to his situation. He snatched his hat, glaring at Simon. "I suppose I'll have to think on it." With that, he plopped the hat over his face again and folded his arms across his chest. "Now, kindly leave me alone." His mumbled words terminated further disturbance.

Flabbergasted, Simon glanced at Artyom with raised brows. He shrugged, then picked up the thread of their earlier conversation.

CHAPTER 4

"Come along, Mary," Ann Nightingale-Temple said, stopping in the doorway of the conservatory the following Monday. "We have work to do." The aroma of tropical blooms and freshy-turned earth filled the humid room.

Mary Nightingale-Temple, once Grand Duchess Maria Nikolaevna, set a china cup in its saucer, demurely swung her legs off the chaise lounge, and planted her feet softy on the stone tile. She shook the morning paper and folded it neatly before setting it aside. "Simon suggested that I read a newspaper every day," she said off-handedly. "He said it would help with my understanding of the local syntax and give me an idea of what happens in the community. I hoped this room would be out of the way of the servants."

Mary reached for a pot of a still-steaming tea, eyebrows raised in invitation. "What is this work?"

Ann declined the tea, fluttering a note she held in her hand. "I'm afraid there's no time for tea," she said, tucking a strawberry blonde curl behind her ear. "We're needed at Walkergate Hospital." She traced the neat script with a manicured nail. "This is a note from the director.

He says, *'Our nurses are overwhelmed by the number of sick being trucked into the hospitals daily, directly from the ships. Even with the help of VAD nurses, we can't keep up.'*

"VAD nurses?" Mary said.

"Volunteer Aid Detachment nurses," Ann replied as she turned toward the doorway. "You told me that you volunteered at an infirmary with your mother and sisters—"

"Yes," Mary said with interest, "and we assisted doctors and nursing sisters while they cared for sick and injured soldiers."

"And I've shared that information with the director," Ann said. "Come along."

An expression of anticipation lit Mary's eyes as she rose to her feet. Lifting a low-hanging banana leaf out of her way, she hastily followed her mother-in-law into the corridor.

"My time off has come to an end, and your volunteer work is about to begin. Apparently, another wave of the Spanish flu has arrived in England. The first wave last spring stayed in the London area, but this wave has already reached Newcastle."

"Shall I ask for the chauffeur to bring the auto?" Mary said as they entered the foyer, the silk of their day-robes swishing against their rapid steps.

"Already done," Ann replied, gathering fabric away from her feet at the foot of the stairwell. "Michael will meet us out front in twenty minutes. Is that enough time for you to be ready?"

"Yes, Mother Ann. My wardrobe is not yet so extensive that I need time for decisions."

"Is it always like this?" Mary said as she stepped from the motor car, awestruck by the activity outside the hospital.

"Throughout the war, and now, because of the Spanish flu, yes," Ann replied, shifting her hat to shade her eyes from the sun.

"Just look at the lorries full of service men!" Mary said, gawking at the line of military vehicles.

"Come along," Ann said, tucking her hand into the younger woman's elbow and smartly guiding her toward the entrance. "If it's this busy out here, I can imagine what's going on inside. The director and Matron will be waiting for us."

Ann led Mary to the director's office and introduced her. The director and the matron asked questions about her experience. Her frank answers quickly assured them that Mary would be an asset to the hospital.

"Don't worry about the formalities," Matron said. "We'll take care of that in good time. For now, let's find you a uniform. Lady Ann can show you the ropes."

"*Show me the ropes?*" Mary said.

"Follow me, Mary," Ann said, once again taking her daughter-in-law's arm, "I'll explain along the way."

"Matron asked us to work in this ward," Ann said after their mid-day meal. Her hazel-coloured eyes perched above the edge of her mask as she glanced toward the over-long room. "But we'll need to don fresh gowns, caps, and masks before we go in." She glanced toward a row of windows lining the room's outer wall. Wavering fingers of shadowy light fell on the interior.

"Given the number of patients, I expect it will take a while," Mary said, regarding the rows of single beds occupied by nondescript, dishevelled men.

"Yes, I expect it will take us until teatime," Ann replied as she tossed her soiled garments into a bin. "Let's get to it. If you have any questions, just ask."

As they worked their way from one bed to the next tending to the needs of the ill men, familiar words wafted toward Mary's ears. Small hairs on the back of her neck prickled. She turned toward them, narrowing her eyes to isolate the source. *Russians!*

"Mother Ann," she said quietly. "Russians are here!"

"Yes, dear," Ann replied, "we have a community of Russians in Jarrow; many are exiles, some are recent immigrants."

"Mother Ann," she said, whispering near Ann's ear, "what if they recognize me?"

"I doubt any would," Ann said, glancing toward the end of the room, "especially with the mask and cap covering your face and hair. Just don't speak near them."

Mary's ice-blue eyes widened. "What if I forget?" Raised, blonde brows punctuated her concern.

"Alright," Ann said, accepting Mary's discomfiture. She paused momentarily as if to consider the predicament.

She slid a finger under her watch brooch. "We're almost finished. Why don't you refill the medical carts. I'll address the patients' needs, then we can go home."

———◆———

A while later, Charles sauntered into the conservatory, where he found his wife and daughter-in-law nibbling on an assortment of watercress and cucumber sandwiches. A three-tiered serving stand of sweet cakes remained untouched.

"Here you are!" he said, rubbing his hands with relish as he surveyed the sweet cakes. "I'm famished!"

"Join us, then," Ann said, waving her hand toward a vacant chair.

"What did you think of the hospital, Mary?" Charles said, accepting a steaming cup from the butler, Tompkins. "Were you invited to assist?"

"Oh, yes," Mary replied, her shifting posture suggesting her interest. "They put me to work straight away! We all wore masks and caps and white coats, and we had to wash our hands over and over. None of that was required in Petrograd."

"We're not privy to the reasoning," Ann said, rubbing crumbs from her fingers, "but I'd never dispute the orders. If these new methods prevent us from contracting illnesses, I can only be delighted."

"Will you be returning soon, then?" Charles said as he reached for a sandwich.

"Yes," Ann replied. "We've been asked to return on a

regular basis for at least the foreseeable future. The director says this is a particularly nasty strain of influenza and expects it to spread significantly before it lets up. Could be many weeks—months even, I expect."

"Mother Ann," Mary said earnestly, "do you think I could become a nurse like you?"

CHAPTER 5

"Where are you two off to so early on a Saturday morning?" Simon said, shaking his newspaper closed when Ann and Mary appeared in the morning room, smartly dressed for an outing.

"We've been so busy at the hospital," Mary replied, a blush staining her cheeks, "that we haven't been able to go to London."

"We're off to my dressmaker," Ann said, smiling at her daughter-in-law. "Mary's garments are ready and some of them need fitting."

"We'll catch the early train and hopefully be home before tea," Mary said.

"When are you leaving?" Richard said grumpily as their conversation gripped his thoughts.

"Michael is bringing the car around now," Ann said. "We must be on the next train, to ensure we're back for dinner."

"Give me five minutes," Richard said, tossing his napkin on the table and racing from the room. "I'll come with you."

"Alright," Ann said as he thundered up the staircase, "but hurry! The train won't wait."

With that, the women disappeared down the hall, heels clacking on the floor of the tiled foyer.

"Lord Richard will be right down," Mary said before Tompkins could close the great oak doors behind them. "He's coming with us."

———

"Will you be returning home to Jarrow Hall with us this afternoon?" Ann asked her son as the train doors opened at Charing Cross station.

"Don't count on it," Richard said as if to deter her interest in his activities. He stood on the platform and offered his hand to her.

"We can wait—"

"Mother, don't," Richard said, reaching for Mary's hand. He glanced about the station as they cleared the platform, as if deciding on his escape route. "If I'm here, I'll see you. If I'm not, don't look for me." He tipped his hat and marched toward the nearest station exit.

"Well, he's certainly snippy this morning," Ann said with a huff. "Come along, dear. The taxi stand is this way."

———

Richard flipped up his collar against the rain and wind and stuffed his hands in his pockets. He wandered aimlessly, wondering what to do next. As his belly grumbled loud enough to interrupt his thoughts, he found himself standing on a familiar corner. The *Eel and Martlet* stood across the street, offering warmth, a place to dry his wet coat, a meal, and a visit with Sally Winton.

He waited as a passing lorry meandered through the intersection, then strode toward the pub's entrance, relieved to finally have purpose in his day. "So much for returning with Mother," he said to himself as he pulled open the door, anticipating an amusing afternoon followed by an entertaining night with Sally in his arms.

He stood inside the doorway waiting for his eyes to adjust to the changing light. Reaching into his jacket pocket, he located his billfold and counted his cash. *That'll do for a game or two tonight. I'm sure I'll win enough to keep me going for a while, especially when Sally spots me a glass of her employer's rot-gut whiskey.* Satisfied with his plan, he sauntered into the pub, hailing Sally where she waited on a table.

Ann linked arms with her daughter-in-law and together they marched up the rain-soaked stairs of the dressmaker's shop.

"It seems the rain has let up," Ann said, stopping on the landing to close her umbrella. She grinned with anticipation. "Ready?"

"I suppose so," Mary said, her face clouded. "I still worry that someone will recognize me." A tremor rippled down her spine.

"My dear Mary," Ann replied, the peacock feathers in the brim of her green felt hat fluttering as she hooked the umbrella over her arm and took Mary's trembling hands in hers, "you know you needn't worry. The shops that I frequent ensure utmost discretion." She held Mary's eyes, giving her hands a little shake. "Ready?"

Mary nodded and followed Ann toward the doorman.

"When we're finished here," Ann said, "we'll stop by Garrard's and see whether your jewellery is ready."

"It was generous of Mr. Garrard to serve me himself," Mary said. "Do you think he was sincere when he said he liked my designs?"

"Of course!" Ann said. "It's not every day that the designs and jewels of a Romanov heir appear on his desk. I think he was quite impressed."

Most of Mary's dresses and gowns required minor adjustments and would be delivered within the week, but she was able to take away two day-dresses and two gowns, as well as undergarments, shoes, gloves, a day coat, an evening coat, and three hats.

She also collected her jewellery and leftover gems from Garrard's, confident in the knowledge that they would soon be safely stowed in the iron safe hidden in Charles Nightingale-Temple's chamber.

<hr>

That evening, as Mary donned the second of her dove-grey gloves, Simon knocked on the jamb of the doorway that joined their rooms.

"May I come in?" he said with a roguish grin.

"Of course," Mary said, turning toward him as she buttoned the last glove. "What do you think?" She twirled with effect, showing off her glittering gown and jewellery. She lifted the gossamer overlay of russet, revealing a sombre grey silk beneath. "This fabric is from France, the latest creation of M. Doucet. He doesn't sell to just anyone, and although he allows it to be used creatively—in the new Art Deco designs—each design must be tasteful and discrete. He does not approve of any fashion that is revealing." She twirled again, appreciating the fall of the fabric.

"Frankly," Simon replied, "I agree with M. Doucet. If anything is to be revealed, I'd prefer it to be for my eyes only." His eyebrows wiggled up and down, causing Mary to erupt in giggles.

"Simon, stop! You'll ruin my effect."

"I beg your pardon, madam," he said, bowing deeply. "The yellow diamonds in your necklace and ear bobs are perfect with your ensemble."

"You don't think it's too bright, do you?" Mary frowned with concern. "I mean … I'm supposed to be in mourning, not gaily attired."

"Not at all, but if you doubt me, ask Mother." He offered his arm, and she inserted a gloved hand at his elbow. They walked slowly toward the stairwell.

"She won't say anything. She approved my designs and helped me with the selection."

CHAPTER 6

Early one morning, a young man knocked at the kitchen door of Jarrow Hall. He wore a light wool jacket against the autumn chill, and the toes of his boots were wet with grass dew.

"Pardon, sir," he said, his words thick with a Russian accent. "I speak to Lady Ann?"

"It's a little early for a house call," Tompkins replied. "What's it about?"

"My old grandfather needs medical aid," he said. "The neighbours say she will help."

"I'm sure Lady Ann would want to help you," Tompkins said, scratching his chin in thought, "but she's at the hospital."

The man hung his head, tears filling his eyes.

"Wait here," Tompkins said, not wanting to turn away a man in need. Lady Ann would not approve.

"Zima," he said, catching Simon's valet at the foot of the stairs. "Are you heading up? Is Lady Mary still here?" Simon's valet nodded. "Will you take her a message? Tell her there's a Russian fellow here. I think he needs help."

"Where?" Zima followed the pointing finger to the back door and greeted the young man. He introduced himself and listened to the man's plea. "Wait here," he replied in Russian, then left the man standing where he was while he went in search of Lady Mary.

"You speak Russian?" the young man said to Zima's back. "In a fine house like this?"

"Pardon, my lady," Zima said, entering the conservatory. "A man from the Russian quarter—Dimitri Mikhailovich Semenov—is at the back door. He has an elderly grandfather who is very ill and is asking for Lady Ann's assistance."

"Did you tell him that she's at the hospital?"

"Yes, my lady, but his need sounds urgent."

"Very well," Mary said, dabbing a cake crumb from her chin. "Ask him to wait while I dress. If you see Mrs. Z, please send her my way."

"My lady," Mary's maid said, entering the chamber in a swish of silk skirts, "tell me what you need. I understand you wish to hurry."

"Buttons, Mrs. Z," Mary said, "always the buttons." As she spoke, Mary turned her back to Mrs. Zima and buttoned her own sleeves. Pulling on a light woollen jacket that matched her rust-and-cream-striped skirt, she mused aloud, "Let me think … I'll need a car, my medical bag, and—"

"My husband has asked Michael to bring the car

to the back door, and I have your bag here." Mrs. Zima opened a cupboard and lifted the leather bag that Mary carried with her when she and Ann did volunteer work in the poorer communities. "Wear this," she said, handing a felt-brimmed hat to Mary. "It will cover your hair, and the brim will shadow your face. The Russian quarter is risky. Someone might recognize you."

Mary nodded, taking the hat and selected a simple pin to poke through it. She glanced at the buckles on her Mary Janes to assure herself that she had fastened them, snatched the bag and a pair of gloves, and started toward the servant's stairwell.

"My lady, your cloak!"

"Of course," Mary said, waiting for Mrs. Zima to settle the cape on her shoulders.

"I'll get my things and be right behind you," Mrs. Zima said, heading up the stairs to the servants' quarters.

Dimitri Mikhailovich Semenov sat in the pull-down seat next to Michael, guiding him through the Russian quarter to a three-storey brick building on Martin Street. While Michael stayed with the car, the young man led Mary and Mrs. Zima up a staircase to a small flat on the second floor. The smell of boiled beets and cabbage permeated the hallway.

Two doors off the stairwell, Dimitri Mikhailovich Semenov opened a door and invited them into the flat he shared with his parents and grandfather. Mary scanned the main living space, noting that, despite the poor furnishings, it was clean and tidy.

Once the young man had introduced his parents, his mother ushered the women into the sleeping quarters where an elderly man rested on a steel-framed bed and straw mattress.

"My father-in-law, Igor Petrovich Popov," the woman said in Russian.

Mrs. Zima repeated the introduction, then stationed herself near the door, ready to act as Mary required.

The woman introduced Mary to the family patriarch as she approached the bed, then stepped out of the way.

"A basin of warm water," Mary said matter-of-factly as she surveyed her patient. Moments later, the basin sat on a small table near the bed. Mary washed her hands and dried them on a cloth from her bag, then examined Igor Petrovich Popov, his hooded blue eyes watching her every move.

"I believe you have pneumonia and need to be in hospital immediately, Mr. Popov. Do you understand?"

"I don't understand what you say," he replied in Russian, gently clasping Mary's wrist.

The remark caught Mary by surprise. Amongst themselves the Zimas, Artyom and his sister Varvara Crocker, and Mary had decided that it was best to speak only English if they were to assimilate well into English society. Rarely was a Russian word exchanged among them. She hesitated momentarily, then repeated her diagnosis in Russian.

Mr. Popov gasped. "A Russian-speaking nurse?" he said. "Here in Newcastle? How can this be?"

Mary dug into her medical bag hoping to hide her regret, immediately realizing her folly.

From the doorway, Dimitri Mikhailovich Semenov explained that they had no money to pay for hospital care. "Perhaps you can explain a remedy for the house?" he said.

"A home-remedy?" Mary said in English. "No, that's not possible. Mr. Popov must go to the hospital immediately." She glanced at Mrs. Zima. "We'll take him in our motor."

"But … no money," Dimitri Mikhailovich Semenov said again.

"If there is an expense," Mary said with authority, "I'll help you find a way to pay it. Mr. Popov is too frail. He needs hospital care immediately."

As the men carried Mr. Popov out the door and down the stairs in a fireman's chair of crossed arms, his daughter-in-law caught Mary's arm. In her hand, she held a collection of coins.

"Please, can this be enough?" Tears filled her eyes.

Mary knew that the coins she held would feed the woman's family for days, maybe weeks, but their love of Mr. Popov would be their sacrifice.

Mary wrapped her slender fingers around the woman's hand, securing the coins in a fist. "No," she said softly, in Russian. "Not today."

"God bless you, lady," the woman said as Mary marched smartly toward the stairs.

"My lady," Mrs. Zima scolded later that evening, "you took a great risk speaking to that family in Russian. You have been working hard to learn defences, and everyone watches out for you. You must take better care!"

"You are absolutely correct," Mary said, distressed to think of the jeopardy in which she had placed everyone. "But I would not do anything different were I to do it again. Mr. Popov's life was in peril."

The next morning, Mary returned to the hospital for her shift. Before she started her rounds, however, she went directly to the bed of Igor Petrovich Popov. Relieved to see him sleeping peacefully, his breathing less laboured, she sighed and headed for the corridor.

In the hallway, she met the ward doctor, a lean man who stood a hand shorter than her. She asked about the patient Popov's prognosis.

"I heard that you insisted the man be brought in," he said. "I commend your decision. The patient would have died, otherwise." He eyed the young woman, deep in thought. "I understand that you have applied for nursing studies."

"Yes, Doctor," Mary said with a nod.

"I will be happy to endorse your application," he said with a kind smile.

At the end of her shift, Mary returned to Mr. Popov's bedside, greeting his grandson as she did so.

"You look familiar," Mr. Popov said, his voice raspy.

"I've seen you before." He grabbed her wrist with gnarly fingers and drew her closer. "You speak Russian. I am old soldier from Imperial Guard. Who are you?"

"I-I know only a little Russian," Mary said in English. "My family lived in Russia when I was young. Now England is my home."

"But I know you!" he said. "Such a pretty girl."

"No prettier than every other Russian girl," Mary said, smiling kindly. "Just a common Russian girl trying to be an English woman." She smiled reassuringly first at the old man, then the young one. She freed her arm gently and straightened to leave. "Do take care."

As she strode purposefully along the hallway, she began to shake, recalling Mrs. Zima's warning.

CHAPTER 7

"Oh, Simon!" Mary said excitedly as they prepared for bed the following Friday. "You can't imagine what happened this past week!" Sitting before her vanity table, she gazed into the mirror and spoke to his reflection as she took up her hairbrush.

Standing behind her, Simon leaned forward and kissed her crown, relieving her of the brush as he did so. He straightened and began brushing her hair. "This reminds me of those early days on the run," he said. "You kept asking me to help you with your hair. Artyom teased me mercilessly."

"I heard snippets of those remarks," Mary said, her smile full of reflection. "I think that's when I realized how much you cared. At that point, though, I was in too much pain. I couldn't appreciate all that you'd done for me. You saved my life." Teary eyes found Simon in the mirror.

"We saved each other," he said, resting the brush on the table. "You were telling me about your thrilling week." He reached for her and led her to the bed. "Sit. Tell me."

Mary relayed the series of events concerning Mr. Popov's welfare, watching Simon's countenance darken as the enormity of the risk donned on him.

"Have you visited your patient since?" Simon said, taking her hand.

"Not since the morning when he asked who I was. I was afraid to go back, but I've asked after him. He will be in the hospital for a while longer."

They sat side by side on the bed, holding hands.

"So, what's next?" he said, stroking her cheek.

"I plan to take greater care with my identity," she said adamantly. "I also have two thoughts that I'd like to pursue. First, I want to spend more time in the Russian quarter offering medical services to those in need. I will take Mr. or Mrs. Zima with me as translator, so I need only speak English. Second, I want to use some of my money—maybe sell some jewels—to establish a fund for them, so they don't need to worry about making ends meet if they run short. A trust of sorts. Will you help me?"

Simon heard the passion and longing in Mary's voice and assured her that he would. "So long as you promise never to go alone, and you take great care to hide your identity." He chewed his lower lip in thought. "Father may have some ideas about setting up a trust fund. We can talk with him tomorrow."

"I promise," Mary replied, feeling her heart begin to race. "I realized that I didn't just put myself at risk. I put everyone at risk! What if someone is harmed because of me? I don't know that I'd have the strength to manage it."

Simon seized her trembling hands and held them

firm. "None of us wants to experience that," he said, drawing her into his arms.

When her trembling eased, he slid from the bed and selected the sherry decanter from the small table between two Queen Ann wing chairs. He filled two sherry glasses and handed one to his wife. "Drink this," he said. "Hopefully, it will deter nightmares."

Soon after, he placed the empty glasses on the mantle and lifted the bed covers.

"There's one other matter," Mary said as she snuggled next to him. "Igor Petrovich's hospital bill. I will pay it, of course, but … to ensure that it doesn't reflect on me personally, might you make the payment in your name, or better yet … anonymously?"

"Consider it done!" Simon said. "When you have the invoice, I'll submit payment immediately, in either fashion."

Mary flung her arms around his neck, thanking him profusely. Moments later, Simon welcomed her tokens of gratitude, each kiss followed by mutterings of oranges.

A few days later, Charles accompanied Mary to a two-storey sandstone building in Newcastle upon Tyne, a historically stylish building where the firm of solicitors who had represented the family for decades occupied much of the upper floor. With the guidance of a senior solicitor, Mary established a trust that would offer financial support for Russian refugees, especially those in medical distress.

On a subsequent visit, she delivered several jewels

to the solicitor and asked his assistance arranging their sale, explaining that the proceeds would be used as the basis for the trust. "Let me know if the fund runs low," she said to the solicitor. "I'll bring more jewels."

Satisfied with the outcome, Mary encouraged Mrs. Zima to spread the word through the Russian quarter that a special fund had been established by an anonymous benefactor.

"How do you propose to spread the word?" Mary said mischievously.

"I will simply tell the priest!" Mrs. Zima said, her accent still significant. "Telling the priest is like telling every ear only once! The entire quarter will know about the fund—within the week!"

CHAPTER 8

Richard hastened from his room, buttoning his dinner jacket as he headed toward the stairs. *Hopefully a shot of whiskey will steady my nerves and get me through another endless dinner with the newlyweds. They haven't been here three months, and already their constant displays of affection make me nauseous*, he thought. *Spanish flu be damned! I'll take my chances elsewhere. Far away from here! From England!*

A scowl shadowed his countenance as he contemplated cocktails and a boring meal with his family. "God, save me!" he said sotto voce, stepping from the bottom stair. "The *last* thing I want to do right now is listen to my brother drone on about his adventures in Russia. I'd give *anything* to skip another tedious dinner."

As Richard approached the salon, he realized that he was not the first to arrive. He recognized the voices and their intimate conversation. He hesitated near the entrance and pressed his back into the wall before he could be seen, straining to hear the quiet exchange between his brother and Mary. His heart pounded with interest.

"Your mother has been so helpful these past weeks," Mary said, her barely-audible accent tainting her words with a peculiar lilt. "She's introduced me to her dressmaker so I could have a wardrobe made, and she's introduced me to Mr. Garrard, the jeweller, who used some of my designs for the jewellery I'll need—"

Richard could no longer resist. He peered quickly through the doorway, then back, pressing into the wall again. His scowl deepened, this time at their tender moment. Simon towered above his wife protectively. Mary, although tall and slender in her own right, appeared petite next to his brother. Her chin tipped upward as she peered into Simon's eyes. *God save me!* Richard groaned.

"If you need anything else," Simon said softly, "I'll take care of it. You don't need to use your mother's money or your gems unless you want to."

The sound of ice clinking against crystal left Richard imagining his brother at the beverage trolley. Ice tipped into a cocktail shaker. *God! I wish it was whiskey!* Liquid burbled into a glass. Richard licked his lips with yearning, his fingers forked in anticipation of a companion cigarette.

Richard peered covertly around the doorway once more, catching their image in a gilt mirror hung on the opposite wall. *Look at them. They haven't a care in the world. As if Simon didn't have everything already—favoured firstborn, titles, wealth, position, the ear of royalty—now a Russian princess for a wife and her wealth, too!*

"Thank you, Simon." Mary's voice quietened as she gazed up at her husband, inviting a kiss. He obliged with a small touch to her forehead.

Hmm, the answer to my financial predicament could be

at hand, Richard schemed dreamily, leaning into the wall yet again. *As well as a way out of England.*

When his brother wondered about the tardiness of others, Richard clenched his jaw with determination and pushed away from the wall, straightening his dinner jacket.

"Good evening," he said, his voice devoid of cheerfulness. He strode smartly into the room, a calculating smirk hovering on his lips. "Mother and Father will be down in a minute."

"That's timely," Simon said pleasantly. "I was wondering that very thing. Cocktail?"

"Whiskey," Richard replied, glancing about with indifference. "Where's the damned footman?"

"He's abed with some seasonal malady," Simon said with a shrug. "We're short-staffed tonight, so I'm doing the honours."

"We'll have a dirty martini," Charles said, as he and Ann entered the room. "It's all the rage in London lately. Are you up for it, Simon?"

"Certainly! They were popular in Russia, too," Simon said. "Two dirty martinis coming up and a whiskey for Richard." Simon hefted the whiskey decanter and poured into a stout glass. In response to Richard's wiggling finger, he poured a double shot.

Richard snatched the glass and turned away from the trolley, leaving Simon to concoct cocktails for their parents. Instead, he sidled up to Mary. "You're looking lovely this evening, Princess," he said. "Did you steal your jewels from Mother Russia?"

Mary took a step back in response to Richard's snide question, wondering how the man who looked so like her husband—but for the ginger hair—could be so different in personality. As yet, she knew little of the nature of Simon's family, except for Simon's brief insight into Richard's black-sheep behaviour. Now, his searching eyes seemed to pierce her soul. She might have dismissed the sensation, but small hairs rising on her nape suggested caution.

"Um, no," Mary replied, her hand rising to cover the pendant at her neck. "These are mine. P-part of my in-inheritance." She smiled at him wanly, wishing that she had misread his greeting. "I would never steal anything!"

His expression remained unchanged, but for the narrowing of his steel blue eyes, shadowed by pale apricot brows.

Blood pounded in Mary's ears. Her mind raced as she steadied herself against a possible threat. *Calm down, Mary,* she thought, pressing a clammy hand into the skirt of her dress as a distraction. *In the past five months, you've survived two attempts on your life and the murder of your family. You're being over-sensitive. Surely, Richard means no harm. You're safe here.* She inhaled deeply, held her breath for a count of ten, then slowly released it, feeling the surge of adrenaline subside.

"And now you have an abundance of riches and can afford such luxuries," Richard said, openly assessing her appearance. His eyes seemed to pierce her fragile armour. "How convenient for you."

"Yes, well," Mary said, lowering her eyes to break his scrutinous glare, "this is so, but here I hope I'm safe from thieves and assassins. If I were in Russia, I would not be safe to wear such things." *Why do I feel intimidated?* Once again, she forced herself to be still.

Simon appeared at Mary's side with two martinis. He handed one to his wife, then cradled her elbow possessively in his free hand. Surreptitiously, he placed a kiss near her ear. "Alright, Sparrow?" he said quietly, his dark brow wrinkled with concern, as if he had seen her reel away from Richard.

Mary turned her puzzled gaze toward him and nodded. "Richard and I were just discussing the jewels I've inherited from my mother."

"Indeed," Richard said, downing the remainder of his whiskey in one swallow. "How fortunate that you both have your own wealth! Take care you don't squander it. Once lost, it's difficult to regain." He bowed abruptly and headed toward the hall.

"Where are you going?" Simon said, his raised voice startling his parents.

"Out!" Richard replied defensively as he disappeared through the doorway.

Simon and Mary looked at one another questioningly.

"What's going on?" Charles said, approaching them.

"I have no idea," Simon replied with a shrug. "Mary?"

Mary shook her head, while Ann glided purposely

from the room. "Richard! Come back!" Contrary to the norm, Ann's voice sounded shrill and confused.

Richard's muffled response sent her huffing back into the salon, while Simon went after him instead.

"Honestly," Ann said, her flawless complexion stained red with frustration, "why could he not simply say he wanted a cigarette? The box is sitting right there on the mantle."

Richard stormed up the stairs, his long legs taking them two at a time. Simon followed, reaching to grab his brother's arm before he could advance along the hall.

Richard swung around to face him. "Get off!" he said, shaking Simon's grip loose. "What do you want?"

"I want to know what's going on," Simon replied, feeling anger boil in his belly. "You've been acting like a spoilt child ever since I returned. You may have issues with me, but you have no right to treat my wife as you do." His eyes narrowed to night blue, reflecting his ire.

"What are you saying?" Richard said defensively, beads of perspiration pearling along his forehead. "How could I possibly offend someone I hardly know?" He turned abruptly and took a step, only to be halted again by Simon's grip on his arm. He spun toward his brother, snarling. "I said *get off!*"

Without thought, Richard's right fist slammed toward Simon's jaw. Simon leaned right. The fist missed its target, landing hard on Simon's left shoulder. Simon's responding right jab caught Richard's jaw, followed by a sharp left jab to his belly.

Richard staggered backward, crashing into a wall, knocking a pastoral painting askew. He bent forward, rubbing his jaw and gasping for air. Simon paused his advance, unintentionally giving Richard an opportunity to redirect.

Richard charged, but his brother deftly stepped aside: not quickly enough, however, to avoid a glancing blow to his cheek, the scrape of Richard's signet ring drawing blood. Richard's momentum propelled him into a small chest on the opposite wall, where he sank to the floor, momentarily stunned.

"I suggest you quit now," Simon said with a snarl, steadying a small vase teetering on the chest, "before you cause serious damage."

Richard rose angrily and staggered toward Simon with intent.

Simon grabbed him by the collar, redirecting the misstep and preventing a tumble down the staircase. He yanked Richard's face toward him. "What's going on?" Simon said viciously, shaking the fist with which he gripped his brother's collar.

A while later, Simon marched back into the salon, pausing inside the doorway to run slender fingers through his disheveled auburn hair and straighten his evening attire.

"Where's Richard?" Mary said, fretfully looking beyond Simon. "Is he coming back?" Anxiously, she inched forward on a lavender silk armchair.

"I'd say not," Simon replied, his rancor cooling. "Let's just say that he can't tolerate the idea of spending another evening with us."

"I'll speak to him," Ann said, rising from her chair.

"No, Mother," Simon said, stepping into her path, resting his hands on her gloved forearms. "Leave him. He'd be poor company even if you were to successfully convince him to return."

"Simon," Mary said, noticing a purple welt blooming near his right eye, "what's that?" She rose from the chair to better examine the injury, raising her gloved fingers toward the soft scab forming in the centre.

"Richard and I had a bit of a set-to," he replied, fingering the throbbing cheek. "He said he's leaving for London and wants the evening for himself." His arm snaked around her shoulder.

"But—"

"Mother, let him go." Simon turned his attention toward Ann. "Richard said he has important business in town and refused to say anything more."

"What business?" Charles, who had been silent to this point, rose menacingly to his feet, his jaw twitching in time with the pulse throbbing at his greying temples.

Mary searched her husband's scowl, trying to see what lay beneath.

"He wouldn't say, Father, but I mean to find out."

—⋅—⋅—

Richard marched into his room at the end of the hall, his mind racing to organize his thoughts. He snatched his carryall from the wardrobe and began stuffing clothing and toiletries into it. *I'll crash at Sally's for a few nights*, he thought. *She won't mind.*

He hastily changed from his dinner garments into casual trousers and a jumper and glanced in the mirror to ensure that no trace of Lord Richard Nightingale-Temple remained, noting a slight bruising on his jawline. Sally had no idea who he was, and he liked it that way. She treated him as a barmaid's equal, not the son of an earl. *Maybe the bruising will reinforce that opinion.*

He slipped into his heavy, tweed jacket and, with carryall and cap in hand, crept toward the back stairs. He stopped abruptly and turned toward Simon's chamber, recalling the overheard discussion of jewels and cash.

Before he could take another step, he heard two maids chatting about turning back the beds as they ascended toward him. He ducked into an alcove out of sight. As the young women moved past him and disappeared into his brother's room, he released a long-held breath and made a hasty escape down the same stairwell.

Only a few staff remained in the kitchen, finalizing preparations for the next day and clearing away the evening mess. The remainder of the staff had already retired for the night. Richard kept to the shadows of the hallway and escaped observation by ducking through the kitchen door into the frost-covered back garden.

He crossed the driveway, stepping on frosted grass to mute his footsteps. Soon he was on the main road into town. The night was chilly. He paused near a stand of fir trees, staying to the shadows. He pulled his tweed cap over copper waves and stuffed his hands into worn leather gloves.

He marched on, heading for the train station. Under the first streetlamp he encountered, he glanced at his wristwatch and noted the time. *The last train leaves for London in twenty minutes. If I keep up this pace, I'll make it easily. That means I'll reach the pub before it closes. Sally will spot me a whiskey before we retire. Ah, good old Sal!*

—————

The day following Richard's disappearance from Jarrow Hall, Simon reviewed his brother's peculiar behaviour with his father while they relaxed in the study.

"As you know, I managed to find Richard a clerical position at the War Office," Charles said, lounging in a worn leather chair, ankles crossed and feet resting on the corner of his desk. "But I couldn't bring myself to trust my own son to work on top secret material. Given his track record of gambling and drinking, it would have been too risky. So, I had a position found for him in the outer office."

He shook his head in dismay. "Unfortunately, he was often late for work. Or he wouldn't show up at all." Charles swung his feet to the floor, steel blue eyes narrowed with impatience. "If he'd paid attention, he could have gleaned any amount of tactical information. In that regard, it's fortunate that he was more often a cad than a clerk."

"Regardless," Simon replied, "now that Mary and I are more settled, should we not wonder about it? He had a security pass, after all, and he has the aptitude for finding underhanded ways to fund his bad habits."

He jumped to his feet, seemingly agitated with the need to press his point. "Now, we have the additional concern that he could do any number of things that would compromise Mary's safety, too."

Charles inhaled, aghast at the comment. Then he shrugged with a sigh of defeat.

CHAPTER 9

September and October had proven overwhelming for all of the hospital staff, Ann and Mary included. Exhausted, they continued to report for their shifts each day as the volume of patients and the intensity of the Spanish flu escalated.

"Hopefully, we'll see the crest of it in the next day or two," the director said as he reported the statistics of the past week during their pre-shift update. "Remember to keep your masks up and wash your hands. If you develop any symptoms, excuse yourself immediately. The last thing we want is a spread of the disease within the hospital staff, too."

Gowned and masked, Mary accompanied Ann to the first ward of their shift: a smaller room of eight beds in the men's wing.

"Lady Ann," a man said, his voice croaking, as he grabbed her wrist.

The contact startled Ann. Her hazel eyes snapped to the man's face, perspiration pooling on his forehead as he gasped for breath, his grip shaky. She glanced at the list of occupied beds and confirmed the name: *John William Temple.*

"John!" Ann said a little too loud.

"I'm dying," he said, forcing each word through a spasm of coughs. "I know it. My wife, my children."

"Now, John," Ann said, "keep yourself calm. You'll only make your condition worse." She glanced about the room. "Sister Mary!"

———·—

Mary excused herself and stepped away from the patient she had been examining. "Yes, Sister?"

"This is John Temple, cousin to Lord Charles." Ann focussed a look of concern in Mary's direction. "Please stay with him a bit. I'll return shortly."

Mary read the worry on her mother-in-law's face and nodded. She took the hand of John Temple between hers and introduced herself.

"I'm going to examine you while Sister Ann speaks to the doctor." She spoke reassuringly as she pressed him gently into the bed. "I'll just take a look at your chart first."

She inserted a thermometer under his tongue, but the sudden fresh air caused another coughing fit. She paused, offering him a sip of water, and tried again. She recorded the information in his chart, then grasped his wrist as she checked his pulse against the ticking seconds of her watch pin. She continued to record the results of her assessment, then mopped his brow.

"So … tired," he said, gasping each word. "My … wife. The … children." His hand dropped to his side. Eyes closed, he drew laboured, wheezing breaths. Mary seized his hand for reassurance.

Ann arrived a short time later, accompanied by one of the doctors. John's eyes twitched but failed to open. Mary continued to hold his hand, saying nothing while the doctor reviewed the medical chart and recent entries she had made. He replaced the chart, filled his ears with the tips of his stethoscope, and applied the chest piece over the patient's lungs.

"Definitely the Spanish flu," he said, "complicated by a bacterial pneumonia inflection." He rolled the patient to reveal his back and moved the chest piece, listening again. "Well advanced, typical rhonchi gurgling and rattling in the bronchi are continuous." He glanced at the patient, then turned his eyes to Ann, shaking his head.

"Thank you, Doctor," she said. "If you don't mind, I'd like to sit with him for a while. Mary, dear, will you see to the other patients?" A tear slid down the side of her nose and disappeared into her mask.

Mary nodded and walked away with the doctor. "Excuse me, Doctor," she said, "would you happen to know whether his wife or children came in with him?"

"I'm sorry, I don't have that information," the doctor said sadly. "Why don't I ask another sister to relieve you for a few minutes? You might enquire at the front desk."

The matron did indeed have an answer for Mary. "Hannah Elizabeth Temple, wife of John William Temple, was admitted with him," she said. "She's in poor condition as well. No mention of children."

"Thank you," Mary said. "Which ward is she in?"

"The women's wing," Matron said, "Ward H, bed four."

"Ward H," Mary said, turning toward the women's wing, "that's a highly infectious ward, too!"

"Yes, be sure to wash your hands and put on a fresh mask, gown, cap, and gloves—and don't stay too long. Discard everything when you exit."

"Yes, Matron." Mary rushed toward the wing, hoping she would not be too late.

———•—•———

Had Mary not been wearing a fresh, white cotton mask, she would have noted the smell of death and dying. The room was silent, but for the occasional whisper of one sister to another or a sister to a patient.

This is a sorrowful room, she thought, feeling its weighted cloak bear down on her shoulders.

She found bed four easily. Spying a diminutive figure burrowed beneath a pile of blankets, she approached warily.

"May I help you?" a sister said as she neared.

"Um, I'm from the highly infectious ward of the men's wing," Mary said in a whisper. "Mr. John William Temple was admitted a while ago. I'm told he arrived with his wife, Mrs. Hannah Elizabeth Temple."

"You have the correct bed," the sister said, whispering in return. "This is Mrs. Temple."

"Is she able to respond?"

"She has the Spanish flu and pneumonia," the sister said. "She's been in and out of consciousness and has a dry cough. So long as she remains quiet, she won't cough. Try not to upset her."

Mary nodded and approached the bed. "Mrs. Temple? Hannah?" she said softly, reaching for the woman's hand. "Can you hear me?"

Hannah's eyes opened slowly. She blinked in response.

Mary introduced herself and explained that she had come from her husband's ward.

"Is he dead, then?" the woman replied, her voice a whisper of sparrow wings, devoid of emotion.

"No, but he's very sick."

"My children," the patient said anxiously. She coughed.

Mary placed a hand on the woman's arm. "Shh…"

"You must take my children," the woman said. "Not the orphanage." She coughed harder. "Water." Her hand wrapped around Mary's, her eyes pleading. "Not … orphanage!"

"Sister!"

Mary glanced at the nurse calling to her.

"You should go now."

Hannah squeezed Mary's hand. "You … take my children!"

"I will," Mary said sorrowfully, wondering what the woman meant.

By the end of their shift, both John and Hannah were dead, leaving Mary frightened for the children and the promise she had made.

With heavy hearts, the two women clambered through the door held open by the chauffeur and settled into the auto for the drive home.

"What can you tell me about their children?" Mary said hesitantly as they reviewed the deaths of the two family members.

"Not much," Ann said, seeming to welcome the diversion. "We've only met them randomly over the years. Different circles, you see." She twiddled her fingers in thought. "Three children: boy, girl, boy. John, the eldest, is about eight. Elvira is about six, and I believe William is four. They're very polite, well-mannered. Cousin John was an accountant, so they've had a good home. Hannah saw to it that they were well cared for. They're all members of our church."

"Ah!" Mary's mind raced. "I believe you pointed them out one of the first Sundays I attend church with you."

———

"Charles, will you contact the Ministry of Health and Social Welfare, Child Services, this morning?" Ann said, spreading jam on a piece of toast. "We must find out where the Temple children are and arrange for them to be brought here immediately."

"Of course," Charles replied, taking a sip of coffee. "To be clear, though, we are simply sheltering them until a proper home can be found; we're not taking them on indefinitely. I'm too old to be raising young children—unless, of course, they arrive naturally." He winked at

Mary knowingly, then sobered. "Poor John and Hannah."

"But it must be a good home, yes?" Mary said. "Surely we'll have a say in the quality of the home."

"One would hope," Charles replied, folding the newspaper that he had been reading before the women entered the breakfast room.

"I'll ask Mrs. Wright to open the nursery," Ann said.

CHAPTER 10

Richard rolled onto his back, growling with pain. Hundreds of needle pricks stabbed his frontal lobe, spiking the memory of a night's imbibing. He rolled onto his side again, hung his head over the edge of the bed, and vomited into a chamber pot conveniently placed on the floor in line with his pillow. He spat viciously, trying to rid his mouth of the aftertaste of bile and booze.

Slowly, he lowered his feet to the floor, placing his elbows on his knees and supporting his pounding head while the room rotated around him. He moaned and leaned toward the chamber pot, grateful for the dry heave.

Swiping the back of his hand across his mouth, he cracked his eyelids and squinted at the room in which he had awakened every morning for several days.

A firm rap pounded on the door.

"Who is it?" Richard said hoarsely, blood throbbing behind his eyes.

"You know who it is, lover," a feminine voice replied. "Open the door, sweetheart. I've brought you something to eat, but my hands are full, and I can't turn the knob."

Richard reached for the wrinkled sheet that moments before had snaked between his lanky legs. He wrenched it from the bed and wrapped it around his waist. "I'm coming," he said, moaning again as he staggered toward the door.

Sally marched into the room and set a tray on a small side table.

"There you are," she said cheerily, hands on round hips, chest thrust forward. "Breakfast! Just as you like it. Black tea. Plain toast. Good for your sour stomach, you always say!"

Richard squinted at the tray, emitted a guttural sound from deep in his throat, and padded into the water closet, leaving the sheet to drop behind him.

Sally picked it up, folded it neatly, and draped it over the end of the bed. "Really, Dickie," she said to his disappearing back. "I don't mind your staying over, but the least you can do is respect my things! I don't have much, but I've worked hard for all of it!"

Richard switched on the light and peered into the small mirror above the sink. Leaning toward it, he saw a pale face with several days' growth of red beard. He scrubbed at it, opened his mouth, and stuck out a white-coated tongue. He scowled, unimpressed. *Why am I here?* he wondered, pressing fingers into his temples. *If it weren't for Sally, where would I be? Indeed!*

He pissed into the toilet, pulled the chain, and staggered back into the room, scratching his copper chest. "Run me a bath, will you?" he said, reaching for the cooling cup of tea.

"Oh, Dickie," Sally replied, the impatience in her

voice expressing her frustration. "You should be running your own bath. I'm not a servant, you know. Makes me wonder how you get along on the days you're not here." She wandered into the bathroom and turned on the taps.

"Sometimes," she said, hands on hips again, "you act as if you're some rich la-dee-da from the other side of town instead of a clerk. Next thing I know, you'll be asking me to curtsy or something."

Richard took several sips of the tea and a bite of the dry toast. "Thanks, Sal," he said, kissing her on the cheek as he headed toward the bathroom. "You're a swell pal—"

"Pal!" she said impatiently, flicking her hand as if to dismiss him. "I need to go down. Customers are starting to queue at the door. Hurry up!"

"Give me fifteen minutes," he replied as Sally closed the outer door into the hallway.

Richard reclined in the tub and closed his eyes, wondering how he was going to come up with the money he needed to repay Sally and get to France. He had frittered away the last of his annual allowance a month ago, and still had two months before he would see another penny. He could not ask his father for more without risking the man's wrath, and his mother's hands were tied; he had milked her for all she could spare.

Simon's unexpected return had curtailed his intention to raid the attic for cast-off heirlooms that he might pawn to pay for pending expenses. *If only he'd returned a week later,* Richard thought, *I'd have been safely away.*

Abruptly, Richard sat up, the sudden movement

causing small waves in the tub and a spike of pain behind his eyeballs. *Jewels!* he thought, recalling the overheard reference to the Romanov jewels. *And cash! If I can find the jewels and cash, I won't need the silver! Plus, they'll be lighter to carry, easier to conceal, and, eventually, easier to sell! I must go back. If I don't, I'll always be indebted to Sally for putting me up and, although she doesn't know it, for buying my ticket out of here.*

Feeling more purposeful than he had for some time, Richard climbed out of the tub. *If I can repay Sally, she may be able to think kindly of me in the future.* He shuddered at the thought. *Better she thinks I'm some sort of cad, than a discredited toff!*

As he towelled himself off, he spied his razor and shaving soap left discreetly on the edge of the sink. Eyeing himself in the mirror, he scrubbed his jaw with his knuckle again. "I guess you're right, Sally girl," he said aloud. "I could use some tidying up."

Fifteen minutes later, a freshly-shaven Richard closed the door to Sally's room and exited down the back stairs, carryall in hand. He knew that if she or her employer spied him, he would be cornered for the rest of the day. Drinking her employer's rotgut was one thing; having her pay for it was another. He had no qualms about taking from his family—they could afford it—but not from someone like Sally.

He checked his wristwatch, realizing that if he was going to make the train, he would have to increase his pace. He plopped his cap on his head, buttoned his coat, and tried not to think about the painful explosions behind his eyes.

CHAPTER 11

Sally told her employer that she needed a toilet break. She raced up the back stairs, wondering why Richard was taking so long. Free booze—at her expense—usually drew him down for a tot immediately after his morning tea disappeared.

She inserted the key in the lock, but before she could turn it, the door slid ajar. It was unlocked. *Odd*, she thought, *I know I locked it behind me earlier.*

Slowly, Sally pushed the door to her room open, peering into the shadows, looking for Richard. She flipped the light switch, illuminating the dishevelled room she had left earlier. Nothing had changed except for the empty teacup, a remnant of toast, a distinct absence of Richard, and an uninvited stranger.

"Who're you?" a deep voice said flatly from the window curtain's penumbra, startling Sally.

"This is my room," Sally said firmly, fists resting on her shapely hips. Her heart pounded with anger when she heard the voice of an unknown, uninvited stranger in her room. "Who the hell are you?"

She remained by the door and glared at the man seated near the window wearing a navy trench coat, his face shadowed by his fedora. "And where's Dickie?" She slid toward the water closet, keeping her back to the wall. "Dickie, are you here?"

No answer came. Sally struggled to quell a rising sense of foreboding.

The dark figure struck a match and calmly lit a cigar. "That's what I'd like to know," he said, his voice husky.

Sally's face puckered at the acrid smell. A plume of smoke wafted from under the man's hat.

"I don't know where he is," she said impatiently, glaring at the intruder, "do I? If I did, I wouldn't be asking you, would I?"

She felt her glare waiver with her rising sense of confusion and fear. "Look, mister," she said, her voice and determination quivering. "Obviously, Dickie isn't here. And I sure as hell don't know where he's gone."

She stepped to the side of the hall door and pointed to the corridor.

"How about you get out of my room before I call my boss! If he gets a hold of you, they'll be serving you up as chopped veal at the Ritz tonight!"

The man slowly unravelled from the chair and strode casually toward the door, where he paused and scowled at her from under the brim of his hat. Then, he disappeared down the hall toward the back stairs.

"And don't come back!" she hollered after him. She dusted her hands and slammed the door. Steadying her quaking body as the adrenaline rush subsided, she leaned into the wall, pressing her hands into her chest, praying for calm.

CHAPTER 12

Not long after departing the *Eel & Martlet*, Richard darted across Whitehall, headed for King's Cross Station. A light breeze sent white clouds scudding inland, making way for blue sky and sunshine. In the distance, he saw, to his surprise, his father and brother entering the War Office Building. *What are they doing in town? I expected them to be in Jarrow for a while longer.*

Covertly, he approached the building. Without thought, he groped in his pocket for his wallet, wondering whether he still carried his security identification. Fingering through the billfold, he spotted his train ticket to Dover. The ticket he had purchased with a loan from Sally. *Train ticket!*

He ducked behind a pillar and jerked his wrist to reveal his watch. A moment later, he raced in the opposite direction, hastily concocting a new plan. As he jogged over shrivelling puddles, he resolved to trade in the ticket that would take him out of England for a round-trip economy ticket to Jarrow on a slow train. *I'll take the train home, collect a few more personal items, and maybe some jewels and silver to finance my plans,* he thought, swallowing a sly smirk. *Even if I'm discovered, Mother will turn a blind eye so long as Father and Simon aren't there.*

With spare change from the ticket swap, Richard bought a meat pasty and a bottle of ale, both of which eased his headache, allowing him to sleep the remainder of the journey.

———

When the train arrived in Jarrow, it was late. The temperature had dropped considerably since he had left days prior, and a light snow had begun to fall.

He pulled a handful of coins from his pocket and calculated whether he would have enough to pay for a motor cab to and from the Hall, concluding that he may have just enough to get him home. *I'll find more cash in the Hall. At worst, I know Tompkins keeps the household allowance in his office.* He raised his arm and flagged the next cab.

Richard ordered the driver to drop him at the gate and walked the remaining distance to Jarrow Hall. As he had done many times in the past, he entered with stealth through the kitchen entrance at the back. Removing his shoes, he made his way up the servants' stairwell to his room on the second floor. He dumped soiled clothes from his carryall onto the floor of his closet and restuffed it with the satchel of papers he had taken from the War Office, fresh clothing, and other necessary items. Satisfied that he had what he would need, he snatched his carryall and returned to the back stairs, where he stashed it under the stairwell.

Recalling the conversation about the Romanov jewels

that he had overheard between Simon and Mary, he crept along the hall toward his brother's room. He opened the door slowly, turned on a table lamp, and furtively opened drawers and closet doors, searching for clues that would reveal the hidden gems. *Nothing!*

He tiptoed to the door leading into Mary's room and used a sliver of the lamp light to determine whether she was abed. Satisfied that she was not, he pressed the door wider and searched her room as well.

His search of the second room proved successful when he found a pouch containing a variety of notes, including British pounds in a dresser drawer. He whistled softly at the significant sum and stuffed the cash into the inner pocket of his tweed overcoat.

Eventually, he accepted that the jewels were not to be found. Returning to Simon's room, he switched off the lamp and crept back along the hall toward the back stairs.

Careful not to step on floorboards that had retained their squeak since before his childhood, he crept up two flights to the attic above the servants' quarters. At the far side of the attic, under the eave, he found a chest of silverware and other small items that had been treasured by his grandparents.

He quietly turned the contents out of an old satchel, serendipitously leaning against the chest, and began removing the silverware. He doubted his parents would ever miss them. Several minutes later, he hefted the bag and decided that he could carry it and his carryall back to the train station, should he be unable to locate a motor cab.

Richard set the two bags on the landing at the yard door and crept into the butler's office. As expected, the drawer in which the household money box was kept was locked. He cast about for a ring of keys. Finding none, he snatched a letter opener and jiggled the lock until it released, and the drawer opened. Fortunately for him, the money box itself was not locked.

Richard stuffed the cash into his pocket next to Mary's notes, closed the drawer, and backed out of Tompkins' office, satisfied that the room appeared as neat and orderly as he had found it. He jammed his feet into his boots, tied the laces, and stepped quietly into the yard, taking care not to bang the door.

Richard walked hastily along the path to the great gate, keeping to the fresh, snow-covered grass. At the manor gate, he headed toward the train station, hoping to find an eatery where no one would recognize him.

He recalled a pub on a side street near the station and hesitantly opened the door. Seeing no one familiar, he sought out a dark corner and ordered a meal.

An hour later, he made his way to the station just in time to catch the last train to London. Instead of returning to the *Eel & Martlet*, however, he headed for a cheap inn located across the street from the station and rented a room for the night.

Mid-morning the next day, Richard entered the London shop of a less-discriminating silversmith. In exchange for a sad story he received a payment which, when added to the funds secured from Jarrow Hall, would be sufficient to see him through the next several months. *If I stay away from pubs, gambling houses, and women.*

Outside the silversmith's shop, he hailed a cab and ordered the driver to take him to Victoria Station, where he bought a ticket for the first train to France the following morning. Half a block away, he found an inexpensive inn, rented a room for the night, and asked the desk clerk for an envelope.

He spent the afternoon working through a plan that would hopefully transport him to Constantinople with little difficulty, where he hoped to eventually win an interview with the sultan and generously share the information he had taken from the War Office.

Once he was satisfied that he had considered his options thoroughly, he pulled out the wad of pound sterling notes and counted out a sum equivalent to Sally's loan. He wrote a note of apology to Sally and stuffed it and cash into the envelope. On the envelope's face, he carefully wrote Sally's name and address, then set it in the centre of the paltry desk.

On his way out the next morning, Richard paid the clerk for the room with enough extra to have the envelope delivered to Sally post haste. Finally, with a clear conscience, Richard boarded the train to Dover. "Constantinople, here I come," he said sotto voce as he settled into his second-class seat.

CHAPTER 13

Since accepting the position in September, Simon had been training as an intelligencer in the London MI6 offices. The training he received followed on the heels of what he had already unwittingly learned in Petrograd, while in the company of Bruce Lockhart. The recent training, however, had provided an opportunity to learn the finer points and advanced skills. Ever the academic and sportsman, he embraced the training with zeal.

Artyom, too, embraced the training he required to become a proficient code breaker and linguist. He was grateful to Simon for helping him find intriguing employment, and grateful to the Nightingale-Temple family for allowing him temporary housing in their London townhouse on Grosvenor Crescent while he settled into his new way of life.

"Being a code breaker is vastly different from being an Imperial guard," Artyom said one evening as they walked through St. James Park on their return to Grosvenor House in Belgravia.

"I'm aware of that," Simon replied, "having done a bit of it on RMS *Guardian*, but you have the skills required to do the work. Like me, you just need to think differently." They walked in silence, enjoying the autumn dusk. "Say, why don't we go out tonight? See what mischief we might get into?"

"So long as we're not out all night," Artyom replied. "Mr. Denniston is a stickler for punctuality, and focus."

"Artyom and I were thinking of a night out," Simon said as Zima set a light meal on the table. "We'll eat quickly and be out of your hair." He grinned as his valet's eyes met his. "Do you have easy access to that special trunk we brought from Petrograd?" Simon winked as they both remembered the shenanigans that he, Lockhart, and Artyom pursued in Russia.

"Yes, my lord," Zima replied, his eyes twinkling with thoughts of their pending mischief. "Shall I take it to your chamber?" In response to Simon's nod, the valet disappeared into the kitchen, but not before Simon sent Mrs. Zima his appreciation for the Russian meal that she had prepared for them.

Before they joined the Nightingale-Temple staff at Jarrow Hall, Mr. and Mrs. Zima had been employed by Simon when he lived in Petrograd. Mr. Zima served as Simon's valet and general aide, and Mrs. Zima oversaw the day-to-day management of Simon's apartment. On those occasions when Simon and his companions determined to make mischief, Zima, and occasionally his wife, may have been involved.

When Simon led Artyom into his chamber a short

while later, the trunk sat in the middle of the room, the lid flung back to reveal its contents.

Soon, the two men, dressed as scoundrels, slipped down the back stairs and out into the alleyway. They scoured the streets of London for the next several hours, hoping to find something remarkable.

"Well, this has been a disappointing night," Simon said. "Not one interesting lead for us to investigate."

"True," Artyom said forlornly, "but I've enjoyed the outing and the company nonetheless."

Simon snickered as they rounded the corner to Grosvenor Crescent. Given the late hour, Simon expected the lamplight to be overwhelmed with darkness. Instead, droplets of faint mist sparkled with reflected light as it swirled on gentle, unseen currents before dampening the pavement.

Simon stopped abruptly, grabbing Artyom's arm and dragging him into the shadows.

"What is it?" Artyom said, instinctively lowering his voice to a whisper.

"Look there!" Simon pointed at the figure positioned across from the entrance to his family's home, just beyond the cast of the gas lamp. "See him?"

Artyom nodded.

"He seems awfully interested in the house."

"Come on," Artyom said, perking up. "We need to get closer. Something about him seems familiar, yet suspicious."

They circled around the street, keeping to the dark

shadows cast by the tall dwellings.

"I can't believe it!" Artyom whispered. He raised his collar against the night's chill. "He looks like he could be *Okhrana!*"

"He could well be Russian police," Simon said, his voice low as he chewed on his lower lip, contemplating. "We've been expecting someone to approach Mary. Vasiliev is still after the crown jewels and is certain we secreted them out of the country, but I never would have thought of *Okhrana.*"

"You think Vasiliev is behind this?"

"Who else? We've tried to keep it secret." Simon pulled his cap lower. "The only ones who know anything about the Romanov jewels are my parents, you, Mary and I, and the former Romanov tutors. None of us would disclose that information to a stranger. Mary's jeweller is also aware that we have gems, but he doesn't know the story behind them, and the King's jeweller would certainly not tell."

"Come then," Artyom said. "Let's see what this fellow knows."

Silently, they approached the man from opposite sides, hoping to block any attempted escape.

As expected, as soon as Simon stepped into the lamplight, the wide-eyed peeper turned, running directly into Artyom. Artyom efficiently turned him about, pinning his arms.

"What business brings you to this neighbourhood?" Simon said gruffly. "Why are you watching my house?"

The man struggled against Artyom's hold without success.

"Answer me!" Simon said, grabbing the peeper's lapel, his face so close that he could smell cheap whiskey and stale tobacco on the man's breath. A soft belch of fear boosted the odour of boiled cabbage that permeated his clothes.

"I-I don't know," the man said, his voice sounding youthful, terror in his eyes. "I was told to watch who comes and goes. That's all."

"How long have you been watching?" Artyom said, pulling on the peeper's arms.

"Ow! A few months, maybe."

"What have you seen that's worth reporting?" Simon said, the effect of his narrowed eyes lost in the dark.

"N-nothing here." The peeper hung his head and kicked his toe into the pavement. "Just you two and the old couple, regular like. Sometimes, the other old couple and a pretty, young miss."

"You mean to tell me that you've been standing here for months and that's all you've learned?" Simon said, incredulous, his mind racing to imagine all that had occurred at the house over the past months.

"N-no, I've followed you. I know you have something to do in that building on Horse Guards Avenue. And I know you live in Jarrow sometimes."

Simon waited for him to speak further, noting the washed-out Russian accent.

"Who sent you?" Artyom said, jerking his arms again.

"My Uncle Ivan sent me a letter. He said that he

would pay me well if I could report that a young woman lived at this address. He sent me a picture of her."

"Do you have the letter with you?" Simon asked.

"In my pocket." His nose pointed unwittingly to the bulky left pocket of his worn, black leather coat. He twisted, trying to inhibit Simon's search of it.

Simon pulled the letter from a tattered envelope, trying to catch the photograph that slipped free. It landed on the pavement face-up under the gas lamp. As Simon bent to retrieve it, a young Mary with light brown hair falling over her shoulders smiled up at him. His stomach seethed with anger … and fear. He tore at the letter and stepped into the light, scanning the Russian words.

"Ivan Vasiliev is your uncle?" Simon said, flabbergasted by the revelation. "How did he know to send you here?"

"I d-don't know. He wrote to me last month from Turkey. I asked around. Are you Charles Temple?"

"No," Simon said, wondering what Vasiliev was doing in Turkey. "Charles is my father."

"Ah! Then you must be Simon Temple." The young man focussed intently on Simon. "Uncle Ivan told me to find out if you're married."

"And why would he want to know that?" Artyom said with another jerk on his arms.

"It's kinda odd, I think, but Uncle Ivan says one of the dead Romanov princesses is missing. He thinks maybe she lived, and you know something about it." Vasiliev's nephew eyed Simon bashfully. "Say, the pretty miss, is she the princess?"

"If she was, I wouldn't be telling you," Simon said.

"She's a real looker, that one!" Vasiliev's nephew said, nodding toward the photograph, whistling softly.

The sound of Simon's slap shattered the quiet morning and sent the young man's cap skidding across the damp pavement. "Don't ever speak of my wife again," he said through clenched teeth, realizing his gaffe immediately.

"Blimey! He's right then? One of them princesses lived, and you married her!"

Simon jerked his head at Artyom, indicating that he could ease his hold on the peeper.

The young man stooped to retrieve his cap. "Can I go now?" he said, rubbing the welt on his cheek where Simon's hand had struck.

"No," Simon said, the word thunderous. "You're coming with us."

Artyom grasped the young man's arm tightly as they marched behind Simon. At the corner, Simon flagged a cab and instructed the driver to head for MI6 Headquarters.

———

A while later, Simon sat opposite the young man, while Artyom hovered in the corner of an MI6 interrogation room. Simon grilled Vasiliev's nephew, Denis Vasiliev, gleaning all he knew of his uncle's assignment, how long the boy had lived in London and why, and what he stood to gain once he reported to Vasiliev.

"What do you think?" Simon said, speaking to Artyom privately in the hallway outside while a constable stood guard inside the room, monitoring the nephew.

"I don't think he knows much … yet," Artyom replied. "I believe him when he says that Vasiliev merely asked him to watch for Mary and report back to him where she could be found. Vasiliev might well instruct him to do more once the boy sends his report. Somehow, though, I doubt the boy is sinister enough to carry out any dastardly deeds, leastwise alone."

"I agree, but I don't want him to bother Mary," Simon said. "I want to speak to him once more, then I'm going to have him held under suspicion that he's a Russian agent until we have certainty."

Artyom relieved the constable and resumed his position in the corner of the room.

"Alright," Simon said harshly, "this is what we're going to do. I'm going to ask you questions, and, if I don't like your answers, I'll ask again until I do. Understood?"

The young man swallowed hard. "Y-yes, sir."

The answers to Simon's second barrage of questions were the same as the first, leaving Simon feeling that further interrogation was not the answer. He needed a thorough background check; he needed to know whether Vasiliev's nephew was truthful or a good actor. Not knowing left a knot in Simon's belly, and he recognized it as a fear for Mary's safety.

Simon reached across the table and grabbed the throat of the nephew's shirt, his face drawn close to Simon's. "Listen to me, and listen well," Simon said with a viper's hiss. "I have two things for you to keep in mind

… always. First, you will be detained for as long as it takes for a thorough background check to be completed. It we find anything contrary to what you've already told me, the remainder of your time in England could be very unpleasant. Second, if I ever catch you near my wife—or any of my family—again, I assure you there will not be a third time." He shook the collar held firm in his fist. "Am I clear?"

"Y-yes, sir. Y-you won't, sir."

Simon lifted a decanter toward Artyom and poured out two glasses of aromatic whiskey in response to Artyom's nod.

"Just when we thought we'd end the evening on a low note …" Artyom said.

"It took a rather interesting turn, don't you think?" Simon said, finishing the sentence with a growl. "He's just another one of Vasiliev's unwitting puppets. The letter reveals more information than the lad realized; otherwise, he wouldn't have been so careless."

"You still have the letter?" Artyom said, raising his eyebrows in surprise. He notched the ankle of one lanky leg over the other.

"In my pocket, along with an outdated photo of Mary," Simon said, handing his friend a glass of the peaty spirit. He set his own glass on a marquetry-inlaid mahogany side table and drew out the envelope before sitting in a matching chair right angle to Artyom.

They both took a moment to appreciate the aged scotch, Simon flipping the envelope front to back.

"The return address is as the lad said: Russian Embassy, Constantinople." He pulled out the letter, written in Cyrillic, and handed the envelope to Artyom. He read the letter slowly, looking for clues. "It's signed by Vasiliev, too."

"I presume Vasiliev is there to investigate whether Russia should send financial aid and, if so, to which party: the Ottomans, or the leader of the rumoured revolutionary force," Artyom said. "But what do you suppose led up to the letter being sent? And why watch this house, not Jarrow Hall?"

"He's obviously in possession of some information that suggests we returned to England; but that would have been easy to guess when Yakov Yurovsky reported back to him that we took the train to Arkhangelsk last summer and boarded a British ship," Simon said, swirling the remainder of his whiskey before emptying the glass. "And Yurovsky knows Mary is with us. If Vasiliev's sent his nephew to watch this house, I can guarantee you that he has someone watching Jarrow Hall, too. Perhaps now we need to take further precautions."

"I have an old army friend working at the Russian Embassy in Constantinople," Artyom said, rising to set his empty glass on the whiskey tray. "I'll send him a note in the morning. See what he knows. I understand, though, that the number of Russians arriving in Turkey is high. Visa and residency applications of White Russians hoping for asylum means great pressure on every embassy. We may have to wait."

"And, while you tend to that," Simon said, setting his glass on the tray as well, "I'll telephone Mary and put her on alert." He stretched, reaching for the ceiling. "If your contact comes up empty, I may have to catch a train to Constantinople."

"Simon, what is it?" Mary asked the next morning, her words breathless as they rushed across the telephone line. "I was just about to leave for the hospital."

"Sorry to make you run, Sparrow," Simon replied. "It's Vasiliev. He's found us." Simon relayed details of the encounter with Vasiliev's nephew the evening before.

"Do you think it has something to do with Mr. Popov?" Mary said. "Have I truly put us all at risk? Am I safe working at the hospital?"

"This intelligence is out of Turkey," Simon replied. "We'll have a better idea in a day or so. I'm only calling now so you'll take extra care. I'll call you as soon as I have more information."

CHAPTER 14

Mary glanced out the window, her thoughts occupied by her telephone conversation with Simon. Most of the deciduous trees along the drive were bare of leaves, their autumn coats mouldering along the edges of the lawn, while abandoned nests clung precariously in the exposed limbs. Without conscious thought, she sliced the letter opener embossed with the crest of the Temple Martlet through the flap of an envelope from Durham County.

"Mother Ann!" she said, excitement laced through her words. "A letter has come about the children!" She tugged at the long-awaited correspondence with a shaking hand.

"Why don't we take tea in the conservatory?" Ann said, approaching from the study. "While we wait for it, we can review the letter's contents."

"An excellent idea," Mary said, tucking the letter into its envelope before slipping it into her skirt pocket. "I'll stop by the kitchen to request tea and meet you there in a moment." Before Ann could respond, Mary disappeared through the blue baize door into the servants' domain, effervescent with anticipation.

Mary read the letter, scrutinizing every word. "This

is quite orderly," she said. "We're given a list of steps to follow with recommendations for greater success. The sooner we follow the steps, the sooner we'll be considered for guardianship."

"And, presuming they have no issue with our qualifications and submission," Ann said, "they'll summon us for an interview."

"I'm glad tomorrow's Saturday," Mary said dreamily. "We can work through the list and submit it on Monday." She sighed heavily. "Just imagine young children running about. Won't it be fun?" *I hope we can keep them*, she thought.

"It will, indeed," Ann said, infected with Mary's happiness. "And it will fill the time while you and Simon get around to having children of your own."

Mary's eyes darted toward Ann as the unexpected comment sliced through her heart. She ducked her head before Ann could read her face and coughed daintily. "Of course," she said. "I hadn't thought of it that way. Simon and I haven't really talked about children."

"And why would you?" Ann said oblivious to Mary's discomfiture. "You're both young and you've only been married a few months. You have lots of time to think about starting a family."

Mary accepted the cup of tea poured by the housekeeper and sipped gingerly, her moment of joy crushed by the thought of having her own child. *That will never happen*, she thought. *I could never bring a child into the world, knowing the possibility that they could inherit bleeder's disease. Dear Simon! How am I ever going to tell him?*

Over the weekend, they assembled the information required for approval by the Ministry of Health and Social Welfare for the guardianship of John Garmansway Temple, Elvira Rose Temple, and William Smoult Temple.

"I think we've earned a cocktail," Simon said Sunday evening as he straightened the pages into a neat pile.

"I agree," Mary said, rising to her feet, shaking with anticipation. "I'll just change for dinner first."

As she climbed the stairs to her room, she wondered whether the three orphans might one day form the family of which she dreamt. *That would certainly go a long way to softening my news when I announce that I won't bear a child.* A shudder ran up her spine as she stepped on the landing. *And then there's Simon's titles. Will they even pass to an orphan? Oh my, what trouble will I cause?* "I should have thought this through before I agreed to marry him!" she chastised herself, tears welling in her eyes.

Late the following week, another letter arrived from Durham Child Services with a summons to meet the following Tuesday. Mary promptly telephoned Simon to report the appointment time.

"That's exciting news," he said. "I can't imagine any hiccups. I'll put my request in for leave now. See you tonight, Sparrow!"

On Tuesday morning, Mary and Simon presented themselves at Durham Child Services, completed guardianship papers in hand. A receptionist accepted the documents and asked them to wait while she delivered them to the superintendent.

Mary lowered herself slowly into one of the worn, wooden chairs lining the reception wall. The room was chilly. Grateful for the warmth of the mink stole tacked along her collar and draping over the lapels of her coat, she folded her gloved hands in her lap. Her head hung in contemplation, all expression sheltered by the brim of her felt basin hat.

Simon reached for a hand and held it tenderly. She glanced sideways, giving him a demure smile.

"Nervous?" he said.

"A little," Mary said. "I hope we pass inspection."

"I can't imagine why we wouldn't," Simon replied. "I'm looking at this guardianship as a trial run for when we have our children." His smile was broad and sincere as he raised her gloved fingers to his lips.

"Please follow me," the receptionist said, interrupting their private conversation. "The superintendent will see you now."

Mary rose abruptly, snatching her hand away before Simon could detect her racing pulse.

Simon rose, brushed the creases from his trousers, and offered his elbow to Mary as he buttoned his tweed jacket.

An hour later, Simon and Mary returned to the hard, wooden chairs in the reception area. A tear slid down the side of Mary's nose. Quickly, she glanced out a nearby window as she dabbed at the trickle.

"Alright?" Simon said, turning to face her.

Mary nodded. "I was just thinking of all that must be done before the children arrive," she said.

"We still have to meet them," Simon replied, "and they need to agree."

"I know," Mary said. "I'm worried, though. What if they don't like us?"

"What's not to like?"

"Nothing, I suppose." Mary shrugged. "I so want them to like us."

"They will." Simon wrapped his arm around her shoulder and hugged her to him.

"Sir, madame?" Mary and Simon glanced at the receptionist. "Follow me, please. The children have arrived."

Hesitant footsteps shuffled on the tile floor outside the meeting room before the door opened slowly to reveal the three children. They stood side by side in the doorway, the young girl holding a hand of each of the boys. Their eyes were fixed on their shoes, as if a spot had been missed when they were polished.

"Hello," Mary said, rising from her chair when they

entered the room. She walked slowly forward, hoping not to startle them. "I'm Mary."

She dropped to a demure squat, facing them at their eye level. "You must be John," she said, extending her hand to the older boy. "And you must be Elvira!" Her smile was wide and genuine as she spoke.

"Yes, madame," the girl said, bobbing a curtsey. "*Elvie*, if you please, and this is William, but we call him Willy." She gave Willy's hand a shake, then dropped it.

"How do you do?" the small boy said, extending his hand. "Are you going to be our new mam? I don't want a new mam! I liked my old one!"

"Shhh," Mary said, caressing his small head. "I don't need to be your mam, but I would like to be your friend, if you'll let me."

"I suppose that would be alright," he said hesitantly, ducking his chin to his chest shyly.

"Are we to live at your house?" Elvie said.

"Yes," Mary said, "if you like, that is."

"Why can't *you* live with *us*?" John said firmly.

"I suppose we could," Mary replied, "but I think it might be a little crowded. Do you suppose you might have a look at our home first?"

"Alright," John said, as if contemplating his predicament.

Mary rose, smiling down at each child.

"May I introduce you to my husband?" she said.

They nodded.

She led them toward Simon for a proper introduction.

"Hello." Simon slid forward on his chair. "I'm Simon."

"How do you do, sir?" John said, sniffing as he extended his hand. "You smell like oranges! We love oranges, don't we." His siblings nodded with enthusiasm.

<hr>

Seeing that the meeting was running smoothly, the superintendent drew Simon into the hallway, leaving Mary and a governess to entertain the children.

"Will you take them?" he said abruptly.

"If the decision was up to me, I'd say yes. But my wife must agree. We will need time to talk about it."

"Will we?" Mary said, walking up behind him. "I think we've done enough of that. I agree with you."

"Then no further discussion is required," Simon replied with confidence. "We have enough information to satisfy our concerns. When can we take them home?"

"As I'm sure you can appreciate," the superintendent said, "we cannot simply give children willy-nilly to anyone who expresses an interest. While we have your paperwork and the children seem to approve, we must visit your home to ensure it's suitable. You say you live with your parents ..."

"If you're concerned about adequate housing," Simon said, chuckling, "I can assure you that the house is more than ample enough to support three children. When can we expect you?" Before the man could answer, Simon spoke again. "The children have been without proper family for weeks. If there is any possibility of abbreviating the process, please tell us how."

The superintendent considered Simon's comments. "Very well," he said. "I will come by tomorrow. In the meantime, please say nothing to the children. I would hate to get their hopes up."

Simon nodded, feeling a knot of anxiety build in his belly. *What if they really don't like us? What if we aren't enough?*

The superintendent was shown into the salon where Simon and Mary awaited him. He reviewed the final paperwork with them and had them sign where needed.

"You'll appreciate that we would normally make enquiries about your capacity to care for three children," the superintendent said, "before the paperwork is signed. However, the reputation of the Nightingale-Temples is well known. It helps that the children's father was a blood relative. We will finalize everything at once. That should shorten the process. Now, the tour, if you please."

Simon and Mary took the man on a tour of the house, indicating rooms where the children would sleep and play, as well as accommodation for a nanny and eventually a tutor. When they returned him to the front hall, the superintendent seemed content with what he had seen.

"We will need about two weeks to organize things," he said. "Once the children are living with you, we will visit on a regular basis for the first while to ensure they are content and well-provided for. Time between visits will eventually lengthen to once a month. But we must follow protocol, you understand."

As the great doors closed behind their guest, Simon hugged Mary, a great sigh of relief seeping through him. "This is going to be great fun!"

When a Durham County sedan finally drew to a stop at the front entrance of Jarrow Hall, Michael opened the car door, inviting the three children to step out. Each disembarked, tugging a small valise containing all their worldly possessions, which Michael dutifully offered to carry to their rooms. Bewildered, the children released their cases, each of the boys seeking one of Elvie's hands.

Beaming, Simon and Mary stepped forward to greet them. Then, although they were introduced to their nanny, Simon and Mary escorted them into the house. The children were taken on a tour of the main floor, the second-floor bedrooms, and the third-floor nursery, including their sleeping quarters. Following the tour, they returned to the salon for refreshments.

"What will become of the household goods and other items?" Simon said, sidling up to the superintendent and escorting him into the salon.

"The Temples were renting the cottage," he said, "but the goods within belong to the estate. The plan is to sell the goods, with the proceeds to be given to the children by way of a trust fund."

"Very well," Simon said. "I will arrange for two men and a van to collect everything next week. We have space for storage in the stable. If the children need something from there to make them feel more at home with us, then we will have it to give. Once you've set a value on the goods, I will send you a draft."

"No need," the superintendent said, surprised. "The goods were to be sold, presuming they could not be stored." He shrugged as if relieved to have the matter settled.

CHAPTER 15

When staying at Grosvenor House, their staff was minimal. Zima, Simon's valet, assumed the additional responsibilities of butler and footman, while his wife or an undercook covered the duties of lady's maid, house maid, and cook. While Charles and Simon might spend a work week in London, other family members visited the city infrequently, usually to run errands. As their visits were rarely more than a day or two, the children remained at Jarrow Hall, in the care of the nanny.

A fire burnt brightly, lending a sense of coziness to the breakfast room as November raindrops pattered on the external windows. Zima refilled four coffee cups, then cleared the breakfast table while the family discussed their plans for the day.

"We should be able to make the eleven o'clock train to Jarrow," Simon said. "Father and I want to stop by the Admiralty to enquire after news of Richard. How about you two?"

"Mother and I had success with our shopping yesterday," Mary said, looking satisfied as she dabbed a napkin at the corner of her mouth. "We even managed to complete most of our Christmas shopping." She reached up to pat her recently coiffed hair and smiled affectionately at the older woman seated opposite her.

"I quite like your new hair style, Sparrow," Simon said. "It suits you."

"I've never worn my hair short," Mary said bashfully. A rosy stain crept up her neck and rested on her cheeks.

"And Mother, your hair is lovely … as usual," Simon said.

"Thank you," Ann replied. "I'm afraid I'm not as adventurous as Mary. Maybe one day I'll surprise all of you, but not yet."

"We'll need to organize our purchases before we leave for the station, but we'll make the eleven o'clock train easily," Mary said as she pushed away from the table. "Coming, Mother Ann?"

The women promptly departed, heading toward the lobby and the stairs to the chambers on the second floor.

"I'm so looking forward to getting home," Mary said as she climbed the stairs. "I already miss the children desperately so."

⸻

Twenty minutes and a cab ride later, Charles and Simon were ushered into Smith-Cumming's office. He was not alone. Charles knew Smith-Cumming well enough but could not recall having met the second guest. Simon, on the other hand, strode straight into the stranger's embrace.

"Father," he said stepping away, "allow me to introduce

Bruce Lockhart—"

"Former Acting Consul-General, Moscow," Lockhart said, interrupting Simon. He bowed respectfully as he extended a hand toward Charles.

"Bruce," Simon said with delight, slapping his friend's back in comradery, "Captain Smith-Cumming mentioned someone from Moscow was in town. I'd hoped it was you." He cocked his head with curiosity. "Why are you here?"

"It's a long story," Lockhart said, shrugging. "Perhaps we can catch up over dinner one evening. In the meantime, I can say that I was forced to depart Moscow under— *ahem*—questionable circumstances, and ..." He stuffed his hands into his pockets, kicked at the floor with a toe, and deferred to Cumming.

"Of course!" Charles said before either could speak. He grinned at Lockhart. "I recognize your name. You're the one who encouraged the hidden messages in those damned Russian souvenirs!"

"Guilty, sir," Lockhart replied, abashed. He glanced at his superiors before continuing. "Given my unexpected availability, I was asked whether I might assist with queries into Lord Richard's whereabouts. Do you mind?"

"I certainly don't," Simon said, eyes bright as he recalled the time the two young men had spent together in Russia. "An extra pair of eyes is always welcome. Father, Bruce taught me most of what I know about espionage and intrigue." Simon's grin widened. "If anyone is going to find Richard, Bruce is the man."

"Nonsense," Lockhart said. "You had all the tools.

I just showed you how to use them." He twisted from Cumming to Charles and back.

"Gentlemen," Cumming said, calling for their attention as he rose from his chair, clasped his hands behind his back, and carefully positioned his artificial foot to ensure a steady stance. "If you're finished reminiscing, may I recall your attention to the matter at hand?" A momentary silence filled the room. "Shall we move on?" He waved his arm toward vacant chairs.

Both men nodded. Simon shook himself free of worrisome thoughts of Richard and focussed on matters at hand.

"A peculiar matter has been brought to my attention," Cumming said. "Not wanting to point fingers, but sensitive to the matter at hand, a young woman from the secretarial pool advised that, on the day of Lord Richard's termination, she saw him riffling through the filing cabinets as she was leaving for the day. Not knowing of his termination, she presumed he was simply carrying out one of his tasks. Several days later, she was asked to provide her supervisor with certain files related to the division of the Ottoman Empire amongst Britain and its allies. She was unable to locate them and, when canvassed, no one else in the pool had seen them. We are now left to wonder …"

"Whether Richard made off with them!" Simon jumped to his feet as he finished the sentence. "That could well be! He was awfully protective of his satchel when Artyom and I met him on the train the day his employment had been terminated. But … when I jokingly accused him of stealing government secrets, he offered to let me inspect it. I declined, feeling rather foolish for accusing my own brother of stealing."

"Hmph," Charles said, "it seems you may have had reason to do so after all!"

"I regret, Lord Charles, that I am obliged to file a report. Lockhart, why don't you bring them up to date. Your man did, after all, find the lad."

"He's been located?" Simon said in disbelief. He swivelled his attention toward Lockhart. "Already?"

"Not by me," Lockhart said, explaining how another agent had been tracking him. "I've just been supervising from afar, if you will."

Before continuing with further details, Lockhart withdrew a silver case, opened it, and offered cigarettes all around. Noting no takers, he lit one for himself, then continued, including Richard's train ride to Jarrow with one carryall in hand, his departure from the hall a short time later carrying two bags, and another brief stop … at a silversmith's establishment, from which he emerged toting only one carryall.

"This morning," Lockhart said a few minutes later, "I learned from the night clerk of the inn where Richard stayed last night that before he checked out this morning, he gave the clerk an overstuffed envelope and asked that it be delivered immediately to a Miss Sally Winton. Miss Winton is the young woman with whom—my colleague advised—Richard stayed recently and who happens to reside above a pub known as the *Eel and Martlett*."

He jabbed the stub of the cigarette into an overflowing ashtray and continued. "If you ask me, Lord Richard may have pilfered some of the family silver, which he then sold to fund his efforts."

"I'll have the name of that silversmith's shop, if you please," Charles said, interrupting the tale.

"Of course," Lockhart said. "The clerk speculated that the envelope likely contained cash, as Lord Richard then gave him a tidy sum to have it delivered, paid his bill, and left. He also told me that Lord Richard said he intended to catch a train to France. The last I saw of Lord Richard, he was boarding a train to Dover." Lockhart removed his pocket watch, noting the time. "His train left half an hour ago."

Leaning toward Simon, he added with a chuckle, "He was a lot easier to follow than Lebedev and Vasiliev."

"What the hell is the boy up to?" Charles said, scratching his chin in consternation.

"He appears to have a plan," Lockhart said. "What would you like us to do next, Captain?"

"Since you're still waiting to hear," Cumming said, directing his comment to Lockhart, "whether you'll to be charged by the Bolsheviks for plotting the assassination of Vladimir Lenin, you won't be returning to Russia any time soon. I therefore suggest that you and Lieutenant Temple follow after Lord Richard. See whether you can discover what the young man might be up to?"

"Brilliant!" Simon said, with a little too much enthusiasm, a surge of adrenaline coursing through his veins.

Cumming chewed his lower lip in thought, then glowered at the two young men. "In the meantime, Lord Charles," Cumming said, "may I suggest that you return to Jarrow as you've planned and determine whether you can glean a purpose for Lord Richard's return home. If you learn anything new, perhaps you'll send a telegram?"

"Certainly," Charles replied smoothly. "I have several engagements in Jarrow next week. Should I be rescheduling them and return to London?"

"That won't be necessary," Cumming said. "You'll be kept informed as matters progress." He turned to the two younger men. "On the other hand, I'll expect to be debriefed immediately on your return."

"Yes, sir," Simon and his friend again replied in unison.

"Off with you then," Cumming said shooing them out of the office.

"Oh my gosh, Mary!" Simon said, stepping with indecision as he glanced at his pocket watch. "The children!"

"I'll explain things to Mary," Charles said, trailing behind them. "Your mother and I will keep them safe. And don't worry: Mary will understand."

On the street, Charles tugged at his pocket watch, then flagged a motor cab.

"I've just enough time to stop at that silversmith's shop," he said as he entered the cab. "With any luck, the silver will still be intact."

"You plan to buy it back?" Simon said, his voice incredulous as he closed the vehicle's door.

"Of course!"

CHAPTER 16

As the cab pulled away from the curb, heavy rain drops began to beat a tattoo on the roofs lining the street. Simon and Lockhart hastened toward the train station to purchase tickets for the next train to Dover.

"I reckon Richard has a two-hour lead on us," Lockhart said once they were seated and the train underway. "Hopefully, he has a wait for the next ship to Calais."

"Why do you think he's headed for Calais?" Simon said, watching as the countryside slid by, framed by the train's window.

"It's a guess, really," Lockhart replied. "Ships are crossing the Channel from many ports, including Folkstone and Portsmouth. Most of the Dover crossings end in Calais. Hopefully, we spot him before his ship of choice departs. That will give us certainty."

When the train stopped in Dover, the men spent no time lingering at the station.

"According to departure postings, we have less than an hour to find Richard," Simon said, climbing a rock wall for a better vantage. "Hopefully, he's here. Look for a tall redhead." He scanned the swarm of milling naval crew and passengers. "Look there! The far side of the dock."

"I see him," Lockhart said, encouraging Simon to climb down. "Quick! We can't lose him!"

The two men set off at a jog toward the vessel near which Richard mingled with a group of passengers preparing to board.

"You keep an eye on him," Lockhart said. "I'll get the tickets."

Simon and Lockhart separated once aboard the ship. Unfamiliar to Richard, Lockhart was able to approach him without suspicion, while Simon endeavoured to keep out of sight.

"Mind if I sit here?" Lockhart said, nearing a vacant spot on the bench occupied by Richard and another gentleman.

"As you wish," Richard said, snapping out of his reverie. He squinted at Lockhart, who stood with his back to the autumn sun, then slid to his right to make allowance. He reached for his carryall and placed it securely between his feet.

"Going somewhere grand?" Lockhart said casually.

"Maybe," Richard said defensively. "What's it to you?"

"Absolutely nothing, mate," Lockhart replied with a smirk. "Just making conversation."

"Not interested," Richard said, crossing his arms over his chest to end the exchange.

For the remainder of the sailing, the two men sat

side by side in silence. When Richard finally rose to make his way to the ramp for disembarking, Lockhart sauntered behind him at a distance, allowing Simon an opportunity to catch up.

"We should stop him on the dock!" Simon said impatiently.

"Not yet," Lockhart cautioned his companion. "We need to know where he's going. He wasn't forthcoming."

Richard strolled with purpose along the side of the road, heading toward Calais Ville.

"He's likely heading for the train station," Simon said, slowing his pace.

"Yeah, but a train to where?" Lockhart said. He grabbed Simon's arm and pulled him behind a hedge when Richard looked over his shoulder.

"Paris would be a good choice," Simon said, resuming the tail. "From there, he could catch a train anywhere."

"We'd better keep up, if that's the case," Lockhart said. "If we can learn where he's headed, we might be able to answer a few of our questions."

CHAPTER 17

A while later, Richard purchased a train ticket and walked toward the platform.

"Excuse me," Simon said approaching the ticket wicket moments later. "My brother told me to buy a ticket to the next station—" he jerked his head toward Richard—"but I've forgotten which one."

"That would be Paris, Gare du Nord," the older man said, grumbling in French as he reached for the appropriate ticket. "Not very thoughtful, your brother. He could have waited for you." In exchange for Simon's fare, he stamped the ticket and pushed it through the wicket.

Simon turned away from the wicket, loosely holding the ticket toward Lockhart. Lockhart blinked confirmation and stepped forward. "One ticket to Paris, *s'il vous plaît*," he said, "Gare du Nord station."

On board, the companions again separated, each maintaining a clear view of Richard's seat. Several hours later, they disembarked and followed Richard to the next ticket wicket. Lockhart stepped in line behind him and sidled close as he requested a ticket to Marseille.

"I beg your pardon," Lockhart said deferentially to Richard when he turned away from the wicket and bumped into Lockhart.

"Learn to stand back, man!" Richard said angrily before stomping toward the platform.

"Next!" the ticket seller said, glaring at Lockhart.

Lockhart's gaze swung from Richard's departure to the wicket and back again. "*Pardonnez moi*," he said to the seller, and marched in Simon's direction.

"What's up?" Simon said as Lockhart approached.

"Richard just purchased a one-way ticket to Marseille," Lockhart replied. "We'd better cable the Chief before we go further."

Fifteen minutes later, as the departure call for the train to Marseille was announced, Lockhart snatched the telegram from the clerk and strode purposefully toward Simon. "We're to follow him," Lockhart read aloud. "Hurry!"

Tickets in hand, the two men clambered up the steps of the last rail car and meandered toward their seats as the train began to roll. Fortunate to find two seats at the opposite end of the car in which Richard had boarded, Simon and Lockhart took care to ensure that, while Richard was easy to observe, he would not see them.

CHAPTER 18

"Father Charles!" Mary said, striding purposefully toward her in-laws' chamber shortly after their return to Jarrow Hall. "Something is incorrect!"

"What is it, my dear?" Charles said, hastening through the doorway. "What's happened?"

"My chamber!" Mary said leading him along the hall. "Everything is upset!"

"Likely Richard," Charles said matter-of-factly as he glanced about the room. "Have you checked Simon's room?"

"Not yet," she said, heading toward the passageway. "I came directly to you."

Charles followed, peering beyond her into the room.

"It doesn't look disturbed," she said, puzzled. "Perhaps we should check the drawers."

"Hmph!" Charles said opening a closet. "This has been turned out, too." He stood, hands on hips, and spun slowly in a circle. "Clearly, we have been burgled. It *must* have been Richard, but just to be certain we should conduct a thorough search of the Hall to determine whether anything except the silver, which I've recovered, was taken."

He whistled softly as he thought. "Fortunately, the safe is hidden in my room. If Richard is responsible, he wouldn't know to look for that. He wasn't home when it was installed."

"The jewels are safe, then," Mary said, starting to feel relieved. "Mother's money!" She gasped, her heart beginning to pound. "I left a pouch of foreign currency …"

She hastened to her room and opened the drawer where she had left it. "It's gone," she said woefully, fists resting on her slender hips. "The pouch is gone!"

Charles reached for the green velvet cord near Mary's bed and tugged it to summon Tompkins.

Ten minutes later, Charles had explained the situation to Tompkins. For the next hour, they searched the chambers on the second floor. Richard's soiled clothing was found at the foot of his wardrobe, the evidence needed to confirm him as the culprit. With a sigh of relief, Charles concluded that nothing had been stolen other than Mary's money and the silver, but he instructed Tompkins to conduct a thorough search of Jarrow Hall the following morning … just in case.

CHAPTER 19

As the train from Paris slowed into the Marseille station late in the afternoon, Richard's belly rumbled loudly. With carryall in hand, he wandered into the street looking for accommodation and a restaurant, aware of the need to be thrifty. November was approaching, and he had no idea how long it would take him to reach his ultimate destination.

Half a block away, a neon sign flickered and buzzed. The highlighted words "Cheap Rooms" drew him into an ancient inn.

"Our rooms cheap, but clean," the portly innkeeper said proudly, his droopy mustache quivering as he spoke.

"Oh, yeah," Richard replied doubtfully as he dropped coins into the man's open hand. "I certainly hope they're cleaner than your reception hall." He tromped heavily on a cockroach scurrying toward his foot, then strode toward the stairs leading to his assigned room on the first floor.

Vermin skittered along the hallway, disappearing under floorboards. His skin crawled at the thought of what might be in the bed. The room was small, scantly furnished, and smelled of a potent cleaning solution. It boasted one dim light bulb suspended from the ceiling, and a large enamel bowl and pitcher on a table next to the wardrobe.

He removed the cord fastened around a curtain, passed it through the handle of his carryall, and tied the cord over a rod in the wardrobe. He snatched the bar of soap next to the bowl and rubbed it around the curtain cord, hoping the soap would deter cockroaches and fleas from reaching his suspended case.

Simon and Lockhart followed Richard to the old inn, then scouted for an obscure observation point.

"Looks like he may be here for a while," Lockhart said. "You stay here, while I'll look for a telegraph office."

"If we're to be here for a while, I'll look for nearby accommodation."

About fifteen minutes later, Richard appeared in the doorway of the inn and sauntered along the street in the opposite direction. Simon straightened, ready to follow. Richard stopped, peered through the dirty window of a questionable café, then entered. A chime over the door announced his arrival.

Simon moved along the street until he had a clear view of the table at which Richard had been seated. Keeping an eye out for Lockhart's return, he settled behind a pillar and kept watch.

Within the half hour, Lockhart reappeared. "We're to stay here and keep watch," Lockhart said. "Where's your brother?"

"In that café," Simon replied, as his own stomach rumbled loudly.

"Any luck with accommodation?"

"Yes," Simon replied. "This inn behind me looks reasonable. Keep an eye on Richard, and I'll get us a room." Soon he reappeared and confirmed that he had rented a room with two beds. "My feet will be hanging off the end of the bed, but at least it's a place to rest and the window overlooks the entrance of that one." He pointed to the one across the street where Richard had registered.

His stomach rumbled again. He shrugged in response to Lockhart's grin and handed his friend a rubbery croissant stuffed with white cheese dried at the edges and a thick slice of ham. "Compliments of the innkeeper."

"Don't suppose he gave you anything to drink," Lockhart said. "I'm parched."

Simon reached into his pocket and pulled out a bottle of orange soda. "It's all *she* had to spare. She promised to do better with breakfast. That's the only meal she offers. These were left over from this morning."

They chewed on the day-old fare, envying Richard's obvious enjoyment of his own meal.

CHAPTER 20

To his surprise, when Richard pulled back the covers of the bed a few hours later, he discovered starched and ironed white sheets. Exhausted from his long journey, he shook out his clothes and hung them in the wardrobe before collapsing into the crispness of the linen and falling into a deep sleep.

A loud rap on the door startled Richard from his slumber. He rolled onto his side, the room aglow with light filtering through frayed slits in the curtain. He rubbed his eyes, promptly recalling where he was.

"What is it?" he said, trying to collect his thoughts.

"*De l'eau, pour votre lavage, monsieur,*" the innkeeper's wife said cheerily from the other side of the door.

"*Un instant,*" Richard replied, wrapping a sheet around his waist as he snatched the empty water jug from the table and opened the door.

"*Bonjour,*" the middle-aged woman said, holding out a water-filled jug, her eyes twinkling in appreciation of the young man's partially-clad body and dishevelment.

"*Merci*," he said, handing her the empty jug with one hand while he held the sheet fast with the other.

"*D'accord*," the woman said, chuckling as she too juggled the exchange of the jugs.

A while later, covert questioning of the innkeeper took Richard to a sinister-looking locksmith named Germain, who specialized in black-market passports. Given the dispute over Ottoman territory, Richard did not want to arrive in Constantinople with a British passport. *Perhaps a Spanish one would be better,* he mused. *At least Spain has no territorial interest in Turkey.*

"He's on the move," Simon said, catching sight of his brother's bright hair. He rose abruptly, dropping his napkin on the table; then he snatched his jacket from the back of the chair and hastened into the street.

Lockhart swigged the last mouthful of his espresso and promptly followed, tidily spitting a collection of coffee grounds into the gutter.

"I wonder where he's off to?" Simon said. "He must have slept well. He seems to have a lot of pep this morning."

A few minutes later, they stopped outside the locksmith's shop and waited in an alleyway.

"Now what?" Simon said impatiently.

"When he comes out," Lockhart said, casually leaning against a nearby building while he lit a cigarette, "you follow him, and I'll find out what he's up to."

———•◦•———

Richard read the red and silver sign above the locksmith's shop—*Entreprise de serrurier Germain*—and muttered aloud his gratitude for the French he had learned in school. A chime over the door announced his entrance.

"*Oui*," the locksmith said once Richard explained his need, "I can make you a Spanish passport, but I don't think there are many Spaniards who have hair the colour of yours, *monsieur*. Or with such an English name. Perhaps you will consider a new name?"

"Like what?" Richard said impatiently.

"I suggest a Spanish name, if you don't want to be noticed." He studied Richard for a moment. "Perhaps *Ricardo Tempolo*? Easier for you to remember, *oui*?"

"Yes, I suppose you're right." Richard scratched his crown in thought. "What would you suggest I do about my hair?"

"My wife, she has a shop around the corner," the locksmith said. "While I make the passport, you visit her. She will help, yes?"

"Yes," Richard said, accepting a slip of paper on which the locksmith had written an address. Richard adjusted his cap, tugging it lower over his brow, and turned toward the door.

"*Attendez*," the locksmith said rapping his fingers on the counter to detain Richard. "Where is it that you go?"

"Turkey," Richard replied, wondering why it was any of the man's business.

"Perhaps you would like a French passport and a French name?" the locksmith said, one dark brow raised in query. "You do realize that most people—French, British, Greek, Armenian, even the Turks—speak French. It is the common language spoken by most parties."

"What?" Richard said, taken aback. "I thought it was English!"

"*Non, monsieur. Français.*"

Richard released the doorknob and turned to face the locksmith, chewing his lip in thought. "Alright," he said, abashed at his oversight. "A French passport it shall be."

"And your name, *monsieur?*" The locksmith raised a brow. "Your name is the same in English and in French, just pronounced differently, *oui?* Or perhaps you prefer something totally different?"

"No, leave my name," Richard replied, disappointed that his attempt at a disguise had been thwarted. "I'll take a French passport and colour my hair. That will have to do."

"That is perhaps a wise decision, *monsieur.* Unless you tell a good lie, it is better to stay near the truth."

The wait outside the locksmith was short. Once again, Richard strode along the street with purpose. Simon increased his pace and followed him to a salon. A sign in the window assured clients that all treatments, including colouring, cuts and styling, were available for hair, as well as manicures, pedicures, and other personal treatments. As Simon read the sign, his brows rose toward his hairline. *Whatever does it mean to have hair 'threaded'? And what is Richard planning?*

Several minutes later, Lockhart caught up with Simon.

"Apparently, the locksmith conducts other projects apart from smithing for a clientele less scrupulous than most," Lockhart said. "The proprietor hinted at forgeries, especially passports."

"Of course," Simon replied. "Presuming he's headed to Turkey, he won't want to appear with a British passport." He scrubbed at the bristles sprouting on his chin. "If so, then it makes sense that he's planning to colour his hair."

While Simon continued to wait in the shadows of the street outside the salon, Lockhart went in search of espresso. "If he's colouring his hair, he'll be a while," Lockhart said.

"Ah, *oui!*" the locksmith's wife said. "Many of my husband's *clients*, they like to change their hair colour." Peering at his wavy red hair, she selected a packet of hair tint. "I think perhaps light brown. New growth will be *trop orange. Trop évident!*"

Richard realized that the locksmith's wife was correct: maintaining the colour of his hair would be time-consuming and expensive. The root growth would have to be monitored almost daily if he was to remain a brunette for any amount of time. Grateful for the woman's advice, he paid close attention to the manner of her application and purchased several packets of the tint before he departed.

CHAPTER 21

"I need a drink," Richard muttered to himself as he wended he way back to the locksmith's shop. His hands quivered as he examined them. He licked his lips, imagining the peaty taste of the whiskey that he craved, and the company of an easy woman in a flapper dress. *No corset!* He smirked, glancing about for a bar.

An easy stride brought him to a *débit de boisson* on the corner before the locksmith's shop. He pressed his sweaty hands into his jacket pockets and licked his lips again. Thoughts of Sally's silky thighs drifted through his desperate brain as he clutched the doorknob and pulled.

He stood in the entrance, inhaling the stale odour of smoke, sweat, and ale. Scanning the room, the barman caught his eye.

"*Bienvenue, monsieur,*" the barman said, waving Richard toward the bar. "*Entrez, s'il vous plaît.*"

"Uh," Richard stammered as he approached. He shoved a hand into his pocket, retrieving a few coins. Spying an English penny in the mix, he realized that he had not had a drink since he left home. *I've been so preoccupied that I haven't thought of cards, whiskey, or women in days.* The coins fluttered in his shaking palm.

"What can I get you?" the barman said, switching to English. "Ale or whiskey?" He winked at Richard. "Perhaps *monsieur* has an eye for a lady?"

"Uh." Richard hesitated again, remembering his purpose, the limited funds in his pocket, and how badly he had lost at cards not so long ago. "Uh, no. Thanks. I've made a mistake." He turned abruptly and strode out of the bar, gulping as if he had been holding his breath.

Moments later, he calmly continued toward the locksmith's shop.

"I was about to say 'so much for devious intentions'," Simon said, "but there he is!" His face scrunched in an expression of amazement. "Hmph, I wonder why he changed his mind?"

Once again, Simon and Lockhart picked up the tail and followed Richard to the locksmith's shop, then back to the inn. As he approached the café, Richard ducked inside, appearing a few minutes later with a sack in hand and a mug containing a steamy beverage. He scanned the neighbourhood, missing the two men hiding in the shadows, then opened the lobby door and disappeared into the inn.

"Looks like he's planning to stay low for a while." Lockhart pushed away from a building. "Hungry?"

Simon nodded absentmindedly.

"I'll nip into that café and pick us up something decent to eat."

"Sure," Simon replied, wondering, not for the first

time, what his brother was up to. "I wish I knew for certain where he was going."

Simon and Lockhart sat in the breakfast room, enjoying the food Lockhart had purchased and keeping an eye on the door of the inn across the street. By the time Richard reappeared, they had finished the simple fare.

"Now what?" Simon said.

Lockhart dabbed his mouth with a napkin and rose with Simon, donning his jacket once again.

Richard marched along *Rue Longue-des-Capucins*, then turned right onto *La Canebière*.

"He's headed toward the Old Port," Lockhart said. "Perhaps he'll be looking for a ship."

"A ship!" Simon said quietly.

"According to the locksmith," Lockhart said, "he's headed for Turkey. He asked for a French passport."

"A French passport!" Simon said. "Why, he only has school French! How does he expect to pass as a Frenchman if he can't speak the language?"

"You tell me," Lockhart said. "He's your brother."

As they neared the port, Richard paused, glancing left and right, then disappeared into a wooden building. A sign offered passage to a variety of Mediterranean ports, including many in Africa and several other countries such as Italy, Greece, and Turkey. Soon, Richard exited the building and strode toward *La Canebière*.

"Let me make enquiries," Lockhart said. "Your resemblance to your brother is too obvious, especially now with the dye job."

———•—•———

"There he is!" Simon said, pointing from his perch at the end of *La Canebière* early the next morning.

"The information from the ticket vendor appears to be accurate," Lockhart said. "Now what?"

As Lockhart spoke, Simon pushed away from the perch and approached Richard with determination. Richard failed to notice his brother's approach, seeming distracted in thought. By the time he realized that the angry man stomping toward him was Simon, he could only side-step the advance and hasten toward the pier.

"I've come to take you back to England," Simon said, his determined steps pushing to reach Richard before he could board the ship.

"I'm not going back," Richard replied. Startled by Simon's grasp, he yanked his arm free and shoved Simon off balance.

As Simon tripped over a coil of hemp rope, Richard quickened his pace. Smoke from the sole passenger ship readying to push off billowed white, reaching toward the morning's sun-kissed sky. A blast of the ship's whistle temporarily drowned the screeching of gulls, as they flapped out of their roost in a cacophony of complaint.

Simon recovered his footing and lunged after his brother. Richard swung his carryall wide, knocking Simon off balance. Simon's heel struck a cleat, tripping him backward. Lockhart grabbed him by the elbow to break the fall.

Furious at Richard's determination to escape, Simon

twisted free of Lockhart's grasp and chased after his brother, intent on catching him before he could reach the gangplank.

"Get lost, Simon!" Richard said, lifting his foot to step on the plank. "I'm not going back."

Determined to thwart his brother's intention, Simon swung hard, his right fist connecting with Richard's belly. Richard moaned, dropped his carryall, and swung wildly, catching Simon in the jaw. Within moments the two were dancing up and down the pier, swinging and grabbing whatever was available of the other.

"I said that's enough," a marine guard said, his French accent exaggerating the command. He reached for Simon's collar.

Taking advantage of the brief distraction, Richard retrieved his bag and swung it hard with two hands. The strength of the swing caught Simon across his back, forcing him forward across the wharf and head-first into the murky sea water.

A second guard grabbed Richard, pulling him in the opposite direction. Simon surfaced, splashing with surprise and spewing salt water before paddling toward the wharf. He reached for a gaff offered by the first guard and clambered back onto the pier. A trickle of blood snaked from a gash on his forehead.

"*Monsieur*, if you intend to board this ship, you will show me your ticket," the guard said angrily, releasing Simon.

"I don't have one," Simon said, licking sea water

from his lips. With annoyance, he swiped at the blood seeping into his eye, smearing it across his brow. "I'm with the British Admiralty. This man"—he thumbed toward Richard—"is to return to London with me."

"I have a ticket," Richard said, confidently producing it, "and he has no authority or reason to seize me." He returned the ticket to his pocket and arrogantly glared at Simon.

"Sir," the first guard said to Simon, "unless you show me evidence of your authority to seize this man, you'll come with me. Otherwise, without it, you have no authority in France." When Simon shook his head, smearing sea water and blood from his eyes, the guard pointed impatiently toward the shore. "*Allons-y! Maintenant!*"

The guard shoved Simon toward the street. Simon stumbled, another fall thwarted by Lockhart. Lockhart and the other guard clasped Simon's soppy sleeves and guided him toward the exit, leaving wet footsteps to dry in the warming sun.

"I'll find you," Simon said over his shoulder, yelling to be heard over the bellow of the ship's whistle. "I'll bring you back! You'll answer for what you've done!"

Richard narrowed his eyes, glowering at his brother, likely for the last time. Then he ducked below deck to join other passengers.

"*Monsieur,*" the guard said to Simon, "I recommend you leave the pier now; otherwise, I will be forced to call *les gendarmes.*"

"Alright! Alright!" Simon said, frustrated by the

encounter. He shook free of grabbing hands and turned to watch the ship pull away from the wharf, fists clenched by his sides.

"Let's go!" Lockhart said, raising an arm to guide Simon off the pier.

Simon jerked away and tromped ahead.

Halfway down the steps to the cabin, Richard hesitated and turned toward the wharf. He shaded the sun from his eyes and watched his older brother angrily storm toward the shore. *What have I done?* Had someone told him that the pain he felt in that moment was heartache, he would have scoffed at such a ridiculous thought. What had become abundantly clear was the sense of finality when he realized, and accepted, that he might never see his family again. Might never see England again.

Feeling the nausea of doubt settle in his gut, he dragged himself back to the deck, not taking his eyes from Simon's back. As the ship pulled away from the wharf and straightened into the channel, Simon became a speck in his vision, until he disappeared completely.

Richard set the carryall between his feet and braced himself against the rail, gulping the fresh sea air as if he would never breathe again.

CHAPTER 22

The morning after their return to London, Simon directed a cab driver to drop him at the War Office Building.

Simon checked his pocket watch as he strode toward the entry guards, then withdrew his clearance card. Recognizing the young man, the guards waved him through. He arrived in the intelligence office with three minutes to spare and was instructed to wait while the clerk announced his arrival.

"The captain will see you now," he said a minute later, and led Simon into the office.

"Good morning!" he said. "I hope I haven't kept you waiting." He glanced at Lockhart. "Have you filled him in?"

"Yes," Lockhart replied.

"When I received Lockhart's cable from Marseille," Cumming said, directing his remark to Simon, "I realized that Lord Richard must have a purpose."

"I agree," Lockhart said. "Each step he took seemed part of a greater plan. The ship he boarded is headed to Malta. After that ..." He shrugged as he drew on a cigarette. "I'll cable some of my contacts and ask them to look out for him. If I hear anything, I'll report back."

"You on the other hand, Lieutenant Temple," Cumming said, "were given orders, which you failed to obey. You were to follow him; not apprehend him. We must learn his plan before we can stop it."

"I'm sorry, sir," Simon said, hanging his head in shame as he recalled his behaviour in France. "It won't happen again."

"Indeed," Cumming said. "I understand how emotions can get the better of one, especially family. However, I suggest you ensure that indeed it does not happen again."

"Yes, sir," Simon replied sullenly, wishing he could crawl under the cracked linoleum on which he stood. He focussed on his discomfiture and struggled to bring his emotions under control.

"Say," Lockhart said, stuffing his hands in his trouser pockets and rocking on his heels, "is Vasiliev's nephew still in custody?"

"Gosh!" Simon replied. "He should have been released by now. He said something about Vasiliev being in Turkey when Artyom and I detained him, though."

"Then I suggest that, tomorrow, you two make it your business to find him and bring him in for further questioning." Cumming glanced at his desk clock. "In the meantime, Lockhart, since there's not much left of the day, why don't you show Temple around the department. Other distractions have deferred an appropriate opportunity for a proper introduction before now."

CHAPTER 23

For the next while, Lockhart led Simon through the neo-Baroque building, showing him the layout and introducing him to key individuals, allowing time for questions when introductions were made to various department heads and instructors.

"Let's grab some dinner," Lockhart said, glancing at a wall clock. "I'll show you the field locations another time."

"Say, we should invite Artyom along," Simon said as they neared Room 40.

•

"By the way," Lockhart said as the three men strolled along the hall, "you might be interested to hear the latest news from Moscow. We've been so distracted with Lord Richard's situation, that it slipped my mind." He glanced covertly at his colleagues and stepped closer as he continued to speak with a lowered voice. "You know Maxim Lebedev is dead."

"We do," Simon replied, chortling, although his expression was serious. "We saw him fall to his well-deserved death last summer. He and Yurovsky followed us from Yekaterinburg. We were on a train headed north to Arkhangelsk, hoping to catch a ship home."

They exited the building, stopping to salute a young soldier who held the door for them.

"They trapped us in the last car and a fight ensued," Artyom said, continuing the story. "Mary recovered one of the pistols bouncing around the car and wounded Yurovsky. She intended a kill shot, but the train lurched, and the bullet struck his hand. Wasn't pretty."

Lockhart pointed across the street toward a restaurant, eyebrows raised for approval. Simon nodded, and they stepped off the curb, keeping pace with the traffic.

"Lebedev attempted to escape as the train neared a station," Simon said. "He tripped out the door and flew over the railing, landing on a track. A moment later, he disappeared under the wheels of a second train rolling into the station behind us. When the trains stopped, station guards secured Yurovsky. I managed to convince them to release him to my custody. We in turn released him to British security when we arrived in Arkhangelsk."

"And you know that Yurovsky and Vasiliev were to stand trial right about now?" Lockhart said. Simon and Artyom nodded.

"Well, Yurovsky was released in advance of his trial. Not enough evidence. He has—I've been told—been engaged by the Bolshevik security force and passes himself off as a secret police officer." He raised his hand to still Simon and avoid an interruption. "Vasiliev disappeared in advance of his trial. No one has been able to explain his escape, but my suspicion is that his family bought his freedom."

"Good God!" Simon said. "That explains a lot. We have news out of Turkey that confirms he's there." He knuckle-tapped his chin, deep in thought. "Mary said that she's felt safe in England, until recently. Her experience in Newcastle's Russian Quarter, combined with the knowledge that Vasiliev is free and using his nephew to threaten her …" He shook his head in sober thought. "Has ended that. Now she'll have the added worry about the children."

"Sorry to be the bearer of bad news," Lockhart said, "but I thought you should know. I have had contacts watching Yurovsky. I agree with you: Vasiliev is the concern. He'll be followed too … as soon as we find him."

"We're close on that note," Artyom said. "I've heard back from my former colleague. He now works in the Russian Embassy in Constantinople. He says that Vasiliev is in and out often."

Simon couldn't sleep. At first, he thought the whiskey that he drank with Artyom and Lockhart before turning in had kept his mind racing. When images of Richard's sneering face as the ship pulled away from the dock in Marseille, combined with not knowing what his brother intended when he arrived in Turkey and the peril in which Mary and the children could be placed if Vasiliev or his thugs were to attack his family spun through his thoughts, he accepted that sleep would evade him. He tossed off the bedclothes and swung his feet to the floor.

Donning a pair of woollen trousers, a brown jumper, and a tweed coat, he shoved his feet into his leather boots. As he crept down the stairwell to the foyer, he wrapped a cream-striped muffler around his neck and fastened his cap securely about his ears.

Quietly, he opened the front door, dragging it closed behind him until the latch snicked shut. He glanced left and right along the street as he pulled on his gloves and followed the plume of his breath down the stairs.

Without realizing where he was going, Simon strode smartly to that part of town where he would find the *Eel and Martlett*. Eventually, he stood under a lamp post across the street, pondering whether to go in. He checked his wristwatch. The publican would be shouting "time" in less than an hour. *What have I got to lose?*

Simon pushed the door open, allowing a breath of fresh air to waft before him into the smoke-filled establishment. Lockhart had not described Sally to him, but he knew her instantly … not simply because she was the only serving girl on the premises, but because she was pretty and blonde, and he knew the type of woman his brother favoured.

He caught the eye of the barkeeper, shouted for a whiskey-neat, and retired to a vacant booth in the corner. Moments later, the blonde server appeared at the table with his drink.

"Do I know you?" she said, eyes full of curiosity.

"Afraid not," Simon said, keeping his chin down with the hope that the brim of his cap covered enough of his face for her not to notice his resemblance to Richard. "Never been here before."

"Odd," she said, "you seem familiar … yet not." She shrugged and turned away. Spinning on her heel, she turned back to him. "Might your name be Temple?" she asked.

"Afraid not," Simon said again, with a silent prayer for forgiveness. He may tell untruths as an intelligencer, but he regretted telling deliberate lies. *Not yet; maybe later.*

"The resemblance is uncanny," the server said.

"Oh? How so?" Simon replied.

"It's nothing really," Sally said. "It's just that, well, I have a friend—his name's Dickie. He used to pop around often. But, well, I haven't seen him in a while. You remind me of him, somehow."

Simon scanned the room. The two remaining patrons were clearing their tab with the publican. "Care to join me for a drink?"

"Oh, I don't think so," Sally said. "Thanks all the same. I have work to do, and I shouldn't drink with patrons." She glanced at her employer as she lowered herself into the opposite bench. "But I suppose my feet could use a break before I close up," she said.

Her smile was lovely, and Simon found himself appreciating her friendly nature and sparkling green eyes. No wonder Richard fancied her. "Tell me about this Dickie. Do you miss him?"

"I do, yes," she said. "I'm worried about him. One day he was here and then"—she threw her hands in the air—"he was gone." She leaned toward Simon. "Confidentially, and I don't know why I'm telling you, except that you sort of look like him and all … He was visiting me in my flat above." She looked toward the ceiling. "He was still up there when I came down to start my shift, but when I went back up thirty minutes later, he was gone. And there was this shifty fella in a long coat and fancy hat, sitting in my window and smoking a cigar! I mean, the gall of him! Smoking in my room! Dickie never smoked in my room." She sighed. "I do miss him so. He never had a tinker's penny, but he was good and kind."

"Sally! Time to lock up, love."

Sally turned to the publican and waved. When she turned her attention back to Simon, he was already standing. As he pulled his cap over his ears, he reminded himself to slouch, hoping to avoid further comparisons.

"Thanks for the company," he said, placing a few coins on the table. He nodded, snatched his gloves, and hurried out the door.

CHAPTER 24

Mrs. Zima surveyed an assortment of boxes received earlier in the week, which were now stacked in Mary's chamber. "So many lovely things, my lady! I'll be kept very busy, especially with the sequinned dresses and the satin shoes!" Her Russian accent bent the words in an odd manner.

While Mary and her siblings had been taught by their English tutor, Sydney Gibbes, and had learned to speak it with a British accent, Mr. and Mrs. Zima had learned to speak English as recent as their arrival in Jarrow in 1918. They had no need to speak English until Simon elected to remain with the Romanovs when they were detained in Tolbosk. On his instructions, Simon's retainers packed any clothing and other items left behind by him, together with their own personal possessions, and while he ensured they had safe passage to Jarrow.

"You might also like to see what's in here," Mary said, placing a nondescript package on the end of the bed. "A courier brought it a while ago."

"What can it be?" Mrs. Zima said. "I see no shop name on the wrapping."

"That," Mary said, "is because it's from the jeweller."

Mrs. Zima withdrew a small pair of scissors from her chatelaine and snipped the string that secured the brown paper wrapping. Spreading the paper, she revealed several small boxes, each impressed with 'Garrard & Co.'

"May I, my lady?" she said tentatively, fingering the boxes.

"Please," Mary said with a wave of her hand.

Mrs. Zima admired the various pieces of jewellery as she gingerly removed them from the boxes, especially the unique ones designed by Mary. Her eyes gleamed with appreciation. "It is a privilege to have this moment to appreciate my lady's new wardrobe and accessories, and the lovely jewellery." She swept her arm across the room. "Never in all of Russia would I have had such an honour bestowed upon me. My husband and I are truly grateful to Lord Simon for all he has done for us! And now, to be able to serve our tsarina!" She curtsied as deep as her aging knees would permit.

"Mrs. Z," Mary replied, taken aback by the woman's gratitude. "You and Zima served Simon well in Russia. You kept his secrets, and you brought his possessions safely to England, all at great risk to yourselves. Plus, you left behind all that you knew and undertook an adventure into the unknown."

"Not unlike yourself, my lady," Mrs. Zima said, her eyes dark, seeming to reflect old memories. "Were it not for Lord Simon, my husband and I would never have known the joy of being together. Would never have known what it is to feel safe and respected."

She retrieved a lacy, white handkerchief from the pocket of her black, silk dress and dabbed her eyes. "The Nightingale-Temple family will always have our gratitude and our loyalty."

Spontaneously, Mary hugged the older woman, then released her, blushing. "I apologize, Mrs. Z," Mary said, sniffling as she fumbled to retrieve her own handkerchief. "Please forgive me." She sank onto the bed, unable to control the tears that flowed freely.

"My lady, what is it?"

"I don't know, Mrs. Z," Mary said, sobbing. "Suddenly, I just feel the need to cry. My mind is racing with images of my parents, my family, their deaths: the overwhelming sense of loss!" She braced her elbows on her knees and hid her face in the handkerchief.

Mrs. Zima quickly retrieved fresh handkerchiefs from a drawer. "Here, my lady."

Mary looked up, red-faced with sorrow and exchanged the soppy fabric for fresh ones. She set one on her lap and blew her nose with the other.

"Only you can know your sorrow," Mrs. Zima said. "But I have my own, and I can feel my loss of family—a child—as greatly as you feel yours. Sometimes, it takes my breath away, and I wonder why each day I rise again." She sat next to Mary and wrapped an arm around her trembling shoulders.

Mary turned toward her, sobbing harder. Mrs. Zima held the young woman. Together, they sat quietly until Mary had spent her heartbreak. Mary pushed away and blew her nose again.

"Thank you," Mary said, mumbling into the fresh handkerchief as she mopped her face with it. "I have been trying to keep 'a stiff upper lip' like the British say, but suddenly I couldn't hold it in any longer. I'm sorry you had to witness my breakdown."

"Think nothing of it, my lady," Mrs. Zima said in Russian, breaking her promise to speak only English. She stuffed her own handkerchief in her pocket with a final sniff. "I am here to support you, however and whenever you need me. And I don't say that as a servant. You have replaced the sore in my heart for the child that I lost. It is presumptuous of me to say, I know, but you have become that child. A blessing that I never expected."

Mary began to sob again, falling against the older woman, welcoming her affection. When her sobbing ceased, she straightened, kissing Mrs. Zima's cheek as she did so. "I am the one who is blessed," Mary said. "My mother was my confidante, but she is gone. In her place, I've found you."

The two were quiet for a few minutes as Mary collected herself with a sniffle.

"Now, what shall we do with this remarkable jewellery?" Mrs. Zima said, collecting the boxes into a manageable pile.

"I have an idea," Simon said. His baritone voice from the doorway startled both women.

"You do?" Mary replied, turning an alarmed gaze

toward her husband.

"Here, let me see if I can remember," Simon said, closing the distance to the chest. He glanced at his wife with curiosity, wondering what had caused her discomposure. Mary's nod to carry on was negligible, but clear enough for him to understand she would explain later. "This was my grandmother's chest. I saw her access a secret compartment once when I was a small boy. I've always been curious, but never had an opportunity to investigate."

Simon approached the highboy and opened the third drawer from the bottom. To the uninformed eye, the façade suggested two lower drawers. Inside, however, the single drawer contained a maze of compartments designed for sorting shawls and wraps, stockings and gloves, and other small items.

Carefully, he lifted the box for stockings and gloves and revealed a long, shallow space beneath. He pressed on the bottom of the space, releasing a hidden lever that opened it slightly. Simon caught the edge with his thumb and lifted it to reveal further velvet-lined compartments for necklaces, rings, and other jewellery.

"Will this do?" he said, grinning at the expression of delight on their faces.

"Ingenious!" Mrs. Zima said. "This will do very well, my lord!"

"I'll wear this set this evening," Mary said, taking the top box from Mrs. Zima and checking inside. A dry sob escaped on a sigh, surprising the three of them.

"Mary!" Simon said, alarmed, "are you alright?"

"Yes," Mary said, blushing. Her eyes fell on Mrs. Zima, and she smiled warmly. "Very fine indeed."

Opening the box wider, Mary revealed a necklace, the pendant of which was a tear-drop shaped piece of transparent, red amber, its clarity marred by the shape of an ancient honeybee. A pierced miniature crown at the top of the pendant formed the bail through which a delicate byzantine chain passed. Tiny copies of the crown formed the settings of the matching earrings, from which smaller pieces of the same red amber dangled, each speckled with golden flecks of pollen.

"These are outstanding, Sparrow!" Simon said snaking his arm around her waist. "Is this one of your designs?"

"Yes," Mary said shyly, mopping her nose. "Mama loved her pearls, but I can't bring myself to wear them just now. I think the amber makes a nice substitute."

"With this dress?" Mrs. Zima said, holding a burnt-orange silk dress, accentuated with a diaphanous drape veined with golden thread.

"Exactly," Mary replied, fingering the fabric. She smiled demurely when she saw a look of endorsement on her husband's face.

"Shall I leave you to change?" he said, leaning toward the door. "I hear Zima coming up the stairs. He'll want to see me dressed as well."

"Certainly," Mary replied, "but will you ask your mother to lock these up for me?" She handed the remaining assortment of boxes to Simon.

"Excuse me, sir, my lady," Zima said from the doorway. "A courier has just delivered this package and insisted that I deliver it to you personally—and immediately."

Seeing that Simon already held several boxes, he handed it to Mary.

"I wonder what it could be," Mary said, tearing at the wrapping. "There's no return address. Oh, wait! There's a note." She withdrew an envelope, opened it, and tugged out a folded page.

"*My dear Grand Duchess,*" she read aloud, her forehead puckering with a frown, "*We cannot tell you of our delight to learn that you have arrived safely in England, still in the care of Lord Simon and Captain Egorov. As soon we are able, we shall visit. In the meantime, please accept our heartfelt condolences at the loss of your family. The contents of this parcel are rightfully yours now.*"

Mary glanced at Simon, then at the package. She hefted the box within, noting the weight of it.

"That must be from the tutors, Gilliard and Gibbes!" Simon said, his smile evaporating to a frown. "Don't open it!"

He dropped the jewellery boxes on the bed and lunged toward Mary. Before he could reach her, she had set the parcel on the bed and slid aside the string that held the lid fast.

Inside, she found two weathered leather pouches. She forced open the mouth of one and stuffed her hand inside. "Money!" she said, opening the pouch's mouth wider. "Coins and bills and—"

"The remainder of the cash that I received when I sold some of your mother's jewels," Simon said, placing a hand over the items to stop her. "You'll recall that, when your family was removed to Tobolsk, I gave a quarter of the jewels and cash to each of the tutors and Artyom, and I held the last quarter. Your mother wanted nothing to do with it and insisted that I keep it for her. Just before your family was sent to the Urals, I divvied it up, hoping that at least one of us would be with you when it was needed."

Gently, he removed the pouch from her hands and set it out of her reach. "Please, don't open anything else," he said, stilling her hand as he ominously repeated his earlier warning. "I expect that the other pouch contains half of the jewels we recovered on the night of the execution. Leave it for another day. Please." His steel blue eyes held hers, pleading.

With a gasp, she snatched her hands away, as if they had been held over a fire.

"I'll clear this mess away," Mrs. Zima said, gathering up the wrapping before silently leaving the room.

"I'll prepare your evening attire, sir," Zima said, following his wife, "and await you in your chambers."

CHAPTER 25

"Isn't it remarkable how a moment of joy can vanish in an instant," Mary said, wandering toward the window, arms blanketing her, head down. "I feel as though I carry the burden of my family's execution. It twists like a knife in my heart." She felt her knees buckle and slumped into a nearby armchair.

Simon crouched beside her, rubbing her hand as if to recall her focus. "Are you alright?" he said, his brow furrowed with vertical lines of concern.

"Yes," she replied, fingering tears from her eyes. "I was surprised, that's all. I'm glad you stopped me from opening the rest." She sighed deeply, searching for calm.

Instead, her eyes shot open, and shivers ran down her spine. "Vasiliev!" she said in horror. "Now he has even more reason to search for me!"

"Uh, he won't know that we received this," Simon said calmly. "Besides, he wants the *crown* jewels. These are the property of your family, not the state, and nothing remotely like the crown jewels. Their value could never finance his goals."

"I suppose," Mary said, "but I can't help feeling that he has eyes everywhere, and these items will only reinforce his belief."

"Excuse me, sir," Mrs. Zima said, reappearing in the doorway. "Perhaps my lady would like to rest for a few minutes before she dresses for dinner. I've brought a cool cloth for her eyes."

"I think I'll need more than a cool cloth, Mrs. Z!" Mary said soberly. "Simon, please put the jewellery boxes and the tutors' pouches in the safe." She watched Simon collect the items. "I'll join you in the salon shortly. I have a great need for a large vodka!"

"Alright," Simon said, collecting the boxes and pouches, a quizzical expression rearranging his features. "There's more to be said about Vasiliev, though. When we meet in the salon, I'll tell you about an encounter Artyom and I had with his nephew, and Lockhart's latest news."

"Before we do anything else," Mary said, "I need to see the children. I don't want to wait for them to come down to the salon to say good night. Let's go up to the nursery now!"

Simon poured a whiskey for himself and, against his better judgement, a double vodka for his wife. "Are you certain you want to drink this?" he said, holding the crystal glass to show her the measure.

"Yes," she said, rising from the velvet settee.

The salon was still but for their quiet conversation. Charles and Ann had yet to arrive. Mary approached Simon where he stood between the unlit fireplace and the beverage cart and held out her hand. Neither spoke, seeming instead to be contemplating the earlier events.

"Throughout my life, I have heard men expound on the virtues of vodka and its ability to remedy all troubles." She held the glass to her nose and sniffed. "I shall now test that theory!"

She touched the glass to her lips, glanced at Simon—noting his raised brow—exhaled in preparation, and promptly drank it all. Her hasty consumption resulted in a fit of coughing, which subsided only after she drank a glass of water proffered by her husband.

"I warned you not to drink it all at once," Simon said, chuckling as he helped her to a chair.

"It always looks so easy when a man does it!" Mary said, protesting between coughs. She cast a red-faced, teary gaze at him.

Simon deftly handed her a starched, white handkerchief as an unchecked chuckle freed itself. "Would you like another?" he said struggling to keep a sober face.

"No, the result is clear: my test failed," Mary replied dabbing her cheeks. "It does *not* make matters any better?" She plopped into a chair, her hands falling to her lap, fingers fidgeting around the starched linen. "I'm left wondering why men maintain this constant lie that a shot of vodka solves everything! Unless," she seemed to reason, "one considers that it does temporarily take one's mind off the reason for such a choice. I think I shall henceforth choose to embrace reality, rather than seek oblivion."

"Pardon me," Michael said, appearing in the salon carrying a silver tray upon which sat a small envelope.

"A message, my lord."

Simon took the envelope and pushed his thumb through the seal. He tugged free a note and read. "It's from Artyom," he said, grinning. "We've been invited to dinner tomorrow evening. He suggests that we arrive early enough to visit with his handsome nephew."

"That will still be too late for us to be taking the children out," Mary said fondly. "Perhaps I'll arrange a picnic luncheon later in the week and Varvara can bring Arthur here."

"That's a jolly idea," Simon said encouragingly.

"I enjoy spending time with Artyom's family," Mary replied. "In Russia, I likely would have had little opportunity to do so."

"Circumstances were different then," Simon said in agreement. "You may, on a future date, have met Artyom and his sister, but I doubt you would have had occasion to meet Henry Crocker."

CHAPTER 26

The morning broke crisp and clear over Jarrow Hall's estate. Sunshine reflected off frost-covered grounds as if a dusting of miniature diamonds had fallen during the predawn.

Simon rose onto his elbow and gazed lovingly at his wife. "Good morning, sleepy head," he said as she began to stir.

She rubbed her eyes as she stretched, the movement broadening her grin into a smile. "Good morning, husband," she said. "It's awfully bright in here, is it not?"

"Nonsense! The light is perfect," he said, leaning forward to kiss the tip of her nose. "As it reflects in your eyes, I'm reminded of age-old water trapped in the Arctic icebergs. Brilliant blue! I could almost dive into them."

She squealed with delight when, in the next moment, he rolled above her, tracing demanding kisses down the curve of her neck to her breast.

"I was going to ask you," he said his voice muffled against her warm skin, "if you would like to ride this morning, but …" He nudged her slender limbs apart with his knee. "I'm now thinking that a different kind of ride might be in order."

Her legs wrapped around his waist, resulting in his roguish grin. He seized her arms and pinned them above her head.

"Who says we must be restricted to one form of ride," she replied, rising to meet the rhythm of his demands.

A while later, they nestled in the afterglow of their lovemaking, sweat-glistened skin cooling. Simon tugged at the coverlet and tucked it around Mary.

"About the other kind of riding," she said, her voice sounding evocative. "With whom would you prefer to ride: a woman in love, or a shy, young boy?" Her chuckle was deep, alluring.

"If I had my choice," he said, "you'd be mounted ahead of me, impaled by—"

"Simon!" Mary said, rising above him, haloed by her golden hair. "While that may be a delightful image, I can list a number of reasons why that will not be possible."

"Fine, then," he said, placing a hand on either cheek, drawing her face toward him. "If I'm not to have my fantasy realized, you may decide." He kissed her nose chastely, then her mouth thoroughly. "No, wait! I know your preference! Shall I lend you a pair of my trousers?"

"Not necessary," she replied, rolling away from him. She reached for her pink silk robe, which had puddled on the floor next to the bed the evening before. She stood and faced him, slowly donning it, aware of the effect that her movement had on him. "In addition to all of the lovely outfits that I ordered, I added a few pair of trousers and some shirts." She inhaled, thrusting her chest forward, prideful. "I now have my very own *gentleman's* attire!"

"Well done!" Simon said, sliding off the opposite side of the bed and donning a dark blue woollen robe. "Breakfast before or after?"

"Oh!" Mary replied. "After. I haven't felt such large muscles between my legs for months." Her eyes widened as her tease hit its mark.

"Large muscles!" he said. "Have you not been mounting my substantial muscles these past many weeks!" He lunged toward her.

"Besides," she said, nimbly dodging his reach. "Riding has a way of working up a voracious appetite."

She squealed again, successfully dodging another attack by crawling through rumpled bed linen. On his third attempt, she tugged the green cord next to the bed, summoning Mrs. Zima to help her dress.

"Oh, God!" Simon said, slouching onto the edge of the bed. "I'm done for now. I'd better leave before I'm discovered in my lady's bed chamber and reprimanded for chafing her tender neck with my whiskers!" He kissed her quickly on the cheek, then opened the door to the passageway that connected his room to hers. "I'm going to sneak an orange from the kitchen. Want one?"

"Yes, please." She quirked her head sideways and smiled. "Have I ever told you that I love how you always smell of oranges?"

Simon shook his head.

"You smelled of oranges when you came to Petrograd, but after we were locked up in Tsarskoye Selo, that disappeared."

"Oranges were hard to come by," Simon said. "I don't think I ate another orange until we returned to Jarrow." He rubbed his chin as he pondered. "They're still hard to come by. Thank goodness Cook can pick them from the tree in the conservatory if there's none to be found in the town." A knock on the door interrupted his musings. "Meet you downstairs in twenty minutes," he said, then disappeared into his own room.

CHAPTER 27

When Richard had removed the confidential documents from the cabinet in the War Office and formulated a plan to leave England, he had given no thought as to whether he would return. He believed only that, if he could reach Constantinople in a timely manner, he could become a wealthy man. He had information that would ensure the sultan retained, at the least, Britain's assigned interest in the Ottoman territory. *Britain be damned!*

Richard clasped his carryall to his chest as he tried to find a comfortable position on a wooden bench bolted to the floor of the latest fishing boat hired in aid of his journey. He had been travelling for weeks and had begun to wonder whether the information he carried would be of any use in the dispute over the Ottoman Empire. If he arrived too late, no one would pay him for the intelligence he carried, and his efforts would be for naught.

He pulled his woollen cap over his eyes and slouched. By extending his long legs, he was able to brace a foot on a stanchion, ensuring that he would remain seated in the event he nodded off. Sleep evaded him, however, as he recalled the events that had brought him to his current predicament. He drank too much, ran up gambling debts he could never repay, spent too much time in the company of women he would never respect—excepting Sally—and worst of all, he had stolen from his family.

At least I don't owe Sally anything. His stomach clenched in regret. *Except perhaps an explanation regarding my hasty departure.* "Sorry, Sal," he said aloud.

Once again, he tightened his grip on his bag and shifted his weight to his left hip, wishing for a good night's sleep in a clean bed with fresh linen. "Wealth does provide some comforts," he said sotto voce to the empty cabin.

"What you say?" the captain of the ship said in broken English as he descended from the deck.

Frustrated, Richard pushed against the stanchion and righted himself. Gazing out the salt-pocked porthole, he felt for his wristwatch. *Thirty minutes before we dock,* he thought.

"Nothing," Richard replied to the captain's query. "I was just pondering how much longer it will take for me to reach Constantinople." He retrieved the pouch in which he kept his money and gave it a shake. *I thought a train and a couple of boats would get me there. I didn't expect to spend so much time between each mode of transport, nor to require so many more boats at so many different ports. I'm tired of sea travel. So much for being a man with a mission!* An unexpected groan of weariness escaped his lips.

"Ah, yes," the captain said with an empathetic frown. "Always the purse, she gets smaller."

As the vessel neared the small port of Mikonos, the

Mediterranean sun melted into the horizon, casting its final glow on a row of ancient windmills. Richard sighed as he contemplated again how many more fishing boats and how many more days it would take to reach his destination.

"Come now," the captain said, beckoning Richard to disembark. "You sleep—" He pointed toward a nearby inn. "Come back when sun, she go up. My wife brother, maybe he take you Constantinople. If no …"

The man shrugged, raising his hands as if inviting God to intervene, a gesture that Richard had learned early on suggested someone else might.

CHAPTER 28

The evening chill bit into Mary's thinly-clad feet as she stepped from the motor. Stars shone brightly in the cloudless sky, their path lit by a full moon leading to the front entrance of the Crocker's home. Simon and Mary ascended the small flight of stairs, their frosted breath floating before them.

In an instant, the hunting-themed, carved wooden slab sprang open, revealing several smiling faces. They all stood silent for seven heart beats before hosts and guests began speaking at once.

Just as quickly, they stopped when Henry pushed himself to the entrance. "Alright!" he said, taking control. "How about we all step back and allow our guests entry? Come into the parlour and we'll have a welcoming drink."

"We were just remarking the other day," Simon said, as vodka-filled glasses were passed around by their host, "how not that long ago Henry and I were employer and valet, now, he outranks me. And, once Artyom served Mary's family, putting them all above his own life. Now, in my opinion, and in Mary's …" He took his wife's hand and gave it a little shake of affirmation. "Now, we are fast friends."

"I couldn't have said that better," Mary said. "We should toast to it!"

"To friends and heroes," Varvara said, raising her glass.

Mary nodded her glass of vodka toward Artyom, then to Simon.

"May we never forget the bonds that tie us," Artyom said. With a mischievous look in his eye, the former guard tipped his glass and emptied it. But for Mary, the others copied the gesture.

Mary remembered too well the effects of hastily-downed vodka and took a small sip, avoiding eye contact with Simon.

"Now!" Henry said. "How about some champagne to rinse our mouths!"

A cheerful discussion followed regarding the merits of rinsing one's mouth of an exceptional vodka with a gargle of French champagne. As the boisterous banter subsided, the nanny appeared at the doorway of the salon.

"Pardon, Madame," Nanny said, her hand firmly fastened around Arthur's.

"Papa!" the little boy said, wresting his hand free and running to his father. He wrapped his arms around Henry's shins. "Up, Papa, up!"

"Thank you, Nanny," Varvara said. "When dinner is served, you may retrieve him. Please tell cook that everyone is here."

The nanny bobbed and disappeared.

"Such a beautiful child," Mary said, admiring him.

While Simon and Artyom caught up on recent

events, Mary chatted with Arthur, who told her all about his mama and papa and his toys.

"See my toys?" Arthur said, tugging Mary's hand toward the doorway.

"Oh! I'd like that very much," Mary said, stooping to his eye level. "Perhaps I might visit another day and spend some time with you in the nursery. Would that be alright?"

"Uh huh," he replied.

"I suppose it won't be long before you two start a family," Henry said, sidling to Mary's side, his smile sincere.

"Oh my!" Mary said, rising. "Perhaps. Uh … I mean … we haven't really talked about it." She turned her shoulder toward the other men, who were ensconced in conversation. "And we are now guardians of three orphans …"

"I'm sorry," Henry quickly apologized. "I spoke out of turn."

"N-no," Mary said. "No apology required, Henry." She lowered her head to conceal her flushing cheeks. "So much has happened these last months. We're still trying to settle ourselves … and the children … and then there's my work at the hospital."

"We, of all people, can understand how upside-down lives can become when forced to flee a perilous situation," Varvara said, reminding them of her hasty marriage to Henry and their ensuing flight from Petrograd to escape the clutches of Vasiliev. She reached for Arthur. "And how chaotic it is to add children into the mix." She shifted Arthur onto her hip and kissed his rosy cheek.

"Truly, Mary, I do apologize—" Henry said.

"What's this?" Simon said. "Mary? You've gone awfully pale."

"It's nothing, Simon," Mary said. "We were just admiring this handsome little fellow." She caressed her finger along Arthur's cheek. He reached for her hand and giggled. "Master Arthur and I have just set a date to play in the nursery. Is that not correct, Master Arthur?"

Arthur smiled shyly at Mary, then turned his face to hide in his mother's collar, terminating further discussion by inserting his thumb into his mouth and scrunching his eyes shut.

At the other end of the house, a door banged; the sound of a gunshot echoed throughout the cottage.

"Simon!" Mary clutched her chest, her voice and Arthur's howl sounding strangled even to her own ears.

———

In an instant, Simon reacted, catching Mary as her knees buckled and she slumped toward the floor. He turned, carrying her to the forest green settee, aglow with the flicker of logs burning in the hearth.

"Henry," Varvara barked as she strode toward Mary, "take Arthur to Nanny!" She glared at the three men hovering above the young woman. "Away with you! Give her space to breathe."

"What happened?" Mary said, eyes fluttering, her voice barely audible. "Why are you all staring at me?"

"You fainted, Mary dear," Varvara said, rubbing

Mary's hand vigorously. "Take a moment and tell me how you feel."

"I feel ... I don't know! Oh my!" Mary replied, as if struggling to untangle her thoughts. She sat up, swinging her feet delicately to the floor. "I'm sorry to cause you worry." Her eyes seemed to search for Simon. When they found him, she gasped. "A gun! I heard a gun!"

"A door slammed, Sparrow," Simon said, kneeling before her as Varvara moved aside. "No gun. You're safe." His attempt at a smile failed.

"Thank goodness," Mary replied, still trembling. She accepted Simon's hand and rose to be near him. "The sound was a shock. Please forgive me." She cast a tentative smile toward the others.

"Cook says dinner is ready?" Henry said as he re-entered the room. "Mary, are you alright? Shall I defer service?"

"Please ... not on my account," Mary said, linking her arm through Simon's. "I'm recovered." She smiled valiantly. "Truly."

Later, Simon settled into a salon chair to enjoy cognac with the gentlemen. Mary accompanied Varvara to the nursery to say goodnight to Arthur.

"I can't help you with your love-life, Artyom," Simon said, responding to his friend's lament. "But I may have an idea that might help pass the time."

"I'm listening," Artyom said.

"The horses will always appreciate exercise," Simon said, amidst a burst of laughter. "Take them out whenever you like."

"I will, thank you!" Artyom said, his cheeks stained with a pale blush. "By the way, I thought I saw the stable lads working some ponies the last time I was in the yard. Am I correct?"

"Indeed," Simon replied with a nod. "They breed ponies as a hobby, then sell them off when they're trained. Some are placed in the mines to work, while others go into business elsewhere. Any proceeds are used to help mining families who may be in need. Why?"

"I was thinking of little Arthur," Artyom said. "Perhaps I could teach him to ride?" He looked to Henry, who had been following the conversation.

"That's a smashing idea," Henry said. "And I'm certain that little Arthur will enjoy the activity."

"He'll need some help, at first," Artyom said. "He's still young, but he can learn about the stables and the ponies now and, until he's able to ride alone, he will ride with me."

"Our three charges will be assigned ponies soon," Simon said. "Perhaps Arthur can learn with them."

<hr>

As Mary followed Varvara to Arthur's room, she took the opportunity to extend the invitation for a picnic luncheon, of which Varvara heartily accepted. The nanny had already prepared him for bed, but he waited for his mother to read him a bedtime story and tuck him in.

"Come with me," Varvara said once Arthur was settled. "There is something you should know."

Piqued with curiosity, Mary followed, waiting patiently for Varvara to speak.

Further along the corridor, Varvara invited Mary into a study. A low fire burnt in the hearth, warming the room. She gestured for Mary to sit near the warmth, poured two glasses of sherry, one of which she handed to Mary, and sat in an opposite chair.

"I find studies warm and welcoming," Mary said. "For some reason, they remind me of my father."

"This is my favourite room, too." Varvara sipped the sherry thoughtfully. "Has Simon ever told you of my experience with Major Ivan Vasiliev?"

Mary's head snapped to face Varvara, her face devoid of expression. "No," Mary replied hesitantly.

"Please don't be shocked that he hasn't," Varvara said. "It happened long before you and Simon met—as adults, at least. I know that you and Simon first met when you were children. He's likely forgotten that story."

"Regardless, you haven't," Mary said flatly, her expression dull.

"I try, but sometimes …" She shook her head. "Please don't find fault with Simon, or Artyom. It is my story to tell, and I will tell it now."

Varvara rolled the stem of her glass between her fingers, her thoughts elsewhere. A shudder ran through her, causing her hands to shake, and she set the glass on the table. When she began to speak, it was in a whisper, as if the man himself stood before them.

She described how she had been introduced to the major during a military celebration; how he had taken an interest in her; how he had forced himself upon her and blackmailed her into becoming his mistress.

"If I didn't meet him when he instructed and do what he wanted, he said he would harm my husband. I had no choice." Tears flowed freely down her cheeks. "If I resisted, he beat me. It became difficult between my husband and myself. I couldn't let him see the bruises, so a distance grew between us.

"Then one day, Vasiliev went mad. He challenged my dear husband to a duel on horseback, a-and he k-killed him." A gut-wrenching sob escaped through the hands that covered her face.

Mary gasped and set her own glass on the table, falling to her knees at Varvara's side and wrapping her arms around the trembling woman.

"Artyom witnessed the entire event," Varvara said when she recovered enough to continue. She swiped at her tears and retrieved a handkerchief from her pocket. "After that, Vasiliev became more demanding, more violent. I had to escape, but Artyom and I were at a loss as to how. Then, we had the good fortune to meet Henry and Simon on the train from Vologda to St. Petersburg." She released a deep and weary sigh, shaking her head. "Artyom insisted that we speak to them; that they would help me escape."

Varvara lifted her head and gazed warmly into Mary's eyes. "And they did. And here we are." She gave Mary a weak smile.

Mary hugged her again. "You have been safe here, yes?"

"Yes, safe and very happy," Varvara said, motioning Mary toward the other chair. "Please, your dress."

Mary rose and sat in the vacated chair.

"When Artyom mentioned that Vasiliev has been haunting you, I determined to warn you of his wickedness," Varvara said.

"I have so many questions," Mary said in awe of the information, "but they can wait for another day. For now, I believe you are still safe. Ivan Vasiliev is after the crown jewels; he thinks I have them."

"You are correct," Varvara said. "Vasiliev has likely assumed that I escaped to England, but he doesn't know where. I'm certain that he could find out if he wished, but his attention has been diverted."

She dabbed her handkerchief under her nose, then replaced it in her pocket. "As you say though, the jewels are of greater value to him, so I don't feel threatened just now. If he ever realized how close we all are, things could change, especially when Henry is away at sea and Artyom is working in the city. On those days, I have no protection ..."

"Then, together we will work something out," Mary said, reaching for Varvara's hands. "It is because of the jewels that he is a threat. Jewels which I don't have, by the way. I only have the jewels that my mother gave to

Simon for safekeeping: her jewels, not the crown's."

"I know," Varvara said easily, "Artyom told me that." She squeezed Mary's hand. "I wanted you to know that he truly is a wicked man, and that you are not the first one to gain his attention or disfavour. You shall not face this wickedness alone."

"And neither shall you," Mary replied.

CHAPTER 29

With Christmas in mind, Ann extended an invitation to the Crocker family to share the meal at Jarrow Hall. Ann told Mary in confidence that she hoped the abundance of young people at the table would help to fill the void left by her youngest son. The burden of worry for his health and safety was sometimes too much for her to bear.

During the course of dinner, Varvara happily shared that she and Henry expected to welcome another child by the summer. An exchange of joyful congratulations followed, including the odd remark of jovial encouragement aimed at Simon and Mary and the beginning of their family.

Although the festivities were such that no one else noticed the sadness in Mary's eyes, Simon did, and he promised himself to speak with her soon. *Perhaps,* he thought, *the expectation of a child would help her through her mourning.*

***

"A toast!" Simon said above the din, catching Mary's eye.

Henry snatched up the canisters of sherry and cognac and mingled through the room, filling glasses as Simon waited patiently.

"The past few years have been challenging. Even dangerous!" Simon's gaze touched each of them. "And this year"—he paused as Mary approached—"was particularly harrowing. For now, at least, we are all here and safe. To family and friends, and to our safety!"

"Hear, hear!" they said in unison.

"The times are still uncertain," Charles said. "Who knows what the next years might bring. But we must be prepared. We must do our best to protect our families, our friends, and our country. People will look to us for leadership and guidance, in this community and elsewhere. We must prepare ourselves to step up wherever we're needed."

"That sounds rather ominous, Father," Simon said. "What do you know that we don't?"

"That's a discussion for another time," Charles said, glancing toward the children.

"Of course," Simon said, catching the eyes of adults. "Happy Christmas, everyone!" He again raised his glass of amber cognac.

"Hear, hear!" Mary said. She transferred her glass to a free hand and mussed John's hair, gaining her an affectionate look from the young boy at her side.

"Hear, hear!" the company replied, raising their glasses to the cheer.

Arthur squirmed for his father to set him down and

ran circles around his parents shouting, "Hear, hear … hear, hear!"

CHAPTER 30

The last of Richard's chain of fishing boats arrived in the Sea of Marmara, destined for Constantinople. Near the end of the afternoon, a deckhand pointed toward a hill with a jabbing finger. "*Iya Sofya!*" he said repeatedly, until Richard nodded and smiled as if he understood.

"Forget the sultan," an Irish shopkeeper told Richard after he had offered to buy the man a cup of local coffee in exchange for information. "He's useless. You want General Mustafa Kemal. He'll listen to your story. Just make sure you have a good reason for betraying your country to help him. If he suspects a trap, he may choose to pay another way." The man drew his forefinger across his throat, then laughed huskily at his own humour and lit an aromatic cigarette.

Richard gulped audibly. In his heart, he knew that his treachery would be labelled a betrayal to his country, but he had buried those thoughts with his determination to prove himself to his father. He needed his father to see that he could achieve something, too. Although he never expected to receive a hereditary title or land, he refused to be overlooked just because he was the second son.

As Richard's thoughts tumbled together in a nest of chaos, the shopkeeper rolled the lit end of his cigarette against the heel of his shoe and tucked the remnant in his shirt pocket. Then, he excused himself and disappeared inside the restaurant.

Several minutes later, he reappeared, followed by the proprietor and a waiter laden with a variety of dishes.

"I was up with the dogs," the Irishman said. "I'm famished. Join me in a meal, and I will tell you more about the modifications you must make to your plans."

In response to the invitation, Richard's belly emitted a loud rumble, resulting in chuckles and an agreement that eating was in order. Once their plates held döners, chunks of cheese, sliced tomato, olives, and yogurt, the conversation continued.

"Kemal demobilized the sultan's troops in the wake of the Armistice of Mudros," the old man said, "then, he returned to Constantinople. So far as I know, he's still here. If he is, you'll find him at the Ministry of War headquarters.

"Just beware of any Allied forces that you encounter within the city," the old man said, lifting a fresh cup of coffee to his lips, then replacing it in the saucer without drinking. "It's still occupied. Each party wants to defend their piece of the pie! The Turks especially want to hold on to what's left of the Ottoman Empire. I, for one, am interested to see how this new country unfolds. I retired here from military service, and the last thing I want is to be forced back to Ireland."

Richard acknowledged the old man's words with a nod and reached for his cup.

"How about something stronger? A whiskey maybe?" He winked at Richard. "To mark the passing of Christmas," the old man said matter-of-factly.

Richard's eyes snapped wide over the rim of his cup, fixed on the Irishman. "Christmas!" he said, bewildered. "I've completely lost track of time. Is this Christmas Day?"

"Yesterday," the old man said. "Soon, it will be 1919! Let's hope the new year is better than the previous five years."

"Indeed," Richard said, silently hoping his plans had not been thwarted by time. "I'll seek out General Kemal tomorrow—"

The old man stretched his arm across the table to halt Richard. "He mightn't be there, see. 'Cause of the holiday."

Richard frowned.

"New year, daft boy. The administration offices will likely be closed until the new year. All I'm saying is be prepared to wait." The old man looked over his shoulder for the proprietor. "Now, about that drink."

"Oh, no, sir," Richard said. "I haven't had a drink …" He retrieved his purse and dug into it.

"Put that away," the Irishman said, patting Richard's hand. "I expect you're low on coins after your travels."

"As a matter of fact," Richard said, then stopped. He peered earnestly into the man's weather-worn face. "Thank you, sir. I hope one day I'll be able to return the favour. For now, please excuse me. I haven't had alcohol since I left England, and for once in my life, my head is clear and full of purpose. I'd rather not cloud it just now."

The old man nodded sadly and waved Richard on his way. Throughout the remainder of the day, Richard dodged the occasional British and French soldiers cheerfully celebrating their few hours of leave while he endeavoured to track down General Kemal.

By the end of the day, Richard had located the Ministry of War. As he gazed at the sunset-lit building across the street, his belly rumbled. Realizing that he had not eaten since the meal with the Irishman, he decided a full stomach and a good night's sleep were in order. He headed toward the dock, hoping to find another inexpensive inn.

"I give you room for good price," the innkeeper said, his English far superior to others Richard had encountered during the past many weeks. "My brother, he feed you." The man pointed out the door to the left and held up two fingers.

Once Richard had inspected the room and stowed his carryall, he meandered along the street, grateful to find the recommended café two doors down, rather than two blocks.

Soon, an array of sample-sized dishes of traditional fare began to appear on the small table at which the soon-to-be-traitor sat. Quickly, he lost himself to the flavours and textures of a cuisine that was contrary to anything he had eaten in Britain: subtly spiced beef kebab; lamb tagine made with honey, apricots, and cinnamon; delicately-flavoured rice; stuffed aubergine and other fragrant vegetables. He licked his lips often, trying to isolate familiar flavours.

"You like?" the restauranteur asked, a hopeful smile illuminating his sun-browned face.

"Delicious!" Richard said, rubbing his contented belly.

When the owner brought him a slice of baklava, Richard asked for a cup of coffee.

"You bring friends, yes?" the owner said when Richard tipped his head to catch the last of the coffee.

"I'll recommend your establishment to everyone I meet," Richard said with a disinterested grin, doubting that he would meet anyone who would care.

CHAPTER 31

Simon entered Mary's bedchamber as silence settled on the Hall. He closed the passage door behind him. His winter beard framed a lustful grin when he noticed her tying the blue bow at the neck of her nightdress.

"Such a wasted effort," he said as he encircled her in his arms and kissed her crown. A light scent of lilac reminded him of the palace tour she had given him in Petrograd some years ago. "It's been a while since we've had the opportunity to prepare for bed unaided." He tugged gently at the blue ribbon. "I'm glad we insisted that the staff not interrupt their New Years celebrations to attend us." He leaned away to better see her face. "New scent?"

"Yes … and no," she said, smiling sheepishly. "There was a time, before … before, you know … when a renowned perfumier approached my mother and asked whether they could name a line of colognes after my sisters and I. Olga's was rose, Tatania's was jasmine, mine was lilac, and Nasty—um, Anastasia's—was violet. I found a case of the four scents in a perfume shop in London and bought it on a whim. I doubt I'll find more. It's just another remembrance of my family." She gazed through the partially closed drapes, beyond her reflection. A layer of fog shrouded the garden below.

Simon tightened his arms around her, eyeing their reflection in the window. "I'm remembering our wedding night." He kissed her hair before resting his chin on the top of her head.

"Although I had no scent to wear at the time," Mary replied, snuggling against his woollen robe, "it was delightful. We didn't have much on the ship, and the cabin was nothing compared to these fine rooms, but it was a special time. I'll never forget it." She turned to face him, wrapping her arms around his waist. "I'm glad we had that time to ourselves. Here, it's challenging to find time alone, especially now with the children and my work at the hospital."

Simon released her, catching her hand, and led her toward the bed. He sat, pulling her toward him. He gazed intently into her eyes as he slipped her robe off satin shoulders, feeling her skin quiver beneath his fingertips.

A while later, Mary nestled against Simon, her mussed hair splayed across his shoulder.

"I'm sorry," he said, tracing his finger along whisker-stained skin. "Once again, I was ill-prepared. I should have shaved first."

"As I recall," Mary said, smiling, "there wasn't enough time."

"That's true," he replied with a chuckle, "but my beard

must come off before I return to work."

"No harm done," Mary said with a giggle. "I'll recover."

"Lovemaking and beards aside," he said, his voice tender as his arms wrapped loosely around her glowing skin, "I watched you the other evening—playing with Arthur—and saw your reaction to Varvara's Christmas news of another child."

Mary dipped her head and closed her eyes, remaining silent.

"Until now, we've taken care not to create a child," he said, "but, when I saw your reaction to Varvara's announcement, I determined that we must have a conversation about it." He tipped her chin, raising her face and waited for her to open her eyes.

When she did, tears pooled in them, overflowing and escaping over the crest of her cheek.

"Why are you so sad?" he said, sitting taller. "Do you not want children?" His eyes widened. "My gosh! We've never talked about children, and I'm amazed that I don't know the answer to that question. Sparrow, I am so sorry." He clutched her to him, kissing the top of her head while she sobbed.

When the crescendo of her outburst subsided and calm returned to her, Mary pushed against his chest, straightening. "I do want children," she said, raising her eyes to meet his. "Desperately so. But I will never bear a child, Simon. I can't."

"But, why ever not?" he said, surprised at her revelation. "You are wonderful with children!"

"Think about it," she said, swiping at her wet cheeks. "Think about my brother, Alexei. How ill he was. How careful we all had to be around him. We were always fearful of anything that might make him bleed. Remember?"

"Yes, I remember," he said, "and I'm reminded of something Queen Mary said too, before I left for Russia. She said that she and the king were always worried about their children, and whether they might suffer from the 'bleeder's disease'. I think she mentioned that other members of the family suffered from the same disorder, including Queen Victoria."

"I've heard doctors refer to it as 'hemophilia' or the 'royal disease' too," Mary replied. "It is indeed a family disorder, and that reinforces my decision. I simply cannot bear a child who would be condemned to live such a life. Even I could be at risk!" She reached for his hand and kissed it. "Remember the concern you and Artyom had stemming the blood loss after I was shot?"

"I do, indeed," Simon replied, observing her intently. "You have good arguments. We should give the matter serious thought."

"No, Simon," she said firmly. "There is no thought to give. I will not do it!" In a softer voice, she continued. "I cannot. I have given the matter a great deal of thought, and I know what that will mean to your family. Without a male heir, your titles will be lost."

"Damn the titles!" Simon said, grasping her hands. "Listen to me, my sweet Sparrow." His voice was urgent and earnest. "You are the most important thing in my life, and I will not risk a pregnancy, either!" Simon snatched her to his chest and held her fast. "It is decided then … we shall not have children."

A deep, mournful sigh issued from each of them, and Mary's tears flowed freely once again.

———•——

Mary sat at her dressing table and gazed in the mirror, watching Simon behind her. His gaze fell on her as she told him about her days with the children.

She turned to face Simon, wrapping her arms around his waist. "Our little orphans have taught me how to be a mother," she said with a sigh. "I wish there was a way to keep them. Being the middle child, I learned how to care for younger children. I think I could be a good mother." She reached for his hand. "If it weren't for …"

"You make parenting seem effortless." Simon interrupted, fondly squeezing her hand. "I'm not so sure about me, though. I often wonder whether I'd need a manual."

"Unfortunately, there's no manual for parenting," Mary replied, "which I find odd, since there are so many parents. I suppose they're all so busy being parents that they have no time to write about it. It's mostly hand-me-down advice, isn't it? Or simple trial and error. Or, if they're able, they hire a nanny and hope she knows what to do."

"And that's not always reliable, is it?" Simon said. "It all becomes muddled when we try to avoid repeating hurtful things, too."

"I suppose we'll just have to do our best, for the time we have them," Mary said. "And try not to inflict our negative experiences on them."

"Simon?" Mary said, her voice still sounding troubled as she reached for her robe. "What are we to do about Yurovsky and Vasiliev? I know you said that Yurovsky is working with the Bolsheviks and seems to have embraced their principles. But, what about Vasiliev? After all that he's done, do you think it possible for him to change from an Imperialist to a Bolshevik?"

"No, I don't," Simon said, sitting on the edge of Mary's turned-back bed. "He will pretend to support the Bolshevik notions only so long as they serve his purpose. At heart, he is driven by power and wealth. He's worked hard to acquire the armaments and other assets required to overthrow the control of Russia, and, I believe, he still has them. There was no time to expose his stash before Britain was forced out of the country. I presume he still has it all tucked away in the countryside."

"If that's the case," Mary said, "then he will still be looking for the crown jewels, unless he accepts that they disappeared during the early days of the revolution."

"Exactly," Simon agreed. "And given that Artyom and I encountered his nephew lurking outside Grosvenor House, I doubt very much that he has embraced anything to do with the revolution. Nor will he share with the revolutionaries all that he has acquired. However, he will definitely use it to further his family's desire to rule all of Germany and Russia."

"Which brings me to my point," Mary said. "So long as Vasiliev is alive, I'm at risk. And, if I'm at risk, then anyone close to me is as well, including the children and Artyom's family." She retied the blue ribbon, wrapped her arms around herself, and began pacing across the room.

"Ah! So, Varvara told you?" Simon straightened, as if to argue the withholding of information.

"Yes, she said it was her story to tell, not yours. Don't worry; I'm not upset that you didn't tell me." She approached him where he sat on the bed, feet firmly planted on the floor. She placed a hand on either shoulder, then kissed the top of his head, feeling the tension in his body ease.

"I had planned to have this conversation with you in the morning, but … *carpe diem*!" Simon said. "Since we're both wide awake now …" He retrieved a decanter of burgundy-coloured sherry from a nearby side table and filled two glasses. "I propose that we engage security guards to watch over you. Perhaps two to start. One will work outdoors as a groomsman; the other will work indoors as a footman. At the same time, we'll refresh your self-defence training."

"A good start indeed," Mary replied, accepting the proffered glass. "Sometimes, I've worried that you're overprotective. That you've forgotten what you've taught me." She sniffed the sherry's delicate fragrance, watching light refract through fine cuts in the glass, sending colourful rainbows dancing off the walls.

"Never!" Simon replied, sounding incredulous. "You're

one of the most capable women I know!"

"Truly?" Mary said, surprised at his revelation.

"Of course," Simon said. "Do I need to recite all that you've overcome since we met?"

"No, no," Mary said, waving a hand to end his praise. "I'm relieved that you're able to see the greater circumstance and that you have the connections to make things happen. To keep *us* safe." She raised the glass in salute and sipped gingerly, contemplating.

CHAPTER 32

" Lady Mary," John said as Mary closed the storybook that she had been reading, "why do you have guards now? You didn't have them when we first came here."

Mary set the book on the night table that stood between the boys' beds. For a moment, she focussed on a tapestry of young boys cavorting in a jungle meadow. Her mind flashed to a memory of her nanny reading *The Jungle Book* by Rudyard Kipling when she and Anastasia were young. They had tormented the nanny with antics of dancing monkeys until the woman's sides ached from laughter.

Mary closed her eyes, willing her thoughts to focus on the present, on John's unexpected question. *How do I answer so that he's satisfied without scaring him?* She opened her eyes to his questioning face.

"The Nightingale-Temples are important people," she said, catching the eye of each child, "both here in Jarrow and in London. Sometimes, folks take exception to decisions they might make." She stroked his auburn waves. "And ... you know how someone else's words or actions might make you angry—"

"Like when John takes my puppy and runs away with

him?" Willy said, hugging his stuffed puppy to his chest as he scrambled across to John's bed and onto Mary's lap.

"Yes, sort of," Mary said. "You see, when adults behave that way, their behaviour can be more severe."

"Like a fist fight!" John said, raising his fists and punching the air. "Pow. Pow, pow!"

"Yes," Mary said nodding, "sort of." As Simon often did, she chewed her lower lip, contemplating the safety of their three wards. "They might certainly intend harm in some fashion, like a fist fight."

She shifted Willy's weight and held him firmly. "Not everyone intends harm, but just in case someone might take exception to something said or done by a member of this family, Lord Simon and I decided to take great care to ensure that we all remain safe."

She reached for Elvie and the boys and hugged them to her. "Especially you three. That's why we have the guards. They're here to protect us and, if you should ever have a concern about your safety, you must find one of them or another adult immediately."

"I know we're safe here," John said. "But what about when Elvie and I go to school?"

"You may not see them," Mary said solemnly, "but at least one guard is always there. I recommend that you do nothing to draw attention to them. Otherwise, you might put yourself or the guard in a dangerous situation." She kissed the top of Willy's head and met John's eyes. "Do you understand?"

"Yes, Lady Mary."

Willy twisted in her lap and flung his arms around her. "I'm safe with you, Lady Mary."

CHAPTER 33

Richard stood in the shade, to the side of the stairs that lead up to the entrance of the Ministry of War building. He set his valise between his feet and retrieved a wrinkled handkerchief from his jacket pocket to wipe his clammy hands. He stuffed the handkerchief back into his pocket, snatched up the case, and took the steps two at a time, keeping to the shadows where he could remain inconspicuous. He clutched the handle of the case that he had stowed in his carryall in a death-grip, eyeing everyone in the vicinity.

At the top of the stairs, he paused behind a pillar and waited until the sentry was distracted. Then, he fell in step with a group of Ministry workers, hunching his shoulders in the hopes of lessening his height.

Inside the foyer, he sought another shadowed area and concealed himself behind a second pillar. The vaulted ceiling echoed the various languages that assaulted his ears, and not for the first time he found himself wishing that he had Simon's gift for languages.

Some ten minutes later, he spotted two French officers strolling into the lobby, accompanied by a handsome man with neatly-cut blond hair and a trimmed moustache, in his late thirties by Richard's guess.

"*Merci*, General Kemal," the older officer said gruffly in French. "This has been a most enlightening meeting. I hope you will keep in mind the favours that France is prepared to accommodate should you agree to work with us."

"Your policies and theories are most interesting," the younger officer said before Kemal could respond, earning a scowl from his superior. "I believe *Kemalism* is a term widely used on the streets."

"*Kemalism?*" the general replied, his amusement obvious. "A new word to be sure, and one I will have to keep in mind, especially if it's already used on the streets!"

Great! Richard frowned. *The locksmith said he doesn't speak English. I hope my French is adequate.*

When the French officers marched smartly past the pillar that obscured Richard from view, he moved silently to catch up with the retiring General.

"*Excusez-moi, Général*," Richard said, matching Kemal's stride, "I wonder if I might have a few minutes of your time?"

"Make an appointment with my aide," the general replied gruffly without a glance.

"But, sir," Richard pled, keeping pace with the general, "I have travelled a long way and at great personal expense."

Kemal paused, scrutinizing the young man from head to toe.

Richard removed his hat and bowed his head, knowing his British accent and rudimentary use of French likely gave away his origins.

"I suppose I must believe you," Kemal said. "Disheveled clothes hanging too loose—not eating well?" He raised a dubious eyebrow and continued. "Unkempt hair and beard, shoes in need of a spit polish. Not a military man, I venture."

"Please, sir," Richard said earnestly, turning the rim of his hat in circles and wishing he had a whiskey to hand. "I've been travelling for almost two months. To be honest, I haven't much money and have used what little I have on transportation. As you've surmised, I'm not a military man. I can assure you, however, that you won't regret listening to me. I promise."

"Very well," Kemal replied, seeming to appreciate Richard's desperate state. "I can't imagine that you would have any information of value to me, but I'll give you five minutes. I have a meeting with the British and can't be late."

Kemal led Richard into his office and closed the door, indicating that Richard should sit in the wooden guest chair. "Speak," he said, pointing to a small table clock. "Time is ticking."

Richard placed his case on a vacant chair and, as he introduced himself, withdrew an assortment of maps, memos, and briefs. He inhaled and let out a long breath as he organized his thoughts, realizing that his next words had to hook the general's attention, or everything he had done thus far would amount to nothing more than a wasted effort. He closed his eyes and prayed silently that all of the French he had ever learned, in school or otherwise, would come to his rescue now.

Five minutes passed, then ten. The general excused himself and crossed the austere room. He opened the door and called to a young man who appeared to be typing reports.

"Please continue," he said, returning to Richard's side to examine the papers neatly covering his desk. "I've delayed my meeting with the British. Drink?"

Richard swallowed hard. He had not had a drop of alcohol since he had stormed out of Jarrow Hall months ago. The last thing he wanted was to start again, but how was he to decline the offer and risk the opportunity to work with Kemal? "Thank you," he said.

Kemal poured two glasses of whiskey and handed one to Richard. He raised his own glass in salute and took a large swallow. Richard sipped gingerly. The peaty liquid trickled warmly down his gullet, leaving a familiar comfort behind. He licked his lips with pleasure and sipped again. Then set the glass aside.

"This information will require considerable thought," Kemal said forty-five minutes later. "And we have yet to discuss a price." He glanced at the clock. "I am obliged to attend this meeting with the British. Your enlightenment puts me in a position I hadn't expected. Each of these parties—France, Britain, Greece, Italy, and so on—they all want a portion of the Ottoman Empire. With this information, I can push back. It's inevitable that they'll claim a piece, but perhaps we can retain the larger and best part of it."

He gazed at the desk clock again, as if not seeing it. "Come again next Wednesday," he said. "I would like you to repeat this information to my colleagues. They will want to hear your observations and ideas, and I am most certain they will have questions. Unfortunately, several of them have returned to their homes to celebrate the new year. In the meantime, I suggest you put some effort into improving your French."

"Yes, sir!" Richard replied, hastily collecting the pages and sliding them into his case.

He shook the General's hand vigorously and walked out of the War Office with far more confidence than he had when he had entered.

"Welcome," the owner of a café said as Richard paused outside. "Come in. Turkish coffee or … English tea? Perhaps something stronger under the table?" He waved Richard into his establishment. "Sit where you like."

"Whiskey," Richard replied. His belly lurched in response to his disappointing choice. *You're weak, Temple!*

He found a small table in a back corner of the shop and withdrew his papers, intending to revisit the information he had presented to Kemal and make notes of further points he would stress the following Wednesday.

Retrieving a fountain pen from his valise, he glanced at the stillness of his hand, dismissing the thought when the owner appeared with an amber-filled glass. He raised the glass to his lips, deeply inhaled the fragrance, then tipped the contents into his mouth. Savouring it as he swallowed slowly, he waved the glass at the proprietor, requesting another.

"Perhaps, sir, some food?" the proprietor said when he set a third glass of whiskey on the table.

Richard fought to focus on the man's question. "Excellent idea!" he said, feeling detached from his body, a slight slur tainting his words. "And a coffee."

He stacked the pages and slid them back into the case, disappointed at his weakness.

While he awaited his meal, Richard contemplated how he would pass the next several days, and the merits of touring the city. *It wouldn't hurt to have something more to talk about than just a military coup d'état,* he thought. *Besides, who knows how long I'll be stuck in this hellhole. I doubt I'll be returning to England any time soon. Maybe I'll start with that famed Haiga Sofia ...*

Fumes of a whiskey-ladened burp reminded him of the risk he had taken when he accepted the glass from Kemal. *Damn!*

CHAPTER 34

During the week between Christmas and New Years, Ann and Mary had returned to their hospital duties. Readying for their return to London, Charles and Simon reviewed estate business and security with the housekeeper, the two security guards, the butler, and the groundskeeper, then drew up a plan that would keep operations running smoothly and safely while they were occupied in London.

"I'd like to add one more matter to your list, if I may," Simon said before concluding the meeting. "For this, I've invited Mr. and Mrs. Zima to join us."

He opened the door to the study and invited the couple in. "As you know, a security concern arose a few weeks ago that has resulted in the engagement of the guards." He nodded toward the two men. "We have since confirmed that the leader of that threat is someone Lady Mary and I encountered while in Russia. Mr. and Mrs. Zima are well aware of the nature of Ivan Vasiliev and the harm he is capable of inflicting."

Both Zimas gasped, eyes wide with shock. Mrs. Zima's hand flew to cover her mouth. "No! Please God, not him!"

Simon turned to the others. "As you can see from their

reaction, this is a serious matter. Vasiliev is looking for Lady Mary, believing she has something he needs. Which she doesn't, by the way, but that's irrelevant. We are, however, greatly concerned, not only for my wife's safety and that of the children, but for everyone living on the estate."

"My lord," Zima said, "what must we do to keep our Lady Mary and the children safe?"

"As you well know, Zima, Vasiliev is wicked, and he employs thugs to carry out his demands. He's also very determined."

The Zimas nodded in agreement.

"I will engage more men, men who will protect the estate and all of its residents. This needs to happen quickly, so no one comes to harm."

"Yes, my lord," Tompkins said. "Whatever we can do to help."

"Tomorrow morning," Simon said, acknowledging the commitment, "I will ask for an inspector from Scotland Yard to be sent out to help you arrange the additional protection. While you await his arrival, I'd like you to give some thought to hiring local chaps who have returned from their service during the war. They must have a good understanding of security and protection, be familiar with firearms and other defence methods, and be prepared to use them, if necessary. I don't want vigilantes. I want fellows who think clearly and logically. They must also be prepared to fit in, to work on the estate, or in the Hall. When the inspector arrives, he will decide how many we need to hire, then he will conduct the final interviews."

"My lord," Mrs. Wright said, "may I suggest at least one woman—if one can be found—who might fit into the nursery routine, so the children are not unnecessarily alarmed?"

"Good idea, Mrs. Wright," Simon replied. "I'll leave that to you and Mrs. Zima to investigate."

<hr>

During that same time, Henry received word that he had been promoted to the rank of commander and that a small ceremony would be held at the Admiralty on the following Tuesday when he and other officers would receive medals recognizing their role in the North Sea during the Great War. To Simon's surprise, he too had been requested to attend the Admiralty's ceremony, in uniform. A scramble followed as he and Zima searched for the trunk containing his uniform, aired it, and ensured its fit.

Neither Simon nor Henry had been adequately prepared for the ceremony. In Simon's opinion, a 'small gathering' amounted to ten or twenty people, not fifty or more. While they expected that Henry would receive the Victory Medal for his heroics during various 1918 North Sea campaigns, Simon was unable to explain the purpose of his invitation.

At the appointed hour, one of the admirals, acting as host of the ceremony, walked onto the stage, signalling for quiet. He began first with a few welcoming comments as stragglers hastened to their seats, then nodded toward the back of the room.

"Please rise," he said as the doors opened to admit the king, in a naval full dress uniform, and his entourage.

A great hush fell over the room as the king made his way to the stage. At the centre of the stage, he accepted the salute from other senior officers standing in a crescent facing the audience. He then turned to face the audience and acknowledged their salute. A small military band began playing *God Save the King*, for which all attendees remained standing. During the distraction, two seamen placed the king's chair in the centre of the crescent.

Formalities concluded, guests were invited to resume their seats, and the ceremony commenced. Simon observed that, although the monarch's attendance had not been written into the program, the organizers seemed aware of his plan to attend. When the time came for certain medals to be awarded, the king rose and handed them out.

Simon was astonished when his name was called to receive the 1914-15 Star for his efforts while onboard the RMS *Guardian* in August of 1915 and the Victory Medal, neither of which would usually involve the King's attention.

"I see, young man," King George said as he pinned the medals on Simon's chest, "that you are out of uniform."

"Sir?" Simon said, regarding the monarch.

"You're wearing the uniform of a Lieutenant of the Royal Navy, are you not?"

"Yes, sir," Simon replied, still puzzled by the monarch's comment.

"Then, indeed, you are out of uniform," the king said,

eyes twinkling as he handed Simon a package of cuff stripes and epaulettes. "For your exceptional and much appreciated service … Commander!"

"C-commander?" Simon said, his hand rising to accept the package.

"We are most grateful, my boy," King George said sotto voce, winking as he offered a congratulatory handshake. "I wonder whether you might stay behind. I'd like a private word."

"Of course," Simon replied as he saluted the monarch.

"An equerry will guide you," the king said, acknowledging the salute before turning to greet the next recipient.

Not long after King George V concluded the ceremony with closing remarks, Simon followed an equerry into a private room reserved for the meeting.

"Commander," the king said, striding into the room. "Thank you for waiting."

"Your Majesty," Simon said, dipping his chin smartly, arms hung stiffly at his sides.

"Two further matters have brought me to the ceremony today," the king said. "First, I'd like to acknowledge your efforts in Russia as my private emissary to the Romanovs. I'm certain you will understand if we do not hold with usual custom. The matter was too private for public display." He turned and nodded to the equerry. A few minutes later, a blue ribbon trimmed with red and white stripes hung from Simon's neck, supporting the Maltese cross of the *Royal Victorian Order*, an honour bestowed for service to the Royal Family.

The unexpected knighthood left Simon speechless. He nodded smartly in thanks.

"Now, please sit down, Sir Simon," the king said, gesturing toward a pair of chairs and a service of tea.

They waited while the equerry poured the tea and closed the door behind himself.

"We haven't had an opportunity to catch up," the king said, "since you returned last summer. I've received reports, but I'd like to hear what you *didn't* report."

While the king's words were sincere, Simon observed a flash of guilt or regret—perhaps both—in the monarch's eyes and a deep furrow in his brow.

As requested, Simon elaborated on his written report regarding his travel to Petrograd in 1915, his involvement with the Romanov family, and his escape, together with Mary and Artyom, from Yekaterinburg in the summer of 1918.

The king listened without interruption, but for the occasional heavy sigh accompanied by a head shake.

"While I'm unable to speak of it publicly," the king said when Simon's story concluded, "I feel solely responsible for the entire fiasco. Wish as I might that I could go back in time and act differently, I cannot."

The private room, decorated with masculine furnishings, fell quiet, the monarch deep in thought.

"Now," King George said, rising from his armchair,

indicating a conclusion to the meeting, "I'm sure you have plans for the remainder of your day, so I'll let you get on."

"Sir," Simon said, standing before him. He nodded and turned on his heel.

"By the way, my wife and I are planning a dinner party—just family," George said. "We would like to invite you, your wife, and your parents to dine with us next week. We're excited to see Maria again." With a heavy sigh, he added, "The question is whether she has any interest in meeting with us."

Simon stiffened at the invitation, anticipating the consequences.

CHAPTER 35

The day broke overcast with a mix of rain and snow. Richard flipped his collar up, covering his neck against the chill; nonetheless, he was grateful for the determined sun piercing the grey clouds like a blade carving through freshly-baked bread. The lingering effects of the previous evening's imbibing stabbed at his temples and pricked his eyes.

By the time he reached the Ministry of War, the pain had eased. The brisk walk had cleared his head, and the modest sun had begun to warm him. Outside Kemal's office, he was greeted by the young man he had seen typing the previous week.

"Come," the man said, rising from his stool.

Richard cupped his hand over nose and mouth and blew into his palm, sniffing quickly. *Keep your distance! You reek of stale whiskey, fool.* He groped in his pocket, fingers searching for a mint.

The clerk led Richard through the foyer and up a staircase to the floor above. The rooms appeared larger and brighter on the second level. Dust motes danced in sunbeams poking through ornamental coverings over ceiling-high windows. His guide stopped outside a pair of carved doors and rapped twice. In response, the right door flung open wide to reveal General Kemal.

"Mr. Temple," he said, extending his hand, "please come in."

Richard squeezed his arm against his valise as the door closed behind him like a death knell. For once, he was grateful for the time he had taken to tidy his appearance. *Steady on*, he cautioned himself. *Don't let them see any weakness.*

"Good morning, General," he said, willing his pounding heart to slow, hoping the General was immune to sweaty palms and boozy breath.

"Let me introduce you to my comrades," Kamel said, guiding Richard toward a large table, around which sat several uniformed men.

"I was just giving them an overview of our meeting last week," Kamel said when introductions were concluded. He snapped his fingers, beckoning a private who stood near the door. "Coffee all around, I should think," Kemal said.

"Apple tea for me," one of the generals said.

"Shall we begin, Mr. Temple?" Kemal asked, inviting Richard to lead the meeting.

Richard faltered once, then, with determination, he found his stride. As he spoke, he passed around his pages of evidence indicating that the British did not, and would not, have a strong position to support their claim for a portion of the territory. He rolled maps of Turkey onto the long table, identified the areas in which Britain had interests, and explained where he perceived their weaknesses.

"Of course, Britain wants control," he said, "but it is no longer a priority. Financially, she's weak. Years of war have depleted the federal treasury. I expect to see a push now to restore England and damage caused to its infrastructure. Any action in Turkey will be half-hearted." He scanned the faces of the officers. *At least they're still listening*, he thought.

"While Britain's administration focusses inward, on rebuilding, I believe that you"—he gazed around the room—"you will have an opportunity to seize control and rule yourselves. That is, if you wish t-to step out from beneath control of the British ... and the sultan," he said, suddenly feeling anxious. "I can't speak for the French or any of the other nations that intend to benefit from the partitioning of the Ottoman Empire, but, if their economy is anything like that of Great Britain ... all the more power to you."

His listeners said nothing, their expressions impossible to read. Since no one interrupted, he continued. "I must also disclose that I have no military training, and I am not a strategist. Plus, I am too young to have been invited into any top-secret meetings." *A snicker from two of the generals and a few smirks: I'll take that.*

"However, I am the son of a former naval officer who is now a British politician. During my relatively short life, I have heard things. Combining that with my limited experience working in Britain's War Office, I have formed my own opinions and my own suspicions, which I am freely sharing with you. That is all.

"General Kemal," Richard said, turning to the man seated to his right, "I have heard your praises sung in the streets and a new term—*Kemalism*—used to define your ideas and theories." He swallowed hard, recalling the young Frenchman who had made the same comment the previous week.

He picked up a pencil, using it to tap the palm of his hand for emphasis. "I believe you have what's needed to govern a new Turkey. A government for the people by the people. A government that will lead its people into a modern age."

"Hurra! Hurra!" the other officers said, uniting their voices.

Kemal rose to his feet and thanked his colleagues for their support. "Well," he said to them, "what do you think? Should we believe this young man? He is, after all, a traitor to his own country, is he not? And, as he says, inexperienced. If you ask me, he is asking a room full of experienced generals to act on the mere opinions of an untested brat!"

Richard winced, feeling a stab to his temples. A snake of fear curdled in his belly as he grasped how tenuous his situation was.

"Perhaps," said a middle-aged man seated at the far end of the table. He narrowed his eyes on Richard before he spoke. "Or perhaps he is simply a British businessman with a product to sell. Hm?" He raised a dark eyebrow to Richard.

"U-uh …" Richard stammered, rising to his feet to

answer the man's question. "Thank you for stating my situation kindly, sir." He bowed slightly to the far end of the table. "It is just so. Without me bringing this information to you now, you may well have come to the realization months or years down the road. With my insight, you will have the opportunity to make plans that will further your cause and lead to their implementation sooner. You will gain the power and control in advance of anyone realizing your intention. If I didn't believe it, I wouldn't have come all the way from Britain to waste your time."

Richard paused, allowing time for further questions. When none came, he continued. "As has been clearly stated already, my circumstance is now such that I shall not be returning to England any time soon."

A chuckle of awareness rippled around the table.

"I would like to offer my services as a consultant," he said, wishing he had a glass of whiskey in his hand. "To provide insight into the British mind and its military tactics, if I may." *In for a penny, in for a pound.*

The following week, Richard found himself summoned to the Ministry of War offices on two further occasions. As Kemal and his colleagues digested proposals disclosed by various nations, Richard's perspective helped them understand the subtleties.

"We'd like to take you up on your offer," Kemal said at the end of the second meeting, "to engage you as a consultant." He led Richard toward his office. "Come, we'll have a drink in my office to seal the arrangement."

Richard remained only long enough to consume the whiskey, then strolled with Kemal through the main lobby, toward the grand entrance.

"Our coffers are close to empty, but we will do our best to ensure you are paid as you deserve. As we rebuild the treasury, we will increase the pay accordingly."

"I'd be honoured, sir," Richard said, relieved to know that he could earn an income. "Until next time …" He stepped through the door, held open by Kemal, and smiled at the early spring sunshine.

CHAPTER 36

When Simon reported his knighthood to his parents and Mary the following weekend, they were delighted to share his news. The following evening, they celebrated with champagne and a fine meal of roast lamb with mint sauce, prepared by the cook.

Toward the end of the meal, Simon told them of the monarch's dinner invitation.

"As it happens, he and the queen will be in London for several weeks, hosting or attending various state events and attending to other obligations." Simon shrugged. "Given that Father and I are in London often as well, the king suggested that we dine at Buckingham Palace, rather than commuting to Sandringham, which would require that we stay with them at least one night, if not two."

"That sounds lovely," Ann said, her eyes alight with expectation.

"It does," Charles said, "but I think we must defer to you, Mary. We wouldn't want to place you in a stressful circumstance."

"Thank you, Father Charles. I appreciate your thoughtfulness," Mary said, glaring at Simon. "If you don't mind, I'll need to give it some thought." She pushed away from the table, the napkin in her hand fluttering as she set it on the table. "P-please excuse me."

Charles and Ann watched her march from the dining room. Simon hastily followed after her. "Mary, wait!"

———

"How can I go to dinner?" Mary said. "My family is dead, because he and others like him failed to help!" She paced across her bedchamber, wringing her hands. Tears dripped from her chin as painful memories of her father begging countries for asylum resurfaced. "I don't want to see any of them!"

"You're perfectly right, Sparrow, to feel as you do," Simon said, rising from the edge of the bed where he had been perched. "I tried to tell the king, but he wouldn't hear my protest. Regardless, I have no qualms about sending regrets."

"But you will be seen to have insulted him!" she said forlornly, stopping abruptly before him. "I can't embarrass your parents, or the memory of mine."

"My parents will understand," Simon said, taking her by the shoulders. "It's settled. We shall decline the invitation." His words were firm as he peered into her pooling eyes.

Mary blinked several times to clear her tears, then reached for a lace handkerchief in the pocket of her robe. "It is not settled," she said. "We will go." The set of her shoulders conveyed that she would brook no argument.

"My brave Sparrow," he said with admiration, kissing

the bridge of her nose before he embraced her again. "Very well … I will confirm a date with Mother and Father, then let the equerry know. But if you change your mind …"

"I won't," she said, pushing away from him with a heavy sigh.

———

When the Nightingale-Temples arrived at Buckingham Palace, an equerry handed their coats to a footman and escorted them to the monarchs' private salon.

"Come along, Sparrow," Simon said sotto voce, as if he sensed Mary's last-minute reluctance, "you can do this. I have complete faith in you." He claimed her hand, gloved in midnight blue, and tucked it into the crook of his elbow.

Mary's hand trembled in his grip, but she repaid his encouragement with a tenuous smile and squeezed his elbow. The dove grey silk of her gown shimmered in contrast with his white tie and black tailcoat. As a reminder of her mourning, her gown featured a diaphanous overlay of midnight blue, with dainty, matching strands of three dark sapphires that dangled from her ears.

The footman left, closing the doors to the salon. Simon and Mary hung back, allowing the monarchs time to greet Charles and Ann. When Simon began to move forward, Mary pulled her hand away.

"I can't do it," she said in a whisper, turning toward the closed doors.

"Maria!" the king said, striding purposefully toward them. He stepped to block her path, pleading with sorrowful eyes. "Please …" He reached for her hand.

Mary stood rigid, hooded eyes glowering at him.

"Please," the king said again, his misery sincere, "allow me to extend my utmost apologies and tell you that I take full responsibility—"

Mary snatched her hand away, seething. "You *are* responsible!" she snapped, her words full of quiet loathing. "Your cowardly actions killed my family!"

Stunned by her words, the others froze, uncertain of what next to do. The king straightened, his chin dropped in shame. Silence cloaked the room.

"I cannot argue with you," he said, finally raising his eyes to hers. "I can only ask that in time you might …"

"Might what? Forgive you?" Mary spat her response, her voice thickened with her Russian accent, which rose shrilly as she continued. "The time in which I won't see my siblings marry and have families? The time in which I won't see my parents age and become grandparents? Your cowardice killed them and left me an orphan!" Tears flowed freely as she sobbed.

Before she could speak another word, Simon withdrew his handkerchief. "Sir, please excuse us." He wrapped an arm around her shoulder and guided her toward the door.

"Maria," the king called after her, his voice full of anguish.

Mary stopped and shook free of Simon's arm. Head high, she turned toward King George. She stood proudly, facing him with defiance. Eyes flooding with tears, she waited.

"I … am … so sorry," he said, unchecked tears drenching his face. Shoulders rounded, he hung his head again.

Mary stared at him, her face devoid of emotion. He was the image of her father, a man she had known to be kind and supportive in the past. Yet now, he was the man who had failed her family when they had needed him most. The room began to spin. As her vision clouded, her knees buckled. Beside her, Simon was unable to stop her fall as she collapsed to the floor, but he was able to soften it.

When awareness returned to her, she was on a sofa. She heard Ann's voice. "Stand back. Give her some air."

Mary slowly opened her eyes, feeling Ann's hand under her head. "Water," Ann said. Mary dutifully sipped.

"Charles, pour some water on your handkerchief." Gently, Ann dabbed salty traces from Mary's face, examining her condition as she did so. "Your pulse is strong and steady," she said encouragingly, fingers resting on Mary's inner wrist. "Alright?"

Mary nodded, lifting herself to a sitting position. "Yes," she said. "What happened?"

"Justifiably so," George interjected deferentially, "you have soundly berated me and reduced me to a humility lower than I thought existed." He looked behind him for Simon. "I believe your husband wishes to take you home." He stepped back to allow Simon access.

"I apologize for my outburst, sir, ma'am," Mary said, abashed, as she swung her feet on the floor. "Regardless of how I feel or what I believe, I had no right to say what

I did." She toyed with Simon's handkerchief.

King George knelt next to her and once again claimed her hand. "You had every right. I let you down … all of you, and I will carry my failure to my deathbed."

Mary knew the king's pain and regret when their eyes met. He squeezed her hand.

"I think, sir, that I would not be pleasant company this evening." She rose to her feet, gently assisted by the king. "Perhaps another time."

"Of course," George said, stepping back to join his wife. "You will always be welcome, Maria."

Simon's hand found Mary's arm to steady her. She lingered for a moment, then gazed at the royal couple.

"Mary," she said, "my name is Mary. *Maria Nikolaevna Romanova* is no more." She discretely shook free of her husband's hand and curtsied deeply. Then, taking Simon's arm, chin raised, she strode calmly toward the door.

<hr>

"How are you, Sparrow?" Simon said later as he scrambled into bed next to his wife.

"Exhausted," Mary said flatly, a dry sob interrupting her even breathing. "My parents would have been mortified to hear me berate any king, let alone a beloved cousin and the king of England! I behaved miserably and embarrassed your parents. How will they ever forgive me?"

"Oh, don't worry about them," Simon said casually. "They understand the circumstances and will stand by you."

Her eyes pierced like daggers.

"Ah! You want to know what *I* think." Hand over heart, he chuckled. "As a matter of fact, you have my admiration. I could never have spoken to King George as you did. But you had two things going for you."

"Go on," Mary said, eyeing him dubiously.

"You lived and, no matter how much you deny it, in theory you are the Tsarina of Russia, and … in his opinion, his peer. And he knows he failed you," Simon replied. "If he didn't feel that failure so deeply, he would not have tolerated your outburst."

"Gosh," Mary said quietly as she smoothed the covers over her lap.

"I doubt that you will ever hear of it again," Simon said.

Mary looked at him quizzically.

"Well, think about it. The equerry had left the room. Only the six of us remained. Do you honestly think George and Mary would disclose these events to anyone else? Mother and Father won't speak of it, unless we do. So … it's a closed matter."

Simon wrapped an arm around her shoulders when he saw her lower lip begin to quiver. "Shhh," he said, speaking quietly into her ear as he stroked her glossy hair. "Shhh!" He held her until she stilled, then released her, sensing her determination to be free of him.

"Well, then," she said. "I suppose the worst is over. The only shadows remaining over me are your brother and Vasiliev."

"Not really," Simon replied, dabbing at her wet cheeks

with the cuff of his night shirt. "Richard can't hurt you; he's not here. And, if he has committed treason, I doubt he'll ever show his face in England again."

"Then I shall not think of him," Mary said, squaring her shoulders, "until I must. Now, I need only worry about Vasiliev and his next treachery!"

"And therein lies a curiosity of its own."

"How so?" Mary said.

"How much of a threat can Vasiliev be, if he's in Turkey focussed on duping senior parties there," Simon replied. "With any luck, he'll forget about the crown jewels."

"But he still has tentacles …"

CHAPTER 37

Hands stuffed in pockets, Simon leaned against the brick wall of a chemist, across the street from the *Eel and Martlett*, contemplating the whereabouts of his brother. He and Lockhart had spent many months communicating with various connections located throughout the Mediterranean, focussing on Turkey, trying to pick up a thread.

Soon after Richard's departure from Marseilles, an alert colleague of Lockhart's spotted him near a dock in Malta. The contact was able to confirm that Richard had been making enquiries about transportation to Constantinople.

Hoping that by now his brother would have written to Sally Winton, Simon reluctantly mulled over the best way to approach the young woman, this time as himself. He sighed heavily, pushed away from the wall, and brushed his jacket, smoothing any creases.

He waited for a lorry to ramble by before stepping into the middle of the road, dodging an ale wagon as he strode toward the entrance of the pub. It was too early for the pub to be open for patrons. The locked door proved it.

Simon straightened his grey fedora, pulling it low on his forehead. Rounding the corner of the pub, he entered a shaded, dead-end alley. At the foot of the alley stood the ale wagon he had skirted earlier. While the driver and his sidekick wrested a keg from the wagon, powerful dray horses waited patiently.

Next to the gaping doors through which the barrels disappeared, Simon spied a separate entrance. He tried the knob. It was unlocked.

He pushed the door ajar and stepped onto a small landing. The door closed behind him, leaving him in a murky darkness while he waited for his eyes to adjust. To one side was another door, which he surmised would give entry to the warehouse. On the other side, a steep stairwell rose to the second floor. He stood quietly, listening to the sounds of the pub and identifying one sound that seemed out of place.

He followed the humming up the stairs and along a narrow hallway. A floorboard squeaked underfoot and the humming stopped.

"Who's there?" a woman said, sounding alarmed. "Bert, is that you?" The door swung open, revealing the shapely, young woman with blonde hair.

"Good morning," Simon said, "I'm—"

"Patrons aren't allowed up here," she said firmly. "You need to—"

"Miss Winton?" When Simon removed his hat, the light from within her flat lit his face.

"Dickie!" the young woman said, opening the door wider. "Why so formal? Where have you been? Come in you fool!" Her eyes examined him further as he stepped toward the door. "What have you done to your hair?"

"Miss Winton, please forgive me," Simon said. "That is your name? Sally Winton?"

"Yes," Sally replied. "Wait! I know you. You're the one who came to the pub awhile back. You look just like Dickie! Are you sure you're not related?"

"As a matter of fact," Simon said, "I'm his older brother, and I must apologize for misleading you the last time I was here." He waited, allowing her thoughts to process his admission. "May I come in?"

Momentarily stunned, Sally nodded curtly, then stepped aside and ushered Simon into her quarters. "Dickie's brother?" she said with surprise. "I didn't know he had a brother. He never spoke of his family." She looked up at Simon, frowning. "Is something wrong? Has something happened to Dickie?"

"Allow me to introduce myself properly," Simon said, eyeing her flushed appearance. "My name is Simon Nightingale-Temple." He reached for her elbow. "I say, Miss Winton, are you alright? Perhaps you should sit down." He ushered her to a chair. "May I get you some water?"

"I-I don't understand!" Sally said, shaking her head to Simon's suggestion of water. Instead, she motioned for him to sit in a worn armchair opposite her. "Is Dickie alright?"

"I can't say," Simon said, concerned for her welfare. "May I presume that, since you're asking, you have heard nothing from Richard since we last spoke?"

"Richard? Oh, you mean Dickie!" Sally said. "I received a note from him last week. He wrote that he was on a boat, travelling through some Greek islands. I don't understand why he would be in Greece. Do you?" She lowered her head, gazing with interest at her fidgeting fingers as if she had never seen them before. "At least he's safe."

"And you've heard nothing from him or anyone else since then?" Simon hung his fedora on his knee and regarded her intently. "How are you feeling now?"

"I'm fine. You surprised me, is all. And … no, I've heard nothing." She shook her head from side to side. "I was hoping—oh, I don't know what I was hoping." She sighed deeply, the red hue of her skin easing. "See D-Dickie and I … well, we never … we never committed to one another. I-I was always just here. If he needed me. And that was usually when he ran low of cash in between pay packets." She raised her head, her eyes locking with Simon's. "D'you know what I mean?"

"I have a reasonable idea," Simon said, pausing long enough for her to collect herself. "In our family, Richard is considered a bit of a scoundrel. He's lived a wild life and has usually spent his annual allowance well in advance of his next. Between drinking, gambling and fast wo—" Simon withheld the last word, not wanting to give offence. "*Ahem*, let's just say he liked a good time."

"A scoundrel! Who receives an allowance?" Sally said, flustered. "What kind of a man is he? Are you saying he wasn't employed at the War Office? That he was some rich la-dee-da?" She shook her head. "I'm confused."

"Perhaps I should start from the beginning," Simon replied, wondering why he felt the need to tell her anything.

He began by re-introducing himself, then his parents. He explained that they had heard nothing of Richard for months, not since his remarkable departure from England.

"So," Sally said, eyeing Simon dubiously, "Dickie isn't an orphaned clerk who worked at the War Office? He-he's rich!" She jumped to her feet again. "He-he lied to me all along?" She plopped into the chair, tears budding in her eyes. "How dare he use me like that! I suppose next you're going to tell me that he's married!"

"To my knowledge, he is not married," Simon said with assurance, "but I'm afraid I can't speak to any other falsehoods. He did work at the War Office for a time, however."

Without understanding why, he felt an urge to provide his brother with some credibility. "Although he did receive an annual income from my parents, I wouldn't say he's rich. He's somewhat of a spendthrift, and that would explain how he might've found himself on your doorstep from time to time."

Sally sat quietly, eyeing him as he spoke.

"May I ask how you two met?" Simon said, cocking his head with curiosity.

Sally appeared calmer. A smile began to grow from her pursed lips as she lovingly recalled their first meeting and the times that he had arrived unexpectedly seeking refuge with her.

"The last time he stayed for almost a week," she said, dreamily. She lowered her eyes. "Do you think we'll ever see him again?"

"I certainly hope so," Simon replied. "But without knowing where he went or what plans he may have had, I can't be certain."

The room fell silent as their thoughts searched for Richard.

"Miss Winton," Simon said a few minutes later, "I will continue to search for my brother, and I will let you know if I hear anything at all." He rose and turned toward the door, disappointed that he had nothing new that would help locate his brother. "May I call upon you from time to time … as a friend?"

"I suppose," Sally said, "but I can't imagine why."

CHAPTER 38

Each weekday, the chauffeur drove Ann and Mary to Walkergate Hospital and returned later in the day to collect them. The hours they kept at the hospital were long and gruelling. The wave of Spanish flu that arrived in September had all but dissipated, replaced with more common strains of flu, pneumonia, bronchitis, and other infections and diseases. Toward the end of winter, it was rare to receive a patient with Spanish flu symptoms. However, whenever a case was reported, hospital staff promptly organized and prepared for it.

By the end of a particularly challenging week, Ann and Mary both claimed exhaustion and took to their beds soon after they had eaten an early meal.

"Tompkins, please inform Lord Charles and Lord Simon that we are not unwell," Ann said Friday evening as she led Mary up the stairwell to the second floor. "We are merely tired and in need of rest."

The butler nodded, seeing the fatigue ooze through their rounded shoulders, marked by their slow treads on the stairs.

"They will simply have to manage without us for one evening, Mary," she said flippantly, dragging herself up the staircase by the railing.

"Otherwise, we shall fall sick and die," Mary said, "and they shall have us not at all!" She giggled softly, then sobered. "I will ensure a thorough wash before I fall into bed and ask Mrs. Zima to have our garments laundered carefully. My skin crawls with the idea that we may be carrying the influenza virus on our skin."

"No one has said that this flu is carried on the skin." Ann paused at the top of the stairs and turned toward Mary, seeming alert to the possibility.

"I know," Mary replied, "but just the thought of it makes me feel unclean!"

"Then I shall scrub too and hope that the fresh air will keep us well," Ann said. Tompkins knows to insist that everyone sleep with an open window, and that the Hall is aired twice a day to keep the fresh air flowing!"

"Hopefully," Mary said, "our preventative measures will keep Jarrow Hall free of illness."

———

An hour later, Michael met the train from London and raced to assist Simon, who was struggling to help his father exit the first-class coach.

"Ah! Michael, there's a good man," Simon said. "Father is unwell. We must get him into bed as quickly as possible."

On learning that his mother and wife had already taken to their beds, Simon insisted on sitting with his father through the night.

"We'll need warm blankets, a bed warmer, and hot tea,

I should think," Simon told Tompkins. "Father has a chill."

"Very well, my lord," Tompkins replied. "I'll attend to it immediately. I have also taken the liberty of opening the windows for each of your chambers, per Lady Ann's instructions."

"Opened the windows!" Simon said, surprised by the directive. "My father has a chill. Open windows will compromise his condition."

"To the contrary, my lord," Tompkins said. "Lady Ann has ordered that we all sleep with windows ajar. Apparently, the doctors insist on it."

"Very well," Simon replied, "but please ensure that we have adequate bed covers."

"As you say, sir," Tompkins said, leaving Simon and the valets to care for Lord Charles while he assembled the requisite items.

A ray of bright sunlight pierced Mary' slumber. She swiftly raised a hand to cover her eyes, then made a small crack between her fingers to check the time on the miniature carriage clock near her bed.

"Eight fifteen!" she said aloud, stretching her aching muscles. "I certainly was tired!"

She rolled onto her side, expecting to see her recumbent husband beside her. She did not, and given the tidy state of the linen, he had not been. She tugged the bellpull as she swung her feet to the floor and reached for her woollen robe.

"Good morning, my lady," Mrs. Zima said a few minutes later. "You slept well?"

"I did indeed," Mary replied, indicating that a tray be set on the bench at the foot of the bed. "Tea for now." She stretched as she headed toward the toilet. "I'll just be a moment."

"Take your time, my lady," Mrs. Zima replied as she set out garments for the day. "The fire needs lighting."

"Did my husband and Lord Charles not return last evening?" Mary said, casting her eyes toward the empty bed.

"Yes, my lady. He and Lord Charles returned on the last train. I understand that the master was feeling unwell, so Lord Simon had him put to bed in his own room."

"Unwell!" Mary said. "You should have said so earlier! Does Mother Ann know?"

"I don't think so," Mrs. Zima replied. "Lady Ann still sleeps."

Mary re-tied the belt of her robe and hastened along the hallway to her father-in-law's chamber. Clearly, Charles' bed had been slept in, but the room's shadows hid him from view.

"Simon!" she said quietly, spying her husband dozing in a wing chair. "Where is your father?"

"Shhh!" Simon silenced her with a finger to his lips. "He's been awake on and off all night. He seems to be sleeping fitfully now, though," Simon said quietly, pointing toward a mound of bedding. "Can we speak outside?"

"Of course!" Mary replied. "But not before I see for myself."

As she neared the bed, Charles' dark, wavy hair became visible. Gently, she placed the back of her hand on his forehead, anticipating the heat. With her free hand, she checked his pulse. *A little fast,* she thought. Then, she lowered the blankets and tested his cheek. *Hot, but not burning.* She leaned in closer, lowering her ear to listen to his breathing. *Congested. Hopefully, just a cold.*

She stood back and gazed at Simon. "Come to my room, the fire's been lit," she said, still whispering.

In her room, Mary poured a cup of tea for Simon. "Breakfast?" she said, delaying Mrs. Zima's departure.

"I'd appreciate that," Simon said as his stomach rumbled on cue. "Maybe two oranges?"

"You look tired, darling; have you been with your father all night?"

"Yes," Simon replied, stifling a yawn. "I couldn't leave him. With all the talk in London concerning a resurgence of the Spanish flu, I needed to be certain he hadn't been infected."

"You should have called me," Mary said impatiently.

"I would have, but Tompkins said you were exhausted," Simon replied as he lowered himself into a pale blue satin chair. "If his condition had worsened, I would have called you regardless." He accepted the cup of tea from Mary and took a sip.

"I'll bring egg and toast, and oranges, shortly, my lord," Mrs. Zima said, closing the door behind her.

"Father was restless from time to time," Simon said, picking up the thread of the conversation, "but I haven't seen any change to warrant waking you."

Mary tapped the tip of her nose, deep in thought. "Would you mind sitting with him for another few minutes while I dress?" she said, reaching for the bellpull.

"Certainly," Simon replied sleepily. "I'll just top up my tea and take it in with me. Ask Mrs. Z to bring the tray to my room?"

Half an hour later, Simon reluctantly crawled into his own, chilly bed, having been informed by Mary that he could expect to sleep alone until the illness passed.

"You wouldn't want to infect anyone else if you are carrying the virus, would you?" she said.

He easily agreed with her, recalling so many occasions in the past when his mother had delivered similar edicts, all to the benefit of the entire Hall. That did not stop him from wishing for the warmth of his wife, however. He heaved a forlorn sigh and promptly fell into a deep sleep, knowing that his wife had his father's welfare well in hand.

"Father Charles," Mary said, her voice soft with worry, "Can you hear me? How do you feel?" She felt his forehead for fever with the back of her hand again, sniffed his breath for foulness, then cupped his stubbled cheek, noting stripes of grey in his dark whiskers. *He's warmer than he was an hour ago*, she thought. *I must keep his temperature down.*

Charles eyes flickered beneath closed eyelids. He moaned,

raising an arm to cover his eyes. "It's bright in here," he mumbled. "Close the curtains."

"They are closed, Father," Mary replied, "but I'll turn down one of the lamps."

The silk of her skirt swished as she moved toward the lamp and clicked the switch. "Is that better?" she said, placing a cool cloth over his forehead.

"Yes," he said, the word sounding forced.

"I know this may be difficult, Father," Mary said, "but you must try to tell me how you feel."

Mary watched as Charles ran his tongue around the inside of his mouth. "Thirsty," he said.

"I can help with that," Mary said, wiggling her hand beneath his head to help lift it and tipping a cup of tepid tea to his lips.

Charles sipped the tea, swallowed with difficulty, and sipped again. The small exercise clearly taxed him. Mary withdrew her hand, and his head slid into the pillow.

"Cold," he said. "Ache."

"I can help with that, too," she said, peeling the top comforter back long enough to drape him with blankets warmed by the fire before returning the cover. "Better?"

"Feels good," Charles said, his voice breathy. His hand shot from beneath the bedclothes to grab her arm. "Tell me: do I have the Spanish flu? Am I going to die?"

"You likely have the flu," she replied, cautiously. "We'll know more in the next few hours. However, you do have a low-grade fever, and that concerns me. Enjoy the warm blankets for now. If your fever spikes, expect an ice bath. If we can keep it from spiking, you'll have a better chance of enduring the virus. Nausea?"

"A little," he said, his voice sounding stronger. "No urge to vomit."

"We have a chamber pot available, if needed," Mary said. "Have you voided since you've been home?"

"Mary!" Charles said weakly. "Private—"

"Now, Father Charles, you know that I need the information if I'm going to help."

"Sorry. No. On the train. Nothing since."

"Hmm," Mary responded. "We'll have to keep an eye on that. In the meantime, I'd like you to sip fluids as much as possible—a cup every hour. Someone will always be here with you. You must do as they say. I don't want your condition worsening."

"Ann," he said, moaning again. "Must speak with Ann."

"I will call on her shortly," Mary said firmly, "and send her in." She squeezed his shoulder and leaned to kiss his forehead.

<hr>

Charles heard the worry in her voice and promised himself that he would do whatever was asked of him. For the first time, he cracked his eyelids and peered around the dimly-lit room. Mary was perched on an armchair that had been pulled close to the bed. A white gauze masked covered her mouth and nose. Beyond her, a maid stood near the door, also wearing a mask.

"You may go," Mary said, dismissing the maid, "but ask Hamilton to come."

"Yes, my lady," the maid replied, reaching for the doorknob.

"Wash your hands with soap and water first," Mary said, her voice firm. "We must do everything we can to keep the illness confined to this room. When you're finished, cover the bowl with a clean cloth and take it with you. Tell cook to ensure everything removed from this room is cleaned with boiling water and Lysol Antiseptic."

The maid washed her hands as instructed before turning toward the door. "Mr. Hamilton's just here ..." she said, nudging the door ajar with her foot.

"My lady," Charles' valet said, creeping into the darkened room. "Tell me what to do."

"Are you wearing a mask?" Mary said as she gently mopped her father-in-law's face with another cool cloth.

"I am," Hamilton replied.

"Good," she said, returning the cloth to a basin of iced water. "Help me lift Lord Charles into a semi-reclining position. Lots of pillows behind him. We must ensure that his body drains downward, keeping his lungs clear. And lots of fluids."

She placed a hand on Charles' shoulder. He smiled wanly in return.

"Father, once we have you sitting up, I'll call Mother Ann for you."

Mary knocked on the door of Ann's chamber and called to her as she opened it. Ann responded with a cough and a moan.

"Mother Ann!" Mary said, rushing toward the bed. Intuitively, she withdrew a fresh mask from her pocket and pulled the bell to summon Ann's maid.

As Mary awaited the maid, she repeated the same examination she had applied to Charles. And, when Ann's maid, Elsie Davis, arrived, she gave the same instructions as she had given to Hamilton.

"Mother Ann," Mary said, checking her pulse, temperature, and comfort, "you and Father Charles both seem to have the flu. He is in good hands now. Davis and I will help you, too."

"Thank … you," Ann replied. "In good hands, too."

CHAPTER 39

Mary stood before the staff gathered in the downstairs kitchen, eyeing them individually as the last arrived. "I cannot tell you enough," Mary said, using her nursing voice, "how important it is that you wash your hands constantly in hot, soapy water."

She cast her gaze around the kitchen, hoping to instill upon the Hall's staff the importance of cleanliness so long as illness remained in the house. "Mrs. Wright, please assign one person to ensure that buckets of Lysol solution are mixed and available for use at all times. Every surface of the house must be wiped with the solution frequently, especially common areas such as the kitchen, bathrooms, and water closets. Nanny will need help, too. Everything in the nursery and the children's rooms will have to be cleaned. Finally, anything removed from the rooms of Lord Charles and Lady Ann must be cleaned with great care. That means a mixture of Lysol in every wash as well. If you have any doubts, concerns, or questions, come to me immediately! Especially if you feel unwell! We must keep this illness in check; I've seen how easily it spreads. I want no one else in this house to fall ill! Is that understood?"

"Yes, my lady," they replied as a chorus.

"Good then," she said officiously. "Let's get to work!"

As the household staff separated, Mary called to Tompkins. "Take Michael and Peter with you up to the attic, please," she said. "We need the portable chamber pot brought down, wiped with the Lysol solution, and taken up to Lord Charles' room—as quickly as possible. I'd prefer it was there when he needs it, rather than the alternative."

"My lady," Tompkins said, already in motion. "Michael, Peter! With me!"

On Sunday, Mary rose early despite the late hour at which she had retired the night before.

"Good morning, darling," she said, spying Simon sitting in a brocade fireside chair in Charles' chamber. "How's Father this morning?"

"Considering the severity of his illness," Simon replied, "I'd say he's alright. But you're the nurse, not me." He smiled sleepily at his wife and rubbed his eyes.

"Have you been here all night?" she said.

"No," he replied. "Hamilton and I have been taking it in shifts. How's Mother?"

"About the same," Mary replied. "Mrs. Z and Davis have been taking shifts with her, while I hover over both." She regarded her father-in-law's reclining figure, arms across her chest.

"Doesn't it strike you as odd that the two of them

spend so much time apart, yet it is they who are sick?" Simon said, musing.

"Indeed," Mary replied. "I cannot explain it." She shook her head in puzzlement. "You, Zima, and the undercook have spent the most time with him this past week. Yet none of you seem ill."

"Not yet, that is. My throat's a little scratchy," Simon replied, opening the hall door with his sleeve. "I think I'll order some honeyed tea and get some more sleep. Hopefully, I'll feel better later. I also hope no one else falls ill."

"Simon," Mary said, pausing his departure. "I'd like to move both of them to one of the larger rooms, so their care can be focussed, and their chambers can be scrubbed."

"Excellent idea! I agree," he replied. "And, if this virus takes hold of me or anyone else, we'll move in with them too!"

———·———

As the day progressed, a room was organized in which Charles and Ann could be lodged and treated together.

"I'm very pleased to see everyone so fastidious," she said to the housekeeper. "Please compliment the staff for me. With any luck, we may have snipped this flu in the bud!"

"*Nipped*, my lady," Mrs. Wright replied kindly. "'Nipped it in the bud' is the correct phrase."

"*Nipped*," Mary said, repeating the word. "Thank you."

CHAPTER 40

Mid-afternoon, Tompkins opened the Hall's great doors to Artyom Egorov. Seeing Mary descend the grand staircase from the second floor, Artyom greeted her.

"Ah! Mary," he said, slightly breathless. "Henry has come home for his lunch but is complaining of nausea and fever. We need help!"

"Wait here," Mary said without ceremony. *The scar beneath his left eye is twitching,* Mary thought. *Simon said it only twitches when he's worried!*

She turned and raced through the baize door in search of Mrs. Wright, reappearing several minutes later.

"You may return to care for Henry. I've asked Mrs. Wright to spare two staff and supplies. We'll be along to help you and Varvara presently. Under no circumstances is Henry to be allowed near little Arthur. Until we arrive, Henry must keep to one room, away from everyone else." Her voice was breathy with urgency and worry. "Go now! We will follow shortly!"

Within half an hour, Mary had assembled two volunteers and a trove of supplies to be driven down the lane by Michael.

With typical efficiency, Mary descended upon the

Crocker house and took control, giving instructions for the preparation and use of a Lysol solution to clean everything, the bathing and caring of Henry, and the overall management of the house and its occupants. Of greatest concern, she told them, was little Arthur's welfare. Everything in the nursery was cleaned immediately, as were all surfaces, including toys, linen, and anything else she itemized specifically.

Once she was satisfied that her instructions would be followed precisely, Mary returned to Jarrow Hall, leaving Varvara and Artyom to oversee the care of the cottage and its occupants.

Mary sent a note to the hospital's director reporting that the flu had reached Jarrow Hall. At Simon's request, she also sent a message to Captain Smith-Cumming regarding his welfare and that of Artyom. Later in the day, she received a reply from the director recommending that anyone at risk of infection remain at home for another week before venturing out.

"So long as you remain well," he wrote, "I would be grateful to see you on duty by Wednesday. We are desperately in need of help."

"Well, I guess that's that!" Mary said, having read the message aloud to Ann, Charles, and Simon.

"Indeed, it appears the director has great faith in your

ability to abstain from illness!" Ann replied with a giggle, which was promptly replaced with a fit of coughing.

"Until this dashed flu struck," Charles said, somewhat breathless, "I would have said the same of you, my dear Ann."

"I can assure you, Mother," Simon said, "that the director is not the only one harbouring that thought. Varvara insists that Mary's quick and efficient response saved the entire Crocker cottage from falling victim to the flu."

On Wednesday, Mary returned to her hospital duties once again. Confident that the household would follow Lady Ann's directions, she turned her attention to the steady stream of patients, both military and civilian, stricken by the latest wave of the Spanish flu.

CHAPTER 41

S imon approached the *Eel and Martlett*, feeling the late March sun warm his cheek in contrast to the chill of the morning. Earlier in the week, he had received a note from Sally Winton advising that she had heard from Richard and invited him to stop by for tea any morning, so long as he arrived before half ten; her workday started at eleven.

Simon straightened his fedora and entered the murky darkness at the foot of the stairs that rose to the second floor. Above him, he heard Sally's humming. He climbed the steps two at a time and strode along the narrow hallway.

When the floorboard squeaked under his foot, her humming ceased. "Hello?" she said, sounding calmer than she was the first time he had visited.

"Good morning," Simon said, calling from the doorway.

"Mr. Temple," Sally said, her voice welcoming, "please come in. Tea's almost ready."

The door opened wider, inviting him into the cozy room. A tea service and fresh baking sat in the middle of a small table. The comely young woman reached for Simon's coat and hat, while her gesture invited him to sit.

"I must apologize for my behaviour during your first visit," she said. "I was taken aback by everything you said." She smiled warmly, pouring steamy brew from the teapot. "I hope you take milk."

"I do, thank you."

Sally nudged a plate of baking toward him. "I just came up from the kitchen. These are still warm." She plopped a roll on a small, chipped plate. "My favourite time of the day. Nothing beats fresh baking."

Simon selected a small meat pie and bit into it. "If I ate here every morning, it could easily become my favourite too."

Sally smiled prettily at the compliment. "I'll be sure to tell cook. She'll take whatever compliments come her way."

They sat in silence for ten heartbeats, Simon waiting for her to speak.

"I promised I'd let you know if I heard from Dickie again," she said eventually. She reached into her pocket and retrieved a small envelope. "This arrived on Monday. Go ahead. Read it."

Simon accepted the envelope and tugged out the letter. "*Dear Sal*", Simon read,

> *It's taken me a while. Over the past several months, I have travelled on many boats of all different types and sizes, and I've met some remarkable people. I left England hoping to avoid conflict but find myself landed in the middle of a left-over chapter from the Great War.*

Today, I received an amazing offer: an opportunity to help change history. I am overjoyed at the possibilities. Must go. I'll write again soon.

Hope you are keeping well.

My best,
D.

"How curious!" Simon said as he folded the letter and returned it to the envelope.

"I'm still confused," Sally said, rubbing her rounding belly. "Do you know where he is?"

"I could venture a guess," he replied, "but I should discuss this with my employer before I say anything more." *Please don't let that be Richard's child.*

"From the sounds of it," Sally said, "I'm guessing that I shouldn't be expecting a speedy return."

"No, I think not," Simon replied, setting his teacup on its saucer.

"That's what I was afraid of." She sighed deeply, resting her hand over the roundness as she thought. Tears began to flood her eyes. "I was hoping he'd return before the baby arrived. That maybe we could …" The tears spilt, flowing leisurely toward her chin.

"So, you're suggesting that Richard is the child's father?" Simon said, nodding toward her resting hand.

"Well, who else's would it be?" Sally said, jumping indignantly to her feet, swiping at the torrent of tears.

"I-I'm sorry," Simon said, rising to face her. "I didn't mean to imply—"

"No, of course not," Sally said, tugging a rumpled handkerchief from her sleeve. "How could you know?"

"Please," Simon said, his hand indicating a return to her chair. "I didn't mean to upset you. It's just that you've never mentioned—"

"There was never a need before," she said. "I still had a hope that he'd be back before anything need be said." Her clasped hands rested on her lap. "This wee one started when he was here last. I presume that he knew he was leaving then, yet he never said a word!" Her hands flew to her face, covering a deep sob. "Will we ever see him again? Will he see his child?"

"I continue to hope so," Simon replied. "At the moment, however, I could only speculate. First, I need to understand where he went and why."

Sally retrieved her cup and sipped her tea. "It's gone cold," she said, her lips pursed in disappointment. The cup rattled against its saucer as she reseated it.

"Miss Winton," Simon said kindly. "I must leave now, but I promise you that I will continue to search for Richard, and I will keep you informed. In the meantime," he said turning to face her, "I'd like to express sincere concern that you appear to be on your own and about to raise a child single-handedly."

"Oh, I won't be alone," Sally replied, swiping her cheeks clear, a determined expression replacing her appearance of hopelessness. "I have my cousin Bert. He'll help. And I can always return home if I must. My folks won't be happy, but once they come to terms with my choices, they'll help me."

Simon opened the door and adjusted his fedora on his head as he stepped into the hallway.

"I'll let you know if I hear from Dickie again," Sally said.

"Will you tell him?" Simon said. "About the child, I mean."

"Perhaps I would," Sally said, "but he's never sent me a return address."

Simon left his business card with her and invited her to contact him if she needed anything regarding the child. *I'll work out a plan that will see her and the child safe. Just because Richard's the father, the child and its mother shouldn't go wanting.*

CHAPTER 42

Richard awoke with a start and for a moment wondered where he was. At once, events of the previous months poured like a waterfall into his consciousness. He stretched leisurely, marvelling that he, Richard the Black Sheep, had become a confidant of General Mustafa Kemal, leader of the sultan's commanders. *What would Father say if he knew?*

"The man is amazing," he said aloud, as if arguing the point with his father. He peered at his reflection in a mirror propped on his dresser.

"He's constantly discussing battle plans with the generals and organizing resistance against the British, Greeks, and French to ensure the Allied powers fail to overthrow the sultan and seize all of Turkey. And, at the same time, he has agents in France monitoring the progress of the Allied powers who are focussed on writing a peace agreement that will divvy up the Ottoman Empire, without allowing any say in the matter to Turkey and other neighbouring countries."

He scrubbed the whiskers along his jaw and stuck out his tongue, an act which summoned the visage of Sally Winton. *If I miss anything of England, it's Sally.*

"And *phwutt!*" he said to his still-listening father. He meandered into the bathroom as his thoughts resettled. "Just like that, the first quarter of the year has passed! Well, they can bully the sultan, but they're not going to push Mustafa Kemal Pasha around! Several generals have tried. Yet, many have pledged to follow him if he resigns his position in the sultan's army."

He turned the taps and filled the bathtub. As the water swirled in the tub, he marvelled how Kemal had convinced the generals that, united, they could hold Anatolia; how, slowly and methodically, they had mobilized their troops and strategically set up camps to protect the country's largest territory. And, when the generals assembled in Erzurum mid-month, he helped Kemal send letters to them, setting out details of those plans.

"Then, Father, while the generals considered his proposal, America's President Wilson inserted himself amongst the Allied powers and is now encouraging a Greek landing on Turkey's west coast! I hope that doesn't mean the general will have to change his plans."

Richard lathered himself with a foamy sponge and slid under the surface for a rinse, mulling over Kemal's accomplishments since he had arrived in December. He glanced at his wristwatch, propped on the shelf above the hook where he had hung his castoff clothes the night before. *Great! I have time enough to record my thoughts in the diary I purchased a few days ago. I may just be a fly on the wall, but sometimes the insights of an observer come in handy.*

———

Forty minutes later, he was dressed for the day and had recorded his earlier thoughts. He chewed the inside of his cheek, mentally wondering what would happen next, when a light rap on the door interrupted him.

He opened the door to see the innkeeper dangling a small envelope addressed to him. Richard glanced at the grinning proprietor, then stared at the envelope bearing the arms of the Ministry of War office, clearly marked *URGENT*.

Richard hastily read the message, stuffed his feet into a new pair of leather shoes, and snatched his jacket from the hook.

"What's this?" the innkeeper asked.

"I haven't a clue," Richard replied, perplexed. "Usually, the message invites me to attend the next day, but this one says immediately!"

He tripped down a flight of stairs to the main floor, leaving the innkeeper following in his wake. Outside, he turned in the direction of the Ministry and jogged through the empty streets.

———

"Good morning, sir," Richard said when the typist showed him into the general's office. "I've come as quickly as I could." He stilled himself and inhaled deeply. "How may I help you?"

"It is I who must help you," Kemal said, gesturing

for Richard to sit on the wooden guest chair as he walked behind the desk to his own well-worn chair. "I've just received word that I've been appointed Inspector-General of the 9th Army. I must leave for Samsun immediately. At the same time, I've received confirmation that the British have asked Greece to land at Izmir. These two events will require my full attention for many weeks …"

"What can I do to help, sir?" Richard edged forward on the chair, keen to be part of it.

"You do not yet have the training to help me now." Kemal reached for a cigarette, offered one to Richard, and shrugged when he declined. "And for me to ensure your safety would be a distraction I cannot risk."

Kemal released a breath of cigarette smoke. "Now is not a good time for you to be seen with me. Not for you; not for me, either."

"But—"

"If you are to continue aiding us with our endeavours," Kemal said, raising his hand to still Richard's objection, "we must keep you safe."

He poured two glasses of whiskey, handing one to Richard. Then he rose from his chair and perched on the corner of his desk, suspended leg swinging with thought. "One of the council members—Ahmet Hamza of Bolu—has family living outside that city several hours from here. He has arranged for a military vehicle to escort you to the farm, where you will stay with his old aunt and uncle for a while. When it is once again safe for you to join me, word will be sent."

"But what am I to do there?" Richard asked, shocked to hear the general's directive.

"I would recommend that you try at least two things," Kemal said, his eyes twinkling. "You are not obliged to do either." He stubbed his cigarette in the burgeoning ashtray. "First, you might learn to speak, or at least understand, the Turkish language. Second, if you are looking for something to pass the time, you might help on the farm. Workers are hard to find, as many have enlisted to support our cause." He chuckled outright. "Who knows, you may even find a nice girl to take as a wife."

"A wife!" Richard rose to his feet and began pacing. "All kidding aside, sir; you need me here, with you." He settled pleading eyes on Kemal.

"Richard Temple," Kemal said formally, "you have been a great help to us since you first arrived. So long as the Allied powers insist on invading Turkey's west coast and keep squabbling with the sultan in Constantinople, I must lead Turkey's defence. This next while, we must take care of ourselves in the only way we know how."

He slid from the desk and placed a firm hand on Richard's shoulder. "Go and pack a bag and return here within the hour. A vehicle will be waiting for you at the front of the building. When you arrive in Bolu, give this message to the uncle of Ahmet Hamza."

Richard swigged the remainder of his whiskey and stared at the envelope addressed to Ender Edem Pasha of Bolu, stunned by the turn of the conversation.

"Go now! Make haste."

CHAPTER 43

Richard hopped from the back of the military vehicle as it rolled to a stop outside a tidy cluster of whitewashed, stone houses. The driver and his comrade jumped from the cab and walked toward him. In broken French, the driver pointed out a stately, dark green, timber-built farmhouse. "That be your home now. Kemal Pasha send for you later," the driver said.

The comrade leapt into the back of the vehicle and began handing canvass sacks of supplies to the driver and Richard. As they stacked everything at the side of the dirt-track road, several men walked toward them from the fields.

"Welcome!" an older man said as he approached. "You will stay for tea?" He spoke French with ease, and the conversation shifted to a more common language.

"We must return to the city quickly," the driver said, shaking his head. "You are Ender Edem Pasha, the uncle of Ahmet Hamza of Bolu?"

"Yes," the older man replied. "*Retired* general. And is this the man we are to host for a while?"

"Richard Temple," the driver said, glancing at his passenger. "The general wrote a note—"

"Richard Temple, sir," Richard said, leaning forward to offer his right hand to Edem Pasha. "Pleased to meet you." As he spoke, he removed Kemal's note from his shirt pocket and offered it to his host.

"I see here," the elder said, addressing Richard as he scanned the hand-written page, "that you have been most helpful to General Kemal and the council of generals." He grinned at Richard as he folded the note, re-inserted it into the envelope, and slid it into a pocket. "We will take good care of you."

As the vehicle pulled away from the farm, Richard's belly felt empty. All that had been comfortable in Constantinople had been replaced with the unfamiliar.

Right, he thought, following the old uncle toward the house. *Learn the language. Help with the chores. Meet the women. Hopefully, the time will pass quickly.*

———•·—

As Kemal had predicted, an aggressive conflict erupted between the Allied forces attempting to protect their interests on Turkish soil and the Turkish resistance led by Kemal. During the ensuing weeks, Kemal led his army on two fronts: against Armenian forces to the east and against Greek forces to the west.

Edem Pasha informed Richard that since his retirement, and having no children of his own, his preference was to be called "Uncle." Although he felt more joy in being an uncle than a general, he was always delighted to receive intermittent updates from his nephew.

At the end of days spent in the fields minding sheep, tending orchards of apricot and apple trees, and assisting the beekeepers, Richard was invited to sit on the veranda with Uncle and pass the evenings drinking coffee and smoking rolled cigarettes. While Richard declined the tobacco, he welcomed the coffee.

After a time, Richard no longer craved whiskey or tobacco. He found that, at the end of a tiring day, the coffee helped him stay alert long enough to grasp the news the old man endeavoured to share. While the primary point of the exercise was that Richard should learn Turkish, he was grateful that his host spoke enough French to ensure that he understood the news in either language. In time, Richard realized, French was rarely required.

***

"What's this?" the old man said one morning as Richard stumbled into the common room scrubbing his head.

"What's what, Uncle?" Richard replied, contemplating the dirt under his fingernails.

"Your hair is changing," the old man said, his face solemn. "Have you been snitching too many carrots and apricots from the garden?"

"Um," Richard said, stammering through a chuckle, "it is, and I have not. I thought I could blend in with most Turks if I darkened my hair. As you can see, my natural colour is quite noticeable."

"Ah!" the old man replied, "now I see it." He peered at

Richard quizzically. "Here many have the Greek heritage that results in a similar hair colour. It was not necessary for you to alter yours."

"I know that now," Richard replied with a shrug. "I didn't know that when I left England."

"It is a good thing that you are not a military man," Uncle said, amused. "You would have no time for such frivolity."

"Indeed," Richard replied. "Nor do I now. I think it's time to reveal all. Don't you agree?"

"I do," Uncle replied. "If you want people to trust you, you cannot have secrets. And while it is a small vanity, it suggests that your intentions might be questionable."

"Yes, Uncle. Exactly so." *And no more whiskey or tobacco!*

CHAPTER 44

Following his meeting with Sally Winton, Simon had hired a private investigator to make enquiries about her situation. If Richard was the father of her child, his family had an obligation to support it and ensure that it was raised well. If not, then he would give her a sum that would see her through the pregnancy and then some; it was not in his nature to see someone do without if he could help.

The investigator had followed Sally for several weeks, including a few days spent in the country with her parents in early summer.

"Nothing about the young woman," the investigator said, "suggests that her story is false. She is highly regarded by her cousin Bert, the landlord, pub patrons, her parents, and their neighbours. No one has ever seen her with a man other than Richard."

He chewed the unlit end of a ratty pipe. "If you ask me, I'd say she's a good girl who happened to get a little carried away." He struck a match and began drawing the flame through the stem of his pipe, releasing small puffs of smoke as he did so. "What you going to do about it, Mr. Temple?"

"Leave that with me," Simon said, tucking a wad of pound notes into the man's open hand and thanking him for his service.

———

Several days later, Simon knocked on Sally's door mid-morning. She stood aside and welcomed him inside, one hand on the doorknob, the other used to brace her back.

"Sit yourself down," she said, waddling toward the kitchen nook. "I'll make us a cuppa and you can tell me why you're here. By the way, I received a letter from Dickie in the late post yesterday. It's there on the table. Since I knew you'd be here this morning, there was no point in notifying you ahead of time."

Simon snatched the envelope as he sank into the old armchair and pulled out the letter. He scanned the first paragraphs, gleaning from the references that his brother had found employment working with a highly-placed officer. Not with the Ottomans; the revolutionaries, perhaps. He also wrote at length about spending time on a farm and learning the local language.

A farm! Simon thought with surprise. *I would like to see that!*

"Thank you for allowing me to read the letter," he said, rising to help her place a tea tray on a small table. "That was unexpected."

"He's always so evasive," Sally said. "Does it make sense to you?"

"Pardon?" Sally's remark cut deeply into Simon's

thoughts, jerking him back to the moment. "A-a little," Simon said, redirecting his attention. "It sounds as though he may be in Turkey, which is where I've suspected he was headed. Bearing in mind the journey that he took through Malta and Greece, that appears to be the primary source of conflict directly in his path. I just can't decide the nature of his employment. Curious, indeed."

"Turkey! Well, if that isn't a surprise," Sally said, appearing perplexed. "I've never heard him mention Turkey. I've never heard him mention anything to do with … anything like that!"

"It is puzzling," Simon said, replacing his cup on the table. "However, I didn't ask to see you this morning to talk about my brother." He slapped his knees, leaning toward her. "I've actually come to talk about you. More particularly, I'd like to help with the support of your child."

"That sounds like a nice way of saying, 'have the child, but keep away'," she said, slowly lowering herself onto a sturdy armchair. "A la-dee-da family like yours won't want a child of mine around your necks." She rested a hand on the side of her bulging belly. "A foot," she said, grinning. "Always kicks when I sit down."

"Shall I pour?" Simon said as he collected his thoughts. Without waiting, he lifted a dainty milk jug and held it toward a cup.

"Just a drop."

He poured the tea and handed her the cup.

"I think you've labelled us unfairly," Simon finally replied. "We wouldn't want to intrude on your life. You've obviously decided to have the child regardless; I commend you for that. It takes strength and determination to raise a child alone."

He sipped his tea, deep in thought. "First, I'd like to provide a stipend, which you may use as you like, but, of course, I hope that you'll use it to ensure that you and the child live comfortably. I'd welcome the opportunity to be involved, and I'm certain my family would be too—when I tell them—but I am also aware that we can appear intimidating. We won't intrude unless invited."

"Exactly how much is this *stipend?*" Sally said warily.

Simon reached into his jacket and retrieved a bankers' draft, placing it on the table. "You will receive this sum every six months, from today onward." He tapped first the amount, then the date.

Sally trapped the draft between tentative fingers and read it. Releasing a soft whistle, she looked at Simon in disbelief.

"Is it not enough?" he said, his brow wrinkled with worry.

"Uh, no, not at all," Sally replied. "I was expecting a few pounds ... not enough to retire on!"

"I want the both of you to be well cared for," Simon said, hoping to assure her.

"Much as I enjoy working here, and the patrons and the money," she said grinning, "this will allow me to live independently. I won't need to ask anyone for help." She whistled again, her eyes bright with joy.

"So, you'll accept my offer?" Simon peered at her,

brows raised with anticipation. When she nodded, he released a long breath of relief. "I'm glad," he said sincerely. "Now, if you'll excuse me, I must be going. I'm expected at Whitehall shortly."

Sally waddled with him to the door. Impulsively, she wrapped her arms around him, the bulge making the embrace difficult. "Thank you," she said bashfully, stepping away. "I'll continue to notify you when I hear from Dickie. And I will definitely notify you when the child is born." She ran a protective hand over the crest of her belly and giggled. "From the size of her, that could be soon."

Simon opened the door and stepped into the hallway.

"With the money you've given us, I'll be able to go home soon. First, I need the words to explain this to my parents." Her attempted grin seemed uncertain.

She's lovely. No wonder Richard came to her. Only a fool would leave her. How desperate he must have felt.

PART TWO

CHAPTER 45

I t was early July before Kemal's summons arrived, delivered to the old uncle by the driver of the latest military vehicle. As the dust from the departing vehicle settled, the old man slipped the envelope into his pocket and held its secret until the evening coffee.

"I see, Richard Temple, that you have accomplished the tasks set upon you when you first came to my home." The old man sat cross-legged on an overstuffed cushion, puffing on his pipe. He nodded gratefully to his wife as she set a tray holding a coffee urn and small cups on a low table and poured for them.

"How so, Uncle?" Richard said, smiling at his hostess when she handed him a cup of thick, strong coffee.

She crossed the veranda and disappeared through the door as evening birds chirped a good-night song to the setting sun.

"You have worked hard in the orchards these many weeks, alongside the others and without complaint. Although I suspect the first week or two caused you aches and pains, and a few blisters. Yet, you said nothing."

Richard cocked his head, listening to the old man. *I don't recall anyone ever praising me before.*

"You have also endeavoured to learn our language," Uncle said, drawing again from his pipe.

"It's helped that only you speak a language I know!" Richard said, amused. "I've had no choice."

The old man nodded as he reached into his pocket. He drew out the note that he had received earlier and pressed it open against his thigh. "This message came today," he said. "It's from Kemal Pasha. It seems our war of independence has intensified. The general has organized a national movement against occupying forces. He also intends to resign his commission with the sultan's army."

Uncle took a puff on his pipe and regarded the note. "He has expressed concern that the country's independence is in jeopardy. Most of the sultan's senior military commanders are backing him. While the sultan has issued a warrant for Kemal Pasha's arrest, the commanders have turned their backs on the ruler and declared the general as their leader."

Uncle paused, allowing Richard time to grasp the significance of Kemal's message. "Kemal wishes you to join him. A vehicle will arrive tomorrow and take you as far as Ancyra. From there, you must find your own way to Erzurum."

"Ang-ka-ra? Her-zur-oom?" Richard said, trying to pronounce the names as Uncle had. "I'm to go east?"

"Yes," the old man said, "I tell you this with a heavy heart. We will be saddened to see you leave." He puffed on his pipe, then set it aside. "And sitting there with your mouth gaping won't get you there any sooner."

"Gosh!" Richard said, realizing the enormity of Kemal's request. He rose, scratching his head as his thoughts raced onward. "I'd better write to my landlord and ask him to send my belongings. He'll want to relet my room."

"Don't bother with your belongings until you know where you're going and how long you'll be there. Take my advice: travel light for now and ask your landlord to store your goods in the meantime."

Richard straightened as the words permeated his thoughts, leaving him with mixed emotions. Small knots twisted in his belly. While he was grateful to return to Kemal, he realized that he was happy on the farm and said as much to his host, emphasising his gratitude for the opportunity.

"Thank you, Uncle," Richard said, suddenly feeling humbled, "for everything." He blinked several times to clear unexpected tears. "If you will excuse me, I think I'll retire. I'll have to be up early if I'm to complete my morning chores before I depart." He bowed to the old general and departed for his room.

CHAPTER 46

Mary sat at her vanity table brushing her hair. Evening songbirds chirped and twittered as if singing their families to sleep. She found their sweet, clear melodies calming.

"Elvie is very protective of little Willy, isn't she?" She set the brush on the table and twisted to smile at Simon. "She told me earlier that she worries about him. She doesn't want him left alone, even with Nanny. She's concerned that he might feel abandoned. It was a good explanation, but I happen to know that she's still feeling an emptiness, too." Her eyes clouded with sadness.

"Come here, Sparrow," Simon said, closing the book he had been reading. He set it on the night table and opened his arms.

Mary rose, as if in a trance, and approached the bed. She sat on the edge and let him draw her into his arms, inhaling as if the masculine smell of him would bring her comfort.

"How are you?" he said. "The anniversary of Yekaterinburg is approaching."

"It is," Mary replied, "but as I've heard many times, the ugliness is lessening, and I find I'm remembering less of that night and more of the pleasant times with my family. The children are a distraction; they make it almost impossible to dwell on the past for very long." She brushed a tear from her cheek. "And that, at least, is a good thing. I miss my parents and siblings so much. I wish I could share the children with them. The three of them are a godsend, and I say a prayer of gratitude every day for the blessing."

"They are indeed," Simon said, hugging her to him. "You and I have experienced a number of horrors that will soften in time ... because of the children." He cupped her face in his hands, staring down at her as if drinking in the sight of her face. She studied him in return. He pulled her to him and stroked her hair, gilded by the lamp light.

As his embrace tightened, Mary aptly conveyed the fierceness of her need for him.

CHAPTER 47

Almost two weeks later, Richard jumped from a donkey cart, thanked the driver for his kindness, and waved him on. Stooping to retrieve his carryall, he turned to face the building where he had been told he would find Mustafa Kemal Pasha: a light-coloured, two-storey building of brick and stone, seconded for use as his official headquarters.

Richard placed a foot on the first step, sighed deeply, then took the remaining steps two at a time. At the landing, he walked through the entrance into the foyer and turned slowly in a circle, taking in the floor plan. Halfway through his turn, he paused and grinned broadly.

Across the lobby, Kemal excused himself from a gathering of men unknown to Richard. Agog, the general strode toward him.

"What have you been eating?" Kemal said, repeating Uncle's question as he struggled to contain his mirth.

Richard's hand snaked through his sun-streaked, ginger hair. "It was time to face the truth," he said, abashed.

"Welcome back," Kemal said, slapping Richard on the back. "Come to my office; we have much to catch up on."

Once in Kemal's office, Richard described his experience in Bolu.

"I'm pleased to hear you report in Turkish," Kemal said, "and to hear of your experience on the farm. You look well, my friend. Now, we must discuss what has happened in your absence and what needs to happen going forward. Later, we will discuss the women."

"Women?" Richard replied.

"Yes, but that must wait," Kemal said with a wave of his hand. "We've more important things to discuss just now."

The general rested his elbows on his desk, collecting his thoughts. "Much has happened since you left Constantinople for the farm," he said with a chuckle. "For both of us, it would seem." His blue eyes fell once again to Richard's hair.

"Ender Edem Pasha may have informed you that many of the sultan's generals, including me, have left Constantinople to further our idea of an independent Turkey. The sultan is displeased, to say the least. Since we left the city many weeks ago, I've been canvassing the generals, who have established military camps throughout Anatolia. They've asked me to lead the revolution, and I've agreed to do so. Shortly, we will be holding a meeting to set out some ground rules for our new republic. I'd like you to help with the drafting of a charter."

"I'd be honoured to help any way I can," Richard said, sitting on the edge of his chair, listening keenly. His skin felt afire with enthusiasm, as if a multitude of invisible creatures skittered under it.

"On another matter," Kemal continued, "and prior

to your departure for the farm, you'll recall that we had begun communications with the Russian Bolshevik government. We asked them to provide us with gold and armaments, and they've promised to oblige. Without that support, we would not have been able to push back against the Greeks and the Armenians. We aren't free of that pressure yet, so we must continue to rely on the Russians. And that reliance comes at a cost. As a result, I have two more tasks for you."

Richard straightened, easing back into his chair. His hands dangled between his knees, strong and steady. He marvelled that the alcohol-driven tremors were completely gone. He squared his shoulders and listened with confidence.

"The Russians are keen to protect their investment and want to ensure that their gold and armaments will be well spent." Kemal cleared his throat, rose from his chair, and asked the typist to bring coffee. "They have assigned a Colonel Ivan Vasiliev to oversee our management. Have you ever heard of this man?"

"Not that I recall," Richard said, shaking his head slowly.

"That is neither here nor there," Kemal said, dismissing the thought with a flip of his hand. "So far, Russia has provided a small advance that will help us rebuke the initial advances of our foes, but we need more. We have been promised delivery of a greater supply of gold and armaments in a few months. As I said, at a cost." He rose, sauntering toward a window that looked onto the street.

"The problem is this man, Vasiliev. He hovers constantly," Kemal complained as he reached for his cigarette case, removed a cigarette, and stabbed it on the case's cover, "and I don't have time to entertain him. I need you to relieve me of his constant scrutiny."

He snatched up a stylish lighter and flicked the wheel, waving the flame beneath the rolled tobacco impatiently. Setting the lighter down, he pounded his desk with annoyance. "It's one thing for him to monitor Russia's investment, but he insists on attending our meetings and voicing his opinions."

"Voicing *his* opinions!" Richard said, aghast. "Not Russia's opinions?"

"*His*," Kemal replied, waving for the typist to set the coffee on his desk and leave. "It's less than half of what we were initially promised, and he acts as if it's twice the amount. You'd think it was his investment!" He drew on his cigarette, then dashed it in the ashtray, releasing a long, smoky breath at the same time.

"As you have proven several times already, you are resourceful. I want you to keep Vasiliev busy so I can focus on the next conflict." He poured two cups of coffee and handed one to Richard. "Will you do that?"

"Yes, sir!" Richard replied heartily. "I believe there are plenty of ruins in the area, and the history is rich." In response to Kemal's raised brow, he elaborated. "I read about Erzurum on the way here."

"Of course, you did!" Kemal said enthusiastically. "As you know, I believe the science of history is critical to the future development of civilizations. By all means, show him the ruins." He exhaled, aggressively releasing broken smoke rings as he contemplated Richard's assignment. "If he gives you any trouble, report back to me immediately." Kemal sipped his coffee, deep in thought. "How's your Russian?"

"Russian?" Richard said, taken aback. "Other than a brief time in St. Petersburg when I was a young child, I've never spoken Russian. I can assure you that whatever tidbits a small child might have learned have been long forgotten."

"I suggest you start again, then," Kemal said. "Vasiliev speaks French, so you won't have difficulty communicating. It would, however, be helpful if you at least *understood* Russian, especially if he or one of his men lets something slip. Don't let them know that you speak Turkish, either. Charm him, but don't let him get too comfortable."

"Yes, sir," Richard replied, wondering where he was going to learn Russian.

"On your way out, speak to the clerk. I asked him earlier to find a scholar to teach you Russian," Kemal said as he watched Richard reach for the doorknob. "I doubt there is a scarcity of Russian scholars in Erzurum these days."

CHAPTER 48

The following morning, Richard entered a nondescript doorway between two shops and climbed a flight of stairs to the second floor. He rapped lightly on the last door at the end of the hall.

An older man, average height with a tidy moustache resting above his lip, opened the door, calling Richard by name. The man eyed him without compunction, nodded, and stepped aside. "I am Cherman Dimitri Pavlovich," the man said, thrusting his thumbs into his vest pockets as he rocked on his heels, a motion that resulted in the protrusion of his slightly-rounded belly. "You wish to learn Russian?"

"Yes, I—"

"There are many aspects to Russian language," Pavlovich said grumpily. "It is not something to learn quickly, and I expect you will fail."

"I just need to understand general conversation," Richard said quickly, before the man dismissed him altogether.

Pavlovich snorted, pushing his lower lip forward as he considered the possibility. "As I said, I doubt you have devotion to learn." He swung his arm toward a table covered in papers and writing instruments. Two chairs sat neatly tucked under it. "Let us begin so you can finish. You may call me Professor."

Richard did not appreciate Pavlovich's attitude or dismissal of his abilities before an opportunity to at least try. He promised himself that he would use his best efforts to prove the man wrong.

By the end of the morning, he was rewarded for his effort: the professor expressed appreciation for Richard's sincerity, and the gruffness softened.

Richard worked diligently to understand the structure of the language and the pronunciation. When his recitations could no longer suppress the rumbling of his stomach, the professor suggested that they end the studies for the day.

"Tomorrow," Pavolvich said, "you spend day with me. I will feed you. Better to immerse the entire day on a contented stomach. For now, you practise."

———

Richard checked in with Kemal every morning on his way to meet the professor. At the end of the last day of the second week, he collected his notes as usual and bid the professor good day.

As he crossed the street heading toward his lodgings, a cadet pushed away from a brick wall and approached him. "Excuse me, sir," he said, handing a note to Richard. "From the general."

Richard thanked the young man and tore open

the small envelope, not noticing the cadet's discrete disappearance.

My office, fifteen hundred hours. Meeting with Vasiliev.

Richard glanced at his watch. *Great! I have thirty minutes to freshen up and reach the Ministry.* He stuffed the note in his pocket and strode purposefully along the street, dodging horse-drawn carts laden with products for sale in the local market.

———

The cadet who had delivered Kemal's note met Richard in the foyer, led him to a meeting room near the rear of the building on the second floor, and announced his arrival.

Richard spied Kemal at the centre of a cluster of men. They spoke amicably on the far side of the room. In response to Kemal's beckoning hand, Richard approached, discretely scanning the faces. He was comfortably familiar with the members of the council of generals; that familiarity was emphasized by expressions of surprise as their owners spied Richard's orange hair. Richard acknowledged them with a slight nod, feeling a prickly blush bloom on his cheeks.

As he neared, Richard realized that Kemal stood amongst three strangers. *The pompous-looking one must be Vasiliev.*

Kemal welcomed Richard into the group, then introduced him, first to the older of the three. *Mid-to-late fifties, balding on top with sparse salt and pepper hair feathered from ear to ear. If I were to add a full head of brown hair and fewer wrinkles …* Richard shuddered. *He does seem familiar!* His gaze shot to Kemal, whose raised brow acknowledged Richard's surprise.

The other two were not familiar to Richard. Rada Makarov, whose hair had not yet begun to silver, appeared to be in his mid-forties, while the youngest, Vilen Nitikin, appeared similar in age to Richard. Richard's eyes connected with Nitikin's as they shook hands. Recognizing keenness in the young man's eyes, Richard made a mental note to learn more about him.

Vasiliev's toady eyes openly scrutinized Richard from head to toe, much as the professor had done two weeks before.

"Mr. Temple," he finally said, his French pronunciation tainted heavily by his Russian accent. "You are very familiar to me. I think we have met before, yes?"

The collective gasp from the Turks may have been negligible to the Russians, but Richard found it deafening.

"H-how so, Colonel Vasiliev?" Richard replied, wondering why an old man might recall a young child.

"Come, come, Mr. Temple," Vasiliev said, his words oily and threatening. "You may change your name, Simon Temple. Even your hair colour. But I know—"

"What's this?" Kemal said, appearing shocked by the revelation.

"Ah!" Richard said, bristling as he locked narrowed eyes with Vasiliev and crossed his arms defensively over his chest. "I take it you've had occasion to meet my older brother, Simon." Richard peered down his nose with hubris. "He lived in Russia for three years. Returned to England last summer."

"Your brother!" Vasiliev said, astounded, his red veined cheeks deepening in colour. "But you look exactly like him! Except for the hair." He blinked several times as a ray of afternoon sun cut through a window, blinding him momentarily.

"Yes," Richard said, sniggering as he ran his fingers through his mop. "My hair—the bane of my existence! And to think I've come all the way to Turkey to step out of my brother's shadow, only to be introduced to someone who has met him!" He grinned at Kemal, his eyes asking for support.

To his relief, Kemal slapped him on the shoulder and laughed with him. "I've just realized, Richard," Kemal said, "that although we have worked closely for some time, we have not talked much about our families. That will have to change!"

"I expect, General," Vasiliev said, "that you will be very interested to learn of Simon Temple's devious behaviour while in Russia, especially during the execution of the royal family!"

This is too personal, Richard thought, relaxing his arms to link his hands behind his back. *I need to change the subject before his comments get out of hand.*

"Sir, was there something you had in mind when you sent for me?" Richard said, turning to Kemal. He felt a heat wave rise from his chest. Fearing he would be unable to breathe in the next moment, he casually inserted a finger into his collar, inhaling deeply.

"Of course!" Kemal replied, picking up on Richard's cue. "I was hoping that you'd have time to show Colonel Vasiliev a bit of Erzurum."

"It would be my pleasure," Richard said with a respectful nod. Richard turned his attention to Vasiliev. "We can start tomorrow if you like. I propose an early start: say, ten o'clock?"

Vasiliev's hooded eyes blinked twice, his sinister brows meeting midway in a scowl. Taken aback by the unexpected turn, he glanced at Makarov and Nitikin. "Of course," Vasiliev said, stiffening as if he realized the trap. "Comrade Makarov will accompany me. Comrade Nitikin will remain behind." He glanced at the aide. "He has work that must be done and has not the time for frivolities."

"Perhaps another time," Richard said, directing his remark to the younger man.

"I look forward to the possibility!" Nitikin replied, his keenness quickly dimming when he caught sight of Vasiliev's black glower.

"If that is all, General," Richard said, "I'll be on my way. I'll need to create a schedule for tomorrow." He bowed smartly toward the gathering and turned on his heel.

"I'll walk you out," Kemal said, stepping in with Richard's stride and closing the door when they entered the hallway. "Keep him busy for a few days, Richard. We have strategies to process and budgets to prepare. I'd appreciate a full report before I'm expected to meet with him again. How are the Russian lessons coming along, by the way?"

Richard grinned. "Alright, I think. The professor didn't think much of me in the beginning, but I think I've proved that I'm worthy."

"Good man," Kemal said, placing a hand on his shoulder. "Keep up with the lessons as long as you can. And … keep your ears open."

"Yes, sir!" Richard gave a mock salute and skipped down the stone stairs to the lobby.

CHAPTER 49

Richard wondered what he was going to do to keep Vasiliev and his comrades occupied now that Kemal's temporary headquarters had been relocated to Ancyra. Filling the first few days in Erzurum had been easy, but, as Richard quickly discovered, Vasiliev was not the least bit interested in the ancient seat of civilization.

Fortunately, there's a lot more to see in Ancyra than in Erzurum. Although, I'll have to be quick about setting an agenda that will keep them occupied until the general departs on another mission.

As an afterthought, he reminded himself to find another Russian scholar. Understanding Russian had already given him a few insights about the Colonel, but the man was guarded in Richard's presence. He had to win the man's confidence somehow.

"A letter for you, sir," Kemal's clerk said, hailing him as he turned toward the corridor that led to the street.

Richard thanked the clerk and flipped the letter to and fro as he continued toward the lobby. Outside, he paused on the landing and glanced down the street. *Ancyra,* he thought with a sigh. *I have a feeling we're going to be here for a while.*

A moment later, he ran his finger along the loose end of the envelope's fold and opened the sheet of paper. He grinned as he realized the sender, then smiled broadly as he read his former landlord's message:

My friend, Richard Temple,

I and my family were most saddened to receive your letter reporting your decision to not return to Constantinople. We leave our door open to you should you return to our welcoming arms again in the future.

In the meantime, do not worry yourself about suitable accommodation while you reside in beautiful Ancyra. I have written a message to my cousin, who lives not far from General Kemal's headquarters. He has a most suitable place for you and awaits your arrival. Your belongings have been forwarded to him for safekeeping.

Until we meet again …

Muttering about the timeliness of the landlord's letter, Richard reread the cousin's address, which was indeed nearby, and strode in that direction, pulling his straw fedora lower to shade his eyes against the determined sun. He glanced toward the castle overlooking the city and squinted against the solid blue of the cloudless sky.

I'll need to keep shade or cool spaces in mind while touring during the peak of the day.

As he neared the last corner, Richard spied a café and marked its proximity to what might be his new lodgings. He stopped and contemplated whether it was too early in the day to eat and realized that it could not be; he had yet to eat that day due to his urgent need to speak with Kemal.

Waiting for his meal to arrive, he contemplated a recent conversation with Kemal. He had pushed his family away and shirked any hope of supporting them or his country for one simple reason: he was the second son of an earl, born into wealth, and envious of everything his brother, Simon, had.

What Richard had realized since then was that the only difference between Simon and him was that Simon would inherit the titles and all the responsibilities attached. Richard knew in his heart that those titles meant nothing to him, especially now.

"I may only be a minor player in the birth of a new era in a foreign country," he had said to Kemal, "but my time at the farm solidified my feelings about Turkey. I've found a land in which I can invest my loyalty and integrity. If you'll have me, I offer my support in any way you need it."

"Your meal, Mister," the proprietor said, standing at the table, arms laden with aromatic dishes.

"Wha—? Oh!" Richard's attention returned to the moment, and he hastily gathered the pages he had been examining while he waited.

"You very deep in thinking," the man said, a bushy black brow raised questioningly.

"Yes," Richard agreed with a chuckle. "I was just thinking that it's time for me to find a home. I have been staying at an inn, but I think I need to find a more permanent abode."

"This is good news, Mister," the man said. "My brother, he has lodgings just around the corner. You eat now, then I take you to meet him."

"Of course, you do," Richard replied, rolling his eyes in disbelief. "My former lodgings were in Constantinople. The owner has referred me to accommodation around the corner. Your brother, no doubt!"

A flurry of conversation followed, during which the proprietor confirmed that he was indeed related to the former landlord. He bowed discretely to Richard and disappeared, only to reappear a short time later with his brother in tow. And, yes, Richard's belongings had arrived, and a room had been made ready for him.

Since Richard's arrival in Turkey, his expenses, even on the road and in Ancyra, had been small. Initially, he had invested in clothes appropriate for the climate, work, and leisure, but little since. His primary expenses had been food and lodging. As a result, he had saved a sum sufficient to afford renting a permanent lodging, but he had not been motivated to do so prior to his conversation with Kemal.

His new flat was small and clean, and, fortunately for him, the rent included the services of Mrs. Sydin, a middle-aged woman who took kindly to him.

Awaking one late-August morning, Richard realized with gratitude that not only had he survived his alcohol withdrawal, but his mind was clear and he was stronger in both body and soul. He had a purpose, something constructive to offer to powerful men inclined to listen to his thoughts. Men who respected him for his insights. *Father would be proud of me*, he thought, then dashed the idea from his mind, realizing that his father would cringe to know that his son was a traitor to Britain.

While his current living arrangements were far from the aristocratic opulence in which he had been raised, he had everything he needed and, to his surprise, he was content. The foreignness of the country had dissipated, fading into the face of familiarity and comfort.

CHAPTER 50

Simon spied a small envelope atop the latest mail delivery waiting in his in-tray. Recognizing Sally Winton's handwriting, he snatched it and tore it open. In her neat hand, she reported that she had received another letter from Richard. If he had time to pop by for tea tomorrow morning, she would have warm biscuits waiting.

He tucked the message in his jacket pocket, making a note not to arrive late.

The aroma of fresh baking and Sally's humming lured Simon up the stairs to her flat. He braced his damp umbrella against the door jamb and rapped on the door.

"Come in!" she said in her sing-song voice.

Simon opened the door to her warm welcome. A tray of fresh tea, baking, and the letter perched on the small table near her armchairs.

"Good morning, Simon," she said from the bathroom, "have a seat and help yourself. I'll be there in a moment."

Simon poured himself a cup of tea and buttered a biscuit, delaying the reading of Richard's letter. He could have fresh baking at Grosvenor House any time he liked, but the pub's baking had a different taste. It wasn't pretentious, just simple and fulfilling.

He took a bite of the biscuit, melted butter and strawberry preserves coating his tongue in delight, and washed it down with a strong breakfast tea. Then, he reached for the envelope as Sally waddled into the room.

"Sorry to take so long," she said. "I'm not moving so quick these days." She rubbed her expanding belly. "I wanted to finish packing a trunk."

"Not long now, I'm guessing," Simon said.

"No," she replied. "I went home a few weeks back, explained everything to my parents and gave my notice here. I leave at week's end for the farm, so I'm packing up all the things that are mine."

She massaged the small of her back. "I've accumulated more while I've been here than I brought with me. Oh! I've jotted my forwarding address on the piece of paper, so you'll know where to find me."

Simon reached for the page, scanned it, and put it in his pocket.

"Have you read the letter?"

"Not yet," Simon said, shaking his head. "I couldn't resist the baking. I'll read it now."

The letter spoke mostly of Richard's mundane, day-to-day tasks to facilitate moving headquarters from Erzurum to Ancyra. The revelation of the new location and the comment in the last paragraph caught Simon's attention, though, and sent a shiver down his spine:

My latest assignment is to manage an interloper, a Russian named Colonel Ivan Vasiliev. He's here

*to monitor a Russian investment. Apparently, he's
a bit of a nuisance, and my employer wants me to
distract him. Quite frankly, he's a smarmy sort of
fellow. Not someone with whom I enjoy socializing,
but orders are orders.*

*Colonel Vasiliev first accused me of being someone
he'd met in Russia. He thought I was wearing a
disguise. That almost lost me my job!*

*I know I've been elusive, but it has simply been that
I haven't had a permanent address. I'm hoping that
will change soon. When it does, I'll let you know.*

Simon folded the letter, slid it into the envelope, and replaced it on the table, marvelling not only at the potential nature of Richard's employment but the fact that he seemed to sincerely embrace the work. Work that had taken him to the epicentre of the Turkish conflict: the headquarters of General Mustafa Kemal and his revolution. And that the work involved Richard having to entertain Vasiliev.

Why? Simon wondered. *And why pit himself against the British?*

Sally nibbled on a biscuit, watching Simon read the letter.

"Any clues?" she said.

Simon cast his eyes toward her, blinking several times as he processed the latest missive. Slowly, he nodded.

"Indeed," he said, contemplating Richard's situation. "I regret that there's nothing hopeful for me to say that would impact on your present circumstance, but on a larger scale, it is significant information to be of value to Britain."

"Oh my," she replied, grasping her belly.

"May I borrow the letter for a few days?" he said with uncertainty. "I'll see that it's returned to you as quickly as possible."

"O-of course."

CHAPTER 51

On one particular Saturday morning as the green leaves of summer began to turn yellow, Simon and Mary sauntered through the conservatory and into the garden. The rattan furniture that had been moved outdoors in late spring remained under the shade of a plane tree, beckoning to them.

Already ensconced in a tray of mid-morning coffee, Simon's parents smiled welcomingly as the young couple approached.

"Please bring us some egg, tomato, and toast," Mary said to the maid pouring coffee.

"And an orange for me," Simon said.

Tompkins appeared a moment later with a silver tray on which rested a small white envelope addressed to Simon in neat handwriting.

Simon examined the envelope, instantly recognizing the return address and the penmanship.

"Who sent it?" Mary said.

Simon grinned but said nothing to the three pair of eyes peering at him with curiosity. He slit the flap, tugged out a small note and read.

"Ah!" he said. "It appears that I have some news to

share. I've been waiting for an opportune time, and now it seems I can delay no longer."

Two maids arrived with their breakfast and discretely disappeared. Simon selected a piece of buttered toast and took a bite, contemplating where to begin. "You'll recall," he said, dusting crumbs from his fingers, "that I visited Richard's young woman a few months back, and that she advised that she'd had no contact with him—"

"And has she now?" Ann asked, leaning toward him.

"As a matter of fact," Simon replied, "I've had occasion to visit her on a few occasions over the past months. I had asked that if she ever heard from Richard, she let me know. Until recently, the communiques have been few and rather vague. 'I've been travelling. I've arrived. I found employment.' That sort of thing, but nothing that could offer anything more than suspicions."

He stirred his coffee and took a sip. "The latest letter arrived several weeks ago. I can tell you that he appears to be safe, but the remainder of the letter has been shared with MI6 and remains confidential. Father had occasion to read that last letter."

"Confidential?" Ann said. "What can he be up to?"

"For now," Simon said glancing at the note, "I suggest we skip that part and get to the next: the reason for this letter. The young woman's name, by the way, is Miss Sally Winton." He waved Sally's note to catch their attention. "What I have neglected to report—until now—is that Miss Winton was pregnant ... with Richard's child."

"What!" the others exclaimed together.

"A child!" Charles said, a frown clouding his countenance. "You didn't tell me that!"

"Continue, please," Ann said, and Mary nodded encouragingly.

Simon relayed Sally's story, and how he had established a trust of sorts to support her and the child.

"I'm certain that, if Richard knew, he would have acted responsibly," Simon said. "For all our differences, I believe he would not have left Miss Winton in the lurch. She is a fine young woman who happened to be caught out. I checked out her history and found nothing untoward. The sum that I offered her has allowed her to leave her job and moved back home. This"—he waved the page again—"this is a note from her to say that she has safely delivered Richard's daughter. Her name is Charlotte Grace, and according to Miss Winton, she has a lovely head of ginger hair just like Richard's."

"How marvellous!" Mary said with sincerity and delight.

"You've been supporting her?" Charles barked impatiently. "Next, she'll claim a right to his inheritance."

"No," Simon said, assuring his parents, "if you'd met her, you would quickly learn that such things don't interest her. She is a down-to-earth person who just wants what's best for her child. I offered the money. She didn't ask."

"Can we meet them?" Ann said. She glanced at her husband's scowl. "Charles, please. The child is Richard's.

We can't turn our back on family. We must find a way."

"I will ask Miss Winton whether she's open to meeting with us," Simon said.

CHAPTER 52

Two days after his revealing conversation with Kemal, Richard and his driver met Vasiliev and Makarov at their hotel. Already, the morning sun suggested the temperature of the day would be high.

As he escorted the two Russians to the car, Richard was pleased to see that the driver had opened the windows, ensuring a breeze as they drove.

Richard opened a rear door for Vasiliev while he explained the topic of the tour for that day would be the ancient city of Ancyra. Vasiliev stifled a yawn as Richard described Ancyra's history, a city founded on centuries of intriguing, powerful, and occasionally faulty cultures.

"We'll start at the top," he said. "Ancyra Castle sits atop a rocky hill and has many well-preserved Roman ruins, as well as ancient ruins of the Ottoman Empire. I'm sure you'll find everything fascinating!"

Richard held the door of one of the few vehicles available for official government events. When both men appeared comfortably seated in the rear, he climbed into the seat next to the driver and directed him through the city toward the castle, noting points of interest along the way.

"Hmph," Vasiliev said, muttering to Makarov in

Russian, "I would prefer to see those structures that are still in use and covered in gold, like those in Constantinople. Like the Harem, perhaps." He chuckled lasciviously.

"There are buildings covered in gold in Constantinople?" Makarov replied in awe.

"Not exactly *covered*," Vasiliev said greedily, "but certainly finished with enough gold that could be used to support the takeover of Russia. To say nothing of the free labour we can assemble from here, once Turkey defaults on its loans to Russia. And don't forget the Russian gold we've seized already, and the armaments! General Kemal thinks the other half will arrive shortly. Little does he know that he won't get it. Every shipment will be half of what he expects, and so long as the revolutionaries keep sending shipments, we'll keep amassing our fifty-percent share until we have enough to fund a revolution of our own. General Kemal, on the other hand, will become frustrated with the Bolsheviks and their lies."

He steepled his fingers in thought as he watched the passing landscape. "Yes, my friend, it won't be long before we have the means and the gold to advance on the revolutionaries who destroy Mother Russia, and to seize Turkey for defaulting on repayment of the entire advancement of gold and armaments."

"Careful, comrade," Makarov said, "someone could overhear, and then what? Hmm? What will the revolutionaries do if they learn our real purpose here?" He chortled and continued. "I don't know about you, Ivan, but I find meandering through ancient ruins boring."

He raised a hand to stifle a yawn.

"Well," Vasiliev replied, "your concerns may be valid, Rada. However, we must remember two things. First, if Russia is to seize control of this new country—Turkey—because it cannot repay its debt when demanded, it will be helpful to know the inventory and assets that will be available to me when I am leader."

"You are correct, my friend," Makarov replied solemnly.

"And second," Vasiliev said, "these people know nothing of our plans: and they won't. They don't speak Russian." He shrugged glibly. "They have no reason to suspect us. They're more worried about receiving only half of the promised gold and armaments needed to push back the Greeks and Armenians."

Richard listened carefully to the exchange, making mental notes for Kemal. *Hmm, all the more reason to show them the 'boring ruins'!*

"Gentlemen," he said as they exited the vehicle at the top of the hill. "Let's have a look around, shall we?" His mind raced quickly through the list of sites he planned to tour afterward, making slight adjustments to avoid any locations that might suggest value. In response to their audible groans, he turned his back to hide a small grin of satisfaction.

Several hours later, the vehicle rolled to a stop outside the hotel at which the Russians lodged. Richard peeked over his shoulder at the two Russians napping in the back seat like cozy kittens. Their heads comfortably rested against one another, a silver thread of saliva dripping off Vasiliev's hairy chin. Like bookends, they both snorted awake when they realized the vehicle had stopped.

"We're back at your hotel," Richard said, stating the obvious to awaken them. "Would you like me to recommend some restaurants for your evening meal?"

"No need," Vasiliev said curtly, "we only eat Russian food. We have been dining every evening at the same fine Russian restaurant not far from here. Perhaps you will join me one evening and enjoy the taste of *superior cuisine.*" His eyes met Richard's as he scrambled out of the auto.

"Thank you. I'll look forward to it," Richard replied, thinking of the many pleasant Turkish meals he had enjoyed since his arrival. *So rigid. No sense of adventure!*

"Perhaps now is the time to discuss tomorrow's agenda, then," Richard said. "I propose a drive to one of the villages. We'll visit some weavers. I'm certain you will appreciate their rug creations and the famous Ancyra wool." Hope that his enthusiasm might be infectious was in vain. "Then we'll return to the city and wander through the market in the old town. Perhaps you'd like to purchase copper items, jewellery, embroidery, or antiques for your wives. You can also purchase food items, like dried fruits, spices, and nuts." He grinned invitingly. "The driver and I will pick you up tomorrow morning at ten o'clock."

CHAPTER 53

S imon rolled onto his side, facing toward Mary. A crack of predawn light peeked through the curtain when a mild breeze shifted it. Below their window, a song thrush welcomed the birth of a new day.

Mary moaned. "No. No!" She murmured the words repeatedly as she began to thrash against the lightweight bed cover. "Mama!"

Simon sat upright, rapidly clearing cobwebbed sleep from his brain. Hesitantly, he placed a hand on his wife's shoulder. "Mary," he said in a soft whisper, giving her shoulder a gentle shake. "Mary, you're dreaming."

Beside him, Mary panted with fear, her eyes pressed tightly closed. "Papa!" Her scream was piercing and plaintive. Beads of perspiration pearled on her forehead as the thrashing increased.

"Mary, darling, wake up. You're dreaming." Simon's belly twisted, knowing the agony of her dream.

"My leg." A hand fell to the scar left by the bullet that had punctured her thigh. "Why?" She screamed again, her sobs gurgling in her throat.

Simon slid his arms under his wife and drew her close, rocking gently, hoping his solace might sooth her.

"Sparrow, wake up, darling. It's just a dream; they can't hurt you now. Your family is at peace. Shhh." His words became a litany as he tried to pierce the nightmare that held her. "Shhh."

"No-o-o!" A moment passed, followed by a deep gasp and a sorrowful sob. Mary slowly raised her head and peered through the dim light. "Another nightmare?" she said, surrendering to its injury.

"Yes," Simon said, holding her close, caressing her silky hair. "Another nightmare."

"Will you hold me for a while longer?"

He kissed her crown. "Forever, if you like."

CHAPTER 54

"A letter for you, sir," the footman said, extending it on a silver tray.

Simon thanked the man and broke the seal. Another note from Sally. He grinned to himself as he slid the letter back into the envelope and put it in his pocket. "From you, Miss Winton, I would expect nothing less," he said, muttering to himself as he went in search of his wife and parents.

"I have Miss Winton's response," he said where they were assembled in Charles' study. "Before I read it to you, I must tell you that knowing her as briefly as I do, I find the response appropriate."

"Get on with it, man," Charles said impatiently. He leaned on a cream and white marbled mantelpiece suspended over a cold fireplace, fidgeting with a small, carved, wooden box. He shook it. It was half-full of Richard's unused cigarettes. "Hmph, likely stale."

"Miss Winton has invited us to visit her parent's farm near Primrose at the end of next week, to meet baby Charlotte and the Winton family," Simon said, raising an eyebrow at the revelation. "The child will be baptised at a nearby Anglican church at the end of October—which I presume will be St. Paul's, as it can't be much more than a fifteen-minute drive. More details will follow."

Before they could speak, Simon held the note up and read with an elevated voice:

While Dickie's family is welcome to attend the baptism, I would like to keep a distance between you and my daughter. I'd like to arrange a meeting twice a year (perhaps around the time each payment is made), during which you may spend time with her as wealthy relatives. I don't want her thinking she is someone special. We will live on the farm, and she will attend school in our community. If she wants more when she's old enough to decide, we can have a discussion then. I hope you find my conditions agreeable.

"I wonder whether Richard knew where her family lived. For that matter, I wonder whether she understands where we live," Simon said, snorting with amusement. "She may wish to maintain a distance, but it could be difficult considering the short distance from one home to the other. It's likely that our farms have overlapping business."

"Do you think she'll give the child Richard's name?" Charles said grumpily.

"I don't know, Father," Simon replied. "Mary and I will attend the baptism. We'll find out then." He glanced at Mary for assurance. "I encourage you and Mother to come with us."

"I look forward to it!" Mary beamed at the idea.

"Whether you attend or not, Charles Nightingale-Temple," Ann said defiantly, "I will. And I intend to respect Miss Winton's conditions as best I can."

"Harrumph," Charles grunted. "Very well …"

CHAPTER 55

Richard originally intended to wait another day or two before delivering a report to Kemal. However, after overhearing the conversation between Vasiliev and Makarov about the shortage of gold and armaments, he changed his mind and asked the driver to drop him at headquarters.

"Just as I thought," Kemal said when Richard ended his summary. "I knew they were up to something. Clearly, they're not to be trusted! I will reach out to my contacts in Moscow tomorrow morning!"

He held up the whiskey decanter. When Richard declined, he filled his glass half full and took a large swig. "Now I understand why I've been receiving enquiries from Moscow: they must have an inkling that something is amiss, too."

He dashed half a cigarette in the overflowing ashtray on his desk and started another. "And these other things: wanting Turkey's riches, using its people as cheap labour, taking control of the country!"

Kemal pushed away from the desk, bolting to his feet as he jammed a fist into an open hand. "By God, they'll not take our county. We have fought long and hard to get where we are. They will not bring us down. We will simply have to find a way to help them depart before they cause more harm. I will speak with the generals tomorrow, while you keep our *friends* occupied. We need this resolved quickly."

"Consider it done," Richard said, contemplating his intentions when he arrived in Turkey to those of Vasiliev and Makarov. "When I arrived in Constantinople, I was running away from another life and had no idea where I was really going. I naively thought I had British secrets to sell and felt wicked for it. I'm grateful that you overlooked my foolishness and allow me to serve you regardless. Hopefully, you don't see a comparison between my situation and their deeds." He shook his head in disbelief.

Kemal sipped his whiskey and listened.

"I know I haven't been here long," Richard said, rising to face the general, "but I've learned far more from you than I've contributed. I've learned what it is to have responsibility and to work productively with others. And I experience daily the sincerity, honesty, and generosity of Turkey's people."

He hung his head bashfully. "I could have had the same experiences in Britain, but, as I've told you, I pushed away from all of it."

"It is always good to know oneself, one's aspirations, and one's limitations." Kemal studied Richard momentarily, his agitation lessening. "I do not compare you: never have." His blue eyes fastened on Richard. "You've done well with the Russians, but it's time for you to start the work I brought you here to do … with the congress."

"I look forward to it, sir."

"Come for dinner tomorrow evening," Kemal said, chuckling as he stabbed the cigarette in the burgeoning, stone-carved ashtray. "I think it's time we discussed family relations, too."

———

"We set out on another mission tomorrow," Kemal said shortly after welcoming Richard into his hotel sitting room. "Sit. Whiskey?"

"No, thank you," Richard said, coughing into his handkerchief as he lowered himself into a dusky-coloured brocade armchair.

"You're not looking too well," Kemal said, eyeing Richard with concern.

"I'm not feeling well," Richard said. "My throat and my ears are scratchy. I expect I've caught a seasonal malady somewhere along the way. It will pass, I'm sure." He coughed again and swiped the hanky across his mouth. "Honestly, I felt fine this morning!"

"Fortunately, I won't need you to attend me for a while," Kemal said, reclining in a nearby chair with a glass of whiskey and a cigarette to hand. "When you're feeling up to it, continue your work on the charter. I'd also like you to scout some office space for us. Our headquarters will be in Ancyra for a while: permanently, if I have my say. I firmly believe that, if a government is going to be accessible to its people, it must be centrally located." He puffed on his cigarette and flicked ashes into the carved dish. "Ancyra is as good a location as any."

"Were you able to sort out matters with Moscow?" Richard asked.

"Yes," Kemal replied. "It was as I expected: the behaviour of Vasiliev and Makarov has been suspected for some time. Apparently, Comrade Nitikin has been looking for concrete evidence, but so far hasn't found anything upon which they can rely. Vasiliev is a clever fellow; he knows how to cover his tracks."

Kemal drew on his latest cigarette and exhaled cautiously, forming a perfect circle. He grinned with satisfaction and continued. "In the meantime, we have been promised a sizeable shipment of gold and armaments in the spring. I have assigned two generals from the council to work directly with Moscow to ensure the shipments are received intact."

Richard stifled an explosive sneeze. "Pardon me, sir!"

"Our meal tonight is a humble one," Kemal said. "I've asked for it to be brought in. Let's get through the remainder of our business and the meal, then you should get home to bed."

"Thank you, sir," Richard said, bracing for another sneeze.

"Once you find appropriate space, start setting everything up. I trust you to make the right decisions."

"Thank you, sir, for your confidence." Richard rose

and poured himself a glass of water from the jug next to the whiskey decanter.

A light rap on the hall door announced the arrival of their meal. As they worked their way through the aromatic courses, Kemal asked after Richard's family, then described his own.

"My early life was rather unremarkable," Kemal said. "My parents named me 'Mustafa' after the Prophet Muhammad—a common name at the time—and so I was until I entered Salonica Military School. For some reason, my mathematics teacher decided that I should be named 'Kemal'—which means 'perfection,' by the way." He scoffed. "An unlikely name, if ever there was one. Perhaps he saw something in me that I didn't. From then on, I was known as 'Mustafa Kemal,' until I started to advance through the ranks; when I became a senior officer, my rank became pasha. Now, I am 'Mustafa Kemal Pasha.'

"In the English system, the rank of *pasha* would begin at *major general*, but no matter the advancement or accomplishment after that, the title of *pasha* doesn't change."

"That explains a lot!" Richard said in awe. "Any titles I may have or receive are referred to as hand-me-downs. I didn't *earn* them; they're titles that belong to the family. My father has most of them now, but my brother, Simon, has already inherited some. For example, as the first-born son of an earl, he is a viscount. He also has a naval rank, lieutenant, if I recall correctly." He snatched his handkerchief from his pocket and coughed vigorously.

"Simon will inherit all titles when my father passes, except the ones specifically assigned to the second son. Fortunately for me, titles aren't a burden for me in Turkey, unless someone like Vasiliev"—he winced—"knows of my family and refers to me as '*Lord Richard*'." Richard hastily retrieved his handkerchief and caught another explosive sneeze.

"Perhaps, my friend," Kemal said, casting his eyes over the empty plates, "it is time for you to find your bed."

Richard agreed as he mopped away another sneeze.

CHAPTER 56

As Richard's malady lessened and he realized his food cache had depleted, he determined that he must visit the local market.

When he returned to his apartment, Mrs. Sydin had just finished her work for the day. She stopped him before he was able to enter his flat and invited him for dinner at the end of the following week, explaining that her daughter, Umut, would be home, and they all would sup together.

"I'd be delighted," Richard said, still sounding nasally. "As you can hear, I haven't been well. I will endeavour to be recovered by then." He bowed toward the woman, who departed in giggles, shaking her head at his gallantry.

"My daughter, Umut, is a tailor's apprentice," Mrs. Sydin said proudly when she introduced their guest.

"That explains why you are so fashionably dressed," Richard said during the meal. "If I didn't know I was in Ancyra, I'd think I was in London or Paris!"

"You prefer European dress over Turkish silk pyjamas?" Umut said in Turkish, her voice sugary with teasing.

Although her eyes twinkled, her deep red lips formed a pout.

"Not at all," he replied, shifting on his cushion to better observe her. "I find the bright colours and the flow of the fabric … attractive, sensuous."

Mrs. Sydin leaned away from the table, as if to examine the two young people. Her dark eyes narrowed as she contemplated their flirting. "Umut," she said, a slight gruffness to her voice. "Let us clear this table and brew some coffee."

As the women cleared the table, Richard admired their graceful efficiency and similar attributes. Long straight noses—almost too sharp—pouty red lips, flawless bronzed skin, and long auburn hair. A twang of melancholy caught in his throat. *Auburn, like father's.*

"Or would you prefer apple tea, Richard?" Umut said demurely, her long hair cascading between them like a silken veil.

"I'd welcome apple tea, Miss Sydin," Richard replied, wishing he could snag his fingers in the waves. "I have coffee at my fingertips all day. Apple tea is a refreshing change." He smiled warmly at both women.

Ela Sydin preferred to twist her long hair into a tight knot when she worked, a practice Richard recognized as practical. At home, she covered her head with a gauzy scarf decorated with delicate embroidery and shiny discs. While her hair cascaded down her back, the scarf held it in check.

Umut preferred to restrain her locks with combs

and clips, much to Richard's pleasure. He enjoyed the movement of light when it cast onto strands that had been kissed by the sun, creating a blend of browns and reds with highlights of gold.

He kept his hands tightly clasped under the table while the women prepared the tea and sweet meats. *One wilful move toward that hair, and that will be it for me.*

As if reading his mind, Umut turned and smiled at him, her large brown eyes, expressive and alluring, leaving him struggling with desire. *If this was another time or another place, I'd have her without a second thought! Where has this patience come from?*

His eyes followed Umut's small hand as it lifted errant strands from her face and coveted the gesture.

Unexpectedly, Sally Winton's lovely face came to mind, with a gut-punch that took his breath away. *Sally made me want to be a better man. Maybe now, with Umut, I might be that man.*

CHAPTER 57

On the predetermined date, the Nightingale-Temple family arrived at the Winton family farm as invited. Having alighted from their vehicle in the farmyard, the initial meeting of the elders became stilted when Mr. and Mrs. Winton took the opportunity to politely express that, in their opinion, Richard should have married their daughter before impregnating her. They accused him of abandoning her.

"Mam," Sally said in protest, "Dickie didn't abandon me. He was well away when I found out I was pregnant. I made the decision to keep the child." She glared at her father. "Can you honestly say that you would want someone else raising your precious granddaughter? Look at her and tell me you would!" She raised her elbow, lifting the child's face to her father's. "Well?"

"No," Mr. Winton said, shame-faced.

"Lord and Lady Temple," Sally said, "please excuse our dispute."

"Yes," Mrs. Winton said, still wearing her starched white apron over a simple grey gown. She stepped aside. "I apologize. Please come in." Abashed, she ushered their guests into a small sitting room stuffed with well-used chairs. A table ladened with tea-things occupied the far end of the room. "I'll just bring the tea." She disappeared down a narrow hallway.

Sally's father entered the room behind his guests. At a loss of what to do next, he fired a questioning gaze at his daughter. Sally chatted easily, inviting the Nightingale-Temples to sit where they liked before offering the bundled child to Ann.

"Do you think we can try, for the sake of our Charlotte, to be friendly, if not friends?" she said, looking to Simon for support.

"I think that would be marvellous," Mary said, her slight Russian accent lending a lilt to her pronunciation. She stood behind her mother-in-law, gazing down at the tiny girl. "Oh, Mother Ann, is she not beautiful?" Her lavender skirt swished as she moved toward the seat next to Ann.

"Yes," Ann said reverentially, tucking a corner of the wrapping away from the baby's face. The same finger lingered on a soft cheek. "Yes, she is." Her eyes rose to meet her husband's. "Charles?"

To everyone's surprise, Charles had been following the exchange and leaned toward Ann with admiration in his eyes. "Our first grandchild," he said, wonderstruck. All signs of resistance had faded. He crouched next to Ann for a closer look, his houndstooth jacket blending with the green of her gown.

As the afternoon tea unfolded, Sally and Simon coached their parents to points of common ground: the child, the farm, and the Jarrow estate. With the mention of livestock, Simon enquired about horses. Catching a glint in the farmer's eye, he enquired whether a tour of the barns might be possible. Moments later, the men excused themselves, buttoning their jackets and snatching their caps as they headed for the door, leaving the women to fuss over the tiny girl.

"I know it's a stretch, Lady Ann," Sally said after a long pause, "to think that a child might be properly raised on a farm." She glanced at her mother and when no comment came, she continued. "While we may not have your wealth, and we don't live in luxury, we are comfortable. I received a good education. I'm capable of running the farm, if needed, but I'm not needed just now. Plus, I wanted to experience life off the farm. When my cousin suggested I help him run the pub, I jumped at the opportunity and moved to the city."

She smiled at her child, snuggled cozily in the crook of Ann's arm. "You must believe me when I say that I had no idea who Dickie really was, er, is. We met at the pub, and he only ever appeared when he was out of pocket. He told me that he was a clerk, that he was a commoner just like me. Although, I did sometimes tease him about the way he talked."

She sighed deeply. "Dickie seemed so broken the last time he came. Usually, he'd stay a night or two and disappear. That time, he stayed for almost a week. I gave him money for a ticket to Dover and he promised to pay it back one day. You can imagine my surprise when the full amount was delivered the next day, with a note that explained he was leaving and had no plans to return."

Ann met Mary's gaze, each seeming to realize the irony that the proceeds of the sale of the family silver had been used to repay Sally, and that Charles had then repurchased the silver soon after.

Ann rocked to and fro, attempting to settle the waking child.

"She's hungry," Sally said, unbuttoning the bodice of her rose-coloured day-dress as she reached for the baby.

"I'm sorry, Miss Winton," Ann said, clasping empty hands on her lap, "that my son left you in such a manner. He was not raised that way." She watched the child suckle for a moment. "I remember Richard when he was that new. Charlotte's hair is much like his was." She dabbed a tear from her eye with a lace handkerchief. "I like to think that he would have married you if—"

"Please don't worry yourself," Sally said interrupting her. "He had no way of knowing before he left. Besides, I'm not so sure I would have married him, anyway." She chuckled. "Can you imagine me a la-dee-da lady of a manor, or Dickie, working the farm with Da!"

On the day of Charlotte's christening, Sally approached the motor car and waited for Simon and his family to disembark.

"I wonder, Lord Simon," she said, "whether you and Lady Mary might spare a moment before entering the kirk. I have a favour to ask."

Charles and Ann gathered with the Winton family around the baptismal font of the ancient St. Paul's Anglican Church in Jarrow. The very church where Charles, Simon, and Richard in turn had been baptised.

To Simon's surprise and delight, he found himself standing to the right of Sally, holding her young daughter Charlotte Grace as the bishop recited the rite of baptism. In response to a question posed by the bishop, Simon agreed to be the baby's godfather. To his right stood his own wife Mary and Sally's sister Gaby, their right hands resting lightly on the child's shoulder, soon to answer a question posed to them regarding their willingness to act as godmothers.

As the bishop repeated the ancient words, Simon wondered at Sally's change of heart. While his family members were still to be considered cousins—which was not far from the truth—so long as neither Charlotte's father nor his circumstance was disclosed, Sally would not stand in their way of a relationship with the child.

CHAPTER 58

One Saturday evening as an autumn storm darkened the sky, Simon hastened up the staircase to the nursery, encountering the nanny as he reached the landing.

"I'm afraid they've started without you, sir."

Simon acknowledged her report and strode toward the chamber from which he could hear the boys' giggles. He paused outside the door and listened.

"Lady Mary," John said shyly, "do you think we'll forget about our parents one day?"

Mary froze as she tucked the covers around him. Before she could answer, Simon stepped back. Leaning against the wall, he watched through the crack between the door hinges.

"Certainly not, John," Mary replied, stroking his dark waves. "Why do you ask?"

"Well," he said, pausing as if to find the correct words, "I can't remember their faces clearly. They're all smudgy."

"Ah! Yes, that is a problem," Mary said sadly. "It is my experience that we remember people and things clearly the more we see them or do for them. If we don't have that opportunity, our memory might fade a bit, but we never forget the people or things we truly want to remember.

I have the same problem when I try to remember my family. Perhaps on the weekend, we can go out to the stable and look for photos in some of your boxes."

"I think I know where they are!" Elvie said, eyes bright.

"Me too!" John said with enthusiasm.

"Are your parents in heaven, too?" Elvie said, appearing awestruck as she recalled Mary's earlier comment.

"Yes," Mary replied, straightening her shoulders. "I've found that, although their images have faded, I remember much about them: and my sisters, and my brother."

"You had sisters and a brother?" John said. "And they died too?"

"Yes."

"Were they all sick, too?" Willy said softly, a frown marring his young face.

"No, sweet child," Mary replied, her palm finding the curve of his cheek. "But they are gone from me, nonetheless."

She sighed, regarding each child before she spoke again. "And I can tell you this: you will always remember your parents, as I do mine. I remember them by their deeds, how they felt when they hugged me, even how they smelled. You'll remember how you felt when they held your hand in theirs, the time they spent with you on a special day at the park, for example. You'll remember how they spoke, how they praised you for your successes, even how they cautioned you to stay out of trouble."

She leaned in close to kiss each boy between their brows, then opened her arms to Elvie, who had been leaning against Willy's bed, and kissed her, too.

"Your parents will always be present, watching over each of you, keeping you safe." She tapped each tiny nose affectionately. "You see, Lord Simon and I are not here to replace your parents. We are merely channelling their love and care for you. We are their representatives, as Nanny is for us when we can't be with you. Does that make sense?" The children nodded as they each reached for a small hand to hold.

"Then I think our parents made a good choice," John said confidently. "Willy, Elvie, and I will do our very best to make them proud, won't we?"

Elvie and Willy nodded solemnly.

"And we'll do our best to make you and Lord Simon proud of us, too!" Elvie said. "Won't we boys?"

"Yes!" the boys said in unison.

"Thank you!" Mary said, reaching to tickle each of the boys. "I'm sure you will."

"What's going on in here?" Simon said sternly, barging into the room, wearing a smile that stretched from ear to ear.

———

"Mary seems particularly happy since we welcomed the children into the Hall," Charles said, buttering a strip of toast before dipping it into an egg cup.

"I believe she is, Father," Simon replied, taking up his napkin to wipe sticky orange juice from his fingers. "They are certainly a distraction. This time last year, Mary was so distraught, remembering the events that led up to the nasty business in Yekaterinburg."

Simon lifted a forkful of sausage to his lips, then set the fork down on his plate—sausage still speared on the tines. "That was a horrible time," Simon said, clasping his hands in his lap. "What she went through. What we three—Mary, Artyom, and I—went through."

His mind spun with thoughts of their escape from Russia and the long journey back to Britain. "She has nightmares, you know. Memories of the execution. They're still so vivid to her. She awakes in the night screaming hysterically. I've noticed, however, that since the children arrived, they've lessened."

"People like to say, 'time heals all wounds'," Charles said, "but I'm inclined to disagree. I had horrid nightmares when I returned from Africa, and they've subsided, I'll give you that. However, it only takes a stressful situation to bring them all back again. I awake in the night in a cold sweat, heart pounding, arms swinging. Occasionally shouting orders." He shook his head at the memory. "Used to scare the living daylights out of your mother!" He chuckled softly. "Dear woman. I don't know how she puts up with me!"

"But it does lessen, yes?" Simon said hopefully. "I have episodes too, but my experiences are nothing compared to yours and Mary's."

"For most," Charles replied, "so long as nothing stressful brings the memories to life again."

"Then I'm doubly glad for the children," Simon

said. "They say they are happy to be here, and they're a delight to have in the Hall. Plus, they keep the staff on their toes. Frankly, I can't imagine what the Hall will be like when they're gone."

Simon picked up his fork and continued his meal, while Charles dressed a fresh cup of coffee.

"I overheard a conversation in the nursery recently," Simon said. "I was delayed, so Mary went ahead to say good night …" Simon recounted the conversation about lost parents.

"John's a thoughtful lad," Charles replied when Simon finished. "Actually … they all are. We are blessed to have them."

"Do you believe that, Father?" Simon said ruefully.

Charles paused, contemplating the question, coffee cup halfway to his lips. "As a matter of fact," Charles said, sounding somewhat surprised at his revelation, "I do!"

CHAPTER 59

Several weeks and many dinners later, Richard, Ela, and Umut felt comfortable in their companionship. The stiff edges of their blossoming friendship had softened.

One evening, when his host suggested that Richard and Umut might step out together on occasion, rather than spending all their time cooped up with an old lady, Richard seized the opportunity.

"Thank you, Mrs. Sydin," he said, looking to Umut with an air of expectancy. "Does that include dinner as well?"

"I think you should direct that question to Umut," Ela said, amused, "since that's where your eyes are directed at the moment."

Umut and Richard broke their eye-lock, turning crimson faces toward Ela.

Ela laughed. "Perhaps, Richard, it is time for you to leave," she said pleasantly. "I've heard rumours that Commander Kemal may be returning tomorrow."

"You're correct," Richard said, rising to take his leave.

He bowed smartly to the elder woman, then the younger, when they came to the door to bid him good night. As he did so, he applied a feather-light kiss to the knuckles of their right hands.

He tripped down the stairs and made his way along the street. As he neared the corner, he glanced over his shoulder, delighted to see Umut standing outside her door, waving good-bye. He waved in answer, backing away as he did so, until he tripped over a tree stump and almost fell. Embarrassed, he waved one last time and turned the corner.

Despite the many efforts of Kemal and the generals to quell the unrest in Turkey caused by disruptive Armenian and Greek factions, a quiet conclusion remained out of reach. Throughout the remainder of 1919, battles continued to lure Kemal away from his preferred role as leader, leaving the generals to pursue the new reforms recommended by him. Russia's representative Ivan Vasiliev nipped at their efforts like a rabid dog.

On those occasions when Kemal's presence was required on a battle front, Richard attended the meetings of the generals as his trusted agent. In that capacity, he recorded discussions and relayed them to Kemal. Any significant response was then carried by Richard back to the generals.

As autumn marched toward winter, Kemal summoned Richard to Sivas, insisting that he be involved with unfolding political matters. Although Richard felt honoured to be among those followers of Kemal who fought to create a new country and a new government, he found himself yearning for the company of Mrs. Sydin and her lovely daughter. He began a chain of correspondence with each of them, which eased the longing. Providentially, he found the return correspondence kept him abreast of matters in Ancyra.

Without asking them to do so, Mrs. Sydin included comments made by tenants residing in her employer's building, several of whom were employed by foreign representatives to the new Turkey. Umut, too, informed him of details casually dropped by unwitting soldiers and government aides who attended the tailor shop for fittings.

Richard scrutinized their letters, looking for critical information that might empower Kemal as leader, strengthen the position of his council of generals, or move a particular battle forward to conclusion.

"Did you put them up to it?" Kemal asked when Richard shared a detail from one of Umut's missives.

"No," Richard said, baffled by the candidness of the correspondence. "They just write what they hear. I do know that you have their undying support. I suppose they hope that this gossip has enough foundation to be useful." He shrugged at his words, accepting that their intent could be misleading.

On one occasion, he reread a recent letter, heartwarmed to see Mrs. Sydin's words of encouragement regarding his relationship with Umut, and those portions of Umut's companion letter that clearly expressed her affection for him. Overwhelmed, he determined to return to Ancyra with marriage top of mind.

"Congratulations," Kemal said as he watched Richard climb into the cab of a military vehicle bound for the city. "You have now met my third recommendation!"

Richard regarded the general with a puzzled expression.

"Work on the farm," Kemal said, holding up a finger. "Learn the language ..." He raised a second finger.

"And find a Turkic wife!" Richard grinned at the realization.

"Please, give my regards to Mrs. Sydin and Miss Sydin, and tell them I send my congratulations as well. Be sure to tell them, too, that their reports are always appreciated."

CHAPTER 60

Richard disembarked the military vehicle later that day and immediately strode off in the direction of the Sydin residence.

"Richard!" the women said together, laughing at the dusty smudges on his cheeks.

"Umut," her mother said, "some warm water and a towel, quickly!"

While the women made dinner preparations, Richard tidied himself. Catching Umut setting dishes on the table, he gently wrapped his fingers around her wrist and drew her to him. "Marry me?" he said, searching her eyes for a reaction.

As his intention dawned, she jumped into his arms, wrapping hers around his neck, dangling like a pendulum. A lingering kiss sealed her delighted acceptance.

"*Ahem!*" Mrs. Sydin cleared her throat as she quietly entered the room and set a large platter of rice and roasted goat meat in the centre of the table.

Umut landed gracefully on her feet and turned to face her mother. Clutching Richard's hand to her breast, she told her mother of the proposal.

"Uh," Richard said hesitantly, "that is … Mrs. Sydin,

if you'll allow me to ask for your daughter's hand in marriage?"

"I think it's a little late for that question," Mrs. Sydin said, eyes lit with joy. "Regardless, I will give my consent. Keep in mind, however, that you have failed to follow the first tradition of *kız isteme*. The rules of asking for the bride's hand should be followed precisely. But, as you know, we are an exception to the tradition: you have no parents to speak on your behalf; Umut has no father to speak for her.

"And, under normal circumstances, we would have to follow the rules of a religion significantly different from yours. Fortunately for all of us, religion is not a factor. Therefore, both of you must undertake to follow the other traditions as best you can, to ensure a proper Turkish wedding." She grinned mischievously, letting her words sink in.

"Of course, Mrs. Sydin," Richard said, bewildered. "Whatever you say. Just tell me what needs to happen, and I'll do it." He gazed lovingly at Umut, squeezing her hand. "The sooner we begin, the sooner we'll be wed!"

"Then let us eat," Mrs. Sydin said, waving an arm toward the cooling food, "and make preparations." Before she lowered herself to the table, she looked Richard in the eye. "I think you should call me Ela or Mama from now on. Enough of the '*Mrs. Sydin*' business."

Two days later, Richard penned a personal note and

dropped it off at Kemal's hotel suite, hoping that the man would return in time to attend the wedding ten days hence.

The following weekend, a few neighbours and close friends were invited to the Sydin home to participate in a modified version of a promise ceremony and engagement party. Richard produced simple gold promise rings. An assortment of small, practical engagement gifts were also exchanged by the bride and groom.

In the early evening, the men were shooed from the home, while the women remained to sing traditional wedding songs. When Umut's neighbour pressed a gold coin into her hand, it signalled the beginning of the henna painting ceremony. "Since your mother could not be here to press the coin," she later told Richard, "our neighbour asked for the privilege."

As the autumn sun rose on his wedding day, Richard stretched leisurely, relishing the last hours of his bachelorhood with great expectation. Aside from those few moments of tranquility, his morning passed swiftly as he ran last-minute errands for Ela, had his hair cut, bathed, and donned his wedding suit.

At long last, he stood with Umut—adorned in a white lace wedding dress and embroidered red cape of her own design—listening to the binding words of a marriage officer. His new, fashionable suit, made by her deft and loving hands, fit him like a second skin. He could not remember ever feeling as proud as he did in that short ceremony.

As it ended, his eyes caught Kemal's fatherly

expression at the back of the room, leaving him to wonder briefly whether he truly saw a tear in the commander's eye.

———

Soon after their wedding, Umut's employer promoted her to military tailor. As such, her responsibilities were directed to the making of officers' uniforms for Kemal's new army, and attire for senior government officials.

Wooed by the wife of an innkeeper, whose husband had enlisted in Kemal's army—thereby leaving her in need of a manager—Ela accepted the woman's offer of employment. During that evening's meal, Ela declared that each member of her family had been blessed with rewarding employment in aid of the Turkish revolution. Given their excellent, combined income, she suggested that they lease comfortable lodgings but continue to live with thrift and save what they could for a later time and need.

Richard's landlord expressed disappointment over the loss of his exceptional tenant, but quickly found them a most suitable house nearby, which happened to be owned by his sister.

CHAPTER 61

Following the Sunday morning church service and their typical luncheon, Simon bid farewell to his family and departed for London. Mary and the children waved good-bye when the motor pulled away from the front drive, then scooted upstairs to change out of their Sunday finery.

"It would not do," Mary said, "for you to wear such grand garments into the barn. Today, we're going to learn how to brush the ponies and muck out their stables!'

The boys hollered with loud cheers, while Elvie turned up her nose at the thought of pony manure.

"Children, you've met Peter Stone," Mary said. "Mr. Stone is the senior groomsman. He will introduce us to the ponies and show us how to care for them."

Peter shook the hand of each child, sizing them up against the ponies, then led them toward a small corral behind the stables. "This one here is Master Arthur's pony," Peter said, scratching the forehead of a sturdy pit pony named Blacky hanging his head over the rail. The ebony pony nickered and shook his head as if agreeing to the ownership.

"We have several pit ponies," Peter said, "but these six would make good riding ponies. You may each pick one."

"What will happen to the ones we don't choose?" Elvie asked as she stroked Blacky's soft muzzle.

"They'll be trained for other work," Peter replied nonchalantly. "They have many options."

"I like the brown one," Willy said decidedly.

"Bet you can't guess his name," Peter said, sharing a grin with Mary.

"Um," Willy said as his face lit up. "Browny?"

"Browny it is," Peter said.

"I like the white one with orange spots," Elvie said, holding her hand over the rail, beckoning. A tall filly with dainty hooves stepped toward her. "Hello Spot!" She rubbed the curious muzzle with affection.

"Master John?"

John crossed his arms over his chest, one hand bracing his chin as he chewed his lip.

So like Simon, Mary thought, pleased at the small revelation.

"I like the one with the star on its forehead," he said. "He reminds me of Da's old horse."

Peter inserted his index finger and thumb in his mouth and whistled. The grey pony trotted from the far side of the corral and nuzzled the groomsman's hand. "We call this fellow Horatio."

"That's a Latin name," John said, stroking the soft muzzle. "My da said it means 'reason'."

"Just so, Master John," Peter said, pleased with the

boy's cleverness. "Horatio keeps the others in line."

"So," Mary said, "you each have a pony." Her fists rested easily on her hips. "Now, you must learn how to care for them."

Peter fastened a lead to the halter of each pony and showed the children how to guide them into a stable, explaining the need to always keep the pen gate closed.

"Ponies are clever, see. Given the opportunity, they'd rather be grazing in the meadow over there than work. But, if they don't work, they don't get fed." He looked at them sternly. "Remember that."

"Yes, sir, Mr. Stone, sir," the children's voices chimed together.

Peter showed them how to tie their ponies securely, then handed them each a brush. "We need to give a pony a good brushing to remove any burrs before we put a saddle on their back; otherwise, the burr will pain the beast."

Mary leaned against the wall of the large stall, appreciating the care and interest each child took in their pony.

"Before they saddle up, Mr. Stone," Mary said, noting the end of the brush work, "the children will need to learn a few more things, don't you agree?"

"Indeed, Lady Mary," Peter said with a grin. "We'll let the ponies enjoy their clean coats for a few minutes," he said, setting the brushes on a shelf and ushering them out of the stall.

In the breezeway, he handed them each a small shovel or pitchfork and lead them into an adjacent stall.

"Ew," Elvie said, curling her nose.

"Ew," the boys said, parroting her reaction.

In retaliation, Elvie dropped her spade and shoved the boys into a small haystack. John rolled sideways coming to a stop just inches above a pile of horse dung.

"Ew!" he said, scampering to his feet and wiping a soiled hand on his trousers. He turned his gaze toward his sister, crouching in readiness for vengeance.

Peter's firm hand grabbed John's collar and stood him square on his feet. He glared sternly at the three children.

"If you want a pony, you will learn to respect its care. This is not the place for fighting." He held their gaze. "Is that clear?"

"Yes, Mr. Stone," they said together, aptly ashamed.

Mary watched Peter deliver the discipline, recalling a similar instance when a royal stable hand had taught her and her younger sister, Anastasia, how to ride. Nasty had tripped over her own shovel and landed face-first in a pile of warm horse apples. Mary had laughed aloud. For her lack of sensitivity, Mary was made to clean the stable of Nasty's horse, while the groom tidied her sister. Eyes alight with amusement, she covered her mouth to hide a grin.

"Right then," Peter said. "Get that muck into this barrow. Master John, I'll show you where to dump the barrow. And, while he does that, you two can spread the clean hay. Then, we saddle up."

"Yes, sir!" The children worked diligently, concluding the task in short order.

Half an hour later, he had talked them through the saddling of their ponies, offering pointers when needed. Anticipating that Willy's saddle was about to slide sideways, Mary held it steady and helped fasten the girth securely.

While Peter instructed Elvie and John how to mount, Mary found a bucket, turned it over and encouraged Willy to use it as a step stool so his foot could reach the stirrup.

"Bravo!" Mary said admiring the three riders. "Well done!"

Peter led the two older children out of the stable, instructing them how to handle their mounts. Mary escorted Willy, one arm wrapped around his waist to keep him steady.

When they returned to the stable, Peter instructed the older children how to dismount and unsaddle their ponies, to brush them down again, and to feed and water them before releasing them to the corral. Mary worked with Willy to ensure that his pony received the same treatment. She watched with pride as the ponies scampered around the corral, the children hanging from the rails in delight of a day well spent.

"Can we ride again tomorrow?" John asked with enthusiasm.

"You may," Mary replied, "but you must always ask Mr. Stone or one of the others to help you. Until you are able to manage everything safely by yourself, you must ask for guidance."

"Yay!" Willy said, hopping up and down. "We can try

again tomorrow!" He threw his arms around Mary's legs. "Thank you, Mother," the little boy said, smiling up at her.

"Mother!" Mary said, squatting to his height. "But I'm not—"

"Yes, you are," John said, resting his hand on her shoulder. "We took a vote, and we agreed that you will be our mother and Lord Simon will be our father. That is, if you'd like to have us." His steel blue eyes held hers fast.

"Oh, John!" Mary said, reaching for the three of them, tears of joy filling her eyes. "Of course, we'll have you!" *I must share this with Simon once the children are in bed*, she thought.

The three children sprang into her arms, knocking her off balance. As she toppled backward into a pile of fragrant hay, they fell with her. They play-fought in the hay to giggles of joy at having cemented their relationship.

As Mary tugged John to his feet, they were startled by a loud harrumph. Mary spun around to face the source. "Father Charles!" she said, brushing straw from her trousers and picking strands of it from Elvie's hair. "We were just—"

"We were just celebrating," John said proudly.

"Yes!" Elvie said. "Lady Mary has agreed to be our mother! Isn't it marvellous?"

"My mother, too," Willy said, taking her hand, turning his small face toward her, an expression of sincerity shining upward. "But we shan't forget Mam and Da, shall we?"

"Never!" Mary said firmly. "We'll have enough love and memories for everyone!"

"I say," Charles replied, grinning as he picked a length of straw from Mary's hair. "That's wonderful news, isn't it!" He stooped down and lifted Willy into his arms. "I don't suppose that you might call me 'Grandfather' one day?"

"Oh, yes, sir!" Willy said, "That would be lovely!"

CHAPTER 62

L ess than a week after his wedding, Richard found himself seated across from Ivan Vasiliev, in a private corner of his favoured Russian restaurant. Vasiliev leaned conspiratorially toward Richard, peering down his nose.

He looks like a mud toad ready to pounce, Richard thought, *but a mud toad isn't wicked, selfish, untrustworthy, and vile.*

"I have seen these many months how the general relies on you," Vasiliev said, twiddling the blade next to his dinner plate. He glanced over his shoulder to be certain no one was nearby, his thin lips pressed tight. "Your services to Kemal could be very useful to my government as well."

"How is that possible?" Richard replied, intrigued. "I can't imagine that I know anything worthy of a Bolshevik interest."

"Mr. Temple," Vasiliev said condescendingly, "you underestimate yourself. You have the ear of the general on all things. And everyone believes he is destined to become leader of all Turkey. I have also observed that he takes your council seriously." Vasiliev steepled his fingers as he spoke.

"All I ask is that you let me know when Kemal makes any substantive decisions. I want to ensure that Russia's investment in this burgeoning new country remains sound. I believe I may rely on your word as truth." He leaned back into his chair, appearing confident in his assumption.

"I see," Richard said, his mind racing, calculating the benefit of such an arrangement. "What makes you think my word is truth?"

A waiter appeared with a bottle of champagne and placed a vessel of ice near their table, interrupting their conversation. They sat quietly as the cork popped free of the bottle and the waiter poured wine into Vasiliev's glass. When he turned to pour a second glass, Richard held his hand above his glass and shook his head. "I'll have apple tea instead, please."

Vasiliev straightened, hands clasped across his ample belly, and narrowed his already narrow eyes when the waiter excused himself. "What! No champagne, Mr. Temple? I have it on good authority that you are partial to drink." He snatched his own glass and downed the effervescent wine with one gulp.

"I regret to inform you, sir," Richard said, "that your *good authority* has failed you. Prior to my journey to Turkey, I admit to a penchant for alcohol, but I have consumed little since I left England—a year ago—and I have determined never to resume that debilitating habit." He reached slowly for the bottle of champagne and refilled Vasiliev's glass.

Part of Richard wanted to spit in the man's face for daring to presume he could corrupt a relationship in which he had invested everything. He admired Kemal and his foresightedness. Besides, Kemal paid him handsomely. He was content.

Although, to be fair, he thought, *if Vasiliev already knows of my history with alcohol, he also knows that I liked to gamble and that I've enjoyed the company of women. And, if he knows that, he likely knows that I've betrayed Britain to be here. Best to hear him out and report back to the general.*

"Where were we?" Vasiliev said. "Ah, yes … we were talking about truth."

As the meal progressed through a variety of tasty Russian dishes, including borscht soup with a dollop of sour cream, breaded veal, and steamed potatoes, Vasiliev made no reference to Richard's past. Instead, he described what information might be of interest, not only to him, but to the Russian government.

"We will pay you in gold for any information that proves to be of value; and, of course," Vasiliev said, concluding the proposal, "you will be free to spend it as you please, no—how do the English say?—strings attached!"

Outside the restaurant a few hours later, Richard welcomed the refreshing chill of the evening. Reluctantly, he accepted Vasiliev's slippery hand before turning to leave.

"By the way," Vasiliev said, his words calling Richard back as he dug in his pocket for his handkerchief, "you have an uncanny resemblance to your brother. You and he must be quite close."

"How so?" Richard said, wiping Vasiliev's slime off his hand. "Place two red apples side by side. Their skins may seem similar. However, either could be over-ripe, woody, or rotten on the inside." He regarded the Russian as he returned his handkerchief to his pocket. "My brother and I may have similar physical attributes as well, but that has no bearing on who we are as individuals."

"In my observations, Simon Temple never acted without first giving a matter great thought. One might even say he was calculating." Vasiliev eyed Richard, as if challenging him to deny the claim, and settled his fedora over his hairless pate.

"Before I decided to leave England, I gave the idea a great deal of thought." Richard gently squeezed his chin between finger and thumb. "I knew I'd be abandoning a great deal, but only now am I realizing the price. If you call that calculating, then perhaps I am. Perhaps I've done other things since then that cause me to question my behaviour as well. I'll have to give that some thought."

He chuckled, surprised to feel a need to protect his brother. "As for my brother, I couldn't say whether he's calculating. Even as youths, we followed different paths. Plus, you'll recall, he was in Russia for three years, while I was working in London."

"Indeed, he was," Vasiliev said breathily, mopping his face with a wrinkled handkerchief. "He also departed Russia in great haste, under a cloud of mystery." He stepped closer and spoke confidentially. "Simon Temple's disappearance has been linked to certain missing crown jewels, which belong to the state. The Bolshevik party is keen to have them returned. They would also like to question him regarding the kidnapping of a Russian princess." He stuffed his hands into his trouser pockets and rocked on his heels with drunken confidence.

"I see," Richard said, appearing disinterested. "I never heard from my brother while he was away, and as I've said, I left England shortly after his return. I know nothing of any crown jewels."

He lowered his head in thought, casually stuffing his hands in his pockets. "Besides, I find it difficult to believe that the Bolshevik party has a need to question my brother regarding a missing Russian princess, when it has been widely reported that *they* murdered the *entire* Romanov family, and a few more besides. Are you suggesting that the reports are wrong?"

"An admirable response," Vasiliev said with a shrug. "I would expect nothing less of you. And I care nothing about a Russian princess. However, with regard to the jewels, I do not believe you, Mr. Temple. Simon Temple has the jewels, and *I* want them back."

"*You* want them back?" Richard said, brows raised at the slip, pleased that he had caught it.

"The party—I meant the revolutionary party," Vasiliev said through clenched teeth, impatiently thrusting his hand forward again. "I will await your consideration and will expect a favourable response when next we meet."

"As you say," Richard replied, turning on his heel to signal the man's dismissal. "Good night."

CHAPTER 63

"Will you return with me?" the driver said, swinging into traffic after dropping off the two Russians for the day. "Or shall I drop you somewhere?"

The unexpected question interrupted Richard's thoughts. "Uh, you can let me out at the next intersection," Richard replied. "I'll walk from there."

Richard waved farewell to the driver and crossed the street in the direction of home. It was a lovely evening for a walk, after a day of driving around the city and managing the two Russians. He glanced at his wristwatch, noting that neither Umut nor Ela would be home for another hour, and decided to stop at a café for refreshment to quench his thirst. Entering an unfamiliar premises, he took a seat near an open window and waved to a server.

"Coffee, please," he said, sliding a few coins over the tabletop.

Before the server could scoop up the coins, a weathered hand stopped him.

"How about two whiskeys?" an older man said, licking his lips. "I'll make it worth your while ..."

Richard considered the man for a moment, then nodded to the server. The coins remained on the table.

The man lowered himself into a rickety wooden chair and grinned, drawing Richard's eye to several missing teeth.

"And what is it that you wish to tell me that is worth the price of a whiskey?" Richard said, curious.

"I've seen you around," the man said, his Cornish accent only slightly slurred. "You have something to do with that General Kemal."

"And what if I do?" Richard said, now wary.

"Me name's Parks, by the way," he said. "Jacob Parks, but me friends call me Jay." He shrugged, unabashed at the disclosure.

"Please continue, Mr. Parks."

The man held his tongue while the server set two glasses of whiskey on the table. Before Richard could count out the additional coins required, Parks downed a glass and winked at Richard. He glanced at the empty glass and grinned again.

"Make that another two," Richard said, collecting the coins. *His information had better be worth the breach of my dry spell.*

Parks leaned into the table, crossing his forearms before him. "Now, what was I saying? Ah, yes! What do I know?"

Parks spoke for several minutes, sharing with Richard his life's story and how he came to be in Ancyra after he had been discharged from the British army.

When his tale ran dry, he reached for the second glass of whiskey and raised it. "To the British!" he said with a derisive chuckle. "And may God save Turkey!" He squinted at Richard, noting the two glasses of whiskey warming before him on the table. "Come on, man. Drink up!"

Richard wrapped his fingers around one of the glasses and reluctantly took a sip. The amber liquid trickled down his throat, leaving him with a warm sense of being. He sipped again, appreciating the ease that seeped through him. He waved at the server, requesting two more glasses.

"Now that's more like it," Parks said. "I hates to drink alone. Now … where was I?" He tapped his forehead, then began again.

"So, just to be clear," Richard said, "you're telling me that you travel between here and Constantinople periodically tending to your own business needs, and that when in Constantinople, you catch up on news imparted by cronies from your old regiment. And that these cronies are comfortable sharing certain confidential information over a pint or two?"

"Exactly so," Parks said, sitting proudly. "Loose lips and all that. They think me enough of a drunk that they can speak openly in my hearing and that I won't recall what was said." He eased himself against the chair's back, eyeing Richard. "You're a bright lad. You grasp the important particulars." He raised his latest glass of whiskey and saluted Richard. "Now, before I become too tipsy, let me tell you the important part."

"Please do," Richard said sardonically, already feeling the effects of the second glass of whiskey. He saluted the old man in return and listened closely.

"So, this Turkish general, whose name you don't

know," Richard said, summarizing what he had heard, "has left the Sultan's employ for a position on Kemal's council of generals, and has agreed to feed important information discussed by the council to the British, in exchange for …?" Richard's brows rose into a solid bar, inviting Parks to finish.

"In exchange for the British promise to place him at the head of the Turkish government instead of Kemal—once it's organized, of course." Parks slapped his hand on the table, suggesting that he had delivered secret information worthy of Kemal's attention. "You must tell the general to watch his back."

"Indeed," Richard said, realizing that the sun had long since set. He glanced at his wristwatch and waved for the server. "Mr. Parks, I thank you for sharing this information." He handed a wad of bills to the server and rose. "It's long past the dinner hour, and my wife will be cross that I have missed one of her meals. You will forgive me, but I must depart. Immediately!" He swayed, eyeing the doorway, and hoped he would reach home without incident.

"I didn't catch your name, friend," Parks said behind him.

"That may be for the good, Mr. Parks!"

"Jay. Call me Jay!"

"Good evening … Jay," Richard repeated as he plopped his straw fedora on his head and staggered through the doorway.

CHAPTER 64

As Richard meandered the few remaining streets to his home, he contemplated his recent dinner with Vasiliev and certain revelations expressed by him. His suspicions about the grand duchess and the jewels were correct, to a point. If he chose to share what he knew with the Russians, Richard could cause Simon and Mary significant harm.

He dismissed further thought, knowing that he would never betray his family to Vasiliev, and turned his mind to the peculiar conversation with Jacob Parks, making a note to record it all in the morning.

"I may be a dishonourable son," he said softly, "but I've yet to reach Vasiliev's level and hopefully never will. If, on the other hand, I was honourable, I'd warn Simon. Regardless, I will inform the general of Mr. Parks observations."

Hands in his pockets, he whistled a tune that a fiddler had been playing outside the café. Rounding the final corner, the bright light of the main street dimmed. Makarov's sudden appearance from the shadow of a cluster of trees alarmed him.

"Makarov!" Richard said jovially, "what are you doing here?" He peered around him. "Where's Vasiliev?"

"*Colonel* Vasiliev is in his room," Makarov replied with a sneer. "He does not know I am here."

"And why exactly *are* you here?" Richard said, managing a modicum of disdain.

"Because I don't like your attitude!" Makarov hesitated. "Most of all, I don't like *you*!"

"My attitude?" Richard said, feeling unstable and wishing he had not had the last two whiskeys. "What are you saying, man? And why would I care whether you like me?"

"You show no respect for Colonel Vasiliev; you're a worthless scum!"

"Worthless scum? Respect?" Richard said, temporarily dumbstruck. "Respect must be earned, and your boss has done nothing to earn mine. Nor, for that matter, do I expect I have his." Richard regarded the middle-aged man, hoping his inebriated sway was less than it felt. "So, what do you plan to do about that?" Fists on hips, Richard rocked on his heels. "Hmm?"

"Perhaps this will persuade you," Makarov said as he jabbed his fist into the softness of Richard's belly. "Or perhaps this." He swung again with a second blow.

Richard crumpled onto the road, grabbing his belly and gasping for air. Makarov towered above him, gloating with pleasure.

"I say, man," Richard said breathlessly as he staggered to his unsteady feet, still guarding his midsection. "That was uncalled for."

"Perhaps you would prefer this!" Makarov's fist

caught Richard's left cheek, sending him spinning across the road. "And this!"

Richard's knees thudded to the packed dirt with the impact of Makarov's fist on his left kidney. Pain shot through Richard's back. He fell forward, face smashing into small stones. Then, his thoughts ceased.

When consciousness returned to him, Richard found himself alone, sprawled at the edge of the dark road. Once again, he staggered to his feet, swaying with the effort to stand erect.

His mouth tasted of blood and metal. He spat a blob of bloody saliva into the dirt and wiped his mouth with the back of his hand. His jaw ached, but his back hurt more. The door to his home was mere paces from where he stood. He tottered toward it, calling for Umut.

"Richard!" Umut said, thrusting the door open. "What's happened to you?"

"Richard, come in," Ela said, reaching from behind her daughter. "Umut, get some warm water and a towel."

Umut administered to Richard's injuries while Ela made tea.

"Tell me what this is about, Richard," Umut said. "Who did this to you?"

"Ah," Richard said, testing the fragility of his injured jaw, "that is the curious thing." He gazed at the two women. "I can't tell you everything, as it concerns Kemal Pasha. However, I can tell you that one of the men whom I have been *entertaining* on behalf of the general has taken exception to my behaviour. I don't have a great deal of respect for either man, but I'm obligated to carry out the assignment. The fellow who roughed me up is the sidekick and henchman. He seems to have hoped that a few blows might instill in me some respect for his boss."

"Humph," Umut said, clearly annoyed. "You smell like one of the drunk soldiers who comes to me with a torn uniform after a night out on the town. And that is one smell too many for me!" She crossed her arms over her chest and glared at Richard. "A man wed to me shall not be wed to alcohol, too. As your wife, I will tend your wounds. But you will not sleep in my bed so long as you are drunk. Mama, please find Richard a blanket. He will sleep on the sofa this night."

<hr>

Ela turned away, raising her hand to cover a knowing grin. She had warned her daughter many times to steer clear of men who drink, Umut being the product of an attack by one such brutal man. Ela sobered and dismissed recollection of the painful experience that, through no fault of her own, stole her youth and cost her a place in her family and her social standing.

Richard sipped his tea, set his cup carefully on the table, and raised his eyes to meet Umut's. "I swear to you, dear Umut, that liquor will never cross my lips again."

He rose to his feet, tucking his shirt into his trousers, kissed his wife's cheek chastely, and bowed to the women. He took the blanket from Ela and headed for the sofa in his study.

———

Richard struggled to pull himself together the following morning. A slight headache and several deep bruises made rapid movement nauseating.

Arriving outside his office mid-morning, Kemal's clerk called to him. "From Kemal Pasha," the clerk said, handing him an envelope.

Richard eased into his chair and read the message.

Dear Richard,

The latest turmoil will soon end. and I expect to return to Ancyra before month's end. If all goes well, we shall remain in that city for some time. As we've discussed, our new government will require office space for our headquarters. I hope you have found something appropriate and that all will be arranged when I arrive. I will require a suitable residence, also, and challenge you to find it.

K

CHAPTER 65

Richard reclined comfortably on the sofa in Kemal's new apartment above the former railway station, now converted into the headquarters for the Turkish National Movement. The general raised a whiskey decanter, offering him a glass.

"No, thank you," Richard said easily. "I recently had an encounter with a retired British soldier. It cost me several glasses of whiskey for information that you may find of value. Soon after, I was attacked and suitably thrashed by Makarov for, in his opinion, disrespecting Vasiliev. And, when I appeared before my wife and mother-in-law dishevelled, drunk, and beaten ..." He shrugged. "Need I say more?"

"As you wish," Kemal said pensively. "I don't think I could survive without it now. The stress of trying to create an independent country is too great. Too many people depend upon me." He placed the glass on a nearby table and lowered himself to the adjoining chair, reaching for a box of cigarettes as he did so. "How about you tell me of this British soldier and Makarov's thrashing before we continue?"

"Makarov's behaviour is troubling," Kemal said when

Richard finished his report. "We will have to think of something that will keep him in line." He stabbed the spent cigarette in the overflowing ashtray and continued. "In the meantime, draft two reports for me: one concerning Makarov's attack, and the other explaining your encounter with this Parks fellow. I will mention the attack to the council, but I'd like to keep the soldier's intelligence confidential for now while I contemplate the possibility of a misguided general and what to do about him."

"What of the battles, sir?" Richard said. "Are you any closer to a conclusion?"

"We're trying," Kemal said, jumping to his feet and pacing across the salon before stopping to light another cigarette. "Just when we think we have the Armenians or the Greeks on the verge of resolution, something shifts, and we lose our grip."

He hammered his fist on a side table, rattling a China vase. "The cursed Armenians just won't give up! Their resistance is sporadic and unreasonable, making it difficult to avoid harming them!"

He leaned against the wall facing Richard, crossing arms and legs nonchalantly. "And the Greeks! It's a constant seesaw over Smyrna and the surrounding area. I hope they're gone before the end of the year. They're irritating both me and the men in the field." He huffed with frustration and resumed his chair. "I don't blame them. We all just want to go home." He paused, contemplating the half-smoked cigarette.

Richard waited patiently for Kemal to speak again.

When he failed to do so, Richard took it as a sign for him to leave. "Thank you for the dinner invitation, sir," he said, shaking his head to decline an offer of a cigarette.

"The meal wasn't as good as a home-cooked one, but what can we expect?" Kemal shrugged. "I've only just moved in. Under the supervision of a good woman," he said, releasing a stream of smoke, "it will improve." He sipped his whiskey, savouring it before he swallowed.

"Yes, sir," Richard replied. "I have references for the staff you'll need. When you're ready, I'll arrange the interviews."

"Very good," Kemal said. "And what about you, Richard? Now that you've found a good Turkic wife, are you happy?"

"As a matter of fact," Richard said, straightening in the chair, "I couldn't be happier! And, I have it on good authority that, so long as I never imbibe again, I will continue to be happy." He bowed to the general. "Thank you again for the idea … of a Turkish wife, I mean!"

CHAPTER 66

Simon waited for Artyom at the entrance to the Admiralty Building at day's end. He stood facing the street, hands clasped behind his back, contemplating the glitter bouncing off random raindrops collecting under the streetlight.

"See anything interesting?" Artyom said, strolling toward him.

Simon shrugged, falling in step with Artyom once they passed through the door. He pulled on his gloves and buttoned his coat against the wind that howled through the trees of St. James Park.

"Interested in a little sleuthing after dinner?" Simon said. "I received another report about Vasiliev's nephew, Denis, this afternoon. I put a tail on him a few weeks ago. He's been busy travelling between here and Jarrow, spying on my family. Apparently, his companion rents a small flat in Shepherd's Bush on the far side of Holland Park. Denis has a flat in Jarrow's Russian quarter, and that is where both of them can be found at the moment."

"Need you ask?" Artyom replied with anticipation.

They hastened through the remainder of St. James Park, along Constitutional Hill toward Grosvenor House.

"Zima," Simon said as his valet served dinner. "Captain Egorov and I are up for some mischief this evening. Is the trunk to hand?"

"Of course, my lord," Zima replied. "I will open it as soon as I've served your meal. It will be ready for you shortly."

The two men finished their dinner, deferring dessert until their return. In short order, they left the House through the servants' entrance, disguised as casual workers, and headed for a tram.

———•·•———

Simon and Artyom hopped off the tram and sauntered in the general direction of the premises rented in Shepherd's Bush.

Under a streetlamp, Simon glanced at his wristwatch. "It's almost nine o'clock," he said. "All good workers should be abed by now. Our destination should be just along this street."

They walked slowly past the address Simon had scratched onto a piece of scrap paper, discretely assessing the building and the neighbourhood.

"Let's see what the back gardens look like, shall we?" Artyom said. "We might find a less visible access."

Clouds scudded across the moon, clearing to light the darkened area. Small gardens backed the buildings. Although the properties had few trees, they did have tall shrubs that offered sufficient shelter. The two men scooted along a row of wintering rhododendrons.

"All dark," Simon said in a whisper. "Per the report." He twisted the knob of the building's back entrance. "Locked. Check the window over there. I think that's the flat we want." His finger guided Artyom to the right.

Artyom gave the window a shove. "Here," he said. Pushing the window wider, he climbed through and waited for Simon.

"Keep your torch beam low," Simon said. "Don't want to alert the neighbours."

"What are we looking for?"

"Anything that might connect Denis to his uncle," Simon said. "This is not Denis' regular abode, so we may not find anything."

Simon rummaged through a pile of papers. Toward the bottom, a small envelope bearing a Turkish postal mark slipped free of the pile. He set his torch on the seat of a chair and pulled the correspondence from of the envelope.

Denis,

I am delighted to hear that you have located Simon Temple. The surveillance report that you sent was very thorough. Well done, my boy. Now, you must look harder and find the Grand Duchess Maria in this Jarrow city. If you find her, you will find the crown jewels. Find the jewels and the revolutionaries will reward us all.

*I, too, have found a Temple. His name is Richard.
While I keep an eye on the Russian gold given to
the Turks, I will woo him until he confirms that the
Grand Duchess is in England with the jewels. It is
just a matter of time. Then we shall have all we need.*

Don't lose heart, Nephew. A new Russia awaits us!

With affection, Uncle Ivan

Simon stuffed the missive into the envelope and
pocketed it, calling softly to Artyom that it was time
to leave.

———

"I'll call Mary tomorrow," Simon said on the tram
back to London.

"I presume we'll be paying young Vasiliev a visit this
weekend?" Artyom said.

"Indeed," Simon replied. "I'll speak with someone
at Scotland Yard tomorrow and make appropriate
arrangements."

CHAPTER 67

On Thursday afternoon the week before Christmas 1919, Ann found Mary in Charles' study.

"Wrapping gifts, are you," Ann said, startling Mary from her revery.

"Mother Ann, your home! Is it that time already?" Mary said. "The days seem to fly by since the children arrived." Mary stood back and admired the stack of small, wrapped gifts. "These gifts are from me. The children have planned an industrious morning on Saturday, during which we'll wrap gifts for the staff who see to them, and they'll decorate a small tree for the nursery."

"Motherhood suits you," Ann said affectionately. "I enjoyed my time with Simon and Richard when they were small." She toyed with a letter opener on Charles' desk. "The servants will be decorating the Hall tree on Christmas eve. The children are welcome to help, too." She hesitated, setting the opener on the blotter. "I've been thinking about inviting the Winton family to join us. What do you think?"

"To decorate the tree?" Mary asked, "or for Christmas dinner?"

"I suspect they already have plans for Christmas

dinner," Ann said, "but I would welcome their company. If they decline, perhaps they'd join us for the tree decorating."

"Why don't I send them an invitation?" Mary said, beaming mischievously. "A letter from little Charlotte's godmother can't go amiss."

"Certainly!" Ann said. "I was hoping you'd suggest that. They might feel an invitation from me too imposing."

Ann watched as Mary tidied the assortment of ribbons and gift wrap and placed the packages into a basket. "I'll take these up to my chamber," she said happily, "and hide them away from prying eyes."

"By the way," Ann said, removing the pin from her hat as she followed Mary toward the staircase, "I spoke with the director today. The number of patients affected by flu has been lessening worldwide, but we were cautioned not to become too casual about transmission. If this virus is to be eliminated, we must continue to wash our hands often, sterilize everything that comes into contact with infected persons, and wear masks wherever and whenever necessary. I, for one, would be delighted to never have that flu again, and I certainly wouldn't wish it on anyone else!"

"We should remind the staff to take care," Mary replied, "this damp, dreary weather seems the perfect time for sickness to flourish."

"The last thing we want is another Christmas lost to illness," Ann said, starting up the stairs. "It's inevitable that someone will be ill. However, if care is taken, perhaps we can control the spread and the degree of illness."

"Pardon me, Lady Mary," Nanny said, appearing at

the bottom of the stairs. "The children are home from school. Master Willy is complaining of a sore throat, and he seems to have a fever as well. He's asking for you."

"Here we go," Mary said, rolling her eyes as she handed the basket to Ann. "I'm coming."

CHAPTER 68

18 December 1919

Comrade Nitikin, if you are able, I invite you to join me at my residence, tomorrow evening 21:00.

R.T.

Vilen Nitikin read and reread the note that had been slipped under the door of his hotel room, feeling the thrill of the unexpected invitation. He had dared to hope that, before he was ordered to return to Moscow, he would have an opportunity to meet with Comrade Temple. He knew of no one in Ancyra who would send him such a note, other than the ginger-haired man who had the ear of General Kemal. Although close in age, he was in awe of Temple and felt honoured to receive such a personal invitation.

The following evening, fearing the wrath of his superiors, Nitikin donned dark clothing and followed the shadows that led from his accommodation to the address Richard had neatly pencilled at the foot of the note. Checking frequently over his shoulder to ensure he was not being followed, he stepped cautiously to the door, scanned the shadows, and rapped lightly.

The door swung open a moment later to reveal a tall, dark figure lit from behind by the dim light of a ceiling lamp. Richard peered into the shadows behind Nitikin as he beckoned his guest to enter quickly.

"This way," Richard said in French, leading Nitikin into the sitting room. He opened the door and ushered Nitikin into a spacious room lined with receiving benches and ample silk cushions.

Richard invited his guest to select a spot near a low table, already set with cups and dishes. "My wife and mother-in-law are in another part of the house. We won't be disturbed." He slid a brocade armchair toward the low table. "Welcome to my humble home." Richard's smile was genuine as he reached for Nitikin's coat.

"Thank you, Mr. Temple," Nitikin said, returning the smile shyly. "I was—am—honoured to receive your invitation. I admire so much the work you do with General Kemal." His pleasure and gratitude danced in his dark green eyes.

"Make yourself comfortable," Richard said. "I'll hang your jacket in the hallway and bring refreshments."

Reappearing a few minutes later, Richard deposited a tray of small savouries on the table, passed a chilled beer to Nitikin, and placed a cup of apple tea near the armchair.

"This was hard to find," Richard said, stroking the brocade arm of his chair. "I found two of them in a small shop one day as I walked along a side street. The proprietor was only too happy to sell them to me cheap. They took up too much space, he said." Richard shrugged. "Many folks in Turkey prefer to sit on cushions. Are you comfortable on the bench? I can bring the other chair if you prefer."

"No, no," Nitikin said. "I am quite comfortable."

Richard gestured toward the beer and the tray of savouries. "Please eat, drink. The savouries are delicious. My mother-in-law made them." He grinned broadly as he added confidentially, "I think she likes me."

Nitikin was delighted to find his host both charming and generous. Some of the savouries were pleasantly spiced, leaving a lingering aftertaste that married smoothly with the chilled beer.

The beer warmed in Nitikin's belly, and he felt himself relax in Richard's amicable company, reminiscing about Moscow and the old Russia, before the execution of the tsar's family.

"It's a shame," he said, "that the entire family had to be executed." His lips twisted in thought as he shook his head. "Living in opulence while the rest of the country starved was not acceptable. However, I don't understand why they all had to die. Surely, they could have been disciplined another way. At one point, I heard rumours that they were to be expelled from Russia. Why that did not happen, I don't know." He shrugged as he took another swig of his beer and shook the remains in the bottom of the bottle. "Hatred and fear can make people do horrid things."

Richard rose, collecting the bottle and cup. "Another?" he said.

"*Oui, merci,*" Nitikin said with a nod. *This room is peaceful,* he thought. *I probably should be on my guard, but I don't feel the need. I haven't felt at peace since before I left Russia.*

<hr />

Richard snagged another chilled beer and refreshed his cup of tea. Returning to his chair, he contemplated the next topic of discussion. He needed to learn more about Vasiliev and what his relationship was with Makarov.

"How do you find working with your two comrades?" he asked, handing his guest the fresh beer. "Comrade Vasiliev strikes me as a grumpy individual."

Nitikin, who had just taken a sip of beer, gagged in response and sputtered his ale down the front of his shirt. He dabbed a napkin briskly along the spatter to keep it from soaking in.

When he finally composed himself, he was chuckling. "Grumpy is a good word to describe the colonel! I have never met a more miserable, greedy, and determined man. He reminds me of a perturbed toad who's been disturbed from his mud bath." It was Richard's turn to choke on a mouthful of tea as Nitikin shook his head and cautiously took another sip. "He is fixated on his rule of Russia."

"*His rule* of Russia?" Richard repeated. "I thought

the whole purpose of communism was to operate as one and not have a ruler. Otherwise, I'd suggest that the Tsar died in vain." He raised a questioning brow as Nitikin casually stretched his legs and crossed his ankles. *Good, he feels comfortable with me.*

"Hmph, I would never suggest that Vasiliev is a communist," Nitikin said. "It is merely a façade. He wants everyone to think he is a friend, but his true desire is to rule Russia as the tsar did."

Richard blinked hard and sat erect, planting both feet on the floor.

"He truly wants to rule Russia? Like the tsar?" Richard said in disbelief. "I thought I was the only one who believed that of him!"

"Exactly so," Nitikin said, aping Richard's posture. "From the first day I was assigned to work with him, I have listened to him plotting to gain control of Russia for Germany. If they are successful, his parents will rule Germany. In turn, with their power and support, they will ensure he rules Russia. He thinks I can't hear his discussions with Makarov when they whisper in the colonel's office, but I have exceptional hearing."

He grinned knowingly before raising the slender bottle to his lips. "They plot all the time. He has promised Makarov to be his right-hand-man! Personally, I think the entire plan sounds fantastical and treacherous." He shook his head, as if incredulous to be speaking the words aloud. "It is just a matter of time now before the revolutionaries in Moscow decide how to interpret, then intercept, Vasiliev's intentions.

"He was sent here to monitor the new Turkish government's use of Russian gold and armaments—which he does." Nitikin nodded his head, confirming Vasiliev's efforts. "However, I am convinced that he is plotting to take over the remnants of the Ottoman Empire and strip the country of all its gold and treasure, which he will use to fund his business in Russia."

Nitikin's remarks surprised Richard; he had not expected him to be so candid. He snatched his glass of tea and took a long draft. *I wonder what he knows about the gold and armaments.*

"Why are you telling *me* this?"

"Because I hate them and their potentate ideas," Nitikin replied venomously. "They are dangerous men. They expect Russians will be grateful for Vasiliev's leadership and that Turks will welcome a change in governance. Vasiliev thinks of none other than himself."

He rose from his chair and looked down upon Richard, fists on hips, the beer bottle dangling from his fingers. "Well … perhaps a little of his parents, too; otherwise, he would not care about their rule of Germany and his relationship with them."

He sipped his beer and set it carefully on the table. "Vasiliev is a wicked villain, make no mistake. I see how you work closely with the general to help the Turkic people. General Kemal is a man of good intention, and he respects your opinions. One day, I, too, will work with a man worthy of my respect. A man who will appreciate my contribution to a noble cause. But first, I must complete my assignment here."

"Ah, yes, your assignment," Richard said, straightening. "I understand that you are also investigating a shortage of gold and armaments."

"You know?" Nitikin's expression of surprise quickly turned to admiration. "Of course you do!" He lifted the beer and viewed the bottle as if contemplating whether to drink it. "I must provide evidence to my superiors of Vasiliev's deception, so that he can be punished. Makarov, too."

"You were sent here to spy on them?" Richard said, lifting the tray of savouries toward his guest.

Nitikin resumed his seat, his lips quirked as if to acknowledge Richard's conclusion, which he confirmed with a nod as he selected a small pastry. "My superiors have always had suspicions. I was assigned to find facts to support them." He popped the pastry into his mouth and chewed slowly, grinning like Lewis Carroll's Cheshire Cat as he savoured the flavours.

"Ah!" Richard said, "and have you found the evidence that you need?"

"I'm getting close," the young officer replied with a chuckle. "On the days you take them from the office, I have time to poke through their records. Just recently, I found another hiding place—loose floorboards under Vasiliev's bed. When I heard them coming down the hall, I had to scramble so as not to be caught. The next time you take them out, I will return."

"Then I shall do my best to take them soon and keep them out all day!" Richard said with a chortle.

"You seem to bring out the worst in him," Nitikin said. "He believes that you are deliberately keeping him from attending meetings with the council of generals."

"I am!" Richard said.

"I believe that you and I are inadvertently working together!" Nitikin leaned toward Richard.

"I believe we are," Richard replied. He regarded the pale-haired officer who stood slightly shorter than himself, intrigued by his guest's observation and forthright disclosure.

"Another beer," Richard said, rising without waiting for an answer. "Then, perhaps, you will tell me how Vasiliev and Makarov came to be working together."

"That is an easy answer," Nitikin said, following Richard to the kitchen, carrying soiled dishes. "Makarov was hired by Vasiliev's family to help him escape from a Russian prison. The Vasiliev family has promised him many things: wealth, status, power. He will do *anything* for them. Have you seen the knife he carries? It's very sharp. Finnish, if I recall. And he does not hesitate to use it, when necessary." He drew his finger knife-like across his throat.

CHAPTER 69

"This man, Simon Temple," Nitikin said, licking foam from his lip, "he is your brother, yes?"

Richard nodded slowly, wondering about the question.

"Then you must warn him to take care."

"Why?" Richard said, feeling a chill of dread creep up his spine.

"Vasiliev, he hates Simon Temple," Nitikin said, clearing his throat, "almost as much as I hate Vasiliev. He rants constantly about how your brother stole the Russian crown jewels from him. He even believes that your brother is married to a grand duchess. But that is crazy, is it not? The revolutionaries have all the crown jewels, and the entire Romanov family is dead … executed."

"I have heard similar claims," Richard said cautiously. "Do you really think Vasiliev is capable of harming my brother from here?"

"Oh, yes." Nitikin leaned forward, resting his elbows on his knees and easily dangling the beer bottle between them. "He has many eyes in England. That is where Simon Temples lives, yes?" In answer to Richard's nod, he continued. "Soon, some of his thugs will try to steal the son of Simon Temple, and—"

"Wait! You must have the wrong man. Simon has no children."

"Ah, but yes," Nitikin said with confidence. "He is the guardian of three orphans."

"Three—"

"Yes, three. The Spanish flu took their parents. They live with Simon Temple these many months now."

Richard was silent for several minutes, marvelling at this revelation. Finally, Nitikin continued the thread of his disclosure.

"Yes, these poor children. So young." He shook his head. "And then I heard Vasiliev order more recently that his nephew should take the wife of Simon Temple from their home in London!"

"What?" Richard shook his head, trying to make sense of his guest's revelations. "Kidnap Mary? That's remarkable!"

"Yes, it is, Mr. Temple," Nitikin said. "Your brother and his family are in grave danger, sir. Vasiliev wants Russia's crown jewels, and he will not stop until he has them."

"Call me Richard, please." He took a sip of tea. "Surely that confirms how dastardly Vasiliev is."

"I am happy that you have agreed to work with me, R-Richard," Nitikin said. "Together we will save Mother Russia from tyrannical rule, and hopefully keep your brother's family safe, too. Yes?"

"Exactly so," Richard said, making a mental note to write to his brother before retiring for the night.

CHAPTER 70

19 December 1919

Dear Brother,

It has been some time since we last spoke, and neither my rude behaviour nor my abrupt departure is anything of which I am proud.

At some point in the future, I hope to apologize in person. In the meantime, I write with some urgent and concerning news.

When I left England, my goal was to reach Turkey. Again, I'll explain later. Here I found employment in General Kemal's office. It's an honour for me to work with such a man of vision. You will find it amusing to know that my French has improved greatly, and I have mastered Russian and Turkish! Once again, more later.

My urgent news is this: as part of my responsibilities to General Kemal, I am to 'manage' Colonel

Ivan Vasiliev and his colleague Corporal Rada Makarov. They have a third, younger colleague— Vilen Nitikin—who works with them as a sort of administrative clerk. Nitikin has been assigned by the Bolsheviks to reveal Vasiliev's true intentions. I trust him.

After a lengthy conversation with Nitikin this evening I have learned several things, the first of which is that you are now a guardian of three young children.

Nitikin also advised that an attempted kidnapping of the eldest—a boy?—has been planned and both Jarrow Hall and Grosvenor House are being watched. Mary may also be at risk. The purpose: Vasiliev wants the Russian crown jewels and believes you have them. Nitikin suspects that, if you're not forthcoming about the jewels, Mary will be the one kidnapped; possibly sold to the Bolsheviks for some sort of reward. I appreciate that from your perspective, this is all hearsay, but you're not here spending days on end with that vile man. He's quite capable, even from here!

Vasiliev has been sniffing around me like an old dog, trying to have me disclose crucial information about Kemal, you, Mary, and the jewels. On Kemal's direction, I am leading Vasiliev on a merry chase, but I can do little to help you from here, other than to warn you.

On orders from his superiors, Nitikin is to discover information that will prove Vasiliev's intent to usurp the revolutionaries and take control of Russia. Talk about grandiose scheming! Vasiliev also intends to take control of Turkey and deplete its resources to support Russia! Although how, I can't imagine. Where would he get the manpower? Unless this is where his wealthy, scheming parents come into it. Nitikin suggested that they are backing him.

If I can help in any way from this end, please let me know. In the meantime, brother, take care of yourself and your (our) family.

Please extend my apologies to Mother and Father, and to Mary. Especially to Mary. I took her money and the family silver to fund my journey. I will repay Mary. The family silver, I fear, is long gone.

Your loving brother,
Richard

CHAPTER 71

On Friday morning, Mary climbed the stairs to the nursery rather than head straight down for breakfast.

"Good morning, Nanny," she said at the doorway to the boys' room. Nanny rose and greeted her, revealing John's empty bed.

"Where's John?"

"I expect he's in the water closet, my lady," Nanny replied. "He's dressed and finished his breakfast." She stacked soiled dishes and set them on a tray for the maid to return to the kitchen. "He found it quite convenient to sleep and eat in the playroom. 'A matter of efficiency' he told me."

"I wouldn't be surprised if he asks to make it permanent," Mary said, appreciating his cleverness.

Willy coughed and moaned quietly. She advanced into the sleeping quarters, transforming from mother into nurse in an instant. Knuckles on forehead feeling for heat, fingers on glands checking for swelling under his jaw, and finally resting on his wrist, noting his pulse.

"Is the window open?"

Nanny nodded.

"Good. Let's open the curtains a crack. Not too much—just enough to give him a sense of the hour.

Continue the treatment we discussed last evening. He should be up and around in a day or two. I'm sure it's just a cold." She leaned down and kissed the restless child. "Where's Elvie?"

"She's still abed, my lady. Her symptoms are similar to Master Willy's."

"I'll check on her now, then John—when he appears."

Mary marched along the corridor to Elvie's room and, after a thorough examination, agreed with Nanny's diagnosis. She returned to Willy's room to advise Nanny to administer the same treatment to both children, suggesting that Elvie be moved to John's bed, and that John sleep in Elvie's room. A moment later, she found John in the playroom, pulling on his coat.

"Off to school?" she asked as she checked him for fever, swollen glands, and irregular pulse.

"Yes, Mother," he said, surrendering to her prodding. "If I'm still well at the end of the day, may I ride my pony? I think both of us could use some fresh air and exercise." He peered at Mary as she straightened. "The school closes today for the holidays."

"If Nanny agrees that you're well enough," she said, narrowing her eyes in thought, "then alright. Dress warmly and stay in the meadow where Mr. Stone and a guard can see you. And return to the stable before it's completely dark."

"Yes, Mother. Thank you, Mother!" He plopped his cap on his head and turned his cheek for a kiss. "I'd better be off. Michael is waiting in the drive."

CHAPTER 72

John was excited to have free time to himself. On the way home, he chattered happily with Michael about his plans during the holiday. When the car crunched to a stop in front of the house, John jumped out before Michael could set the brake.

"You'd better hurry," John said. "Mother will be waiting for you at the hospital."

He thanked Michael for the lift and raced up to his room, where he found Willy and Elvie sleeping. *Nanny must be downstairs*, he thought as he stripped off his school clothes and changed into his riding gear.

"Cook, may I have a carrot for my pony?" he asked a few minutes later.

"Here you are, Master John," she said, taking a carrot from the basket of vegetables the undercook was chopping. "Enjoy your ride."

John nodded his thanks as he breezed toward the boot room. He donned his riding jacket, stuffing the carrot in his pocket, and pulled on his boots. Banging the back door behind him, he continued his race to the stables.

Mary noticed John crossing the yard as Micheal drew the motor to a stop at the front of the Hall once again.

"Michael, please ask Peter to saddle my horse. I'll check on Elvie and Willy and be right down. If I'm quick, perhaps I can catch up with John."

She hastened to the nursery and spoke with the nanny.

"The young ones are fine," Nanny said with assurance. "Their symptoms haven't worsened. They're napping at the moment. Master John asked if he could ride and, since he had no symptoms, I told him he could."

"Hopefully, I can change my clothes and catch up with him," Mary said, scurrying off to her chamber.

Horses and ponies nickered a welcome, craning their necks over the gates, smacking their lips for a taste of the carrot John had brought for Horatio. The grey gelding pawed the straw when John opened the gate to his pen and pushed his nose into John's pocket.

"Hang on mate," John said, giggling at the pony's antics. He pushed the beast aside, withdrawing the carrot.

While Horatio munched on his treat, John brushed and saddled him and led him into the yard. He greeted Peter Stone and asked him to check that he had saddled Horatio correctly, then waved to the guard who had followed him to the stable.

"Mind you stay in the meadow where we can see you," Peter said.

"I will, sir," John replied, mounting the pony. He

urged Horatio along the worn path toward the meadow.

Horatio's trot increased as they neared their destination. When John relaxed the reins, the pony broke into a gallop. John giggled, feeling free and one with the pony.

As Horatio slowed to a walk, John heard a noise in the brush. He reined Horatio to a stop, tied him loosely to a post, and slid under the fence rail to investigate. He followed the panicked cries of what he thought to be a wounded animal.

"I can't see. It's getting dark," he said, talking to the creature. "I'll have to return for a lantern. Stay quiet. I'll find you."

He turned away from the bush and bent to slide under the fence rail. Instead, he was lifted by powerful arms that turned him back toward the bush.

CHAPTER 73

"Help, help!" John screamed loudly, kicking hard against his attacker, twisting to free himself. Trying to remember all the defence moves that the guards had taught Lady Mary. Glad that he had insisted on participating. Glad that he had paid attention. "Help! Help!"

Horatio joined the ruckus, rearing against the fence post. When the reins broke free, he galloped toward the stable, bucking and screaming. He plodded into the yard, yelling and snorting as if calling for help.

"Master John?" Peter called out from one of the stalls, then poked his head out. Horatio nickered, stamping his foot. "Master John?"

Peter dropped the rake from his hand and snagged the pony's rein. As he tethered Horatio to a rail, he hollered for the security guard. "Where's the lad?" Peter said. "You're supposed to be watchin' out for him."

"I was, er, I am," the guard said. "I've been waiting by the corral. I was just about to walk toward the meadow to meet him. It's getting too dark to see him from this distance."

"Well, something's happened," Peter said. "His pony's back without him and seems upset."

"Right, round up the lads, and I'll grab lanterns," the guard said. "We need to find the boy … now!"

John continued to struggle against his assailant, screaming for help until a large hand clamped over his mouth.

"Shut up, you," the man said angrily.

John promptly bit hard into an available finger, grinding his teeth as the guard had instructed, tasting a peculiar mixture of blood, metal, and cabbage. The man screamed, dropping John to the ground.

John scrambled on hands and feet back toward the fence.

Mary strode with purpose toward the stables as she buttoned her jacket and tied a blue and cream paisley kerchief under her chin. She found her saddled horse tied to a post near Horatio but saw no one. The stable was quiet. She called out to John, Peter Stone, and the guards. No one answered. Panic rose in her gorge; her heart began to pound. *Where is everyone?*

Rounding the stable, she glimpsed flickering lamplight on the far side of the meadow and began to run, stopping abruptly. A moment later, her horse raced across the meadow. As she neared the movement of light and shadows, she called out. Silhouettes stopped and waited for her.

"Where's John?" What's happened?" she said as she approached Peter and the lead guard.

———

"Help! Help!" John shouted, calling again and again, seeing a flicker of light at the top of the meadow.

"Oh no you don't," the man said, grabbing John around the waist with one arm. "I'll be paid good money for you!" He struggled to restrain the boy with his uninjured hand. "Quit it will you, or I'll have to get mean!"

In defiance, John wriggled again.

"That's it!" the attacker shouted angrily, jabbing his foot sideways into the back of John's knees, forcing him to the ground.

John struggled against the rope being tied around his wrists, feeling prickly blades of wet, winter grass tickle at his nose. He raised his head and cried out again, receiving a hard smack across the side of his face for his efforts. Stunned, he ceased struggling.

———

"What was that?" Mary said aloud, still mounted. "John?" She jabbed her boot heels into the mare. The mare broke into a gallop. Mary squinted against the darkening sky, listening for clues above thundering hooves. She tugged on the reins as she neared the fence at the far end of the meadow. The mare stopped abruptly, blowing hard. *Too much noise*, Mary thought.

She dropped the reins and slid to the ground, patting the mare's neck. The mare stood motionless, still breathing heavily. Mary advanced toward the fence with stealth, listening.

———

The man pulled John to his feet and pushed him into the trees. John shook his head, trying to focus. *What am I supposed to do now? Oh yeah!* He fell to his knees, deliberately disturbing the dirt. The man stood him up again. He staggered into a young tree and broke the branches. Every step he took, he dragged his feet.

The man glanced over his shoulder. "Damned brat. Stand up and walk properly! They're closing on us." He pushed John forward, deeper into the trees.

John could not understand some the words, but he recognized the accent and the intent.

"You're Russian," he said, hoping his voice was loud enough to be heard as he resisted the shove. "You won't get away with this, you know. They'll catch you. You're going to jail."

"I said *shut up!*" the man said, turning again to glance over his shoulder.

Menacing clouds roiled over the meadow toward the forest, cutting off the light of a slivered moon. In the moment of quiet before the man shoved him again, John thought he heard a twig snap.

"What do you plan to do to me?" John said angrily,

raising his voice. Another shove. He screamed as he tripped over a tree root and fell to the forest floor. Damp soil pasted against his cheek.

CHAPTER 74

Acry, then the rustling of branches. Mary held her breath and listened.

Voices! I hear voices, Mary thought, as she leaned into a tree. *One of them is John!* With slow deliberate steps, she crept toward them. *The other is Russian!*

A bright lantern light slashed across the bush. Enough light for Mary to momentarily see two figures, one large and one small, several yards ahead of her. She dropped to a squat.

"Come on, brat!" the man said angrily. "If they catch me, you're dead. Now get up and walk."

Another slash of light. Men's voices calling out. *Good,* she thought, *make noise and keep him distracted.* She ran along the path, bent low.

A third flash of light. Mere yards separated her from the boy. She fixated on the spot where last she had seen the man and charged. With the fourth pass of the lantern, she leapt, knocking the man off balance. He fell. They rolled. John screamed.

"Run, John, run," Mary said, struggling with the man. "Peter! Over here—"

A gloved hand covered Mary's mouth. Strong hands

pulled her to her feet. "Leave the boy," an English voice said. "We have something better. Come on! Let's go."

Mary deadened her weight, dragging her toes through the soft turf. Strong hands on each arm dragged her, forcing her to run. The distance between them and John grew.

"*Mother!*"

Rescuing voices faded.

The doors of an enclosed box lorry creaked opened. Four hands pushed Mary into the back, and the doors slammed shut as her knees scraped against a cold metal floor, tearing a knee of her trousers. The motor revved, and the ungainly vehicle jumped into action, barreling along a road.

Mary struggled to a sitting position, angrily demanding who her captors were and what they intended.

"Master John," Peter said gravely, gently lifting the boy to his feet, dusting detritus from his face and clothing and releasing the rope. He rubbed John's wrists as if to remove the red chafing. "You alright?"

"I-I think so," John said, nodding his head, his eyes glued to the dark on the other side of the forest. "Lady Mar-, I mean Mother! Those men t-took her!"

"What men?" the lead guard said, bending to John's level.

"I don't know," John replied. "One was Russian for sure. He was trying to take me away, but when they grabbed M-mother, the other one said 'Leave the boy.

We have something better.'"

John began running toward the spot he had last seen Mary. "Mother! We're coming. Mother!"

"Master John, you stay here with the stable lad," the guard said, grabbing the boy's arm to still him. "Brian, walk Master John back to the house. Tell Tompkins what's happened. We need the police, and Lord Simon needs to be informed as soon as he's off the train."

"Yes, sir," the stable lad said.

"Let's take Mother's horse," John said, determined. Peter hoisted him up behind Brian and smacked the horse's rump.

"Hang on, Master John," Brian shouted when the mare broke into a gallop.

Satisfied that John was safe and that Brian would deliver the messages, the lead guard turned to the others. "Spread out. Move!" he said, shouting. "Lady Mary's been snatched!"

By the time the police arrived, the stable hands and guards had swept the forest for clues. Muddy footprints had led them to the location where the large vehicle had been parked.

"Lady Mary's scarf!" Peter said, bending to retrieve it from the muddy road. "And tire tracks too!"

During a canvass of houses further along the road, the police learned that the vehicle was a light blue box lorry with a grocer's logo on the side.

PART THREE

CHAPTER 75

As the lorry rumbled over worn, dirt roads, Mary struggled to sit up. Rough hands pulled her arms behind her and coiled a length of coarse rope around her wrists.

"What do you want?" she said, summoning ire to quell her fear. "Who are you?"

"Too many questions, pretty lady," the English man said as he inserted a cloth into her mouth.

Mary struggled against him, trying to spit it out, but he pulled it secure and tied it tight. Fibers tickled the inside of her mouth, drawing her saliva. She fought the urge to vomit, inhaling deeply through her nose.

The lorry swerved to the left. Mary braced herself to remain upright. Through the rear window, she glimpsed the slivered moon and noted the direction they travelled. *Information is useless without someone to share,* she thought. *At least John is safe.*

She struggled again, testing the rope and finding the knot too tight for her to loosen.

"Keep squirmin' like that, an' it'll only get tighter, sweetheart," the English man said.

Mary stiffened, then surrendered.

"That's more like it," the English man said. "Just sit quiet and relax. We're almost there." He leaned forward into the cab. "Denis, how much farther?"

"Almost there, Sarge," Denis replied. "Another two or three minutes." As he spoke, Denis eased his pressure on the accelerator, shifted gears, and turned into a treed driveway on the right. He advanced to the side of a derelict farmhouse, stopped, and turned off the engine.

"You wait here with the woman," Sarge said. "I'll make sure all is clear."

A few minutes of rough handling later, Mary found herself standing in the centre of an antiquated farm kitchen. While it clearly needed a thorough cleaning, evidence suggested that it had been used recently. Dirty dishes covered the counter and filled a sink. Discarded furniture covers sat in a pile at the end of a sofa.

Firm hands turned her around and forced her to sit on a wooden chair from which old, green paint flecked to the floor. The floorboard creaked as the men moved about the space. Sarge filled a kettle and put it on the stovetop to boil.

"I could use some tea," Sarge said, rubbing his hands together for warmth. "Cold work sitting in that lorry, waiting on you." He scowled at Denis.

"Tea, lady?" Sarge said amicably.

Mary's narrowed eyes shot angry death darts at Sarge.

"I'll remove the gag, if you behave," he said, untying the knot. "If you step out of line, it goes back on. Got it?" Mary nodded. "For now, the rope stays put."

Mary shook her head free of the gag. She turned left and right, rubbing the edges of her mouth on her sleeves. She ran her tongue around the inside of her mouth, scraping bits of fiber into a ball. She spat the wad free, watching it land unintentionally next to Sarge's muddy boot.

"Be nice, now," Sarge said, his voice rumbling with warning.

Simon, Charles, and Artyom stepped off the Friday evening train and strode through the station. Zima and the undercook rounded the corner of the building, hastily pushing a cart of hand luggage. Michael waved a greeting and opened the car doors, then helped stuff the luggage in the boot. As he drove them toward Jarrow Hall, he explained the recent kidnapping.

"Drop me at the cottage," Artyom said, the tick under his eye twitching. "I'll change my clothes and come to help."

Simon and Charles exited the vehicle as it coasted to a stop at the front of the Hall. Both men hopped out and jogged toward the great doors, while Michael drove the staff and luggage to the back yard.

"Father, please remain here with Mother and the children," Simon said racing up the stairs. "I need to be with the search party."

Zima was already laying out clothes for Simon. "My lord," he said, "may I leave you? I will change and come, too. I must help."

"Yes, Zima. Hurry!"

Simon was greeted by an inspector and the chief of police. Zima, Artyom, and Varvara arrived moments later. Together, they received the latest report on the hostage taking.

"It seems, Lord Simon, that the clearest clue we have is the vehicle," the inspector said. "The colour and the name of the grocer have been distributed to all officers, and we are conducting a systematic search of the area at the moment."

"Given the muddy tire marks found at the scene and the tread left on Lady Mary's scarf," the police chief said, "the delivery lorry has likely been stored outside the city. We traced the muddy tracks as far as we could. Now we need to be more methodical. We have lads checking surrounding farmlands too."

"What about the grocer?" Simon said. "Do you know which one?"

"Yes," the police chief said. "Regrettably, it belongs to *Cook & Baker*. But … it was reported stolen yesterday morning."

"What about a description?" Artyom said. "Has Master John been asked for a statement?"

"Yes, sir," the police chief said. "Our detectives are on their way now." He nodded toward a young man and a young woman, jerking his head toward the house. In answer to Simon's questioning gaze, he continued. "We were reminded by your guards that you have a woman on staff, so we've requested one of our woman constables be present because of the children."

"I understand," Simon replied, watching the pair stride toward the kitchen door. "My parents will also be available, if needed. We have two more pieces of information to be considered." Simon showed them the letter sent by Vasiliev to his nephew, Denis. He also reported that he had intended to investigate the nephew's Jarrow premises.

"Excellent!" the lead inspector replied. "I'll send a couple of lads there now." He motioned for two more detectives to come forward and directed them to the property. "If you see anyone at that address, don't go in; call for back up."

For the next twenty minutes, those present discussed next moves and made plans. The radio receiver squawked regularly as cars called in negative findings and more streets were struck from the list.

"Sir," the radio operator called to the police chief, "it's the detectives sent to the culprit's premises. No one is there. Do you have a response?"

"Yes," the inspector replied. "Tell them to enter and conduct a thorough search. If they need help, ensure they have it."

———

Throughout the night, the search increased in area. By pre-dawn, officers were rolling along bumpy country roads.

Half an hour later, as the morning sun broke through cloud cover, a small glint in a bush caught the eye of one of the Hall guards, formerly an able seaman with the Royal Navy.

"Mac, stop," he said, swatting at the driver's arm. "Pull over there." He pointed to an overhang of plane trees at the edge of a furrowed field. "I'm used to looking for glints of metal in a rough sea. This was almost too easy." He explained what he saw and the two vacated the vehicle.

"Stay down," Mac said in a whisper.

The two men crept toward the bushes where the Hall guard had pointed. As they approached, the blue of the vehicle became more evident. Then, they spied the name *Cook & Baker* painted on its side.

"She must be in there," Mac said quietly. "You return to the car and radio our location, and be quiet about it. I don't want any trouble." As he spoke, he reached for his sidearm.

The Hall guard returned a few minutes later, reporting that help was enroute and they were to take no action, merely watch. They waited patiently for another half hour, when other vehicles began crawling into cover behind them.

CHAPTER 76

Mary lay curled on the horsehair sofa. A beam of sunlight broke through a slit in the curtains, aimed at her closed eyes. She tugged a ratty blanket over her face to block it, instantly recalling her circumstance. She lowered the blanket and cracked her eye, scanning the room. Each man sprawled in an overstuffed armchair, snoring quietly.

Slowly, Mary pushed away the blanket and eased her feet to the floor. The men had been kind, untying her hands so she could eat a biscuit and drink tea with them. However, as soon as the tea and biscuit had been consumed, they retied her hands with one end of the rope, then fastened the other end to the leg of the sofa. She rolled her eyes, realizing their folly. Try as she might, though, she could not loosen the knots tied by Sarge.

Mary inched toward the leg of the sofa and reached for the other end of the rope. Finding it looser, she worked it free. Rejuvenated, she tried the end around her wrists once more, forcing the loosened end through the knots. It worked. Moments later, her hands were free. She rubbed them briskly, wondering what to do next.

She knew she should leave right then. The keys to

the van were sitting on the kitchen table where they had been placed hours before, but her ire rose again, willing her to use the rope to her advantage.

Silently, she slid between the two armchairs, ran one end of the rope under the chair leg, and fastened it around Sarge's ankle. Her heart pounded as she ran the other end under the chair supporting Denis and tied it around the young man's ankle. Satisfied with her work, she backed away toward the kitchen.

Sarge snorted. Mary froze. Sarge murmured something undiscernible, rolled his cheek onto the chair's arm, and settled.

Mary tiptoed toward the kitchen table and carefully lifted the key. Safely to the door, she turned the knob and instantly realized the one thing she had failed to notice when they had arrived the previous evening, simply because Sarge had opened the door before she and Denis had entered. The door hinges squealed ... loudly. She froze again.

Sarge snorted again and jolted upright, eyes focussed on the sofa where Mary no longer sat.

"What the—!" He jumped to his feet and promptly fell face-first onto an old rug that covered the plank flooring. A cloud of dust rose, then promptly settled over him. At the same time, his leg jerked, tugging the rope that bound his ankle to Denis.

Denis jumped to his feet, fists at the ready. "Wh-what's happening?" The rope around his ankle pulled tight against Sarge's leg. Sarge yelped. In an instant, Denis found himself prone on the floor next to Sarge.

The men coughed and sneezed amid the flying dust as they struggled to untangle their feet.

Mary threw the door wide and ran for the lorry. She jumped inside and cranked the engine. It groaned and quit. She tried again. No response.

Seeing her captors tripping toward the kitchen door, she jumped from the vehicle and ran toward the road, hoping to find a passing auto. Blinded as she was with her dilemma, she saw nothing as she rounded the corner.

"Sparrow!" Simon said, his voice low. He grabbed her arm and pulled her toward him.

Mary crouched next to him, panting with fear, heart pounding. "They're right behind me!" she hissed.

Through the shrubs, Mary watched as officers circled her captors and secured them. Prickling with anger, she stormed toward Denis and Sarge.

"You harmed my son!" she screamed at the two men. Her arm coiled. "How dare you threaten my family." Her palm connected with Denis' cheek, the force spinning his face over his shoulder.

"And you!" She coiled her arm again, readying for a second strike.

Artyom's hand wrapped gently around her wrist. The other turned her to him. "Not now, Mary," he said, whispering in her ear. The twitch under his eye pulsed rapidly. He gave her a quick hug and turned her toward Simon.

Simon led Mary to the opposite side of the road, now

cordoned off by police. Together, they watched as Sarge and Denis, neither of whom offered much resistance, were guided away from the house.

"What will happen to them?" Mary said, seeing them each placed in a separate motor and driven away.

"They'll be taken in for questioning, then put in cells," Simon replied. "The police will want statements from you and John, then those two will be charged with kidnapping."

"Who are they, exactly?" Mary said, trying to grasp all that had happened since Michael drove her home the previous evening.

"The Russian one is Vasiliev's nephew, Denis," Simon said. "I told you about him."

Mary nodded.

"And I suspect the other is merely a hired thug."

"Sarge," Mary said matter-of-factly. "Denis called him 'Sarge'.

"We're done here," Artyom said, approaching them. "The Yard will take over now. It appears that Denis is not cut out to be his uncle's henchman. He's quite prepared to talk and cut a deal to avoid time in prison."

"Mary!" Varvara said, springing from a police vehicle.

"Varvara!" Mary said with surprise. "Where have you come from?"

"They made me wait in the auto," Varvara said. "I came to help rescue you." She cast about her, giggling. "It appears, however, that I'm not required. You have rescued yourself!" She hugged Mary warmly and wrapped a blanket over her shoulders.

"May we go home for now?" Mary said, once the motor cars began to depart. "I need to kiss my son. Then … I need a bath. I have slept the night with spiders!"

CHAPTER 77

"Mother!" John said, racing across the gravel drive when the auto parked at the front of the Hall.

"John!" Mary said, opening the door herself. She pulled him into a tight embrace and vigorously kissed his cheeks. "My dear boy, are you alright? Did they hurt you?" She pushed him away and examined the scrapes on his face and wrists.

John giggled. "Mother, I'm fine. Really! You're the one they took away. Are you alright?" He eyed her head to toe. "Your trousers are torn, and your knee is bleeding!"

"It's nothing," Mary said. She stopped fussing and drank in the vision of the boy she almost lost. Tears cascaded down her cheeks unchecked. She hugged him again, fiercely. "And, yes," she said. "I'm alright now."

Mary recalled the chaos of the minutes that followed as the other children arrived for a reunion. Charles and Ann awaited their turn to welcome her. They asked after her well-being and slowly relinquished their claim on her to Simon when her fatigue became clear.

"Mrs. Z," Simon said, spying the woman nearby, "I'm certain Lady Mary would appreciate a hot bath."

"Immediately, my lord," Mrs. Zima replied, disappearing through the baize door into the servants' hall.

<hr />

"That puts an end to greedy endeavours for a while," Simon said later as Mary snuggled next to him on her chaise lounge.

"For now," Mary said sotto voce, "but it's not over, is it?" Elvie stood behind her, gently brushing her damp hair before the fire.

Simon kissed the tip of her ear. "No, not at all," he whispered in reply.

"Mmm," Elvie said, "I smell lilacs. I wish my hair smelled like lilacs."

Mary reached behind her and found Elvie's wrist. "You are doing such a fine job drying my hair, perhaps we can scent your hair as a reward."

"Oh, thank you, Mother," Elvie said with a sigh. She leaned forward and kissed Mary's ear.

"Here's your chocolate, Mother," Willy said. Accepting a cup from John, he marked his footsteps with great care as he delivered it to Mary.

Mary accepted the cup and sipped. "Delicious!"

A rap at the door announced the arrival of the nanny.

"Come along children," she said. "I'm sure Lady Mary could use the rest." She shooed the children out and closed the door quietly.

Mary sipped the chocolate and leaned her head against Simon, sighing with contentment.

"Alright?" Simon asked, snaking his arms around her waist.

"Mmph," Mary said, taking another sip. "Here, with my family, I'm safe." She twisted to look up at him. "I suppose I should have been afraid, but I wasn't. Being prepared for a situation makes it easier to stay clear-headed. Everything you've taught me over the years—"

"Shh," Simon said stroking her almost-dry hair. "You've always been capable."

"I know," she said, wriggling into a comfortable position and drinking the last of her chocolate. "What I'm trying to say is I didn't panic. I simply waited and, when I could, I responded to the opportunity."

She felt her husband's possessive squeeze in response. Then she closed her eyes, surrendering to her fatigue.

A short time later, Mary awoke with a start. The fire had died down, and she was alone. She stretched dreamily, then pulled the velvet cord to summon Mrs. Zima, determined to speak with Simon about the safety of her family. Her kidnappers may be in custody, but the real culprit—Vasiliev—remained at large.

———

Mary found her husband and his parents in the conservatory.

"Sparrow! Good morning!" Simon said, rising from his chair to greet her. "We're just having coffee and discussing family safety."

"Perfect!" Mary replied. "I was looking for you with that top of mind." She nodded to the footman when he offered coffee. "Mrs. Zima is sending a small tray for me, too, since I missed breakfast."

"It's here, my lady," a maid said, swinging wide of the fruit-ladened banana tree.

"What have you discussed so far?" Mary said, when they were alone.

"I think the obvious question is: what can we do to thwart whatever else Vasiliev has in mind?" Simon said. "I'm hoping that his nephew will be able to shed some light on the matter. I suspect that Denis Vasiliev is a puppet and merely does as he's directed."

"I think so, too," Mary said. "He seemed to defer to the other one—Sarge—for any action required, but Sarge doesn't have a connection to Vasiliev. I believe he's drawn by any incentive Vasiliev may have offered."

"Exactly what I was thinking," Simon said. "What we need to discover is whether Vasiliev has other thugs working for him in England, or have we captured the only two ... for now?"

"There's really nothing more we can do until we have answers," Charles said.

"Except," Ann said, "we might consider increasing the number of security guards."

"I believe we should too, Mother," Simon said, "I spoke with the inspector about that this morning. More guards will be engaged, and another inspector will be sent from London today: as a temporary measure."

"I have two other matters that I'd like you to think about," Mary said hesitantly.

"Go on," Simon said encouraging her.

"First," Mary said, "I think we should see about having proper tutors come to the Hall to teach the children here, where they'll be safe. The risk of them remaining in the grammar school is too great."

Her eyes found Simon's and she smiled demurely. "As you know, my siblings and I weren't sent away to school. I never thought about it, or whether we were safe. The Imperial Guards were just there. Besides, my parents ensured that we had the best of tutors, and I certainly don't feel that my education … mental or physical … was lacking."

"I agree, Sparrow," Simon said, laughing as he leaned toward her and took her hand. "I have some ideas about how best to accomplish that."

"I'm sure you do!"

"And the other matter?" Charles said before taking a bite of a tea biscuit.

"The other," Mary said, fidgeting her hands in her lap, "concerns all of the children, and …" She gazed at Simon, eyes pleading for understanding. "I-I want to … I want to adopt them!" She sighed as if she had been holding her breath.

"Mary—" Simon said.

"Adopt them!" Charles said, jumping to his feet.

"Father!" Simon said, looking from his wife to his father.

Mary rose slowly to her feet, head high. "Yes, adopt them." She stood by Simon, reaching for his hand. "When I ran after John and found him bound, face smashed in the dirt," she said, her lower lip quivering, "I couldn't bear it. What if they had taken him? Harmed him? The thought of never seeing him again … broke my heart." She sobbed, tears welling in her eyes and falling unchecked.

Simon handed his handkerchief to her and waited patiently as she mopped her face.

"I was grateful when they took me. Grateful that he was safe and alive." She struck the tears with the handkerchief. "I can't bear the thought of losing any of them again … to anyone. I want them!"

"Mary, dear," Ann said, rising from her chair to comfort her daughter-in-law.

"Listen, Father," Simon said defensively. "I know you want a grandson to receive the hereditary titles, but that is the one thing that Mary and I are unwilling to satisfy. We have agreed that we will not curse any child with the possibility of the *royal disease* knowing full well what that entails."

"Hemophilia?" Charles blurted with surprise. "I hadn't given that possibility a thought! Now I understand."

Simon stood by Mary and wrapped an arm across her shoulders. "Yes, hemophilia. And we will adopt the children, titles or not. I agree with Mary. I can't imagine our lives without them."

Anticipating Charles' reaction, they steeled themselves for a vehement protest.

Charles shoved his hands in the pockets of his smoking jacket and regarded the three of them. He rocked on his heels and began to smile.

"Indeed!" Charles said, scratching his crown, an

expression of amazement overtaking his features. "Ever since wee Willy called me Grandfather, I've been flummoxed. I, too, can't imagine a home without them. Go ahead: start the process!"

"You're really willing to relinquish the hereditary titles?" Simon said.

"If it comes to that," Charles replied, abashed, when the others erupted in laughter. "The peerage can only pass to a legitimate heir. Therefore, those would pass to Richard's issue, should he have a son. Some of the other titles may remain with Simon's heirs, while others may well pass to Richard's. However, I believe that, if I present the argument to Georgie in a way that he is able to grant the passing of titles to Simon, he'll do what he can to ensure it happens. Passage of others may have to be approved by Cabinet; in which case, it will be up to Georgie to convince the prime minister, who will then have to convince Cabinet."

"Charles!" Ann said. "You really have given this thought!"

"Well, yes," Charles replied, his embarrassment fading. "But that was before the mention of the royal disease. I've had my doubts, but perhaps if we explain to the king the reasoning behind the matter, he will be more sympathetic: perhaps find a way to make an exception."

"Perhaps," Simon said. "For now, I suggest we wait to see what happens. It will be a long while yet before any transfers will occur, and anything can happen in the meantime."

CHAPTER 78

When Kemal arrived in Ancyra on December 27th, 1919, Richard did not hesitate to enlighten him about Vasiliev's invitation to betray his duty to Turkey, and of his recent evening with Nitikin.

"This is getting out of hand," Kemal said, smashing his fist into his desk. He jumped to his feet and marched to and fro across his office. "We must feed them intelligence that will keep them occupied elsewhere." He grinned ominously. "You tell me that the jewels he seeks were likely taken by the revolutionaries." He crossed his arms and tapped his lip in contemplation.

"I overheard my brother say something to that effect," Richard said with a nod.

"I'd like you to continue building on your relationship with Nitikin," Kemal said. "If he is here to keep an eye on Vasiliev, collaborate with him." He extracted his silver case from his pocket and shook loose a cigarette. "And give serious thought to the manner of Vasiliev's departure."

"I will, sir," Richard replied, sitting calmly in the guest chair. He closed his eyes for a moment and braced himself for the next topic with a deep sigh. "There's something else I need to tell you." He gazed at Kemal earnestly, hoping the general would understand.

Kemal nodded. "Out with it, man!"

"You'll recall my telling you that my brother, Simon, spent three years in Russia."

Kemal nodded.

"I need to tell the rest of that story now."

"Tell me," Kemal said, resuming his chair.

Richard took a deep breath, then told the general of Simon's assignment in Petrograd, how he had returned to England in August of 1918 with a grand duchess for a wife and that, although she had brought some jewels with her, they were family heirlooms, not state jewels. He also explained how Vasiliev's thugs have been threatening Simon's family.

"They are under constant surveillance according to Nitikin, and apparently Vasiliev intends to personally apply pressure on me. Nitikin was unable to speculate what that might be." His steel blue eyes met Kemal's. "Makarov said that Vasiliev had not ordered his attack on me. Now, I wonder."

"A direct threat!" Kemal said curtly and smacked his open hand on the desk.

"There's more," Richard said. "Nitikin suggested that I alert my brother." Richard leaned forward and braced his elbows on his knees. "I took the liberty of writing to my brother that night. I had to warn him."

"Of course you did," Kemal said. "Thank you for telling me." Kemal sat quietly for a few minutes, tugging his earlobe as he contemplated Richard's news. "I return to my original suggestion, Richard. Give serious consideration to the manner of Vasiliev's departure, and let's see if we can't reach a conclusion that is beneficial for both Turkey and your brother's family. Perhaps even for Russia."

"I will, sir," Richard said, heading toward the door.

"Thank you, my friend," Kemal said, rising to his feet when Richard reached for the knob to open the office door. "You have never been anything but loyal to me, and to Turkey. We owe you a debt of gratitude."

He placed a hand on Richard's shoulder, delaying him a moment longer. "Including that wayward general you told me about. I'm told by senior council members that he was easy to isolate and challenge. You may have noticed the council is one less."

Richard nodded.

"He has unceremoniously been returned to the sultan!"

CHAPTER 79

Simon reclined in the study with a cup of coffee and his briefcase, from which he withdrew a folder of mail that had been received and unattended during the previous week. He placed the folder on the desk in Charles' study and began flipping through correspondence: several inter-office memoranda; a few reports from colleagues working cases with him; and one unusual envelope, made of fine paper and bearing stamps of the British High Commission in Turkey, addressed to him in his brother's handwriting. *Curious. Richard?*

He twisted the envelope one way and another as he lowered himself into a leather armchair, then slit the fold of the envelope. *Dear Brother…*

Simon read the letter quickly, without hesitation, then slowly reread it again and returned it to the envelope. *Richard!*

———

"Turkey, indeed!" Charles said, removing his spectacles and plopping them on the mantelpiece after having read Richard's letter. "I wonder whether we'll ever know why?"

"Perhaps he has been looking for a way to make his own mark," Simon replied, sipping tepid coffee.

"Well, his news is a little late, I'd say," Charles said with a snort as he returned the letter to Simon.

"Yes and no," Simon replied. "True, we knew about events here, but we haven't known where Vasiliev could be found, nor what his greater plans have been. Except what Artyom and I discovered when we rummaged the house in Shepherd's Bush and interrogated Vasiliev's nephew and that English fellow. The agents found additional correspondence in Denis' flat, which confirmed the arrangement with Vasiliev."

"Vasiliev is like a dog with a bone," Ann replied with a huff. "He just won't let go. He won't accept that you don't have the crown jewels!"

"Precisely, Mother," Simon said. "We've confirmed that Richard is in Turkey. Now he's provided us with solid information and confirmed what we surmised about Vasiliev." He rose from the settee and placed his empty cup on a tray. "I'll make arrangements this weekend and set off for Ancyra as soon as I can."

"Good idea, Simon," Charles said. "While you're at it, bring Richard back. He needs to answer for a few things."

Mary sat quietly, listening to the conversation and Simon's plan. "I'm going with you," she said matter-of-factly, unable to hold her tongue any longer.

"Now, Mary." Simon smiled at his wife. "I understand you're wanting to tag along, but it won't be necessary, and it will be an arduous journey."

"Simon," Mary said, eyeing her husband. "I'm not asking. I'm telling you that I'm coming and that's that!"

"It's too dangerous!"

"You will recall that I've survived danger before, including a recent kidnapping," Mary protested. "We're discussing Vasiliev! I need to do this!"

"But—"

"Simon," Mary said fixing her husband with a gimlet eye. "I'm coming."

"Of course, you are," Simon replied, relinquishing the argument. "And your company will be most welcome."

———

As it was, their departure was delayed while Mary notified the hospital regarding her indefinite absence and ensured the care, safety, and education of her children. Simon met with Captain Smith-Cumming, too.

"You will recall those superiors," Cumming said, "who so kindly held you up as a sacrificial lamb when you returned from Petrograd. Who chose to imply that you were involved in the debacle involving the murder of the Romanovs."

"I do," Simon replied stiffly, planting his feet flat on the floor, intuitively sensing a need to flee or fight. "Too well."

"There is a risk if I approve your travel to Turkey," Cumming said. "You know Britain's secrets. Vasiliev knows you know. Plus, you will be visiting your brother …"

"And so," Simon said encouraging his supervisor to elaborate.

"Richard, we now know, has absconded with government documents, the value of which remains to be determined. We need to know what he knows, what he took, and whether Kemal has benefitted from any of it. Plus, if Vasiliev hasn't figured out by now that you two are related, it won't take him long. My mind is racing with possibilities, and few are pleasant."

"What would you propose I do?"

"Take great care, for one," Cumming replied. "Don't be reckless. Lady Mary will be with you. If Vasiliev sees her …"

"Or she sees him," Simon replied. "Don't think that hasn't crossed my mind. I tried to dissuade her, but she wouldn't hear my protests."

"Also, you will appreciate," Cumming replied, "that any intel regarding General Kemal's inner circle and plans would be of great value to our government."

"Hmm, let me guess who's asking for that information!" Simon said. "I can just imagine a British attempt at a coup d'état being blamed on me next, just because I chose to visit my brother in Ancyra!"

"That risk will always exist," Cumming said, "whenever you go abroad, so long as you are openly exposed to political discord. Especially when you take matters into your own hands. It's part of the job. Surely, you and Lockhart discussed the vulnerable situations in which you might find yourself, and the risks."

"We have," Simon replied. "I wouldn't worry if it was just me, but I have to think about Mary. She's not one of us; she's just looking for closure. The destruction of her family took its toll. And now she's dealing with the aftermath and legal issues of the two kidnappings." He sighed heavily. "Unfortunately, I agree with her: if she doesn't see an end to Vasiliev's obsession, she won't be able to move on. She will continue to be haunted by the possibilities."

"Agreed," Cumming said. "For the time being, then, report to the British High Commission in Constantinople before you continue on to Ancyra. Think of it as a courtesy call, in the event they have need of your services. Humour them … cautiously. And don't be careless."

The first Tuesday in January 1920, Simon sent a telegram to Richard, for delivery to the address noted on Richard's letter:

R STOP

Leaving by train tomorrow morning STOP

Will contact you when we arrive STOP

S STOP

Richard read the telegram, set it on the table, and poured himself a glass of iced tea. *Simon … here! I can't believe it.* He threaded his fingers through his ginger hair in wonder. Wavy spikes left him looking like an orange porcupine.

He took a sip of his tea, snatched up the paper, and reread the message. "Why, that means he'll be here next week!" he said, muttering aloud. "'We'? Who's coming with him?" He abandoned his tea and went in search of his wife.

CHAPTER 80

Simon and Mary stood on the platform of the Constantinople train station, waiting for the porter to remove their belongings from the baggage car of the Orient Express.

"Excuse me, sir," a stranger in a rumpled brown suit said as he approached. "You are Mr. Simon Temple, yes?"

Simon eyed the fellow, trying to puzzle why he would know of him.

"You exactly as Mr. Richard say," the stranger said, smiling knowingly. "Looking like him without orange hair."

"Mr. Rich—"

"Mr. Richard, he tell me meet you at station. Keep you safe."

"Keep me safe?" Simon replied, casting his eyes toward Mary, brow puckered with confusion.

"Yes," the stranger said. "Come now."

Twenty minutes later, Simon and Mary were waiting in the stranger's motor car, while their luggage was stowed in the boot.

"We go now," the stranger said as he climbed into

the driver's seat and the vehicle began to roll forward.

"Where exactly are we going?" Simon said, leaning forward to speak to the driver's back.

The stranger glanced over his shoulder. "I take you home. Not far. We talk then. Enjoy sights now."

"Oh, Simon, look!" Mary said, pointing at the view as they headed north toward the Galata Bridge. Twisting to see the view through the vehicle's rear window, she pointed. "That must be the Hagia Sophia! I've heard so much about it." She reached her hand to snag the brim of her straw cloche hat that the breeze caused by the rambling motor vehicle, threatened to tear from her head. "I can't believe we're actually here. In Constantinople!"

"Indeed," Simon said. "The city sounds, and the smell of the ocean, are different here. Not like London—full of autos, trollies, and lorries. Most folks appear to be travelling on foot, including those British soldiers." He ducked back into the vehicle to avoid being seen.

"I wish we could stay here for a while," Mary said with a sigh.

"You come," the stranger said, rolling the vehicle to a stop on a side street. "I bring bags. We talk inside." He ushered them toward the entrance. "My wife, she make coffee, good food."

Inside the stranger's home, Simon and Mary were

shown to a small room of one bed, a cupboard for clothes, and an adjoining room with basic toilet essentials. The stranger explained that he was the landlord, and that the room had once been occupied by Richard.

"Not much," Simon said with a shrug, "but it will do for one night."

"It has everything we need," Mary replied. "Come, we shouldn't keep our hosts waiting."

In a salon on the main floor, Simon and Mary were greeted by the landlord, who ushered them toward a low bench covered in striped, blue silk. Its comfortable backing consisted of matching, overstuffed cushions. Colourful rugs of rich reds and blues invitingly covered the floor. Although the benches that hugged three of the walls suggested ample seating, a low table sat before two benches that met at a corner. High windows with intricately-carved coverings invited ample lighting while lessening the brightness of the day.

"Please sit," the landlord said. "My wife, she bring food, drink."

For the next hour, the landlord's wife brought small trays of food for them to sample, and prepared strong coffee in a copper *cezve* before pouring it into small, china cups.

The landlord explained how Richard had come to live with them when he first arrived in Constantinople and found employment at the Ministry of Defence.

"Soon, great Kemal Pasha take Mr. Richard under wing!" The landlord's chest inflated with pride. "Weeks ago, Mr. Richard, he move to Ancyra with General," the landlord concluded. "He live in my cousin's house now, with his new wife."

"Wife?" Simon and Mary said, blurting the word in unison.

"This will be an interesting visit," Mary said, grinning. "I can just feel it!"

Simon wiggled toward the edge of the sofa and set his cup and saucer on the low, ornate table. He thanked his host and hostess for the refreshments and advised that he was expected at the British High Commission at three o'clock.

"Mrs. Simon, you go, too?" the landlord asked Mary. When Mary nodded, he added, "I take you in auto, but first you read this." From a trouser pocket, he withdrew an envelope with Simon's name neatly written across the front. "Mr. Richard send to me. Ask you open now."

Simon opened the small envelope and tugged out the note, straightening the paper on his knee.

S

I apologize for not meeting you. Do not come directly to Ancyra. Instead, I ask that, for your safety, you allow your host to take you to a farm outside of Bolu. I'll meet you there. Will explain later. We will have ample time for discussion and reminiscing, following which we can then decide what needs to be done. I will be notified of your arrival in Constantinople and will depart for Bolu directly.

R

CHAPTER 81

"The high commissioner will see you now," a uniformed clerk said, inviting Simon and Mary to follow him.

Together, the two followed along a corridor lit with afternoon sunlight, which radiated through narrow windows that reached toward the cathedral-like ceiling. Simon squinted to shadow his eyes as he followed the clerk into a darkened interior corridor and up a flight of stairs, Mary one step behind him.

As they passed through carved wooden doors, the chaos of the lobby faded into the quiet of the high commissioner's chambers. The clerk knocked on a second set of doors, opening one marked with a small brass plaque naming the occupant: *High Commissioner Sir Horace Rumbold, Ninth Baronet*, and ushered them through.

"I'll bring refreshments, sir," he said, before turning on his heel and heading back along the corridor.

"Sir Simon," the high commissioner said with the confidence of long diplomatic service, walking toward them with his hand extended. "Lady Mary, please be seated."

He turned toward a comfortable setting of silk brocade armchairs and two-person sofas and a variety of small tables. Assorted marble statuettes, set on pedestals, stood like sentinels along the carpet-lined walls. "I understand," he continued, "that you are in Turkey on personal business."

"We are," Simon said, "but I was asked to report to you on our arrival, in the event you might have need of my, *ahem,* services."

At a light rap on the door, the conversation paused while the clerk to set a tray of coffee on one of the longer tables.

"You may leave," the high commissioner said dismissively.

Rumbold poured out the coffee, describing the current political situation as he did so. "As you can imagine, the sultan is struggling to maintain control of what they call the 'Constantinople Government,' while General Kemal is rousing the Turks to support his proposed 'Turkish Government'."

He held the tray of poured coffee toward Simon. "Just now, we have an obligation to support Britain's contractual arrangements with the sultan," Rumbold said, continuing, "whether we believe in Kemal's intent or not. Most of the sultan's former generals have defected to join Kemal. In turn, most of the military led by the generals have joined the fledgling Turkish military, and Kemal's strength grows stronger every month. I have been tasked to sort out the details of a so-called 'Lausanne Treaty,' and to ensure that Britain's interests are acceptable to all parties."

"I understand," Simon said, dressing a cup of coffee and handing it to Mary before attending to his own, "that General Kemal now has Russia interested in supporting his endeavours with gold and armaments."

"That's true," the high commissioner replied. "As a result, Kemal has placed himself in a precarious position, aggressively pushing for a new Turkey, while attempting to thwart—my sources report—a Russian desire to supplant him. I am also advised by those in the know that your brother, Lord Richard, is in the thick of it. Apparently, he has secured a position as one of Kemal's close advisors."

Simon raised an eyebrow toward Mary, who sat demurely at his side, sipping her coffee. "And what exactly would you have me do on behalf of the British government? I presume that's why I'm here." He focussed a piercing stare on the high commissioner and waited for the man to speak.

"I understand that you are headed for Ancyra and intend to visit with your brother," the high commissioner said. He set his cup and saucer on the table and leaned back into his chair, resting his elbow on its arm. He eyed Simon with consideration.

Simon nodded.

"All we ask is that you keep your eyes and ears open—much as you did in Petrograd—and advise this office if you sense anything untoward that might compromise Britain's interests in Turkey, particularly in Ancyra. I believe you'll know what to look for."

"My assignment in Petrograd was two-fold," Simon

replied, feeling the hairs on his neck prickle to attention. "The first was private, and I am not at liberty to discuss it. The second had to do with finding Vasiliev and his colleagues, and discovering why he had a need for German submarines. Nothing more."

"I am only aware of the submarine incident," Rumbold replied.

"So, you can see that my assignment was not a blanket request to keep my eyes and ears open." Simon pinned Rumbold with a glare. "If you have something particular in mind, please state it clearly. I have no intention of wasting my time rooting around in Ancyra for tidbits that might please your office or that of your superiors!"

"Hang on, Sir Simon!" Rumbold said, raising his hands defensively. "I didn't mean to suggest—"

"Of course not," Simon said, his rigid posture suggesting otherwise. He reached for Mary's hand to reassure her but turned with concern when he realized she was trembling.

She shook her head, indicating that he should continue.

"Unless you are able to express specific concerns that you'd like me to identify, respectfully, I decline your request." Simon rose and strode toward the tall windows, the vast view of the city spread before him, unseen.

Appearing chastised, Rumbold tapped his steepled fingers in thought.

Simon's anger cooled and he resumed his seat next to Mary. She wrapped her fingers around his and squeezed them reassuringly. They waited, their coffee gone cold and unappealing.

"Very well," Rumbold said, "we are aware of General Kemal's movements and imagine he is planning some sort of revolt. It took us a while to insert a man on the generals' council, but he was identified quickly and rejected. Once again, we have no inside man to tell us what Kemal's thinking: his timing, his intentions. If it weren't for some vague remarks about Lord Richard's reason for being in Ancyra, one would think him the perfect plant. But no one can get close enough to him to figure him out. If we were able to confirm that his presence is for the benefit of the British interest, we'd be asking you to investigate the relationship. If that isn't possible, any information that you might provide that would give us insight into Kemal's business would be most helpful."

"I see," Simon said with a nondescript chortle, ire driving his rapidly beating heart. "I'd say that makes two of us, then. I have no idea of my brother's business with General Kemal. My business, although personal, has to do with the ongoing activity of Major Vasiliev. That is all. If, during the course of that business, I learn anything that might be of interest to you and your superiors, I will ensure that you hear about it. I can promise nothing more."

He glanced at Mary and felt his blood pressure lessen. "Come, Mary, it's time we were on our way." He rose and offered his hand to her.

"Uh, there is one other thing," Rumbold said, "if I may."

Simon nodded curtly and reached for his hat, a signal of his impatience.

"People from all sides are pouring into Constantinople, applying at random—or perhaps not random—embassies for refugee status. While you're in Ancyra, we'd be grateful if you could provide a sense of who these refugees are, where they're coming from, how many, etc. … especially Russians."

To Simon, the man's smile appeared cynical. "We've been contemplating opening an office in Ancyra to take some of the load off this office. The additional information would help us write a more thorough report for the home office."

"I can't promise anything," Simon said. "I don't expect to be in Turkey long enough to collect that sort of statistical information." He placed his hat on his head and tucked Mary's gloved hand at his elbow. "If that is all, sir, you must excuse us. We have other business to attend."

"Of course," the high commissioner said, rising. "Thank you for stopping by." He escorted his guests to the doorway. "We'll look forward to hearing from you."

Simon nodded and escorted Mary through the door, tucking her hand into the crook of his elbow once again. Together, they marched purposefully toward the staircase.

"Those are two distractions we don't need right now!" Simon said dubiously. He scanned the street and waved when he spied the vehicle of Richard's former landlord.

CHAPTER 82

The landlord's eyes widened briefly when Mary appeared at breakfast the next morning wearing trousers. He made no comment, but his wife grinned broadly and winked twice at her, a gesture Mary later learned was a sign of approval.

"Comfortable for riding horses and travelling," she explained, slightly abashed.

The woman served a pleasant meal and packed a lunch for their long drive to Bolu.

Toward dusk, the landlord rolled his vehicle off a dirt road, stopping in front of a stately, two-storey log house. As the tires crunched on scattered gravel, a dog barked to announce their arrival.

Before Mary and Simon had their feet on the dusty drive, an older gentleman appeared on the porch. Although he stepped with the aid of a walking stick, his back was straight, his head high and authoritative.

"That must be the general of whom our driver spoke," Simon said sotto voce, dipping his head toward the house.

"Your host greets you," the driver said as he retrieved the luggage from the boot. "You go. Speak French. I bring the bags."

Simon gently placed a hand in the centre of Mary's back, encouraging her forward.

"*Bonsoir, monsieur*," Simon said as they approached the porch. "*Je suis—*"

"He knows who you are," a familiar voice said as its ginger-haired owner stepped through the door. Richard placed a hand on the general's arm as he strode down the stairs. "Simon!" he said, grinning broadly. He embraced his brother heartily, then turned to Mary.

"Mary!" he said, taking her hands with sincerity. "I can't apologize enough for the terror I've inflicted upon you." He held her hands firmly and turned toward Simon, the grin on his face still radiant. "Your note said 'we,' but you didn't explain who 'we' was. I was hoping it would be you, Mary," he said, facing her and shaking her hands gently. "I have so much to explain!"

"Harrumph!" The general's interruption drew Richard's attention to the luggage and the need for further introductions.

Abashed, Richard fulfilled his obligations and welcomed his former landlord, inviting him to spend the night.

"Forgive me, Mr. Richard, I return to city. And you greet your brother," the landlord said. "We visit another time, when you free to be in Constantinople again." He exchanged an embrace with Richard, said good-bye to the general, and waved vigorously once he turned his vehicle toward the road again.

"Come," the general said in French. "No need to

stand like pillars in the dust, Richard. You have greetings to be said, and my wife has made food." He turned away and entered the house.

"Yes … please," Richard said, switching to English. "Come in. You'll want to freshen up, of course. Then we will tell our stories and eat the most magnificent food!" He snatched the luggage off the porch and led the way along a corridor and up a flight of stairs.

"The general insists that you occupy the largest guest room. I'll show you the facilities. When you're ready, please come down to the salon. Just left of the staircase." He set the bags in the room and turned abruptly to embrace first Simon, then Mary. "It may be that compromising circumstances have brought you to Turkey, but I am glad that they have. I am so happy to see you both again!"

Simon marvelled at the change in his brother and was almost positive that he spied a tear in his eye as he turned to leave.

"Simon, Mary," Richard said, welcoming them into the salon. "Meet my wife, Umut."

Simon and Mary exchanged a flicker of a glance reserved for married couples alone, then greeted the petite, young woman standing next to Richard. Carved combs, inlaid with gold, held waves of auburn hair that cascaded loosely down her back. Umut smiled warmly. Reaching for Mary's hands, she welcomed them in French and guided them to the sofas.

The general and his wife stayed with them long enough to make their guests feel welcome, share a meal, and ensure their comfort; then, they left the four young people to catch up on their news. Richard asked after home and parents and congratulated Simon and Mary on their soon-to-be adopted children, leaving Simon and Mary glowing with pride.

When Simon enquired after Richard's adventures, Richard openly and easily shared the events leading up to his hasty departure from England, tactfully avoiding any mention of Sally Winton, and his awkward arrival in Turkey. He also described how it was that he became a confidant of Kemal Pasha, the time he had spent on the farm as a guest of Ender Edem Pasha of Bolu, and his recent marriage.

Richard reached for his coffee cup, shook the grounds loose from the bottom, and set it back on its saucer. "It seems we've talked ourselves to the end of our refreshments." He grinned shyly. "Perhaps we should call it a night and get into the heavy stuff tomorrow. We especially need to discuss Colonel Ivan Vasiliev."

When Mary stiffened at the reference to Vasiliev, Richard continued quickly. "Don't worry, Mary. I took great pains to ensure that no one knows you're here. If you choose to reveal your presence, it will be on your terms. I can assure you that you are safe here. It is my safe haven. I come here for Uncle's wisdom and the solitude."

Mary relaxed and set her cup and saucer on the low table before rising. "Then I will bid you good night,

Richard … and Umut. Thank you for receiving us in this lovely place. Perhaps tomorrow you will show us the farm?"

"I welcome the opportunity!" Richard rose from the sofa and embraced Mary and his brother. "We need not rush to Ancyra. We can take as much time as we require to prepare for what'll greet us there."

Mary nestled into the crook of Simon's shoulder, waiting for sleep to overtake her. "Simon?" she said, her voice a whisper in his ear.

"Hmm?" he responded sleepily.

"Should we not tell Richard about Sally's baby?" She rose on her elbow and gazed at him intently. "She's such a little darling. Surely, he would want to know."

"I've been puzzling through that," Simon replied. "I don't think now is the time. He's just introduced us to his new wife, and we're about to encounter Vasiliev. More news might be too much of a distraction."

"True." Mary sighed. "It's just that we had such a lovely visit with her and Sally and Sally's family during Christmas, I feel guilty not telling him. And he's trying to be honest with Umut. Don't you think he'd want her to know?"

"What you say is important," Simon replied, running his fingers through her mussed hair. "I'm simply suggesting that we wait so he can savour the news when we tell him, and not have it overshadow our current task."

"You're right, of course," Mary said, lowering her

head to his shoulder again. "Good night." A moment later, her slow, sleep-filled breath drifted toward his ear.

In the end, they remained at the farm for several more days, hashing and rehashing what to do about Vasiliev. Eventually, Richard invited the old uncle to join them in the discussion, welcoming his input, especially regarding Turkish custom and the need to avoid scandal.

Once they had incorporated Uncle's advice into their plans, they determined it was time to advance on Ancyra. They thanked their host for his hospitality and sound recommendations, then set off in Richard's borrowed vehicle the following morning. As dusk diminished into a darkening, overcast sky, the vehicle bounced its way into the outskirts of Ancyra, finally rolling to a stop behind Richard's home.

Grinning, Richard stopped at the foot of the staircase. "Before I say goodnight to you," he said with sincerity, "I want to be certain you know how grateful I am that you've come to Turkey. When I sent the letter, it was only to warn you of evil afoot. I didn't expect you to drop what you were doing and come running." He sighed, almost—but not quite—speechless, and placed his hand on his heart.

"Our home is your home," Umut said. "We welcome you and invite you to make yourselves comfortable."

CHAPTER 83

No sooner had the Temples arrived in Ancyra than Richard sent a note to Nitikin, inviting him for another evening of beer and conversation, as well as an opportunity to meet his family. In the meantime, while Simon and Mary planned a day visit to a factory of weavers on the outskirts of town, Richard reported to Kemal.

"Tell me," Kemal said, welcoming Richard, pointing him toward the guest chair.

Richard glanced around the office, marking the familiar sparseness and the half-full ashtray.

"You have good news, I presume," Kemal said encouragingly.

"Actually, sir," Richard replied, twisting slightly in the chair to easily cross his knees. He dangled his free foot while he organized his thoughts. "It was a heartwarming reunion. Better than anything I could have hoped for. Thank you for allowing us the days on the farm. As usual, it had a calming effect on me, and my brother and his wife felt the same. Even when we discussed difficult topics, we were able to find resolution. Umut and Uncle were supportive, too."

"And … what sort of resolution did you reach?"

"Well, with regard to family," Richard said, slightly flustered, "I still have apologies to make … to my parents … and grovelling to do where the country is concerned. I will likely have to appear before authorities and ask for forgiveness, as you can imagine, but … I'm prepared to do that. I want to be on the good side of both England *and* Turkey!"

"And the other difficulty?"

"Ah!" Richard said with a grin. "That, too, is coming along nicely. Among my brother, sister-in-law, and me, we have devised a plan that, if it works, will see Vasiliev gone. We will be speaking with Nitikin this evening to ensure that he is onside."

"And what is my role in this scheme of yours?" Kemal said with a raised brow.

"Uncle recommends—and we agree—that it would be best if you were not involved," Richard said, leaning toward the desk and resting his clasped hands on the top. "Should anything go amiss, you must not be implicated."

"I see," Kemal said, leaning into his chair, resting his heels on the corner of the desk as he crossed his ankles. "I appreciate your consideration." He lit a cigarette, releasing smoke toward the ceiling. "When and where is this plan to be revealed?"

"Whether Nitikin agrees or not," Richard said, "it will be tomorrow evening at the Russian restaurant next to the Antik Hotel. I happen to know it to be Vasiliev's favourite restaurant. He dines there most evenings."

Richard returned his dangling foot to the floor and

air-drew the plan before him, describing the invitation he had sent to Vasiliev that morning, and how Vasiliev preferred to sit at the table in the back, near the kitchen.

"My letter extended an invitation for Makarov to join us. It's a small restaurant. I will be waiting for them at that table." Richard rose from his chair and began to pace casually across the room, his footsteps muffled by the intricately-woven rug beneath his feet.

"If Nitikin accepts our challenge, he will join us only after Vasiliev and Makarov are seated." He chuckled. "His appearance will be an unexpected surprise, hopefully disconcerting the older men!"

"How so?"

"That's where I come in," Richard said sincerely. "As you know, Vasiliev believes that I'm betraying you based on the information we feed him, but he also harps constantly about the tsarina's jewels that he believes my brother and wife stole from Russia. I intend to expose his usual rant in a way that it can be overheard."

Richard came to a standstill before Kemal's desk. "That's it in a nutshell. I don't want to say more. The last thing any of us wants is for this situation to blow up in your face. You could become fodder for the opposition."

"Thank you, Richard, for your consideration," Kemal said, lowering his feet to the floor. "I'll not ask for more information. I will, however, wish you good luck. It's important for Turkey to be rid of Vasiliev, too. The sooner we have a more reliable and responsible Russian representative, the sooner we can focus on our successes without having to think about a yapping dog nipping at the heels of all we hope to accomplish."

"Agreed." Richard rocked on his heels, then settled. "There is one more thing I'd like to offer for your consideration, sir." Kemal nodded. "Nitikin: I find him loyal, dedicated, respectful, and clever. I know he belongs to Russia, but, if ever the opportunity arises, he would be an asset to your office."

"You're correct, Richard," Kemal replied. "He belongs to Russia. But … I will keep your recommendation in mind should anything change." He stood in front of Richard, placing a hand on either shoulder. "Go with Allah and keep safe," he said sincerely.

CHAPTER 84

Surveying his surroundings, Richard sat at a table for four at the back of the restaurant, facing the door, slowly rotating a glass of warm apple tea. There was a smattering of guests closer to the entrance, few electric lights, many and varied candles, and a musician softly strumming a balalaika. *On another occasion, I'd call the place romantic.*

Beside him sat an empty chair where he expected Nitikin to sit. Knowing that Vasiliev and Makarov preferred to sit side-by-side rather than opposite, the two men would be forced to occupy the other two empty chairs.

A row of potted plants obscured vision of the next table, creating a privacy screen of sorts. Richard watched as a waiter seated two smartly-attired, older gentlemen against the pots. They, too, sat facing the entrance, explaining to the waiter that they expected others to join them.

Richard sipped the tea, gone cool from waiting, and rotated the glass in his sweaty hand. He licked the sweet taste from his lips and wiped his hands on the legs of his trousers. *A set-up sounds great in a novel. I expected to be calm, to feel in control, but the anticipation is killing me! What if something goes wrong?*

'Nothing will go wrong', he heard Simon's voice in his ear. *'Trust me. Stay calm. It will work. Vasiliev's ego will do him in. Just remember to breathe.'*

A moment later, his worries were shattered by a jovial conversation projecting from the doorway. Richard straightened. Vasiliev confidently strolled in, followed by his companion, and headed toward the table. When he saw the arrangement, he scowled at Richard.

"I see, Mr. Temple, that you occupy my preferred seat," Vasiliev grumbled.

"I apologize, Colonel, if my placement disturbs you," Richard said as he half-rose respectfully. "But how else could I watch for your arrival?" He bowed in greeting, but resumed his seat, forcing them to sit with their backs to the door. Noting Nitikin's arrival, he rose slowly to his feet again.

"I hope you don't mind, gentlemen—I took the liberty of inviting Comrade Nitikin to join us as well."

Vasiliev's eye's popped wide and round behind his spectacles, while Makarov's mouth gaped like a fish out of water before closing, flat lipped. Richard greeted the young man pleasantly and offered the empty chair next to him.

He cleared his throat before speaking again, struggling to swallow his amusement. "You don't mind, do you?" Richard said, appearing perplexed. "We have enjoyed several fine meals together, while our dedicated comrade here"—he gestured toward Nitikin—"has been left behind like a poor Cinderella. You must agree with me, surely, that Comrade Nitikin has more than earned the right to a fine meal." His apricot brows rose questioningly as he peered at the two older men.

"Hmph! Of course, you are correct," Vasiliev said begrudgingly. Makarov nodded grumpily beside him.

"Wonderful!" Richard said, flagging the waiter. *"Pardonnez-moi Monsieur, une bouteille de votre meilleure vodka s'il vous plaît, et de l'eau pour moi."*

"Where is our usual waiter, Boris?" Vasiliev said, rudely interrupting.

"Boris, he is ill today," the waiter replied. "I'm Aleksandr, and I'm happy to be serving you this evening. Excuse me. I will bring the vodka and the water." He bowed respectfully and disappeared behind a swinging door.

Vasiliev scowled at the waiter's departing back. "I don't believe it! Boris is never ill!"

"I prefer water to vodka," Richard said, trying to draw Vasiliev's attention. "I'll leave the strong drink to you gentlemen."

Once the vodka had been served and they had ordered their meals, he changed the conversation to a more pointed topic.

"Well," he said, raising his glass of water, "here's to our ongoing relationship." He sipped the water, watching a snide expression curve on Vasiliev's lips.

"What I'm curious to know," Richard said, leaning back in his chair as he cast a line to catch a big fish, "is whether you have been pleased with the information that I've passed to you regarding General Kemal's plans, and what more I can do for you. After all, you do pay me a gratifying sum for the information I provide."

Nitikin's eyes rounded at Richard's disclosure. "Mr. Temple, you are *the source* of the vital information that Comrade Vasiliev relies upon?" The young man grinned. "Then it is no wonder you are so confident, Colonel." He turned his head toward his elders, appearing awestruck by their arrangement.

"We have several tasks for you, Mr. Temple," Vasiliev said, ignoring Nitikin as he leaned toward the table, eyes narrowed. He sneered, drawing his lips into a line, and glanced sideways to Makarov.

"Yes," Makarov said breathlessly as he straightened with purpose and poured another vodka, "for one thing, we would like to review the *real* ledgers that account for the use and distribution of the Russian gold. We do not believe that General Kemal is using all of it to fight his battles and advance his control; we believe he is holding back a percentage for his own use. We see his opulent lifestyle: living in hotels instead of a serviceable flat. Clearly, he's lining his own nest."

He glanced at Vasiliev, who nodded for him to continue. "And we have every reason to believe that he is stockpiling the armaments. The battles that he leads against the Greeks and the Armenians don't require half of what Mother Russia sends."

"As I'm certain you're aware, gentlemen, General Kemal gave up his home in Constantinople so he could have the freedom to move where he might be needed.

The hotels in which he has stayed are hosted by those who believe in the revolutionary cause," Richard replied, swallowing hard to control his anger at the accusations he knew to be false. "And only recently has he moved into a more permanent residence, again provided by loyal supporters."

Richard sipped his water and deliberately set it on the table with a thud. "I can assure you that every bit of the first delivery of gold and weaponry has been put to good use. There is no residue." Richard eyed the two men seated opposite him. "As a matter of fact, the latest report suggests a fifty percent shortfall on delivery."

"A shortfall?" Vasiliev said. "Our records indicate that everything received in Turkey has been delivered directly to Kemal's authorities."

"Indeed," Richard said, "what was received has been delivered. But the amount received is only half of what Moscow claims to have shipped. I've seen the ledgers, and no one in Moscow can explain the discrepancy."

"Mr. Temple," Vasiliev said slyly. He reached for the vodka bottle. "I'm a little confused. In one breath you say you want to help us and are happy for the money we pay you, and in a second breath, you challenge our word?"

"No, no, sir," Richard said, feeling the prominence in his throat bob up and down uncomfortably as he searched for an appropriate explanation. "I'm merely repeating what I've heard the council of generals discuss. If you can explain the shortfall, please do. Have you redirected it to help the Greeks or the Armenians? Perhaps the French

… or the British? Richard's eyes widened with awareness. "Please tell me you don't intend to support the British!"

"Ah, Richard," Vasiliev said, sitting back to rest his elbows on the table and steeple his fingers over his ample belly. "How quickly you jump to conclusions. I can assure you that no such thing has occurred. We have merely diverted the excess for our, *ahem*, own purposes."

Richard's eyebrows rose toward his hairline. *Does he realize what he just said?*

"You have diverted the excess? You plan to use Mother Russia's gold and armaments for your own purposes?" Nitikin said, jumping to his feet, clearly affronted.

"Sit down, you fool," Makarov said impatiently, "do you want everyone to hear you? Pour more vodka and keep your mouth shut!"

Nitikin resumed his seat, appearing abashed.

"Tomorrow, I will remind you that this conversation has nothing to do with you," Makarov said, glaring at Nitikin, "and what might happen should you forget that. Am I clear?" Unhurried, Makarov lifted the lapel of his jacket to reveal the Finnish hunting knife that Nitikin had described to Richard: the knife that Makarov preferred to use as an assault weapon.

"Yes, sir!" Nitikin gulped loudly, appearing sufficiently intimidated.

"Let's just say," Vasiliev said, continuing his point before shooting back the remnants of his vodka and waving the glass at Nitikin for a refill, "that we have a more important use to which these riches could be put."

He tipped his head toward Makarov, brow wrinkled as if looking for agreement.

Makarov obliged with a curt nod, waving his empty glass toward Nitikin as well.

"Alright," Richard said, leaning back as the waiter began placing steaming dishes on the table. "I'll see what I can find out, but I can't promise the information will help you."

"I trust you will make every effort," Vasiliev said, his voice sinister. "Otherwise, our young friend's duties could suddenly come to an end." He narrowed his eyes toward Nitikin. The young man cringed.

CHAPTER 85

Richard refilled their vodka glasses several times as they consumed their meal. The table quietened and the heated conversation cooled.

Once Vasiliev mopped his plate with the last morsel of bread, he popped it into his mouth and chewed with pleasure. Then, he pushed the plate into the centre of the table and dusted his hands. "There is one other matter that remains to be discussed, Richard," Vasiliev said, his words oily with impatience and an intimate threat. "The jewels."

Richard regarded his opponents as he pushed away from the table; chewing his lip while he contemplated Vasiliev's recurring threat. "You keep insisting that my family is in possession of jewels that you are determined to have," Richard said thoughtfully. "What if we did have them? What use do you have for them?"

"*The jewels are mine!*" Vasiliev hissed with ire. His chair screeched as he rose threateningly, palms flat on the table, face flushed a purple hue. "Together with the gold and the armaments, they will fund my army's takeover of Russia. Then, I will return Russia to the greatness it had during Tsar Alexander's rule; before the greed of Nicholas II destroyed it! *Nothing* and *no one* will deny me!" His breath came in shallow pants.

"Ivan!" Makaraov quietly spat the warning. "You say too much."

Richard ignored Makarov and rose to meet Vasiliev's stance. "Next, I suppose you're going to tell me that you intend to take over Turkey, too!" He kept his words low, directing them toward the next table. "To strip her of her wealth and use her people as slaves."

"What of it?" Vasiliev said defensively. "I've seen Turkey's gold. It will be useful for my purposes. I will have it, too."

"Ivan!" Makarov said with caution. "Mind your voice!"

"As for her people," Vasiliev said, seeming to calm. He lowered himself into his chair. "They have no value other than free labour." He shrugged. "They are disposable."

"I see," Richard said, feeling at ease as he resumed his seat. "Is there no end to your greed, your obsession with power?"

"How dare you speak to me like that!" Vasiliev said, rigid with indignance.

"Perhaps Mr. Temple needs to be reminded of his precarious position," Makarov said, his words slurred. He patted his chest over the hidden knife.

"I don't think it will come to that, Rada," Vasiliev said scornfully. "Mr. Temple will not repeat anything I've said. If he fails to deliver the jewels within the next three weeks, his sister-in-law will meet with a very serious accident. Why bother with a dogsbody like him when one can speak directly with the pack's leader, *n'est-ce pas?*" He turned to Richard. "By the time my agents in London finish with her, she won't look like the pretty girl your brother married."

Richard bristled as he rose from his chair. "You must be incredibly thick to think that I would betray my brother and his wife." He towered over Vasiliev, fists clenched. "Touch a hair on her head and—"

"And what?" Vasiliev said, glowering at Richard as he rose slowly to his feet again, recoiling like an angered asp. "Come, Rada. I think the coffee will be too frosty tonight."

Richard and Nitikin exchanged a quick glance, threw some paper lira on the table, and followed.

CHAPTER 86

On the street, Vasiliev turned on Richard, fists balled at this sides. The soft light from candles glowing in the restaurant's large windows illuminated the mad glint in his eyes and the perspiration pearling on his forehead. Light just enough for Richard to see that the purple hue remained.

"Mr. Temple," he said, frothing with anger. "If you fail to provide the jewels in three weeks, only you may live to regret it." His right hand slid into his jacket pocket. "*No one* is going to deny me my right to rule Russia."

"What do you mean 'your right'?" Makarov drew his superior's attention from Richard. "What about *me?* *My* right? You and your family have promised me wealth, power, and status for all I have done to help you."

"You?" Vasiliev replied derisively. "You have no presence, no capacity. You're just a *nincompoop!* An *inept nincompoop!*" He flicked his hand as if swatting a fly.

"Nincompoop!" Makarov said, his shout echoing along the street. Effortlessly, he reached beneath his lapel and extracted the Finnish blade, turning its threat toward Vasiliev. "You've had my allegiance for years, and now you betray me? After all I've done to support the dreams of your family!" He shifted, ready to attack. Snorting with his own anger.

Ignoring Makarov's rant, Vasiliev slowly retrieved a small derringer from his pocket, wavering its aim from Makarov to Richard. His free hand wrapped around the handle. His feet planted themselves firmly on the road.

"No!" Mary said, racing toward them from the shadows, her voice deep and threatening. She lunged toward Vasiliev, knocking his hand upward. The gun fired, its bullet lost to the heavens.

Richard glanced at Nitikin, nodding toward Makarov. Together, they grabbed Makarov's arms and yanked him into the shadows, curtailing any further involvement.

"Don't try anything stupid, comrade," Nitikin warned as he relieved Makarov of his killing tool.

"You!" Vasiliev said, gasping in disbelief. "How can this be?"

"Yes, me!" Mary said, facing her foe with determination. "I've come to deliver that which you need."

She saw Simon edge forward, balanced to pounce. Yet, he waited as if to hear Vasiliev's reply.

A smile of realization crossed Vasiliev's face. "You've brought me the jewels? Richard, why did you not just say this?" he exclaimed. "We could have avoided our unpleasant evening!" He held his hand toward Mary, wiggling his fingers in invitation. "Where are they?"

Mary's unexpected response caught everyone off

guard. She twisted his outstretched hand out of her way and drove the edge of her right hand into his throat. Vasiliev gasped and coughed, protecting his throat with his hand.

Adrenaline racing, Mary sank her left fist into his belly with impetus. Vasiliev's free hand flew to the pain.

Simon's words echoed in Mary's ear: *Element of surprise, Sparrow.*

Vasiliev scrambled to his feet, venom in his eyes. "What is this?" His voice was a raspy, high-pitched whisper.

"This is for my family," she said ominously. "For my children!" Efficiently, she drove her anger through the palm of her right hand, its heel striking Vasiliev's nose, forcing the bridge up and back. Vasiliev screamed when the fine cartilage snapped between his eyes. He took a step toward her, tears and blood flooding his face.

"And this! This one is for Varvara Voronov!" Mary said, her movement fluid and thorough. She grabbed the lapels of his jacket and jerked him to her, hammering her thigh deep into his groin. "You will never force your wicked deeds upon another woman!"

"Var-va-ra?" Vasiliev gasped with agony, falling to the dirt road. He curled into a fetal ball, moaning, his hands protecting his latest injury, his bloody mouth gasping for air.

Mary stood over him, preparing to deliver a kick to his kidneys. Panting hard, she hesitated.

"Mary?" Simon said, racing from the shadows. "Before you do more harm, ask yourself whether that will suffice."

Mary glanced as Simon, feeling herself surface from the depths of hatred and rage. She placed gloved hands on her thighs, willing her rapid pulse to ease and nodded. "I suppose."

"Good," Simon replied. "I'm sure the police would appreciate you leaving a part of him for their purposes."

"You're right," she said, still skirting her victim.

"Simon Temple?" Vasiliev said his squeaking voice barely audible. "You too?" His eyes rolled back into his head, and he fainted.

Richard signalled to the shadows for the military police to take over. As they approached, Mary neared Vasiliev again and half-heartedly delivered a kick to his kidneys. Then, hands on hips, she neatly circled him and spat in his face, just as his eyes opened to witness her final blow.

"Murderer!" she said with loathing. "Greedy, power-hungry, abhorrent, scum-of-the-earth murderer!"

"Mary," Simon said softly, turning her to him, wrapping his arms around her. He kissed her forehead chastely and waited again.

Eventually, Mary's arms found their way around Simon, and they stood together quietly as the military police took Vasiliev and Makarov into custody. Mary's even breathing returned, and Simon released her.

"Alright?" he said, peering into her eyes.

"Yes," she said, chortling, "I am now." She gazed at her hands, marvelling as she flexed her fingers. "You were correct: wearing the leather gloves did protect my hands!"

"Right then," Richard said, interrupting them. "I believe our men have what they need, and Mary appears to be satisfied. Vilen, what about you?"

"I am satisfied as well," Nitikin replied. "I spoke with our men seated at the next table and the waiter. Amongst them, they heard enough to file their own reports. The police in the shadows saw and heard enough, too." He chuckled as he regarded Mary. "Remind me never to cross you in a dark alley, Lady Mary!"

CHAPTER 87

Early the following morning, Richard answered a firm rap on the front door of his home and accepted an envelope from one of Kemal's cadets. Wandering into the kitchen, where his brother and their wives were chatting, he opened it and read the all-to-familiar directive aloud:

My office 1300 hours—all of you.

K

Richard cackled, passing the note for the others to read.

"I suggest we leave mid-morning and stop by the military police. We three promised to provide statements," Richard said. "Best to do it while our recollection is clear."

"Agreed," Simon said. "Once that's done, Mary and I should be heading home. I strongly recommend that you come with us, for the reasons we've already discussed."

Richard looked to Umut, a hand resting protectively on her belly. She nodded for him to speak.

"We will," Richard said, reaching a hand toward his wife. "Umut knows everything about me now. I have no secrets from her … or you. I need to make amends to Mother and Father, and clear up matters in London. Otherwise, I'll never be free of my guilt."

Umut narrowed her eyes at him, waiting patiently.

"And," he said finally, "I have no secrets from Ela, either. This morning, Umut and I explained everything to her and told her of my need to return with you. If our return to Turkey is delayed for any reason, she will join us in England. She insists that she won't miss the birth of her first grandchild."

———•—•———

At 1300 hours on January 25th, 1920, Richard, Simon, Mary, and Umut were shown into Kemal's office.

"General!" Richard said warmly, "may I introduce my brother, Simon, and his wife, Mary."

"Sir Simon," Kemal said, eyeing Simon. "You are exactly as Richard has described you." He gave Simon a knowing look, nodding toward the auburn hair. "And you, Lady Mary," Kemal said. "I've heard you had an eventful evening." He reached for her hands and kissed her knuckles. "How are your hands this morning? Shall I have the military doctor tend to them?"

"They're well enough, Kemal Pasha," Mary said, abashed. "Thank you for asking. My husband suggested I wear a lovely pair of leather gloves that I had bought in the market. They provided excellent protection." She flexed her fingers. "See! No harm done." She glanced at their small party, seeing them struggle to contain their amusement, and giggled herself.

"Please be seated," Kemal said, appreciating her humour. He waved his arm toward a brocade sofa and armchairs, recently placed to rest on the large Turkish carpet. "And my dear Umut," Kemal said. He placed a hand on each of her shoulders and kissed both of her cheeks in welcome. "How radiant you look today."

"Comrade Nitikin!" Kemal said, spying the young man entering his office. "Please … join us." He pointed toward the gathering. "Coffee should arrive shortly."

Kemal reclined casually in one of the armchairs, long legs outstretched and crossed at the ankles. He selected a rolled, aromatic cylinder from an ornamental cigarette box sitting on a nearby table, then tipped the box toward the others. Nitikin chose one and accepted the silver table lighter from Kemal.

"Kemal Pasha," Umut said shyly, "may I?" She nodded toward the arrival of the coffee tray.

"First, let me thank you all for coming to my office," Kemal said. "It's a little easier for me to greet you here, where I can be interrupted, if necessary. I'd also like to thank all of you for seeing your plan through to entrap Vasiliev and Makarov. And Richard, thank you for ensuring the police chief reported events to me last night. I presume you have all given your statements?"

"Yes, sir," Richard said. "We took care of that before coming here."

"Have you any news on the welfare of the two

criminals?" Mary asked.

"I'm told that Makarov is still sleeping off his vodka hangover," Kemal said, "and that—in time—Vasiliev will recover from his injuries. Some of his bruises are quite deep. And then there's the broken nose …" He smirked with humour. "You would put some of my men to shame, Lady Mary. Where did you learn to fight like that?"

"Simon taught me … in Russia," Mary replied, glancing at her husband. "More recently, I've had a security guard teaching me." She shook her head, her expression saddening. "I wish I never had to learn or use any of it, but I am thankful that I had the skills when I needed them."

Mary gratefully held out her coffee cup when Umut offered to refresh the contents, and attention shifted to another topic.

Nitikin rose and sauntered toward the coffee tray to refresh his own cup. "Regarding the outcome of last evening," Nitikin said. "First, the military police will determine whether Colonel Vasiliev and Corporal Makarov have committed crimes against Turkey. Once that investigation is concluded and any crimes addressed, they will be deported. In Russia, they will face their crimes against our motherland.

"As Richard and Kemal Pasha know, I was sent to Turkey to observe and investigate the actions of Vasiliev and Makarov. My superiors and the officers of the Comintern Bank have suspected them of embezzlement and fraud for some time, but they required evidence before they could act. We now have that evidence, thanks to the witness statements given this morning, including those of the three agents present in the restaurant." He stirred his coffee and returned to his seat.

"What happens now, sir?" Richard said, turning his attention to Kemal.

"What indeed?" Kemal said with a frown. "As you can imagine, I have given these matters great thought." He reached for the cigarette box and lit another cylinder. "Comrade Nitikin has a report to write for the bank and for his superiors, which I will endorse. The report will describe Vasiliev's plot to steal the Russian gold and armaments for his own purposes—to take over Turkey, enslave her people, and rob her of her treasurers, all in aid of his diabolical intent to take over Russia. How he ever expected to accomplish that is beyond me." He drew on the cigarette in contemplation, then released the smoke.

"I can expand on that," Simon said, straightening in his chair before describing the location at which he and Lockhart, in 1917, had discovered the amassed military supplies, equipment, vehicles—including decommissioned trains—and much more, which Vasiliev intended to use to establish his own military might. "I know he was in the market for at least one submarine. Likely, he would have been successful in 1915, had the Royal Navy not intercepted intelligence regarding a secret submarine base on a remote island in the Arctic known as Bear Island."

"May I ask you to write a report to that effect too, Sir Simon," Kemal said. "Before you leave?"

"Of course," Simon replied.

"In the meantime," Nitikin said, his chest inflating, "I spoke with my superiors this morning. Until replacements can be sent from Petrograd, I will be managing the office—which means a promotion for me—and reviewing all records in search of discrepancies. Once I turn the office over to my replacements, I will return to Russia to testify."

"A well-deserved promotion!" Richard said, reaching to shake Nitikin's hand.

"And you, Richard," Kemal said. "I believe it is time for you to leave, too, yes?"

"Yes, sir," Richard said confidently. He collected his coffee cup and that of Umut's and placed them on the tray. "We were discussing that just this morning. It's time for me to answer for my actions."

Kemal smiled at his protégé with fondness. "You have been a great support to me, my boy. Go as you must and know that you will always be welcome to return."

<hr>

While Mary gave instructions to the porter and the steward for the handling of their luggage during their return passage on the Orient Express, Simon found a quiet location in the salon. He penned a short note to the High Commissioner and glanced at his wristwatch to ensure he had time to arrange its delivery:

Sir,

On two points: I recommend that you pay close

attention to General Kemal. He is worthy of great esteem and Britain's co-operation. Further, refugees are advancing on Constantinople, in vast numbers. Make ready.

Sincerely,
Sir Simon Nightingale-Temple, Viscount Blackett

NOTE TO READER

Thank you for reading *Tsarina's Jewels*, the second book in *The Nightingale and Sparrow Chronicles*. I hope you enjoyed the adventure.

Other readers find reviews helpful for locating books they prefer to read. All reviews are appreciated.

Don't forget to visit my website: www.jerenatobiasen. ca, to read about my other works and inspirations, and to join my Readers Club.

ABOUT THE AUTHOR

Jerena Tobiasen—award-winning author of *The Prophecy*, a 3-volume, historical fiction saga—lives in Vancouver, Canada. If she's not home, she's likely travelling.

Jerena embellishes her writing by visiting foreign lands, wandering through museums and delving into libraries, conducting interviews, and walking in the footsteps of her characters. Her experiences and discoveries enrich the authenticity of her stories.

She has travelled extensively throughout the United Kingdom, Europe, northern Africa, and the Arctic, collecting data for her series *The Nightingale and Sparrow Chronicles*. *Tsarina's Crown*, the first novel in this series, is a first-place winner of the 2023 Hemingway Award for Twentieth Century Wartime Fiction.

Jerena also writes short stories and poetry, some of which you will find on her website. For more information about Jerena and her craft, you are invited to visit her website www.jerenatobiasen.ca, where you'll also find an invitation to join her newsletter.